Spring Into SciFi
2022 Edition

A Cloaked Press Anthology

Published by:
Cloaked Press, LLC
P. O. Box 341
Suring, WI 54174
https://www.cloakedpress.com

Cover Design by:
Fantasy & Coffee Design
https://www.fantasyandcoffee.com/SPDesign

Cloaked Press is Proud to Present:

Greg Eccleston

Mark Bilsborough

Andrew P. McGregor

Nestor Delfino

James Pyles

Barend Nieuwstraten III

Karl El-Korea

Eve Morton

Diane Arrelle

Alex Minns

Sara Crocoll Smith

Elizabeth Estabrooks

J. L. Royce

MR Wells

Nicholas Poe

Table of Contents

Searching for Jodie: "A love story"

by Greg Eccleston

SIX MONTHS (OR SO) AGO

I met Jodie in the 'Bull and Finch'. It was 2020 and I was standing 1.5 metres behind her. She ordered a bottled mineral water for $5, paid with a tap of her left wrist. As she walked from the bar, I noticed a copy of 'A Prayer for Owen Meany' by John Irving, in her canvas tote bag.

It was mid-afternoon and I had just finished my shift at the station. I ordered and paid $9.18 for a schooner of local craft beer and headed in the same direction that Jodie had gone. I did not know her name yet, of course, however she had my full attention. She looked quite like the American actress Jodie Foster, but not so much that you would mistake them for each other.

She started playing a pinball machine in a back corner of the pub. Not something that I saw every day. The machine was called 'World Cup 94' and was almost an antique. I had played it many times myself. It had been recently upgraded to accept scans instead of just cash. I still preferred coins. Jodie had tap-scanned with her wrist and I pretended to read a newspaper.

Half an hour later, I was halfway through my third beer, and she was still on her first credit, easily eclipsing my previous high score. We were in a suburb of Sydney named Rose Forest, close to where I live. 'Bull and Finch' is my local; a place where (almost) everybody knows my name.

So, as I was working up some courage to approach Jodie with a kind of introduction, a couple of men, younger than me, entered. She concentrated on the silver ball, they attempted to engage her in conversation. I could not discern it all, however I did hear "Can we have the next game, baby?".

"No," she said.

"No doesn't always mean no," the taller one of them taunted. He was wearing a sleeveless shirt and looked like he had just come from the gym. And he hadn't skipped arm day.

She attempted to ignore them. The pinball machine boomed the word "CANADA".

I then did something that I had never before done in my life; I intervened on behalf of a stranger. Standing from my barstool, I announced "Gents! The lady is with me."

The eyes turned towards me, except for Jodie's, who was now trapping the pinball with the right flipper. The two men flexed their knuckles and took a step towards me.

My mind: 'I have never thrown an angry punch in my life'. My mind, also: 'If this was a movie, the good guy risks himself to win the girl'. Real life: The gym guy shrugged his shoulders at his colleague, and then they both wandered off back into the main bar.

Jodie nodded a 'thanks' to me and released the silver ball from where she had trapped it. I nodded back (she had already turned around) and returned to my stool and half a beer. She defeated Canada and continued to set an all-time high score on that historic machine, as I half-heartedly attempted to finish the newspaper cryptic crossword. I am not particularly good at cryptics.

***

Sometime later, she sat on the stool two away from me, appropriately socially distanced. After four beers, I had abandoned any attempt at charming seduction and scarcely noticed.

"Thank you," she spoke.

I looked up and into a pair of pale blue-green eyes. Jodie had rounded cheekbones, a dimpled chin, and thick dark eyebrows. Her nose looked like it had once been broken. At a guess, she was about nine years younger than me. I was smitten.

"You're welcome, probably", I managed in reply, instantly regretting that fourth beer.

"Why did you say that, to those men?" she asked, "I am not with you."

"I guess that I didn't want to be a witness. Kelly McGillis would have destroyed me in court". Even when slightly drunk, I usually manage to work a 1980s pop culture reference into conversation, no matter how inappropriate. Especially when slightly drunk.

"'The Accused'," she replied, to my mild surprise, "Yes, that could have been an awful scene. Thank you, again."

There was a voice in my head telling me to sober up as quickly as possible. Or maybe just cut to the chase and ask her for her phone number. Instead I asked if I could buy her a drink.

"Alcohol doesn't agree with me," she said, "but you can buy me some water."

So, I went to the bar, where there was free filtered water. Remembering seeing her buy bottled eau minérale, I paid $10 for two. Returning and handing one of the bottles to her, I said "So, are you from around here?"

***

After about forty-five minutes of small talk, mostly about 1980s and 1990s books, music and movies (we agreed that John Irving is the greatest living novelist, David Bowie the greatest-ever musical genius, but disagreed whether 'The Silence of the Lambs' was the greatest American movie; I thought so, she did not), I realised that we hadn't exchanged names.

"This is a bit awkward," I said, "but I forgot to manage our introductions."

"My name is Jodie," to which I laughed.

"And my name is Anthony Hopkins."

"No."

"How about Hannibal?"

"I don't believe you."

"Is your name really Jodie?"

"Yes."

"J-O-D-I-E?"

"Yes."

"Okay, then. My name is Palmer."

"I believe you," she said, and smiled. "Nice to meet you, Palmer," and extended her hand.

"Nice to meet you too, Jodie," and we shook hands. "Very nice to meet you," I continued. And it was.

I felt a little tingle of excitement. I had not felt a woman's touch in over a year. Then I remembered that I had not had any human contact for nearly that long.

"Oh! I'm so sorry! We should have elbow-bumped," to which I received a puzzled look, as she still grasped my hand, so I continued, "you know, no physical contact, because of COVID."

She gently withdrew her hand, and shyly smiled. "I guess it's too late now," she said.

And it was.

4

***

Several hours later, we were at my flat, drinking bottled water. We had been discussing movies. I have an entire room devoted to my DVD collection, which we spent time inspecting and she described as 'amazing' and 'mind-blowing'. I knew every title in there. In 2020, that probably makes me a bit of a renaissance man. Most retailers do not even sell DVD players anymore.

Jodie sipped her water in a way that a wine connoisseur drinks a particularly good vintage.

Sitting on my expensive and comfortable Italian brown leather couch (with a purple cushion artfully hiding the torn section on the armrest), we were debating 'The Silence of the Lambs' again. I called it a masterpiece. She conceded that point, however argued that Hopkins should have been awarded 'Best Supporting Actor' rather than 'Best Actor'.

"Hannibal was on screen for sixteen minutes!" she exclaimed.

Then we were kissing. To this day, I cannot say that either of us initiated it. It was truly mutual. We were talking. Then, we were kissing.

And it was the best first kiss that I have ever had. As a middle-aged man (somewhat in denial about that), I have kissed many girls and women. Albeit, not for a while. This kiss was the new number one. When our lips first touched, I was light-headed. It seemed like I was seeing stars.

To my eternal credit, I did not force the issue. I have no idea if she would have consented to sex that first night, however it did not matter. Because this is what I said:

"Jodie. Let's not have sex tonight. Don't get me wrong, I am not assuming that we would. And I want to. I do want to. I really want to. But I also think that I am falling in like with you."

"Falling in like?"

5

"I was trying to be cute. Sorry. I know that it's soon, but yeah. I like you madly." And then, quickly "I want to get to know you better. If you feel the same way—and I hope that you do—I think that we should wait." At which, Jodie smiled that same shy smile.

"I understand. Small moves." And then she stood up.

"You don't have to go," I said. "It is late, and you have to work tomorrow." I stood up next to her and we kissed some more. Clichéd or not, I felt weak at the knees. Then, she walked to the front door.

"When will we see each other again?" I asked, hoping not to sound desperate.

"Soon," she said, opening the door to the night.

"Jodie, wait. Where? I don't have your number. I don't even know your last name."

"Don't worry," Jodie said, "You'll find me".

And then she left. I stood at the doorway, watching her walk. The streetlights were off, however it wasn't that dark. Then she stopped and turned around, about forty metres away.

"Palmer," she said, rather seriously, "I do feel the same way."

And off she walked, into the moonlight.

INDIAN-PACIFIC

About four years ago, I took a cross-country train trip. The 'Indian-Pacific' takes three days to travel from Perth to Sydney. I was recovering from the nasty relationship break-down with that bitch Maddison (by the way, why do most people call it a break-up?) and I went on a pre-planned luxury holiday with my elderly mother, flying to Perth and returning on the iconic train.

And I fell in love. Sort of.

Raini was a member of the train crew. It was her job to answer questions, tidy the cabins, serve at mealtimes, and just generally look after the passengers. She was exceptionally good at her job. She possessed a personality which could be described as 'lighting up the room' or in this case, the train.

Raini also had a generous laugh and was just a sheer pleasure to be around. At the end of the first day (when my mother was not there), I told Raini that I had a crush on her. She scoffed at that. But in a nice way.

On day two, in the 'Queen Adelaide' restaurant car, as she took our lunch orders, we were talking about why Mum and I were taking the trip. I explained that it was a treat for my mother's eightieth birthday. Raini smiled her warm smile and turned to my Mum.

"Your son is a good human," Raini said, and squeezed my Mum's hand.

The next day, we said goodbye. The train crew routinely swap places every week in Adelaide, halfway through the east-west journey, in each direction.

On that Adelaide train platform, we exchanged a lovely long hug goodbye; the one and only time that I had any physical contact with Raini. I told her that I would miss her. And then instantly realised that I did not know her at all. She was someone whom I had just met, who was (very) good at her job and was now logging off and going home for a break, probably to her husband and children. I will almost certainly never see her again.

"Enjoy the rest of your journey, Palmer. Look after your Mum," Raini said.

"I am so glad that I met you Raini," I replied.

Her final words to me were "Good humans find each other."

A FEW WEEKS LATER

Every night, for weeks, I visited the 'Bull and Finch', searching for Jodie. I would sit out the back, do the cryptic crossword and look up if anyone started playing 'World Cup 94'.

Googled her, of course. Searched through several social media sites. But with almost nothing to go on other than her first name, that was pointless.

A couple of times, I even mentioned her on-air. I was working as a DJ at a radio station; 2GFO-FM. The 9-12 morning shift. Not a lot of talk, mostly just back-announcing 1980s music. I had mentioned this job to her the night that we met, and she was interested.

So, every now and then, I would announce something like "That was 'Raspberry Beret' by Prince. That 1985 classic was for Jodie. If you have a hit that you want to hear, call 2GFO on…".

Another day: "And a number one from '81, 'Tainted Love' by Soft Cell. I think that a lot of us can relate to that one. Call in before noon to request your favourite sad 80s song."

And: "'I Still Haven't Found What I'm Looking For' by U2, out of 1987. I sure know how that feels. Call us here in the 2GFO studio if you can help. This is Palmer and the time is…".

She never called.

***

After a few weeks of this, one night I walked towards the 'Bull and Finch' and just kept walking. I kicked at a discarded can in the gutter and missed. It was a beautiful crisp and moonlit night. I wished that it was raining.

In my head, I replayed the conversation that we had just before we kissed. As I was showing her my DVD room, Jodie had said "I love this. It reminds me of the old DVD stores. Those places were amazing. So educational. The fact that you have recreated it blows my mind."

There used to be a Civic DVD store in Rose Forest. I knew it well, because I was their best customer, even when it was on its way out of business. It is now a café. It is called 'The Old Civic' and I had never been inside.

So, without anything better to do, I walked there. Before I even entered, I could smell the ubiquitous hand sanitiser (it was vaguely reminiscent of tequila). I walked in through the out door.

And that's when I saw her.

She was sitting at a table, alone, at the back of the café. Reading 'A Prayer for Owen Meany'. A bottle of water in front of her. My heartrate surged as I approached. Guess what? She was wearing a raspberry beret.

When I got close, she said (without looking up) "You know, Palmer, if you are going to search for the girl that you thought you had lost, and you still haven't found her, you need to be much more creative than just going back every night to the same place where you first met her."

I could not even think of a reply. Words, as they say, failed me.

So, I kissed her.

9

THE NEXT FEW MONTHS

Over the next few months, a strange thing happened. I was happy.

Jodie and I spent so much time with each other. We talked about our histories and laughed about our mistakes. Selectively revealing our true selves. We watched a lot of DVDs together.

Jodie provoked my best behaviour and excused my worst. Without ever being condescending, she reassured me. I never wondered about whether our new love was genuine because I was simply too appreciative of our time together, to waste any of it on doubt.

She brought out my long-dormant romantic side. Once, she cut her finger, opening one of my DVD cases. So I 'kissed it better'. It didn't even bleed, so I claimed credit for that.

The sex, when it happened, was fantastic. I was frankly scared the first time; it had been a while. And as I say, I am getting older. But it was perfect, almost effortlessly so.

I flatter myself to say that Jodie enjoyed it as much. Okay, perfect is the wrong adjective. It was not rolling simultaneous orgasms every time (although that did happen). But it was always gentle and encouraging, whilst also being passionate and never disappointing.

Jodie's body was the body of a somewhat mature woman. And it was more arousing to me than any twenty-something that I might have once lusted after.

I avoided using the 'love' word with her. Because of a private promise I had made after the Maddison disaster. No 'love' until after one year. Jodie either did not notice or did not mind.

Everything about my life improved. I was drinking less. I was enjoying my work more. The radio station management gave me a pay rise, based solely, they said, on my 'outstanding performance'. I even got better at the cryptic crosswords.

And I told her my stories. She often asked me to. So, I would go on and on about my life. My unsuccessful golfing career. My failed relationships (especially that bitch Maddison). That time when I spent a night in jail in Monte Carlo because I propositioned Prince Albert's girlfriend in the casino. I even told her the story about Raini, 'the girl on the train'.

Jodie always listened. She never judged. She would sometimes ask questions about details, but rarely interrupted me. Once, after a long-winded and possibly dull comic anecdote, she said "You are a fascinating person, Palmer, and your mind is a strange and mysterious thing."

Which was probably the nicest thing that anybody had ever said to me.

***

She soon moved in with me.

One beautiful Saturday morning, we were lying in bed together, in our flat in Rose Forest, after a particularly satisfying episode of lovemaking, in a ray of light. When Jodie surprised me. "What do you most like about me?"

I gathered my thoughts as best as I could. "You make me a better man. And you understand my pop culture references." Which whilst not being original, I felt was adequate at short notice.

"I believe you," she said. It was exactly what she had said when I first told her my name. Perhaps she remembered that also, as she then segued to "Why did your parents name you Palmer?"

"My Dad was a golf fan. Rather good player himself. He named me after the American golfer Arnold Palmer. I used to hate my name; nobody I have ever heard of is named Palmer. But at some point, I realised it could have been worse. I could have been named Arnold."

She laughed. A laugh I had never heard before. A shy sort of laugh, that accompanied her shy yet challenging smile. The smile that made me want to kiss her, every damn time.

Instead of kissing her, on this occasion, I asked "Why did your parents name you Jodie?"

"They didn't. I named myself."

"Oh," I said, "when did you do that?"

"When it was the right time to choose my own name."

"And how old was that?" I ventured.

"You know better than to ask a lady about her age."

True. Even after months of effectively living as husband and wife, I did not know when Jodie was born. Or where, for that matter. I was not bothered, but I suppose that it was a little strange.

"I don't even care how old you are, or where you are from," I lied.

"I don't believe you."

Ouch. Opting for safer ground, I went for "What do you most like about me?"

"You care about others. You have faults, but you recognise them. And you have so many questions, but you know when it is better not to ask. You have been hurt, badly, but you still trust."

Well, that blew my 'You make me a better man' response out of the water. Clever girl.

"I love you, Jodie."

Shit! Shit!! I had planned not to say that yet.

"I love you too, then, Palmer." Which was the new number one nicest thing that anybody had ever said to me.

"I mean it," I said.

"I believe you," she said.

***

That was the night when I replaced my 'Don't say I love you' vow with 'Don't lie to Jodie' vow. I never again wanted to hear her say 'I don't believe you'.

A week or so later, we were once again lying together in bed, naked. She was in an uncharacteristically playful mood. After a short tickle fight, she started this chat:

"I know that 'Lambs' is your favourite Jodie Foster movie. What's your number two?"

After an appropriate thoughtful pause, "I am going with 'Taxi Driver'."

"Not 'Panic Room'?"

"I don't like horror. And before you say anything, 'Lambs' is a thriller, not horror."

"'The Accused'?" Jodie quizzed me.

"Horror, also."

She nodded and appearing to be searching for another option. "How about 'Contact'?"

"Not a fan of science fiction. Spielberg ruined Indiana Jones when he brought aliens into it."

"Really?" my lover said, "I am surprised. Especially considering that 'Contact' has a main character named Palmer."

"It does?" I said. Oops. I am the self-proclaimed movie expert. But I had just had sex, I was off-guard.

Jodie play-slapped me. "You haven't even watched it, have you?" I considering lying by saying yes. But remembering my recent vow, I admitted that I had not.

"But I've seen the DVD on your shelves?" "You've seen the DVD case. Maddison used to never return the disc to the correct place. She might have taken that one, I don't know. But it's lost. 'Contact' is an empty case."

"Seems like an awful waste of space," Jodie said.

'CONTACT'

So that is why, in late 2020, I spent $AUD 45.23 to online order the Special Edition DVD of the 1997 film 'Contact'. Jodie Foster as Doctor Eleanor Arroway and Matthew McConaughey as Palmer. I probably could have streamed it, but I do love a DVD. I threw out the old empty case.

The new DVD arrived two weeks later, all the way from Kentucky, U.S.A. There was a special thrill in slicing open the cardboard and plastic wrapping, with a small sharp box-cutting knife that I kept for just these ceremonies.

Later, when the first viewing was over, in each other's arms, I felt like Jodie (my Jodie) was going to cry. As the credits rolled (I always insist upon watching the credits), I muted the soundtrack and we lay in silence. The DVD eventually returned to the features menu.

"That's my new number two," I finally said.

"They based that character on me," she said, sadly.

"You could say that about any Jodie Foster character," I laughed.

She moved out of the embrace.

"No, not Doctor Ellie," she whispered.

"Well, McConaughey was clearly based on me. I mean, even the name…," trailing off, feeling stupid.

She was silent. More than usual. So was I. The silence hung in the air, as muted as the DVD features menu that we were both staring into.

***

Things between us were never the same after that. Jodie spent less time with me, and when she was with me, she spoke less, asked fewer questions of me. She stopped answering her phone.

Our penultimate day on earth together dawned with—for the first time—disappointing sex.

We didn't speak of it. We watched some DVDs. 'Taxi Driver' followed by 'The Beaver' and then 'The Hotel New Hampshire'. I wanted to discuss how underrated the latter movie was, but I sensed that Jodie didn't want to hear it. So, we lay in silence again, until …

"I have to leave, Palmer." Instinctively, I knew. She did not mean leaving our flat, this night. She meant leaving my life. She meant leaving me forever.

I stayed mute.

THE NEXT DAY

The next day, I was working at the radio station and I was distracted. I back-announced Bowie's 'Space Oddity' as 'Starman'. Eleven listeners rang in to correct me.

Then, I played a song less than twenty years old, which is strictly against 2GFO-FM policy for the 9-12 shift. The programme manager gave me a serious dressing-down for that.

But I was more concerned as to whether Jodie would be there when I got home. I rang her mobile number and it rang out (she didn't have voicemail). I texted her, without reply. I rang her on the landline, as I often did (yes kids, people still use landlines), however there was no answer.

Sometime between finishing my shift and arriving back at our Rose Forest flat, a thought occurred to me. I had never seen Jodie with her mobile. It was 2020. Even my 84-year-old mother owned a Samsung. Who didn't carry their phone? And why had I never questioned her about it?

Despite these suspicious thoughts, I was relieved when I entered the flat and Jodie was there. Sitting on the leather couch. The same spot where we had first kissed. She was naked.

God, I loved her.

I rushed to her and kissed her, as passionately as that first kiss had been. She responded in kind, for about five minutes or so. Until …

"We have to talk."

Fuck it.

***

"Palmer, I don't want to overwhelm you. There is much to say and we don't have a lot of time. Is it okay for me to ask you to listen?"

"Yes," I replied, "but before I do, I have to tell you one thing. Is that okay?"

"It is," she said.

"You're the best thing that ever happened to me, or my world" (quoting a song, as usual).

"I believe you," she said.

And then she told me this:

"I love you, Palmer. I had never really understood love, until I met you. That day in the pub, with the pinball machine, changed me. You will never know how it did, but thank you."

She smiled, briefly, before her tone changed.

"I am going home soon. And you can't come with me. But know that I will never forget you. I am leaving you a memento. It is a kind of memory drive and it contains much information."

"What kind of info…," I interrupted.

"Please. I am speaking," Jodie said.

"Okay."

"Information that should be immensely helpful, when seen by the right people. It will explain so many things. And potentially solve many problems. You only need to hold it near any mobile technology and it will download. No need to make copies. The file folder will be named Jodie."

"I understand," I said, although I absolutely did not.

"Two final things, my love. One: when I give you this present, I will no longer be able to communicate with you. I will not speak and I will not hear. Two: I am so glad that I found you. Thanks for believing in me, Palmer. You are a good human." And she stood up and hugged me.

What happened next is difficult for me to describe. However, I shall try.

***

Jodie picked up my box-cutting knife from the coffee table and placed it under her right ear. She then cut into her scalp and sliced into her skin, moving above her skull, onto her left ear and then down the side of her neck, shoulder, and arm. There was no blood.

Her right hand holding the knife then cut back upwards towards her left armpit and then peeled back the skin, completely exposing what lay beneath her face, upper body, and left arm.

Sorry that I do not have sufficient words. Again, I will try. It was sort of like a pulsating mound of firm translucent jelly. There were no organs or bones visible. Just a ... mass. It was not gory. It was just ... there. Not shifting yet somehow shapeless.

I was reminded of a popular song "Jellyfish" from the previous year. It was by an indie Aussie band whose name I couldn't remember. It was the same song I had played on radio a few hours earlier. The lyrics included a question about watching jellyfish and then how weird they are. But it was actually about finding love. Jodie adored that song. I'd have to download it.

The rest of the skin (skinsuit?) fell to the ground. Near the top of the mass, there was something resembling a tentacle. As I watched, the tentacle-thing moved towards what used to be Jodie's left wrist. It extracted a small dark object. A second tentacle (for want of a better word) then gathered up the skinsuit. It drew it up over the gelatinous mass and as I watched, it became Jodie again. The skin reformed in a perfect demonstration of the adverb 'seamlessly'.

Seconds later, I was once again looking at the woman that I loved. The only noticeable difference was that her nose no longer looked like it had been broken.

In her right hand, palm up, she held out the object. It looked like a purple Tic Tac. She gestured for me to hold out my own right hand, palm up. I shook my head 'no' and I looked into her blue-green eyes and silently mouthed "I believe you."

Jodie smiled that same shy yet challenging smile that I adored. She placed the purple Tic Tac and (bloodless) box-cutter knife on my coffee table, right next to my mobile phone.

And then she walked out my front door.

NOW

I still work at the radio station. One day, not long after she left, I recorded a three-hour rantfilled broadcast, all about extra-terrestrials living amongst us and whether we should contact them. I was trying to get sacked. I may have been drunk. At the end of the tirade, I played Bowie's 1984 song 'Loving The Alien'. And back-announced it, in a whisper; "For Jodie".

My bosses loved it. Turned it into a podcast. They named it 'Second Contact'. Publicised it and sold advertising spots. It received over two million hits worldwide within a week. You might have heard about it. It was trending in both social media and mainstream news for a while there.

However, I soon realised that my followers were mostly the same people (or their bots) who believed the moon landings, climate change, and COVID-19 were all hoaxes. One prominent group 'Flat Earthers Unite' posted without apparent irony: 'This needs to be shared around the globe'.

So, I managed to convince management to take the podcast down. They were reluctant to do so, it was making them money. But like everybody else, they soon forgot about it.

***

On a clear night, I often find myself searching for Jodie. I take a four-pack of craft beer ($22) and walk to my local golf course. I climb through a hole in the fence and lie in a sand bunker, drink, and stare at the stars. Under the moonlight (as Bowie had sung), this serious moonlight.

I will never see her again, of course. She is far beyond the reach of our extremely large telescopes, let alone my naked eyes. However, it comforts me knowing that she is out there.

And I never did look at the contents of the purple Tic Tac. It is now very safely well-hidden. The mobile phone that was exposed to it has also been destroyed and disposed of, just in case.

I know that is selfish. Perhaps it contains solutions to man-made climate change. And / or the cure for this damn killer virus. And more? But I don't care; I don't want to share her.

Maybe one day I will change my mind. Perhaps. We'll see.

Jodie was better at being human than any human being ever was. God, I miss her.

Greg Eccleston is a writer & professional actor. He has written & had produced the stageplays "Catharsis" & "Girlfriend #33 Stole my Mojo"; as well as the award-winning short play "The Fifth Stage". His creative influences & heroes include John Irving, Robin Williams & David Bowie. Greg lives near the beach in Terrigal, Australia & he has visiting rights to his cat Banderas.

Redemption

by Mark Bilsborough

Erin emerged into the blinding glare of the midday sun. She staggered and fell, face down on dusty ground.

She let the dizziness fade then eased herself to her knees. She was in the middle of an open square, surrounded by crudely assembled low wooden buildings set at the base of a snow-flecked mountain. Men and women hurried past, dressed in rough furs and thick, coarse fabrics. They all paused and stared.

Her head ached. She ran her hand through her hair, or rather what was left of it; close-cropped now, spiky and ragged. A crowd gathered, though everyone looked more curious than hostile. She became conscious that she wasn't in her smart office clothes anymore but wore the same dull, practical frontier clothing of the people around her. Wherever she was, it was a long way from home.

A small man with a shaven head pushed his way to the front. "Jared wants to see you," he said, and led her away. Erin thought of resisting, but her head hurt and she wanted to get out of the sun. The crowd dispersed, talking softly and glancing at Erin until she disappeared into the largest of the surrounding buildings.

"Where am I?" she said.

The small man laughed. "You know where you are. Or you will, when your memory returns." He pulled back a large curtain and led her into an inner chamber. A thickset man with long white

21

hair tied back in a ponytail sat at a wooden desk studying papers. She recognised him straight away—and at that moment she knew exactly where she was. In a virtual prison world.

Jared Anderson looked up and stared at Erin. "Just in?"

"Five minutes ago in the square, Chief," the small man said.

Jared leaned back in his chair and studied her. It made Erin uncomfortable, seeing him without his practiced politician's smile. He seemed meaner, more calculating than she remembered, now that the cameras weren't on him. She remembered his trial and inevitable conviction for embezzlement. Throughout, he maintained his innocence despite overwhelming evidence against him. He was so good at making everyone want to believe him that his ratings stayed high even after the verdict. Now here he was, a prisoner just like her. He motioned her to stand opposite him on the other side of the desk.

"What can you do?" he said.

"Don't you want to know who I am first, or how I came to be here?"

"No."

Erin searched for elusive memory and found fragments. She'd stumbled across something. Been somewhere she wasn't supposed to be. She recalled a struggle. And now this, a smelly room filled with hostile men in a place that just felt… wrong. She tried not to sound panicked. "I can't stay. I shouldn't be here."

Jared looked disinterested. "Leave then. Be my guest—I don't want you. Oh, but you can't, can you? None of us can. So you're stuck here, and you need to pay your way. You're not pretty enough for the whorehouse and you look too stupid to be any use to me. So what can you do?"

She was confused, her brain still fuzzy from her sudden and unexpected arrival. She considered arguing, but that would have to wait. She knew she couldn't afford to antagonise this man. "I'm good with computers."

"Do you see any computers round here?"

"Teaching, then. I can teach."

"Do you see any children? Can you cook? Sew? Build a wall? Fix a leaking roof?"

Erin stood impassively.

"Take her to the kitchens, Gary. Shannon will know what to do with her."

"That's it?"

"Just two things. Do as you're told and don't do anything stupid."

She opened her mouth to say something else but Gary glowered at her and motioned for her to go with him. Jared went back to his paperwork.

Gary said nothing as he grabbed hold of her arm and dragged her to a large room on the other side of the building, laid out with wooden tables and chairs with a huge open fire dominating one wall. A serving bar ran the length of the opposite side, broken only by a doorway leading, Erin suspected, to the kitchens. A woman with long red hair scrubbed one of the tables. She looked up as they entered, her face hard and unsmiling. "What's this, Gary? Another new arrival I don't want and can't use?"

"I'm sure you can find her something to do."

"Why should I take the ones Jared doesn't want? Tell him no." She went back to her cleaning.

"You don't say no to Jared."

Gary grinned at Erin, released her arm and left the room.

Erin broke the silence first. "What happens now?"

"You keep out of my way. Unless you have any talent at all." She frowned. "Which I doubt."

"I can be useful."

"How? You're too soft, like all the other new arrivals. I haven't got time to toughen you up."

"I'm tougher than I look."

"You'd better be." The woman sighed and sat down. She gestured at an empty chair and Erin sat too. "Okay. Not that I have a choice. What's your name?"

"Erin."

"Mine's Shannon. I'll put you in the kitchens. You're too pretty for waitressing—can't let you out here until you've learned how to handle yourself."

"I've waitressed before, when I was a student."

Shannon grunted. "Serving college boys and Professors isn't the same as feeding rapists and murderers. You'll see."

"So I was right. This is a prison world."

"Your brain still mush from the arrival? Look around—does this look like a vacation world? Welcome to the 'Bay."

"Bay?"

"Botany Bay. You know, the place we all get a fresh start. The place there's no going back from."

***

The rest of the people in the kitchen largely ignored Erin. It was a huge and noisy space, with cooking done on large open fires in searing heat. Shannon handed her over to Maria, an older woman with a constant smile who talked softly when she talked at all. A younger man—boy—washing pots caught her eye.

"That's Ben," said Maria. "Don't mind him."

Erin was put to work straight away, preparing vegetables she'd hauled from a storehouse next to the main building. After four hours, too tired to stay awake, she dropped her knife and steadied herself on a low table. Maria gently led her away upstairs to a long, low dormitory in the roof space with the floor covered in dirty mattresses and furs.

"Sleep," said Maria. "I suspect you need it."

Exhausted, Erin lay staring at the ceiling until every part of the dormitory filled with the other kitchen workers. Faced with the harsh reality of her new life what happened before seemed like a dream. Maybe it was.

Her memory was still vague and disjointed but she felt lucky: some people never got over the shock of forced immersion. Some memory loss was part of the design, anyhow. Rob criminals of their memories and maybe you can strip them of their criminality. Just enough to make them unlikely to descend into chaos and anarchy, not enough to lead to accusations of brainwashing and identity tampering. Erin didn't know why the courts even cared: once sent to a prison world there was no way back.

Maybe she wasn't meant to be there in the first place. Perhaps that's why she could remember being surprised that there was anyone else in the building so late, down a corridor where only a handful of people should have access.

She knew she should be grateful. If not for the V-worlds they probably would have killed her, instead of sending her into permanent virtual exile. She wanted to think that it meant they had some sort of conscience, instead of it being a way to silence her without having a corpse to dispose of.

***

For the next few days she barely got out of the kitchen. A relentless, mind numbing drudge of shifting boxes, peeling vegetables and mopping floors, leaving her too tired and busy to think. She was grateful that she didn't have an opportunity to dwell on her hopeless situation.

After a while her bones stopped aching and she found she actually enjoyed the routine. The rest of the kitchen workers largely ignored her, but she'd no desire to encourage them. They looked, almost without exception, like the kind of people she spent most of her life avoiding.

Ben was different, though. Just a kid, barely old enough to be there, but with something approachable about him. Maybe because he was the only one apart from Maria who smiled. Maybe because he didn't shave his head like the other men. She wished she knew what he'd been sent there for, but that was the one topic nobody wanted to discuss. Whatever his crime, he had an innocence about him that made her want to stick close by, both for his protection and perhaps her own.

"Will I get older in here?" he said, when they were taking a break. Marie had stolen some biscuits and the three of them were sitting well away from the rest of the kitchen hands.

"Physically, yes. The simulation should match you to the age your body's at, back in the tank. Mentally? The brain's a strange and complex thing. Your experiences are all in here now. You'll change, certainly, but I don't know if anyone can predict whether you'll turn into the same person you would if you weren't in the simulation. Probably not. I think the people who sent you here are rather hoping it would make you less likely to do whatever you did that brought you here in the first place."

"We shouldn't be talking like this. This is our reality now," said Maria.

"Yes but what if we could leave?" said Ben, with the enthusiasm of the young.

"We can't," said Erin, but her face betrayed her.

"There's a back door, isn't there," said Ben, catching her unease.

"There's always a back door."

***

That night as Erin cleaned the stove after the others had gone up to the dormitory Shannon lingered at the doorway. "You never did say what you were here for."

"I thought no-one asked that."

"I'm curious. For most people what they were is a nightmare they don't want to be reminded of. And, frankly, if I knew some of the things the people in this kitchen had done in the past, I'd have to get rid of them. Some of them are very good with knives; did you noticed that?" Shannon grinned. "Me? I put a pillow over my husband's head one day. Right after he'd hospitalised my youngest, the second time."

"I'm sorry."

"Don't be. I hated my husband. And it's not so bad here, once you get used to the cold and the complete lack of anything interesting to do." Shannon moved into the room, holding something behind her back.

"You, though, are desperate to tell someone all about yourself, aren't you? You're different. I think I was so mad with Jared for foisting you on me to notice at first. I think you have stories to tell." She held up a bottle and two glasses. "Drink?"

They walked out into the main room. The late hour meant the place was empty apart from a large, bearded man slumped against the wall, snoring gently. Shannon led them to comfortable looking fur-covered seats, though Erin found she could only sit stiffly on the rim of her chair. Shannon lit a candle and slowly Erin began to relax. After a couple of glasses of Shannon's crude home-made vodka Erin found herself ready to talk.

"They put you in here for killing your husband? Even though he terrorised you?" said Erin.

Shannon leaned back in her seat. "Apparently I didn't show enough remorse. Besides, ever since they set up the virtual prison system the courts have been giving out life sentences much more frequently. After all, cheaper to send me here than put me in a conventional prison for a year and pay out social security for the rest of my life. They'd already taken my children away—last thing they would want is for me to walk back into their lives."

"We hadn't anticipated that," said Erin. "But I guess every technological innovation influences behaviour in unpredictable ways."

"You got kids?" asked Shannon, moving on to the next question before Erin could shake her head. "Boyfriend? Husband?" Erin felt alone, a feeling made worse by the shadow of a smirk Shannon had trouble concealing. "Best that way. Nobody to miss, nobody to miss you. Clean start."

"Peeling vegetables? Hardly what MIT trained me for."

"You remember what you used to be then," said Shannon." You worked for the people who put us here, didn't you?" Shannon poured them both another glass. Erin realised she was getting drunk.

"Yes, I worked for V-corp," said Erin.

"You created this world?"

Erin shook her head. "Not this one. I worked on leisure systems. Holiday worlds, that sort of thing. Though I helped design the total immersion tanks which make all this possible."

The V tanks. The answer to the inconvenient need to take off your V-band to eat, and sleep, and crap. Nutrient glop which can feed you, take away your waste, even keep your muscles toned with a mild electrical charge. No reason to ever unplug. Once Erin's colleagues rigged their software so you couldn't leave the system even if you wanted to they had, in effect, created the perfect prison. The cost savings were enormous and it wasn't long before a life sentence meant transportation to places like Botany Bay.

"So what are you here for then? Passing through to check it's all working?"

Erin sighed. "I need to get out."

"You can't. You should know that, if you worked for V-corp. That's the whole point. And besides, they'd only put you back in."

"Not if I hadn't been put here by the courts, they wouldn't. My crime—if you can call it that—was to expose some industrial espionage back at V-corps. We're world leaders in virtual world technology and our rivals are desperate to get hold of our secrets. My mistake was to confront the guys about to sell us out before I went public. So I ended up having my face shoved into the tank by my co-workers."

"Everyone's innocent in here, Erin. But if it makes you feel better I'll pretend to believe you."

"It's true."

"Won't help you much though. There's still no way out."

"There's always a way out. There has to be. Maybe not officially, but when we construct these worlds we always add a back door, something only the designer knows about, just in case we can't get out of the system quickly, or get stuck, like I am here.

"Trouble is, I have no idea where, or what, it is. Unless I can find it, I'm trapped."

***

Erin graduated to waiting tables. She ignored the leers and glances—something about her prevented any trouble. Maybe people could sense that she wasn't really one of them.

Jared ate there most days, accompanied by Gary and a man Erin recognised from old news footage: Owen Mason. No way could he hide what he'd done on the outside—his crimes were both violent and notorious. Jared kept him close by as bodyguard and enforcer.

Jared caught her arm as she cleared his plate. "Sit."

Erin looked for Shannon but her friend had her back turned. So she sat. Mason and Gary shifted to the next table.

"Shannon tells me you're settling in well."

Erin shrugged. "What else has she said?"

Jared smiled. "That you know a way out of here."

"She's wrong about that. If I knew the way out, do you think I'd still be here?"

He leaned forward. "Word is that you're a spy for the Company. That you can go home anytime you choose."

She snorted and stood up. "Believe that if you want. I've got work to do." Jared chuckled, but stopped abruptly when he noticed Shannon staring at him.

***

That evening she and Shannon took a bottle of wine and walked down to the shoreline. They sat on a fishing boat moored high on the beach and looked out over the moon-dappled waves.

"How far out can you go?" asked Erin.

"Not far. There's a barrier about two miles out. I guess the coders ran out of time or inclination to give us the whole world."

"Or money. V-corp wouldn't want to set up a whole simulation nobody ever needed."

"When we first arrived the barrier was only just beyond the shore. As the population grows, our world gets bigger." She paused and poured the wine. "Do you think the back door's out there?"

Erin shook her head. "Doesn't work like that. If it's physical, it's more likely to be in the centre of the territory."

"The mountain."

"That would be my guess. We need to try commands first though. Like 'home', 'open', 'gone' …"

"Away, leave, escape…"

"You get the picture. It's unlikely to be a single word though, because that would be too easy to trigger accidentally."

"If you'd designed it, what would you have done?"

"Something simple, that I wouldn't forget. Like 'get us out of here,' or 'I'll see you in hell, suckers.'"

They tried every combination of words they could think of, until the warm soft light of dawn started to creep over the horizon and Erin ran out of phrases to try.

***

Erin climbed the mountain the next day. Shannon had gone to visit Jared, early in the morning, and hadn't returned by lunchtime, leaving Erin to head up the shift. She wasn't sure what that meant yet but she suspected trouble, and that gave her an added urgency. She'd seen the look Shannon gave her when Jared talked to her. And she'd heard the way Shannon talked to him too, like only a lover would. She had no intention of being in the middle when the recrimination started.

The mountain was barely more than a big hill, but there was snow at the top and the climb was steep.

She didn't really know what to look for. Each designer had their own visual signatures. Hers was red lipstick, hidden at random strategic points. Pick it up and you're elsewhere in the simulation, or out altogether. But she couldn't find anything at all. Of course the snow didn't help. She saw a small plateau right at the top, perhaps ten feet in diameter. Unusual to have a flat design right at the top of the hill. She started digging, scooping up great mounds of snow and throwing them off the side. She tried to ignore the cold, but despite the thick furs she wore she knew she couldn't carry on much longer. Then her hands struck something hard. She quickly dug round it, levering it free from the snow.

A body, frozen solid.

Alarmed, she took a step back and almost stepped off the edge. In most virtual worlds if someone dies they automatically snap back out of the game. Not in a prison world though, because if all you had to do to get back into the real world was die the suicide rate would be massive. No, here if you died, the system was supposed to regenerate you, to keep you inside until your own flesh and blood body died of natural causes in the tank.

But what if you were frozen when you died? Or did the act of freezing keep you alive in some way? With horror she realised the answer lay in front of her.

She hauled the body over on its back and inspected it more closely. The dead eyes of a man stared blankly ahead, dressed in light clothes which were no match for the ferocity of the mountain.

She had to get him back down, but she knew she couldn't do it by herself. And then out of the corner of her eye she saw something colourful, now partially clear. She dug some more, until she could make out the full extent of her find. A ring on the surface of the plateau, maybe six feet in diameter, etched in pink.

Now she knew the designer. And now she knew the code. She kneeled down by the body and dragged it over to the ring, making sure they were both completely encircled. Then she said, firmly, "Xyzzy." The air stilled, then with a crack of ozone the mountain disappeared in a bright flash of pink-tinged light.

They reappeared in the main square, right in front of a horse which reared its legs and nearly toppled its rider. "Mr Pink, gaming geek. You are so predictable," Erin said, under her breath. But she'd been hoping the shortcut code would lead her home.

Shocked villagers backed away. Someone must have run to fetch Jared because he appeared very quickly, accompanied by Shannon.

"What's going on?" he said.

"I found him at the top of the mountain. I couldn't leave him there."

He raised his arms. "Have you any idea what you've done?"

Erin looked down at the impossible sight of the frozen body and had a sinking feeling she knew exactly what she'd done.

***

Jared called her for tea the next day and they sat drinking, Mediterranean style, on low cushions. Mint tea, hot, strong and sweet which to Erin tasted like medicine.

"The man you brought down from the mountain has thawed out now, before you ask."

"How is he?"

Jared cocked his ear theatrically. "If you listen very carefully you might hear him. They tell me he does nothing but scream. His mind has completely gone."

"Do you think he was conscious all that time?" Erin knew that would guarantee craziness.

"You tell me, you're the V-world designer. I'm guessing that his body shut down though, and put him in some sort of coma. Probably as close to death as you can get in this place. Maybe that's why he was up there. Maybe he tried to commit suicide. Did you think of that?"

Erin sipped quietly. "I could take him back."

"Ah I dunno. Perhaps someone on the outside will notice now. They might finally believe what I said about this system not being safe enough to use." Jared grinned. "Something's just occurred to me. If you were here accidentally, like you claimed, wouldn't one of the routine monitoring scans have noticed you here and pulled you out?"

"They're not that sophisticated."

"I wonder. Did you say you were uncovering espionage? Or engaged in it?"

Erin changed the subject. "I remember your campaign against the V-worlds back when you were a politician."

"Back before your people closed me down, you mean."

Erin took a good long look at him. With his normal arrogance missing he almost seemed defeated. "You closed yourself down. Or are you trying to tell me you weren't the one who embezzled millions from dubious construction projects? Surely you're not saying V-Corp framed you, just so you'd stop bothering them? Shannon always says everyone claims to be innocent in here."

He smiled. "Ask yourself. Is anyone here behaving like a criminal? There are murderers all around us, yet there's no violent crime. Fraudsters, but no fraud."

"You're going to tell me that's because of your brilliant benign dictatorship, aren't you?" The tea began to leave a sickly taste in her mouth.

"I was going to make a point about crime being more about the environment than the criminal. You people thought we'd all be killing ourselves in here, didn't you? Engaged in sadistic mutilation sprees. Terrorising, raping and pillaging. Sorry to disappoint. Life's tough but there's a community here. We all have jobs to do and people who rely on us."

"Jobs make model citizens?"

"Do virtual prisons?"

"You didn't bring me here so you could give me a politics lecture," she said, refusing the offer of another cup of tea.

He leaned forward. "No. I wanted to ask you about your materialisation in the square yesterday. Very impressive. I need you to tell me how you did it."

"We can't use it to escape, if that's what you mean. It's an in-game transporter, that's all. It's a pretty crude one too. I can get us from the square to the top of the mountain and back again, but that's it. If I knew the designer's cat's mother's maiden name I might have a chance, but, realistically, given how easily I guessed the other code, I think the back door isn't verbal."

"Not physical, not verbal. What's left?"

"Something you do. Something probably related to the scenario we're in, because we V-world designers like that sort of symmetry. But not something obvious or anything which is likely to happen naturally, at least not here."

Erin suddenly felt a chill breeze from the ill-fitting windows. It was getting late.

"I'll walk you out," said Jared with what she used to think of as his politician's smile. She wondered if she'd been wrong about him.

They walked across the square, well-lit by the full moon. The moon was always full, Erin thought absently. Lazy design. As they reached the door to her quarters Jared reached out and touched her gently on the cheek, before she could pull away. Then, abruptly, Jared backed off, still smiling but clearly uncomfortable.

That's when she caught sight of Shannon, in the doorway of the tavern, staring across at them.

***

Erin didn't think anything of it when Shannon suggested they take a trip to the top of the mountain, now that they could get there without a gruelling three hour climb. Maybe they could see something from that high vantage point which might be useful to them. Or maybe they'd find another frozen body.

The code word worked perfectly, as Erin knew it would. The day was still and bright, which took some of the edge off the extreme cold, but still, Erin made sure they were both well-padded with furs.

"Astounding," Shannon said. You can see everything from here." She turned to face Erin. "And, you know, everything's so much clearer here. Just me and you. Alone."

Shannon's face was partially shrouded by fur but Erin could see she had the same hard stare she'd shown her the first day, back before they were friends.

"You remember that story I told you about why I'm in here? I lied. I really did kill my husband. The prosecution tried to make out he hadn't actually slept with his girlfriend. That she wasn't actually his girlfriend at all. But I'd seen them looking at each other, the way you and Jared look at each other."

"There's nothing going on between me and Jared." Erin tensed as she worked out where the conversation was going. "So you killed the girlfriend too."

"But it would have been so much more satisfying if I could have kept her alive. Made her suffer for ever for what she'd done."

Now Erin knew why they were on the top of the mountain. "The frozen man."

"I should thank you for giving me that idea. I wonder what it's like slowly going mad up here in the freezing cold." Shannon moved slowly towards her, backing her against the edge. Erin thought about falling. Painful, but at least then the simulation's regeneration routines would trigger and she'd be safe.

But Shannon was too quick. She grabbed hold of Erin's arm and swung her round, leaving Erin splayed on her back scrambling to get up. But Shannon's strength and determination made her dangerous. Then Shannon was on her, pinning her to the ground.

Shannon raised her fist and Erin knew she had one chance. She relaxed, just like they'd told her in self-defence classes. Then, just as Shannon was unbalanced by the force of her punch Erin tensed and jerked sideways, away from the blow. Shannon fell to the ground and Erin kicked her over onto her back, grabbed her round the neck and squeezed. At first she didn't think about anything except survival. Then she realised that Shannon's twitching was getting less vigorous and she knew she was choking her.

If she carried on Shannon would die, only to be regenerated, probably back down in the village. It might solve the immediate problem, but what then? Shannon would be back, and angry. So she couldn't kill Shannon, but she couldn't let her live either.

But what if Shannon just lost consciousness? Then she'd freeze, alive, just like the madman back in the village. Dead, but not dead. No reset.

She deserved it. She had tried to kill her. Not to mention the unspeakable crimes she'd committed, and the ones she would undoubtedly do in the future.

She wanted to, she really did. She even tightened her grip for a second or two. But that would make her just like Shannon, and she knew she couldn't live with herself. If there was any doubt whether or not she belonged in a prison world, she would have the answer. So she relaxed her grip and eased herself up.

Shannon gasped and rubbed her windpipe. Slowly, she got up off the ground and moved towards Erin, arms out, reaching for her throat. Erin closed her eyes and waited for the worst.

"You should have done it," Shannon said.

And then it all went dark.

***

Erin hauled herself out of the nutrient and wiped the goo off her eyes. She was out.

With hindsight it all made sense to her. By saving Shannon even though she knew it would lead to her own pain and suffering she'd done something unexpected, something that deserved the reward of freedom.

She'd found the back door.

Redemption.

Mark Bilsborough is based in England and mainly writes the kind of science fiction that invariably involves time travel, dimension hopping or both. His stories are dotted around the internet and he's working on a novel. www.markbilsborough.com and @MarkBils are places you can find him.

Space Action Hero

by Andrew P. McGregor

I covered my shuddering mouth and fell to my knees as the screen turned to black. "My wife," I whispered. The execution by our enemies, the Andromedan Scurge, completed my failure as a war hero. Tears fell onto my shaking hands and I squeezed my eyes shut, not wanting to see the concern of the other prisoners of war. "They killed my wife," I growled to the steel-sheeted floor. The image of her white dress, fallen on the dead dirt of a blasted park in the middle of an alien military facility, was still fresh in my mind.

The stench of sweat announced the appearance of one of the other prisoners at my side, and I flinched when he put a light hand on my shoulder. "I know, Hero, but what can we do about it?"

My stinging eyes popped open, and my head snapped to the side. I glared at the stinking man, whose hair fell in ragged white sheets around his orange-suited shoulders. "What can we *do?*" I snarled. The prisoner lifted his hand from my shoulder and took two steps backwards, his mouth curling downwards while his eyes burst wide.

"Uh, I don't know, Mr H-Hero," he stuttered.

"We can escape and save my children."

"Oh, no," the older man stammered, backing away from me. "Not another attempt." The prisoners took notice and stared, while others looked for the exits in the grey-paneled room.

"Help me escape. All of you help me save my children."

Worried stares gazed back at me.

"Scream," I told them, my hands transforming into angry fists. "Start screaming, before I make you scream."

"Uh …" the older man continued backing away. I narrowed my eyes and walked toward him. He sat on a plain white chair, one of many that faced the large black screen, and covered his head. "Scream," I whispered in his ear. When he whimpered, I grabbed his wrist. "Please?" But the man only sunk lower.

I let go of the man's wrist and whispered an apology. He was just an old man, frightened in an alien prison ship. I would have to do it myself.

"Help!" I shouted. "Help, they're attacking me."

I screamed and shouted, as loud as I could, until my throat was sore, and then screamed some more while lying on the cold grey floor. The other prisoners scattered, not wanting to be in the same room when the guards came. And come they did. Two white-armoured guards, human collaborators, charged into the room from one of the exits that the other prisoners fled from.

They ran to me, their batons sheathed and helping hands offered. Their armoured boots clamped tight to the metal paneling, telling me the boots were magnetised. That shouldn't be a problem.

With snot and tears dripping down my face, I turned to regard my captors. I grabbed the hand of one of the faceless armoured collaborators and smiled.

"Shit," the woman behind the helmet said before I yanked her downwards, slamming her armoured head on the hard floor.

"Not again!" the other guard, a man, said before I could turn my attention to him.

I kicked with my right foot and hit him behind the knee. The guard yelped, and the magnets attaching his armoured feet to the floor slipped away under the sudden assault. He fell to the ground, and I grabbed his head, slamming it into the floor.

The collaborators groaned and moved weakly to cover their heads with their hands. I got to my feet, ready to end their lives. "No," I told myself. *I'm better than that,* I thought. Instead, I got to work removing the man's white armour.

The software behind the armour was basic, and it took mere moments for me to bypass the security, using my Terran Government-supplied overrides, a relic from my war days.

The ship's alarms blared in a crescendo, and emergency lights strobed the room. I hastily donned the white suit, which was a size or two too small, and slammed the helmet over the top. The helmet's HUD powered on and the internal screen gave me vision, while the suit's electronic ears picked up the telltale taps of footsteps. I ignored the smell of the other man's breath and faced the two doors.

Hero of the empire, defender of humanity, destroyer of the Scurge, I would not let the approaching guards stop me from saving my children.

Six white-armoured guards launched into the room, batons drawn.

Whack-Whack-Whack. Three guards fell to the floor. Two more danced out of my reach while the last guard took one look at my wild visage and fled.

One of the two remaining guards surged forwards, and I brought my baton down on his back, hearing something snap under the armour. The last guard hit me on the knee, but I barely felt it and head-butted him, knocking him to the ground.

I snorted with satisfaction before turning to charge through the doors, determined to find a way to the armoury, or the bridge, where the ship's antiquated A.I. would be hiding. I found little resistance, and the other prisoners scattered before my vengeful visage. Doors fell to my armoured fists and feet, and the few guards that dared face me soon regretted their mistake.

***

The bridge was strewn with human collaborators, officers, and midshipmen who'd offered little resistance to my explosive entrance. I clenched the captain's small pistol in my left hand as I typed commands into the bridge's secure terminal. I looked up as the main screen flicked to life.

A blue marble set against a starry black backdrop confirmed my suspicions; I was on a prison ship overlooking Earth. The ship was an old cruise liner that must've been captured by the Scurge and put to use, holding their most dangerous prisoners. My secret codes, supplied by the Terran Government, unlocked the ship's controls, allowing me access to the external sensors.

The sensors were limited, but they afforded a view of the docking tube, where I spied a shuttle coming in to dock. It was military grade, built by the Terran Overseers.

"Ship?"

"Yes?" the commandeered A.I. replied.

"How many are aboard that shuttle?"

"I am reliably informed there are four soldiers and an A.I. pilot."

I nodded. "When the soldiers from that shuttle come aboard, I want you to do an emergency decompression of the docking tube."

"That will cause significant damage to the area, sir, and harm the shuttle and soldiers. Are you sure?"

I could hear the reluctance in the A.I.'s androgynous voice, as if it wanted to argue against me, but couldn't due to the codes I'd entered into the bridge terminal. In the ship's mind, emergency decompression might kill some of the other prisoners. I bowed my head and thought of my wife's execution and the threats against my children. If I didn't do this, we were all dead anyway. "Just do it."

The bridge's speakers crackled in response, the A.I. venting its frustration at me. "Emergency decompression is set."

"Good, I'm going down there. Keep a channel open to my armour and update me on what's happening."

With the sleek, blue pistol still clenched in my hand, I ran as fast as my powered armour could manage.

"The shuttle has docked, and the airlock is cycling," the A.I. informed me, sounding upset about it.

"Don't do it, Hero," the old man who'd tried to comfort me earlier said. He stood in the hatchway of a dining room, leaning heavily on its frame. He watched me with glazed eyes as I ran past. "It's too late to bring her back."

"I know, damn it!" I yelled at him over my shoulder. I shook my head, disgusted at the number of collaborators and placid prisoners. Had they no pride? Could they not help?

A loud bang and a whooshing sound came from the corridor ahead before something heavy thudded shut. The bang would be the emergency decompression, and the heavy thud would be one of the ship's emergency metal seals closing to stop the air from rushing out. I reached the end of the corridor and hunted for the docking hatch where the enemy soldiers were going to board. It wasn't hard to find; The escaping air had pulled loose tools and equipment toward a single bulkhead on the ship's dock. I headed along metal gantries toward that point, and panted for breath as I touched the wall, my lungs not working as well as they used to.

I ignored my aching muscles and ordered the ship's A.I. to give me a view of the shuttle. A small image popped onto my HUD. *Good*, I thought. The shuttle was intact, and its docking tube had ripped clear, exposing its side to the open vacuum. It had shifted a little from the sudden blast of air, so if I timed my jump right, I'd hit the inside of the shuttle at a slow enough velocity that I hopefully wouldn't break my limbs. The four soldiers flailed uselessly, but were still alive, floating away from the prison ship at a few metres a minute. A slow, inevitable death for the collaborators.

"When I tell you to open this bulkhead, do it," I told the A.I., which buzzed a sultry affirmative. I shook my head and banged my armoured fists against the metal plating, mentally preparing myself for the leap and trying to work the kinks out of my aching muscles. It felt as if my muscles had atrophied, gone soft in the alien prison, which was impossible; among other military enhancements to my body, nano-machines massaged my limbs, keeping them in peak performance. *What did the Scurge do to me?*

"Now."

The metal sheet, several inches thick, slammed open and embedded itself in a shaft in the ceiling. The damaged airlock waited beyond, as did vacuum and my waiting ride. My magnetic boots held firm against the rushing wind while I steadied myself, holding the edges of the ruined airlock. I searched for the hole in the shuttle, leaned back into the rushing wind, and then leapt forward, flying through the prison ship's airlock, straight for the shuttle.

I waved at the flailing soldiers, who were so inept as to forget any sort of propulsion packs or magnetic tethers on their power armour. "Bye, idiots," I told them. Not bothering to use any sort of communications channel, I instead flipped them with my middle fingers. A second later, I careened into the damaged shuttle airlock, scattering debris and hitting hard against the interior walls of the shuttle.

I'd done this stunt a hundred times before, back in the wars. Overlooking colony worlds at the front of the conflict, I'd performed many space-borne boarding actions, so I knew just what to expect and how to recover. The hit against the shuttle's interior didn't hurt. The white security armour was tough enough to protect my aching body from the impact. The moment I hit, I searched for something solid and latched onto it, which happened to be the edge of a miniature conveyor belt with a cryo-tube sitting atop it. The tube must've been for my capture and incarceration, but I had little time to think about it.

I checked my suit for any signs of damage. They'd banged it up, but it was still airtight, so I monkey-walked my way from the shuttle's tiny airlock into the shuttle's command cabin, using various hand-holds to power my way through floating equipment, clothes and other miscellanea. The shuttle's computer responded to my touch, and my suit interfaced with it, allowing me direct mental control over its systems. I thanked the former Terran Government once again for entrusting me with its old secret codes.

Now I just needed to make orbital insertion, find the military installation where the Scurge were keeping my children, and rescue them. The shuttle's computer informed me there were several defence satellites orbiting on the route, and the shuttle was ill-equipped to get through without being blown to pieces.

"Ship?" I called to the prison ship's A.I.

"Sir?" the ship's voice crackled over my suit's radio.

"Launch every one of your life pods towards the following coordinates on my command."

"Acknowledged."

That should help, I thought. The Scurge would have to take down every pod to make sure the one that carried me didn't make it. The satellites couldn't stop them all …

"What?" I shouted with glee when I discovered the shuttle's private armoury in its memory banks. I hit the digital button that would open the small armoury, and a wall panel at the rear of the small cabin split open, revealing several shock weapons, magnetic clips, a couple of laser welders, and the diamond in the rough, a D-suit.

It was a disarmed model, and patched in several places, as if it'd seen a lot of action over the years. I didn't care. A Destroyer-suit, even a disarmed one, improved my odds of success astronomically. I accessed the digital codes to open the black hulk of the three-metre tall D-suit and climbed in, sealing it tight. A grim smile accompanied my relief when I saw the D-suit was fully powered.

The white armour was superfluous now, simply weighing me down, but in the airless confines of the shuttle I would have to stay within it while also wearing the D-suit. The shuttle's two life pods were the next deck down, and I made haste to them, clamping magnetic boots against metal decking and swimming down an open shaft to the deck with the life pods. I squeezed aboard one pod and locked the hatch.

"Ship, launch all pods now."

"Done."

At the same time I used the neural interface with the shuttle's computer to order the shuttle to release the pods and felt the G-forces crush into me as my pod launched at the Earth.

***

I awoke on the floor of the pod. "Shit." I never blacked out during the war. I activated the D-suit's miniaturised fusion reactor, collected the laser rifle that had survived the descent, and slammed a metal fist against the pod's door. The door popped open, clanging loudly on the hard tarmac of the military base's main road. The overcast sky bled drop pods, a handful of which crashed into low-lying buildings, sending small shock-waves throughout the base. A sign near the chained gates read 'Purplewood Studies,' the name of the facility.

As I leapt onto the road, the suit's scanners detected several enemy non-combatants, human collaborators, running for their lives to the shelter of the nearby sheds. The suit's weapon-alarm pushed a needle of noise into my right ear, and I turned that direction to get a look at the enemy with my biological eyes. Assisted by the suit's automated zoom functions, I spotted three collaborators wheeling a cannon in my direction.

For several seconds, my limbs no longer felt tired and aching. I sent a surge of energy through the suit and ran with unnatural speed towards a side building. At the same time, I set the suit the task of taking out the cannon, and it dutifully lifted the laser rifle in my right hand, automatically lining up the cannon and activating the rifle. The shot took half the antiquated rifle's charge, but the end of the cannon was quickly melted shut.

Two drones, each the size of a fist and equipped with what looked like small grenade launchers, buzzed toward me. The automated targeting of the D-suit made quick work of the drones, draining much of the rest of the rifle's power.

I dived inside the nearest corrugated metal building, crashing through its doorway that was a metre too short for the suit, and immediately halted. A small crowd of cowering collaborators stared at me. The alarm triggered again, and I found the cannon-wielder. The shoulder-mounted cannon was much smaller this time, and only a metre in front of me behind a young woman. I reached over the woman, who fell down, her face turning porcelain, and grabbed the cannon, crushing it in my suit's powerful hand.

"Where are they?" I demanded, using the D-suit's external speakers. I'd turned the speakers up enough that they could be heard over the sounds of falling drop pods outside. "Where is my family?"

"F-family?" the fallen woman asked at my feet while the rest shuffled backwards, not quite believing their eyes.

47

"What have you done with my family?" I demanded, louder this time.

"I-I-I ..."

"We don't know," an older man near the back of the spacious shed said.

"Then who would?" I started forward, stepping over the fallen woman to face the older man. He looked to be some sort of undercover officer; heavy disguising makeup easily penetrated by the suit's sensors.

The older man, short spikey hair and dapper pinstriped suit contrasting with the cold sweat melting his face, stared at death and lost his breath. I took one more step toward him and the woman on the floor answered. "The director, he might know."

"The director of this facility?" I asked, spinning back around. "Your Scurge master? Where is it?" My hand clenched shut as I imagined the Scurge's thin neck caught between the suit's hard fingers, and the small crowd ducked and flinched at the loud clacking noise.

"Director Slitten is two studies northward, on the opposite side of the road. He's the only Scurge talented enough to direct, so you can't miss him," the woman stammered quickly, her voice shaking.

I nodded and stepped back over her, pressing through the ruined doorway and back into the open. The suit detected no more threats, so I ran towards the building the woman had indicated and smashed my way through the wall of the shed, which the woman had called a 'study.' The name induced my spine to shivers as I realised what the name must imply. This wasn't just a military facility; it was a science lab. They were conducting tests on humans here. On my children!

The wall crumpled, offering little resistance to the D-suit's unstoppable bulk. They'd set a large main room up with dirt, trees and bright lights, all pointed at a seat in the middle, while several chairs, some knocked over, filled the room. Several doors led to other rooms, but my eyes were drawn to the five individuals that stood huddling behind one of the large lights. The D-suit's scanners quickly located 'Director Slitten.'

"Scurge scum," I snarled at the gangly creature. Four humans, all wearing dark suits, surrounded the skinny, tall creature who also wore a black suit made by human tailors. The Andromedan Scurge's bulbous green eyes moved like gelatinous blobs as their pupils tracked toward me. The twin-elbowed arms dropped in surprise, so that the long, pencil-thin fingers touched the ground. The thick, high legs wobbled, and the creature sat down on a high office chair. The small, air-tight energy seal that surrounded him shimmered, doing its best to keep the Scurge's atmosphere contained. That was a neat trick. I'd never seen an energy seal used as a personal environment suit before. This director must be one of the Andromedan Scurge's highest-ranked commanders. I smiled; the energy pack would be tiny, and I doubted the energy seal could stop the laser rifle.

Sat down as it was, the Scurge Director still towered over its four human servants. Its grey, trunk-like mouth wobbled from side to side, clearly afraid of the D-suit.

"Where are my children?" I shouted. The Scurge director's four stalk-mounted ears swivelled and shrunk away from the sound while the humans covered their ears. I waited a moment for Director Slitten to recover and then pointed the laser rifle at him. "Where. Are. They?"

Director Slitten raised his gangly arms and started signing with his hands and arms. The D-suit's limited A.I. translated for me. "I'm sorry, sir, but who are you?"

"Who am I?" I asked, aghast. "I am the one who destroys. I am the hero of Terra. I am the black angel of the space lanes. I am Deacon Hero, the Annihilator of the Andromedan Scurge."

Director Slitten stared for several seconds and then seemed to relax back into his chair. "Oh, you. The scourge of the Scurge?" he signed.

"Yes. Me," I growled. My threatening demeanour seemed to have little effect, as if finding out who I was had made me a helpless kitten in the eyes of the alien. I clacked my left hand together. The humans flinched, but after a second looked more interested than scared. The sounds of the descending drop pods died off, and they all relaxed, straitening up as if the danger was over. "You think this is a joke?" I asked while stepping forwards to get within arms-reach of the nearest human. The eyes of the humans opened wide, their fear returning.

Director Slitten signed quickly to the humans present. "Call Starla."

"Who the hell is Starla?" I demanded. I clamped my left hand over the wrist of a middle-aged bald man whose teeth chattered. The bald man's suit ripped while my armoured hand threatened to crush the wrist, and he looked at his Andromedan Scurge master.

"Quickly, now," Director Slitten implored his servants, my rifle pointed at his green, gelatinous eyes.

"Starla! Starla, come up here, please," the bald man shouted. "Help, Starla, run."

I frowned, and the D-suit's electronic ears picked up the fast footsteps of a mid-sized human, running from a room on the opposite side of the room. The footsteps crunched through the dirt in the middle of the room and my rear-scanners identified her as a young woman of average height, wearing a white dress and too much makeup. She stopped when she reached the white chair in the middle of the room, her eyes adjusting to the harsh lights and spotting the D-suit's bulky form bearing down on the humans.

"Starla?" the bald man said weakly, "please tell Mr Hero to stop."

The woman's jaws opened for several seconds and then slapped shut. Her eyes narrowed, and she strode toward me, unafraid.

I gasped and let go of the man's wrists. The laser rifle clattered to the floor, and I turned to stare at the woman with my biological eyes. "But ... you died," I accused her. "I saw you die."

The woman, my wife, shook her head. "No, Deak, I'm not dead, and I'm not your wife."

"W-what?"

She looked annoyed, a perpetual frown on her face while she stepped past me. "Come on, see for yourself." She rounded a small black screen, set up near the back of the room on top of a low table, and touched a button. The screen turned on, and she tapped on it several times. "Come look."

The aches in my muscles returned, and despite being inside an indomitable D-suit, powered by a fusion reactor, my legs felt heavy and I wanted to sit down next to the Andromedan Scurge in his high-back chair.

My wife is alive, but she isn't my wife? I'd had the Scurge under my rifle, but he'd called a small woman, not much more than a teen, to rescue him? My heart slowed as I rounded the screen to see what my wife wanted me to see. My heavy footsteps stopped, and I looked down at the screen, resisting the urge to crouch so that I didn't hurt my aching back.

"Action!" someone called from the screen's speakers. It was the execution scene, the same one I had witnessed aboard the prison ship when they'd killed my wife.

"You see?" my wife implored, willing me to make sense of the execution.

"No ..." I mumbled, "no, it can't be." I stumbled backwards, steadied myself, and turned to crash through the walls to the outside. A small crowd had gathered around the other sheds, watching for the D-suited warrior, ready to run for their lives. Several heads disappeared behind doorways when they saw me emerge, but I paid them no attention, focussed as I was on the large cannon my laser rifle had melted shut earlier.

Except it wasn't a cannon at all.

I ordered the D-suit to open, and then took off the white security suit's helmet and tossed it to the black tarmac's surface, where it clattered loudly. I waited one heart-fluttering moment for my eyes to adjust and then looked again at the cannon.

Mounted on a wheeled cart sat a large camera.

I turned around to look at the large sign that said 'Purplewood Studies,' and now that I had slowed down, saw what it really said: 'Pinewood Studios.'

The 'sheds' were still made of corrugated iron, but signs were plastered over each of them, saying what number studio they were.

"This … this is a film studio? *Hollywood?*" I screamed. I fell to my knees, and my wife, who wasn't my wife, walked to me to show me a small screen embedded in a sheaf of translucent paper. A video played security camera footage. It was live.

On the screen, a D-suited man sporting short white hair and wrinkled eyes crouched next to a raven haired young woman in a white dress.

"Is that …?"

The woman smiled, but her eyes glazed, betraying the sadness she was holding inside. "Yes, it's you."

I opened the suit and stepped out of it, stumbling around until my wife steadied me. I took the security suit off and touched my white hair with wrinkled hands. "What happened to me?"

"It was the D-suits and the gene splicing the government put you through," the young woman explained. "You used them so much during the war, they affected your brain. They've been trying to use therapy and advanced medicines on the old cruise ship to reverse the damage."

"I don't understand, cruise ship?"

"Yes, pop, you were on a cruise ship, with wonderful views of the world you helped save. That's right, you won the war, and we're all at peace now. They'd deactivated most of your military upgrades from your body, but couldn't get rid of the computer in your brain, the one you always used to hack into alien tech. They sent a military honour guard to bring you home. You were making so much progress … Oh, the honour guard, that must be where you got your old suit from." She blinked back tears. "Slitten told our producers not to broadcast live. He knew it would probably upset you. I hope heads roll for this."

"Honour guard?" I thought back to the four soldiers on the shuttle, and then looked at the young woman who'd called me 'pop.' "Just … who are you?" I looked at the baton, still strapped to the white suit from what I had thought of as a prison ship. The baton wasn't a baton, it was a damaged medical device, a scanner of some sort.

"I'm your granddaughter. Starla Hero."

I buried my head in my hands, both elated and saddened.

We won, but my wife is dead. How many years ago? How many years had my memories given up?

"You won the war, but we lost *you*."

She held me and I hugged her back. "I'm sorry. I'll come back. I have to." I had to find out what happened to me, what happened to my wife and the life I couldn't remember.

"I hope so."

I'd tricked myself into attacking a civilian movie studio. I trio of heavily armoured soldiers arrived in a quad-copter, jumping to the ground with rifles drawn, a cloud of deadly wasp drones following in their wake. I let my granddaughter, whose face so resembled my wife's, help me up, and I allowed the soldiers to take me away. I glanced at the screens one last time and stared at the strands of white hair that fell from my head.

Andrew P. McGregor lives in the rural town of Inverell near the East coast of Australia. He writes science fiction and dark fantasy short stories, most of which are collected in the 'Tales of Starships & Apocalypse' series.

Sandwich City

by Nestor Delfino

K roy One could not afford a Birth Credit, and the population control laws in the *Cave* were inflexible. Without Birth Credits, the authorities terminated illegal babies. And Aliss, Kroy's wife, was going to give birth in two months.

Although he felt the weight of the Cave on his shoulders, the guilt he carried was even more oppressive. Guilt for not getting his promotion in school, and guilt for believing that his crooked friend Olsam, jailed again, would return the money he owed him.

"What are we going to do?" Aliss said. "They'll kill our son!" she cupped her smooth scalp with her hands and wept. "It's your fault! I'll kill myself before they take my baby!"

Kroy believed her. He was going to lose them both: his unborn son, and his wife. He scratched his bald head, took a deep breath, and said, "I'm volunteering for Infrastructure."

As if to illustrate what he was volunteering for, the Cave shook. Not violently like other times, but still enough to be considered an earthquake. To Kroy, it felt as if the Cave had shifted, never mind what the Council told the population.

Despite her constant reproaches, Kroy knew Aliss still loved him. She jumped from the bed and embraced him, letting loose another wave of tears.

"No!" she said. "People die in the *Pits*! I won't let you!"

Kroy smiled and gently pried her apart from him. "It's our only chance. I'll work hard and earn enough money to buy a Birth Credit. Our son will live."

***

The way to school felt different today, as Kroy trudged the polished rock streets. He was more aware of the dark, oppressive, encroaching walls of the Cave. Ten thousand people sardined into ramshackle habitats. In reality, just under ten thousand, the maximum limit for sustainability, although there was some room for a few newborns. Strict enforcement of the law was how the survivors of the Third World War had made it that long. But at what cost: no baby could be born unless somebody died first. Only if their parents could purchase a Birth Credit from the *Source*, the Council office that issued the permits, would the baby live, even if the population was not quite at the upper limit.

Sometimes it came down to the wire. Mothers were pushing their babies out, not knowing if they would get to hold them. If no Birth Credit were produced by then, the guards would snatch the baby from the nurse's hands, and take it to the recycling facility. The law was ruthless.

As a teacher, Kroy had to comfort students who would never see their siblings, and frantic fathers who hoped to grab a Birth Credit until the last moment, perhaps by some miraculous government edict—which happened, rarely—, but never came for them. And desperate fathers did desperate things. Some killed themselves in the waiting room. Guards readily offered their thunder-rifles to the fathers, to facilitate the ultimate sacrifice.

Kroy was also ready to sacrifice himself. One way or the other, his son would be born.

The principal looked at him with sad eyes, but he signed Kroy's extended leave papers. Volunteers for Infrastructure had the right, by law, to get time off from their regular jobs.

Usually, they did not return.

At ten in the morning, Kroy reached the tunnels, the entrance to the Pits. Three Infrastructure clerks waited for volunteers behind a long table. Kroy made eye contact with the bald, square-faced man in the middle, and walked resolutely.

Somebody got in his way. A young man, younger than Kroy—he could not be older than twenty—pressed his hands against Kroy's chest and said, "Don't do it! Don't go to your death!"

The square-faced man behind the table jumped from his chair and yelled, "We told you to leave, councilor! File any grievance through the appropriate channels."

But the young man did not leave. He said to the clerk, "I know you're selling Birth Credits in the black market! I'm going to expose you!"

Two large men wearing crowd control gear—Infrastructure guards—emerged from the tunnels and dragged the screaming councilor away.

Kroy approached the table.

"Ignore him, citizen," the square-faced man said. "A politician trying to make a name for himself. The *boss* will have him expelled from the Council soon." He gave Kroy a synthetic smile. "Welcome to Infrastructure! I commend you; it's not every day that a free person volunteers."

Like all Cave dwellers, the boss was entirely without hair, not even brows or eyelashes. It had been decided, generations ago, that hairless people would fare better in the Cave's humid conditions, so scientists played with human genes until they accomplished it. Less risk of parasites.

The man had a big head, and he was fat. Kroy had never seen such a fat person before. Was he consuming more than his daily ration of mushrooms?

As if aware of his newest subordinate's impertinent inspection, the boss said, "We have certain liberties down here, citizen. You'll learn. Do what you're told and don't ask questions, and you'll be rewarded."

Kroy had a few urgent questions to ask that caveman but held his tongue, and looked down. It was dark there, darker even than up top, in the main section of the Cave. His eyes had a hard time getting used to it.

"It's darker in the Pits," the boss said. "You'll get used to it. Here's your first assignment: report to the crew chief in tunnel four."

***

The boilers required constant maintenance. Leaks were common. Anybody who was near a boiler when it sprang a leak, either got their hands burned off, or their face steam-boiled. And yet, it was the safest job in Infrastructure. Replacing worn-out gaskets and pump gears that could not be replaced, but only molten and reshaped, was hard work. And the humidity was unbearable. Kroy was sure not even the engineered mushrooms— the only food in the Cave—could tolerate it.

In the Cave, nothing went to waste. The boilers served essential purposes: they generated steam to run the dynamos and purified the water. There was one last critical task: insulation. The magma from the depths would fry everybody in the Cave unless the heat were dissipated somehow. Insulation alone was not enough, so the boiler served as a heat radiator, sending the excess heat up to the surface.

Up in the main section, when Infrastructure released extra heat for the mushroom crops to reach maturity, people would take off their skimpy rags. Down there in the Pits, Kroy had to wear protective clothing. There was no material in the Cave to craft industrial apparel, so his heavy, uncomfortable, heat-resistant overall was made with human skin.

In the Cave, nothing went to waste.

He was sweating like a pig, which was an old saying from before the war when there used to be pigs and other animals on Earth.

When another sudden earthquake cracked a pipe, and a whistling torrent of steam wrapped him in a cocoon of scalding mist, that uncomfortable overall saved his life. He was catapulted backward and hit the rock wall. Luckily, his overall softened the impact. He sounded the alarm and followed the procedures that had been drilled into him all week long.

Crawling under the widening steam column, he reached the shutoff valve. His greasy human skin gloves slipped from the metal handle. Desperate now, because the compartment was filling up with steam and he was suffocating, he kicked the handle. It turned, and the steam stopped. An eerie silence took over, interrupted only by his uneven, deep gulps for air.

There was no recognition for his heroics, just a brief visit to the infirmary, where a nurse promptly declared him fit for duty.

Kroy was assigned to another section, to replace a previous operator who had perished in a similar accident. When he asked about the Birth Credit, generated after the victim's death, he heard the eternal Infrastructure mantra: "Do what you're told, don't ask questions, and you'll be rewarded."

Two more weeks of boiler work, and Kroy realized he would not make enough money before Aliss gave birth. He needed a higher-paying position. He had to see the boss.

The fat man arched his eyebrows, and then shut one eye and observed Kroy as if he was about to snipe him. It was uncommon that a free citizen volunteered to work the boilers. It was unheard of that a free citizen insisted on working with an insulation crew.

"If you're so intent on doing your part for the sustainability of the Cave, I'm not going to get in your way. Report to crew six at 04:30."

Kroy felt that expressing gratitude would make him look like a fool, so he just turned around and left the boss's prehistoric-looking office, itself a small cave of its own. Made to look like the exposed inner walls of the Cave from where the insulation had fallen off, it gave the visitors a clear picture of what the Cave looked like behind the insulating tiles. The rock in the office was cold to the touch. The stone in the actual Cave's walls would fry eggs. Not that the survivors had any eggs—the last generation that enjoyed foods other than engineered Cave mushrooms had hair on their bodies.

If boiler work was dangerous, this was suicidal: insulating tiles kept falling off the walls, and the ones covering the bottom of the Cave and the boilers, which withstood the highest temperatures, kept cracking. Cracked tiles let the inferno from the depths of the Earth into the Cave.

During the first hour at the job, several tiles came down near Kroy. One bounced off a naked indentation on the rock wall and smacked his hard hat. His head cocked, the hard hat went flying in one direction, and the broken tile in another—laughter from the crewmen. Someone with a strident voice said something about the Pits welcoming fresh meat.

All the action happened in the Pits. The constant earthquakes loosened the tiles, which rained down like brick-sized hail. Entire sections of the wall collapsed on hapless workers. Those who completed the month-long shift alive became legends.

Kroy got up, dusted himself off, and picked up the tile that hit him. It wasn't made out of stone as he had imagined.

"What you looking at, rookie?" said the owner of the strident voice. "Never seen a tile before?" More laughs.

"What is it made of?" Kroy asked the loud, short man.

"What's everything made of around here? The clothes you wear when you're not naked up top? The seals in the boiler? The water you drink?"

Apparently annoyed by the stupid look on Kroy's face, the loud man screamed, "People, you fool, everything here's made from people! The tiles contain ground bone!"

Kroy dropped the tile as if it was some cursed amulet, and a white cloud rose around him when it broke in multiple pieces.

The short man sang, "Bones, bones! Bones from our dear departed! Ain't that right, boys?"

More laughs.

"And bits of rocks," the man with the annoying voice said. "For added strength."

Kroy found out the short man was called Shelgar.

Rookies did not stay rookies for long in the Pits unless they planned to become insulation. Kroy was focused. He learned quickly, and within a week, he was as good as anyone else in the crew. He discovered ways to glue broken tiles together, avoiding the tedious work of melting and forging new ones. The heat was so pervasive that they did not know what to do with it, but the material was not. In the Cave, they recycled everything. But recycling took precious time, and the insulation had to be repaired quickly.

The boss took notice, during one of his surprise rounds— surprising, because the man rarely went down to the Pits. When he heard of Kroy's new procedure to repair broken tiles, he promoted him to crew chief.

Kroy was now in charge of eight young men, all his seniors. And he was the only free citizen. Everyone else was there to shorten their sentence. That was why the boss promoted him, Kroy thought. A respectable citizen in charge of those lost souls, now on their way to redemption.

On one occasion, Kroy was called to the boss's office. A recent earthquake had damaged a large part of the wall in another sector, and the boss wanted to send Kroy and his crew for repairs. Kroy took the opportunity to suggest improvements to the process.

"Why can't we carve out rock from the *border* wall? There are tons! Why is it no crew ever works there?"

"Do what you're told and don't ask questions, and you'll be rewarded," the boss said.

It did not make sense to Kroy. Nobody in his crew knew about the border wall, or if they knew about it, they did not care. Other than the boss and the menacing guards, he was the only free citizen who had touched it. Everybody else kept to themselves because they were in enough trouble already, Kroy concluded.

***

Earthquakes were happening more often, it seemed, as Kroy worked in one of the most hazardous sections in the Pits. He had little time to eat his ration of mushrooms, and rest. He was hungry and sleepy.

You people aren't here to rest, the boss would often preach.

Perhaps it was lack of rest; perhaps it was the increasingly violent earthquakes; maybe it was negligence from Kroy's crew. When a section of the tiled ceiling came crashing down during the third earthquake that day, Kroy knew there was nothing he could do for his men. He felt lucky for not being under the rubble. He felt terrible for being, instead, pleading to the boss about improving their working conditions.

Shelgar was the sole survivor. He had been called to the boss's office right after Kroy's meeting. Shelgar knew things; this was not his first shift. He had been in an out of prison forever and was a repeat volunteer. It was Shelgar who stated the undeniable fact that seven Birth Credits had just been added to the Source's inventory. It was Shelgar who tipped off Kroy that Infrastructure higher-ups got first picks at Birth Credits.

It was Shelgar who suggested he negotiated one with the boss.

Kroy put his guilt aside for the time being and went back to the boss's office. Despite the loss of a crew, the man could not stop grinning.

"I want to purchase a Birth Credit," Kroy said. "I understand us workers get discounts."

The boss was a great negotiator, much better than Kroy. He looked at Kroy up and down as if he was a child who had just asked for a second serving of mushrooms. Clearing his throat and, with difficulty, erasing the grin off his face, he said, "I'm afraid that the Birth Credits have already been allocated." He said that Kroy was welcome to purchase one from the Source, at regular price. And when Kroy asked about the Infrastructure discount, he mentioned something about not enough seniority.

When the boss sensed that his underling was not happy with the answer, he threw in, for good measure, the classic: "Do what you're told, don't ask questions, and you'll be rewarded."

Kroy felt a mix of ire and desperation. Aliss would give Birth in a few weeks, and the Birth Credit seemed so remote.

"Kroy One," the boss said, "you're seven men short."

That was a serious problem that required an immediate solution. If Kroy did not put another crew together, he would be demoted back to the low-paying boiler work.

That night he did not eat and gave his ration to Shelgar, who consumed it ravenously. He did not sleep, either. The boss had said Kroy could try luring seven guys from the boilers if he offered them extra pay, from his own salary, of course. The boss had also noted that if Kroy could improve efficiency, he would get a big bonus.

Even then, Kroy would be short one man. A crew of eight could not compete with the teams of nine. And news of the accident had bubbled up to the city. Nobody was volunteering. He shut his eyes.

The next morning, he made his weekly call to Aliss. He promised he was taking care of himself and lied about the accident. She asked about the Birth Credit, and he said it was going to be a close one because Infrastructure did not pay what the recruiters preached.

She began cursing Olsam again. She had heard the career crook was in jail for a long stretch this time, for stealing from a councilor.

For the first time since the accident, Kroy's eyes brightened. He told Aliss he loved her and that everything would be alright, and hung up. He made another call, this time to the city's jail.

"Well, look who's calling!" Olsam said. "Thought I'd never hear from you again, old buddy."

"Listen," Kroy said, "this isn't a courtesy call. I need you to volunteer for the Pits. Work in my crew, and I'll forget about your debt."

A pause, as if Olsam was considering the offer.

"*My* debt?" he said with feigned consternation. "What about *your* debt? Isn't your life worth more than the money you lent me?"

Kroy had suspected Olsam would bring up that time he saved him, during an earthquake when Olsam pulled him from under a collapsed habitat. He had never told Aliss about it, and now he wondered why. She would have thought better of his friend.

"You have to help me. Aliss will have my baby soon. We need a Birth Credit!" Hearing nothing but the static from the old city communication lines, Kroy said, "Don't you want to get out of prison?"

Olsam scowled. "We're all in prison, one great, big prison. My cell just happens to be smaller than everybody else's, smaller than yours. We're in this miserable prison together."

"Don't tell me you want to rot there, eating half the ration of free citizens and making clothes out of dead ones. This is your chance. If you don't want it, I'm getting someone else. You have one minute."

Kroy was bluffing; no prisoner had volunteered since the accident. His only hope was that Olsam, being in isolation, did not know that. One minute had passed, and he was about to hang up when Olsam said, "I'll do it. For old times' sakes."

***

Olsam was a strong young man who did not look famished in the slightest and had no trouble doing the heaviest lifting. Kroy wondered if Olsam had already done a shift before, but the work was so demanding and the downtime so scarce, that he did not talk much during his few precious sleep hours. He put the thoughts out of his mind, for Olsam had done something good for once: he had convinced old associates of his to fill the remaining empty places in the crew. And to Kroy, that accounted for a lot.

One night, Shelgar sneaked up to Kroy's bunk—a bony, four-legged contraption reserved for the crew chief—and whispered into his ear, "I've got information you might find valuable. It's about Olsam Fanger."

Kroy forced his heavy eyes open and said, "What nonsense are you blabbering about? Go back to sleep!"

But soon enough, Kroy sat up on his bunk. Shelgar claimed to have met Olsam before, in jail and could share some useful tips: how to manage him, how to survive him.

Kroy massaged his temples and looked around. Olsam was snoring at the far end of their section, by the wheel barrels and other tools.

Olsam continued, "I'll tell you only if you put a good word about my work to the boss, so they'll cut down my sentence further."

Kroy had a hard time keeping his voice down. "Good work? You've done everything but good work! Rookies work harder than you! I'm not interested in your lies, and I'm warning you, drop it, or I'll have a conversation with the boss all right, one you won't like."

He dismissed an upset-looking Shelgar with a wave and laid back down. Surprisingly enough, sleep came swiftly, perhaps because Olsam had stopped snoring.

The next morning Kroy had the men work the disaster section that killed his previous crew. The collapsed honeycombed area was so large that the insulating tiles and rocks had piled up on a sort of hill. *So much material,* Kroy thought. He had to recycle it; he could not afford to request new tiles.

It was the toughest day. They moved tons of material into classified mounds. Kroy thought he saw the rocky bottom, as Shelgar used his rudimentary broom to clear the last bits of debris.

Suddenly, everything began to shake.

When the earthquake hit, the dust was kicked up and saturated the air, making breathing almost impossible. There was a thundering roar as if a mountain had crashed down from the upper level, through the Pits, down to the boilers. The bottom was already weak by the enormous weight of the debris piled upon it, and the earthquake finished it off.

The floor collapsed. Screams. Kroy crawled to the edge of the hole and grabbed one of his men just before he fell. As the dust settled, he saw Shelgar, at the opposite side of the breach, in a similar predicament. Olsam was trying to help, although, for being the strongest man in the team, he was letting Shelgar slip. Down to the cracked, steamy boiler below.

"Hold on!" Kroy yelled. "Just hold on!"

Kroy did not have time to run around the hole before Shelgar slipped from Olsam's grip, and went right through the cracked lid of the boiler, diving into the rolling, boiling water. His screams stopped abruptly as furious, white steam began rising through the hole and threatened to suffocate the rest of the crew, until someone down below tripped the safety switch.

Olsam smiled.

The boss absorbed the Birth Credit that had just materialized on account of Shelgar's fiery death, ignoring Kroy's demands for first picks. Kroy's desperation reached untenable levels.

***

Until then, Kroy had followed the rules. But his son trumped the rules. He was done playing by the rules.

How could he get the bonus? How could he repair so much insulation to earn it? Restoring the entire collapsed section should be enough. Where would he find more material?

He brooded through the night, in complete silence. Olsam was not snoring, and Kroy suspected he was keeping an eye on him. He had seen his friend sneaking into the boss's office many times. Could he trust him? In any case, he needed his help.

The answer manifested itself: the border wall. That naked rock boundary had so much material that it was obscene to leave it untouched. He got up and tiptoed to where the crew kept the tools, where Olsam bunked. Encouraged by his friend's snoring, Kroy picked up a wheel barrel and carried it over his shoulders, as quietly as he could.

There was nobody around the forbidden border wall. Guards rarely patrolled that section of the Pits, since no soul dared wander close. All crews were currently repairing sections at the other end of the Pits.

Kroy's fluorescent hard hat cast enough light to determine where to pick at the wall. Hours later, he had filled up the wheel barrel with enough bits of rock to mix with bones and make dozens of tiles.

Before returning to his bunk, he dispersed the rocks around the floor randomly, taking great care to make them look like debris from the last earthquake. Exhausted, he shut his eyes to catch an hour of sleep.

After a few backbreaking nights of covert work, Kroy's crew was repairing insulation at a rapid rate. The boss called Kroy to his office.

"Your crew is doing well. I'm promoting you to senior crew chief."

Kroy thought that he would finally be able to afford the Birth Credit he so desperately needed. "Do I get the discount then?"

The boss's mouth slanted to one side, as if he was about to laugh, but compromised instead on a crooked smile. "You're not senior enough yet. I thought I'd made that clear."

Kroy took a deep breath.

"But, you're on your way to a big bonus."

Kroy was going to work himself to death. He went at it for what seemed like a short eternity; the long nights carving rock from the forbidden border wall were wearing him out. He began imagining things, hidden figures sneaking up to him from the corner of his eye.

Although he had begun carving a large area of the wall to keep it inconspicuous, that section looked lighter than the rest of the wall. He decided to concentrate on one spot, digging a tunnel no wider than two men. When he gathered enough material for the night, he concealed the tunnel's entrance with rocks and dirt.

After another short eternity, when the boss guaranteed him the bonus that would buy his son's life, Kroy went to the border wall one last time. With one week left in his shift, he wanted one last mining trip, just to be sure.

The tunnel was now a few meters deep, and he only planned to fill up a couple of wheel barrels. *Poc-poc,* the pick sank easily. *Poc-poc.* Was there someone behind him? He stopped for a moment and looked out the dark mouth of the tunnel: nothing but the diffuse glow of the distant Pits' lights.

Torrents of sweat dripped from his forehead. Poc-poc the pick continued as if attracted by the increasingly soft, muddy wall until the last hit yielded neither sound nor resistance. The tool went right through the mud.

It took him a short while to realize what had just happened. He pulled the pick back, breaking out a hole the size of a man's head. Air rushed from the hole and filled the tunnel. Cold air. It smelled earthy and was more humid than the mushroom farms up top.

What had he done?

The ground shook in what was the third earthquake that week. Not particularly violent, but enough to complete his work: the muddy wall collapsed in front of him. Another wall lay beyond, this one made of darkness.

All of a sudden, a flash behind him projected his skinny silhouette on the ground ahead. A familiar voice said, "You've discovered something, alright. We might as well explore!"

Kroy turned around and was immediately blinded by the white beam of light coming from where Olsam stood. Olsam pointed the light to the ground.

"Sorry," he said. "Don't just stand there, let's see what you found!" He pushed past his seemingly frozen friend and entered the void.

With Olsam's great torch, which Kroy thought only guards were allowed to carry, a clear picture of their surroundings emerged. This was not a pocket in the rock. This was something bigger. Much bigger. The far end was still enshrouded in darkness.

They walked into the unknown. Shivering, Kroy wondered why it was so cold there. After a few steps, he thought he saw a reflection, while Olsam swung the light left to right, like a blind man sensing his way with a stick.

"Give me that," Kroy said, and grabbed the torch from Olsam. "Look! What's that white stuff? It's all over, beyond that mound over there."

They walked toward it. Half buried in the soft ground, there were bones. Thousands. Hundreds of thousands, enough to make infinite tiles. Kroy thought of the possibilities until his curiosity forced him to think of the impossibilities. What was this uncharted cave? Why was it full of bones? Who built the forbidden border wall, and why?

Olsam snatched his torch back and continued scanning. "Look over there!"

Buildings. Large habitats, like they had never seen before. As they got closer to the first row of them, after walking for about a hundred meters, Kroy realized they were ancient, and some had partially collapsed.

"This type of construction belongs to the surface world!" he mumbled in astonishment.

They walked along the clearly defined street, as Olsam scanned their surroundings with his powerful torch. Suddenly they reached the mouth of a broad avenue. Kroy calculated that this place was much bigger than their section of the Cave, and much, much older. The road was flanked by taller buildings, which he had only seen in pictures in books at school, books about the great cities on the surface, from long ago.

Bones were everywhere—complete skeletons of all shapes and sizes. Little ones were clinging to larger ones. And among the bones, there were mushrooms, growing from the soft, humid ground: millions, billions of them. There was enough food there to feed the entire Cave for years.

They stopped in front of the tallest building. It had a clock at the top of an arched entrance; its double doors had collapsed to the sides. Wooden doors Kroy explained to Olsam, who knew as much history as a preschooler.

Olsam's constant, random scanning was getting on Kroy's nerves. "Give me the torch!" Kroy demanded and began a systematic survey of the building. There was a central hall with a checkered floor. Long, wooden seats lined the walls, arranged in an octagon. Stairs were going up the perimeter. And there were bookcases, with as many books as bones outside.

But what sparked Kroy's attention was the sign above the towering bookcase opposite the entrance: *Sustainable Habitat Library*.

In his astonishment, he glanced at Olsam, who was fumbling for something in his overall. He ignored him and began going up the nearest staircase, which would lead him to the large bookcase, with a richly ornamented wooden desk right against it. As he went up, he caressed the rows of books on the shelves.

Kroy could swear he heard a *click*, and a hushed, hurried voice. "Did you say anything?" he asked. But Olsam did not respond. Kroy pointed the torch toward the ground floor. Olsam was at the entrance, using his fluorescent hard hat for illumination.

"Olsam! Where are you going?"

The darkness swallowed Olsam. Kroy paid no further attention to his friend and turned to the large desk. On it, there was a thick, open book with people's names, signatures, and dates. The last entry was made on August 25th, 2195.

Shills traveled up his spine. *Impossible! That was over three hundred years ago!* The survivors of the nuclear apocalypse had sought refuge in the Cave only four generations ago—right after that civilization-killing event—, so this could not be true.

His gaze shifted to the right of the visitor's book, where a golden plaque, carved in the most beautiful hand-writing he had ever seen, read: *On the third day of July 2150, a two-hundred-kilometer asteroid hit mainland United States of America. The impact melted the Earth's crust. Only we survived, the lucky refugees in our Sustainable Habitat, deep under the deepest oceanic trench, just above the Earth's mantle. Thank you to the brave men and women who built this refuge, thank you to the wise men and women who kept the incoming catastrophe hidden from the world for so many decades. Here, our descendants shall wait for that distant time, when the crust cools, and they can live on the surface once again.*

There were diagrams beside the plaque: an egg-shaped capsule inside a long shaft, under the bottom of the ocean. Anchors. Anchors were critical to the position of the capsule. The anchors were brakes, stoppers. When the swarm of self-sinking melting machines that liquefied the rock under the seafloor failed to shut themselves off, there was nothing solid to stop the Cave from sinking.

Only anchors.

Monstrous metal beams secured the capsule to the walls of the shaft that the self-sinking digging machines melted, quite possibly all the way down to the Earth's outer core. Below the capsule, the shaft had filled with molten rock.

The earthquakes! That was the reason for the earthquakes. The anchors were failing, never meant to support the entire structure indefinitely; they had been designed for emergencies.

Kroy gathered the diagrams and a map of the city and ran out of the library. The map depicted the anchor points. When he came across huge concrete cubes that were almost the size of the library, he knew he had reached the place where the anchors secured the capsule.

The walls were not rocky, nor covered with insulating tiles. They were dark metal. Some sort of alloy, Kroy read in the diagrams. A heat-resistant, shock-absorbing metal that protected humanity's last bastion, fifty kilometers below the bottom of what used to be the Pacific Ocean—now a viscous, churning, global sea of lava.

He saw the borers; giant machines meant to take them back to the surface, someday in the distant future. And he saw the anchors or parts of them at least. As thick as the pillars of the Acropolis. Hundreds of them, going through the metal shell, into the shaft's wall, where there was solid rock.

Many anchors were cracked, their pieces resting on top of the anchors under them, rattling as the capsule shook.

According to the map, *this* was the city, not the section where he had been born. That was the service area to support the city. Under the city proper, the insulation was thicker, hence the cooler temperature.

But what had happened? Some sort of conflict, generations ago? The bones littering the city attested to that. Ages ago, the survivors moved to the service area, and the city was sealed off and forgotten. And now, the capsule was hanging by a thread. If the anchors gave, the whole structure would plummet down into the Earth's gut, to dissolve in the inferno.

He had to warn the Council. He had to save Aliss and his unborn son.

He saw three flashes of light, and he heard yelling.

"There he is!" Olsam was back, accompanied by two armed guards. "You've gone far enough, Kroy. Forget this place and never speak of it."

"You knew about this place?"

"No. But it makes no difference. *Someone* knew. And someone wants to keep things the way they are."

"What happened here? Why did everybody die? Why do we live in the service section? This is no cave! We are inside a huge metallic egg!"

For an instant, Olsam seemed confused. "I don't care! It's still a prison! Now let's get out of here before others find out about it." He grabbed a shaking Kroy by the forearm and pulled him away.

"Hey!" Kroy said. "We must find out what happened here! Can't you see? Whatever it was, it could happen on the other side."

Olsam looked unsure of himself. He put his hands on Kroy's shoulders and said, "Listen. Come back with me, and we'll finish the shift. The boss told me he's willing to sell you a Birth Credit for cheap."

Right, the Birth Credit. His discovery so absorbed Kroy that he had momentarily forgotten his purpose in the Pits. Aliss and his unborn came first. He could find that outspoken young councilor and tell him about the hidden place later. He could not pass up this opportunity.

"You're right!" he said. "Let's go finish the shift!"

"Not so fast," one of the guards said, pointing his thunder-rifle at Olsam, while the other one pointed his at Kroy. "He knows too much," the first guard said. "The boss wants him gone. Step aside!"

Olsam lowered his head, as in resignation, and moved away. The guard aimed at Kroy, who closed his eyes.

He thought of Aliss and his son. He thought of the anchors disintegrating, and the capsule dropping to the center of the Earth. He opened his eyes, eyes that contained the fires of the Earth.

Then he saw Olsam hitting the guard in the face with a bone that looked like someone's lower leg. The bone broke in two pieces, and the guard collapsed; the thunder-rifle went flying in Kroy's direction.

The other guard pointed his weapon at Olsam but had trouble keeping aim because another earthquake hit. The bones scattered all around began rattling, changing position. Still, the guard fired his weapon, and Olsam fell backward, grabbing his neck. With his torch, the guard searched for Kroy, who had crawled away.

Kroy had to get the lost thunder-rifle, but it was beyond arm's reach. And the guard's torch was about to find him. He picked up a large bone and threw it at the guard with all his strength. Lights out. A scream of pain and cursing.

Frantically now, Kroy felt for the thunder-rifle among the disturbed bones. The earthquake was subsiding now. Suddenly, there was a random fire in all directions, followed by more swearing.

Kroy snatched the thunder-rifle, and, from the ground, pointed it at the source of the fire and pressed the trigger. He kept it pressed until the thunder-rifle ran out of ammo.

Only his rapid, anxious breathing perturbed the silence like a tiger trapped in a small cage. When he calmed down, he heard moaning nearby, weak and irregular.

"Olsam!"

A grunt was his answer, and then there was light. Olsam had found a torch where he had fallen.

Kroy dropped the empty thunder-rifle and ran to his friend. Olsam lay flat on the bed of bones and dirt, his chest drenched in blood. But he was smiling.

"I'll get help!" Kroy said.

"I'm done for," Olsam gurgled. He pulled out a key from his skin overall. "My locker. Take the money, buy your Birth Credit. And forgive me…"

That was the last thing Olsam said.

Kroy did not know if other guards were waiting for him by the tunnel. He crawled his way back to the section that had, until that day, been his whole universe.

Nobody was waiting for him. He covered up the entrance the best he could and took the precaution of wrecking the nearest Pits' lights.

The rest was a blur. Kroy went through almost mechanical motions to fetch Olsam's money, *his* money, and then he got his few belongings from his own locker—a picture of Aliss and his wedding ring.

He burst into the *pay* office, collected his shift's regular pay and bonus, and, just like that, took the elevator up top, all the way looking at the picture of his wife as if he could somehow immerse himself in it.

The city lights blinded him momentarily, the same lights he had considered dim before. Shading his eyes with Aliss's picture, he exited the tunnel and almost bumped into some eager youngsters who had just signed up for the Pits, in a rush to make a lot of money or to lessen their criminal sentences. Kroy heard the tired preaching of the councilor, failing to convince the youngsters against signing up.

The councilor. The one politician he had ever seen who did not spend his life holed up in his comfy office.

And the young politician saw him too and remembered him. "You made it!" he said. "Tell me what's going on down there. Nothing will change unless someone speaks up!"

Kroy's gaze went from the councilor to the picture and back to the councilor. He had the money he needed to buy the Birth Credit. He would be happy ever after.

But no. The city-the *capsule* would not last much longer unless the anchors were repaired, unless the whole structure itself were somehow *pulled up*, away from the inferno below, but still clear from the inferno above.

"Listen to me," he whispered into the councilor's ear. "The city is in mortal danger."

***

Life as a schoolteacher was uplifting and rewarding. Kroy's problem was to remain fair; he could not publicly congratulate his son for being among the best students in the school, but he feared that, sometimes, he was treating him harshly in front of the other children.

He loved teaching so much, that he was sure he would still be doing it when his daughter, due to be born in a few months, began attending school.

The school program had been revamped in the last few years. A particular former councilor, now mayor, ensured that every detail of the superstructure that housed what remained of the human race became a mandatory subject of study.

Sandwich City, as the children nicknamed it, represented salvation. Until the day the surface cooled and solidified, the capsule had to be monitored, maintained.

Volunteers were plenty and eager, even though the authorities had eliminated Birth Credits. The expansion of the decrepit service area into Sandwich City had allowed the population to swell, and still be well below the maximum sustainable margins.

Another subject taught in school was the mysterious illness that killed off the majority of the population, long ago, and forced the survivors to seal themselves in the service area. They were so scared of the illness that they never told their children. Doctors were able to trace it to the mutated mushrooms, which poisoned the majority. The frightened survivors had become immune.

One day, Kroy One took his students on a field trip to the Pits so that they could see for themselves the painstaking and dangerous work of the volunteers. The work that kept the habitat safe.

One of them, an old criminal who was serving a life sentence for extortion, bribery, and murder, seemed to work much less than the rest. Kroy remembered him well from a long time ago. He avoided eye contact.

"Children," Kroy said, "Let's go see the repaired anchors."

The noisy children fumbled with their hard hats and followed a technician, in a single line, to one of the immense anchoring points.

As Kroy fell in line behind the last student, the old man said, "Wait! Did you put in a good word for me with the mayor? How much longer do I have to be here?"

Kroy One looked at the boss in the eye and said, "Do what you're told, don't ask questions, and you'll be rewarded."

Nestor Delfino is a science fiction and fantasy author, writing from his home in Mississauga, Canada, where he lives with his wife. A software developer by trade, his first publication was a video game he programmed on his first computer (a ZX Spectrum) when he was fourteen.

Tiamat Descending

by James Pyles

Mission Summary - Subject Tiamat - Security: Top Secret —

The need to colonize one or more exo-planetary bodies after Earth was rendered uninhabitable a century ago has been deemed imperative by the Interplanetary Union (IU) Security Council. Although humanity has heavily colonized numerous planetary, lunar, and asteroid bodies as well as creating a network of space stations in our solar system, those communities are unsustainable long term. Without access to unique provisions from our mother world, those colonies and bases are estimated to have only another 100 to 150 years of life.

*Humanity has evolved to live in a planetary environment, and when a suitable exo-planet was discovered 20 light-years away, a program to send over 10,000 colonists to inhabit that world was initiated. Tiamat was the first of five interstellar sleeper ships designed to carry a complement of 2,460 passengers and crew to colony world 82 Eridani E. Her sister ships, Anubis, Isis, and Osiris were launched 33, 21, and 9 years ago respectively, while Tiamat left the Gateway construction yards orbiting Luna 45 years ago (***subnote**: Ra, the final ship in the series, is scheduled for launch three years from now). The journey to 82 Eridani was expected to take 350 years. With all human life on board kept in cryogenic stasis in the four rotating rings* *around Tiamat's half-kilometer length, only the vessel's AI named Gracie (***subnote:** after Admiral Grace Hopper who was the creator of the COBOL programming language) and several hundred robotic drones called Wardens, monitor ship's operations.*

Five months ago, an amateur astronomer on Ganymede observed Tiamat approaching the outer asteroid belt. Since then, there has been no response from Tiamat's AI or human crew to attempts at communication. Tiamat is apparently under control in that it is continuing to decelerate as it moves sunward and has made several minor course corrections. Best estimate is that Tiamat's present course will take it near Earth and Luna perhaps in an attempt to return to its origin point.

*Interplanetary Union (IU) Corvette-class spacecraft SS Belisama (***subnote:** Registry, Mars - Acidalia Planitia Base), crew complement of six, has been launched to intercept the Tiamat. Belisama will reach the target five weeks later after Tiamat has passed the orbit of Mars. Belisama will attempt to communicate with Tiamat by radio at close range. If no response, the crew is authorized to board Tiamat and access the AI directly and/or revive the command crew and attempt to ascertain how and why the Tiamat has abandoned its flight to 82 Eridani. Answering this question is vital to understanding if the three other colony vessels in transit will experience the same fate as Tiamat or otherwise face unknown dangers at the edge of interstellar space.*

End Mission Summary

"Still no response from the Tiamat, Captain." Belisama co-pilot Margarita Avila was a civilian, but aboard ship, she addressed mission commander Elisha Rush by his IU Marine rank.

"We've been at this for six hours, Avila. So far, besides radio silence, the only unusual thing was finding that one of the SSV's is missing. Damn peculiar since there was no place for a short-range cargo and recon craft to go once they left the inner solar system. " Although born and raised at Copernicus Base on Luna, somehow, he managed to speak in a soft, Texas drawl. He nodded, but didn't try to look behind him and to the right where Margie was sitting.

"Yes sir, that would be Ship-to-Surface-Vehicle 03, the Shepard." She mentally kicked herself for putting in too many details, but when she was nervous, she tended to sound more like one of Shane's drones.

The forty-five-meter length of the Belisama glided a quarter of a kilometer above the main hull of the Tiamat, far enough to clear the four rotating habitat rings of the ship that were just ahead as they proceeded toward the bow. The sleeper ship had a certain grace to it, apart from the wide, modified Bussard-Lightner ramjet at the nose used for collecting interstellar hydrogen. In contrast, the Marine vessel looked like a shoe box with regularly cut angles. It was sectioned into the command module, personnel, and engineering units. Under thrust, looking down at the "floor" led to the fusion reactor and the engines as if the ship were standing on end. When thrust was cut, as it was now with the "Bel" having matched velocity with Tiamat, their ship cruised lengthwise, parallel with the sleeper ship, and nowhere was down. The acceleration couches and working terminals on the bridge stations rotated in spherical frames to accommodate ship conditions, and when maneuvering, those movements felt like an old carnival ride.

"Captain, recommend we dock with Tiamat and perform visual inspection. Access the AI directly. Mission parameters…"

"That was my very next thought, Sarge. Thanks."

Marine Sergeant Joanne Speirs could almost hear the smile in her Captain's voice, but it was still her duty to offer him options within the mission profile. She and Corporal Will Chalmers were sitting beside each other in the back of the command module. They were essentially cargo until they entered Tiamat or in the unlikely occurrence the ship was attacked and she had to man the Bel's missile systems. Her brilliant red hair was tied back but thanks to her Scottish grandmother, it was almost completely unruly, especially in zero G.

If necessary, the lower decks could hold twenty Marines, but this mission was considered critical risk, so the brass, in their infinite wisdom (she rolled her eyes at this), ordered only a minimal crew.

"I'd recommend one of the docking ports forward of the ring assembly."

"Makes sense Avila, although I'd love to find a way to access the forward ring first and learn the status of the crew."

"Sir, in theory, the Bel can dock with any of the four Personnel Descent Vehicles attached to each ring, but the risk of that kind of maneuver given the spin…"

"Just an idle thought, Avila. Have no fear. I'm not feeling suicidal today." He winked even though he knew she couldn't see his face.

"What about docking at the empty SSV bay, Captain? We'd be a lot closer to the AI that way." Cpl Chalmers was newly assigned to the Bel and at twenty, the youngest member of the crew. Green as grass used to be on Earth and only transferred from Luna's Tycho Station to Acidalia Planetia three months ago.

"Use your head, Chalmers." Speirs reached out and swatted him on the shoulder over the lip of their couches. "You read the mission briefing. The Bel isn't compatible with the SSV docking system."

"Sorry, Sarge, I just thought…"

"Next time, leave the thinking to the Captain."

He didn't answer. Like Captain Rush, he was descended from black Americans, but he felt that's where the similarity ended. Rush was calm, even jovial under pressure, tall but slender, while Chalmers was three inches shorter, built like a brick, and took things way too seriously, especially when he screwed up. More than anything, growing up on Luna, he wanted to be a Marine, but now that he was on his first Op, he felt torn between his dreams, duty and the parents and five sisters he left behind at Tycho.

In the cramped cockpit between Rush and Avila and the Marines, Shane Kumar and Leigh Hendricks sat in side-by-side couches. Shane, her grandparents from India before the forced emigration off world, doubled as navigator and robotics expert. She shared her love of machine intelligence with Leigh, a light-skinned blond who had been born and raised on the Jovian moon Ganymede. Shane was a Martian through and through, but never encountered someone she wanted to spend the rest of her life with until meeting Leigh in an advanced AI dynamics seminar almost two years ago.

"It's a shame Cpl Chalmers' idea isn't sound because I'd like to get to Gracie as soon as possible." Leigh was both ship's engineer and AI specialist. "We've already determined that none of Tiamat's four redundant antenna are damaged, so either there's an internal comm fault or, in spite of the ship's-controlled maneuvers, something's wrong with the AI. Fortunately, we can override Gracie's control of individual systems including airlocks, but I'll need to work with her directly to isolate any specific malfunctions."

"We'll get you there, Hendricks. Approaching the forward docking ports now. Expecting to link with Tiamat in under fifteen minutes."

"I concur, Captain." Strict safety protocol required that Avila confirm Rush's decisions but, in this case, it was just lip service. He had five years in the command seat when Margie was still in school. She wasn't exactly attracted to him, although sometimes her husband teased her about it. Rush was more of the father figure to her and the ship. When she had children with Robert someday, she wanted Elisha to be their Papa.

***

"Larry, Moe, and Curly are online and ready for launch, Captain." Kumar and Speirs had spent the last forty-five minutes, deploying three Extreme Lift Flyers or ELF drones in the main access conduit in Tiamat's long, hollow superstructure, standing just inside the second starboard docking port. Speirs was in heavy combat armor while Kumar was using a standard EVA suit.

The ship's primary conduit was a vast tunnel lined with arcane piping, power lines, junction boxes, essentially the underbelly of the leviathan-like machine. Above them, as they were oriented, another, slightly smaller conduit ran the length of the ship from the modified ramjet back through ops and into the fuel modules feeding the fusion reactors and the drive. It was heavily shielded to prevent a disastrous hydrogen plasma leak, but with the ramjet cold, the system was inert.

The space in the main core was to accommodate the movement of large cargo containers to different parts of the ship as well as the equipment modules required for its construction. Faint light sources gave the impression of a chamber of horrors where one might expect to find concealed all manner of apparitions. Not so frivolous a description given the unknown nature of Tiamat's return.

"Alright, get back inside and test the remote connections," said Elisha. He was still sitting in the command couch at the front of the cockpit, the Bel having mated with the Tiamat's port via their ship's anterior airlock.

The core was depressurized and since the only gravity was simulated in the four rotating rings, Shane and Joanne used their suits' magnetic boots to walk to and from their vessel.

The Marine allowed Shane to enter the airlock first. Her armor included a right-shoulder mounted ST15M Rifle which fired Glaser safety slugs. The rounds were designed to bring down a target by exploding inside of whatever they hit, but wouldn't penetrate anything thicker than sheet metal or drywall. Perfect for avoiding a hull breach inside a spaceship.

But while the Marine Sergeant remained cautious, in spite of the foreboding atmosphere, no threat was apparent.

Half an hour later, the initial tests on the three drones having been successful, Rush, Hendricks, Speirs, and Chalmers were in the airlock as it depressurized. Only Leigh was in a standard EVA suit while Elisha and Will had joined Joanne in donning battle armor.

"Now remember, I want you two using the ELFs to do recon fore, aft, and up the pylon to the A Ring. They are our eyes out here. I don't like surprises."

"You won't get any Captain." Margie swung her acceleration couch around to face Shane, emphasizing Elisha's words.

"While Kumar runs the ELFs and updates us with their findings, you monitor and send periodic advisories to the listening posts on Mars and Luna using focused transmission. I don't want the whole solar system tuning in."

"Acknowledged, Captain." Margie found it a little annoying that Elisha kept telling her what she already knew. He trusted her and he liked her, but she had always gotten the impression he'd rather have had a Marine in the co-pilot's chair. IU official policy said otherwise, preferring a mixed military and civilian presence in command, but Rush was considered "old school."

"Three ELFs ready for deployment," Shane said. She sounded enthusiastic, but it bothered her that Leigh was going EVA while she was staying in the ship. Curiosity would prompt Kumar to jump naked into the caldera of a volcano on Io to learn something new. While Leigh agreed to share the risk on board the Bel, at heart, she'd prefer to spend her time digging through endless lines of code in the safety of a lab, building the perfect machine learning routine.

The airlock hatch released and Speirs took point re-entering the core, followed by Rush and Hendricks, with Chalmers bringing up the rear.

Shane switched to an isolated channel and whispered, "You be careful out there."

Leigh answered, "Okay," hearing the smile in her partner's voice. She felt reassured, but having to be careful meant things were dangerous.

Kumar glanced over at Avila who, as she expected, had politely ignored her. Fraternizing between crew wasn't against regs but it wasn't exactly encouraged, either.

"Sending Larry forward while Moe and Curly are going aft." Her panel showed the three ELFs taking off from the landing platforms attached to the core's surface. Jets of cold O^2 gas lifted each body upward silently. Shane could override their course, but their programming plus various sensory units allowed them to be relatively autonomous.

"Have Larry check the other starboard docking bay and the two on the port side. Find out why only ours was active."

"Roger that." Kumar smartly altered the drone's parameters to comply.

Moe and Curly were far ahead of the four explorers as they walked, magnetically attached, toward the rear of the ship toward the rotating interior connections powering the hab rings.

The party was still fifteen minutes from the first ring when Kumar reported in. "Moe and Curly are holding station at the interior hub to Hab Ring A but Larry's found something odd, Captain."

"How odd?" While his power armor amplified his strength many times, his voice still sounded like he was struggling against some weight.

"The other three docking ports don't conform to ship's norms. The temperature reading for them and the surrounding hull is warmer and a quick materials analysis doesn't even read like metal plating. It's more like…something organic. Look, I know that sounds crazy but…"

"Double-check the analysis, but we're already hip deep in crazy so don't worry about what it sounds like. You said this material makes up part of the bulkhead surrounding the ports, how far does it extend?"

It drops off just a few meters aft of the ports but continues forward toward the ship's anterior. I don't know how far yet."

"Send Larry back on its original course and keep an eye on the changes. Let me know what you find out. In the meantime, send Moe up, or rather down Alpha pylon toward A Ring. I want to get a look at the cryogenic creche units, find out what happened to the occupants. Then send Curly ahead past the other ring hubs to the next core partition. We'll join up with the drone there."

"Right, Captain." She wasn't anxious to have the Ring images crossing the monitors since as far as they knew, all of the passengers and crew were dead.

Releasing Curly first, she let it proceed on its pre-programmed course. Then she commanded Moe to take the more complicated path. The interior rotating hub was a massive ring moving between the inner and outer hull. For the drone or anything, including a person, to enter the rapidly moving pylon opening, she had to send it into an access port just forward of the hub. That port led to a car on an auxiliary ring that could be spun up to match the velocity of the drive hub for Ring A. From there, the drone could transfer over and fly down the pylon.

Rush saw the two drones dart away as the four of them approached the area of the first ring hub. While they could feel the vibrations generated by the moving axis, their activity was concealed behind tons of hull plating.

"Captain, we have a problem."

"Go ahead, Avila."

"I was sending my status updates to Luna and Mars when the transmitter went dead."

"Equipment failure?"

"Running diagnostics now. Hopefully, it's just a software glitch, but given how hardened our systems are, I don't think so."

"Keep working on it and let me know how it goes."

"It gets worse, or at least weirder, Captain."

"Yes, Kumar?"

"Larry's telling me that everything from about five hundred meters forward of our position is made up of that same organic substance. Analysis isn't giving me much back. I'd have to get a sample of the stuff into the lab for a positive ID. The best I can do right now is that it's organic, hotter than the ship's interior, and probably living."

"Liv…" Margie felt her throat tighten.

"Any indication from Moe or Curly of similar conditions in our part of the Tiamat?"

"Nothing so far, Captain. Curly is holding station at the bulkhead separating the ring section from the engineering and control module."

"And Gracie," Leigh added over the open comm.

"Everything looks normal except the partition, especially around the personnel hatch. It seems distressed, as if something had made multiple impacts on it. Nothing organic showing up, though. It's 180 meters from the core to the ring. Moe will take another several minutes to get down the pylon. It's having to compensate for the increased gravity effect caused by the rotation plus building atmospheric pressure. The ring section is definitely still pressurized."

"Roger, Kumar. We're just crossing the ring hub section now."

"Captain, Avila breaking in. Maybe you should wait until the report comes back from Moe in A Ring. For all we know, all four rings could be compromised like the front of Tiamat."

"Maybe in the AI section, too," Shane added. "Without going through the partition hatch, Curly can't get an accurate reading of the other side."

"Okay, we'll hold position pending Moe's recon. Anything else from Larry?"

"One moment, Captain. Larry…I've lost contact with Larry."

"What?" Margie had been running her comm diagnostic but swung around again to face Kumar. Was there some sort of alarm or…?"

"No, nothing. Just like the comm. It cut out all of a sudden. No warning of any kind."

"I agree, Captain. The comm is still offline and I haven't the faintest idea why."

"Before Larry stopped sending, did it learn anything more about the organic form it was tracking?"

"Nothing except what I already told you. The entire front end of the ship is no longer the Tiamat. It appears to be some sort of biomass, but exactly what it is or how it's alive has me beat. Wait. Moe is at the top of the pylon. It's bypassing the lift car and using the auxiliary hatch to enter the ring."

"That would be the control bay with the lift car controls and EVA prep chamber."

"It's in. Scanning. Nothing unusual so far. All the EVA suits are in place and the lift controls are on standby. Exits to the hab modules on either side are closed."

"Right. Each ring has a total of eight hab modules, each module holding 15 hib creche clusters."

"I remember, Captain. Two pairs of hab modules, one on each side of a pylon. On the other side of a hab mod going spinward or anti-spinward is a personnel transport module. There's a total of four transports designed to ferry the inhabitants of the ring to the surface of the colony world."

"Have Moe go through the 1A hab entrance. The command crew's hibernation cradles are in there."

Shane took a deep breath and issued the go directive. The drone overrode the locking mechanism and the door slid open. Looking at her monitor, she imagined the hib clusters as a graveyard. Each cluster held six creches for a total of ninety human beings per mod. The creche pods for each cluster formed a circle around a control core, making them look like flowers.

The drone moved into the room slowly.

"Yes, I see the lid on a creche in cluster one, the Captain's. It's open. There are four more open creches scattered across clusters two through six. No occupants. Indicators on all of the others are dark and..." Shane bit her lip to keep from screaming.

"Captain." She tried not to cry but in zero G, her tear ducts filled and then tiny globes left her, traveling randomly in front of her face.

"Send me the image." Margie's tried to make her voice sound neutral but she needed to know what was happening. Then she saw the spectacle and her grip tightened on the sides of her console.

"Captain. Not all of them, but some of the corpses...they look like they've been torn apart. The remains are mummified but...but there are what's left of...I don't know, tentacles, something like that, as if something monstrous had been growing in the creche with the occupant and..."

"Are they alive? Kumar, answer me."

"No...no I don't think so. Nothing's moving but..." She paused. Captain, Curly stopped transmitting. Can you see the ELF?"

"Still too far away. I mean, we should be able to see the separating bulkhead but there's some sort of mist forming in the vacuum messing up visibility."

"With all due respect Sir, I think you and the others should get back to the Bel now."

"Avila, we need to press ahead to learn what happened to the Tiamat. If the remains of the crew don't tell us enough, then the AI is all we have left. Besides, three of us are in advanced combat armor. There isn't much we can't handle."

"That makes me so relieved," Leigh murmured sarcastically.

"You'll be okay, Hendricks. Chalmers has your six and the Captain and I are on point. Nothing gets to you that doesn't go through us first." Speirs tried to sound casual, but she was beginning to wonder if she and the others had walked into a nightmare. Best to keep that to herself and keep the civvie calm.

"Kumar, have Moe recon the entire ring starting with the first PDV; it should be the Clarke. Then have it proceed to the other modules and PDVs just in case anyone revived and tried to leave the ship that way. If everyone is dead, I want confirmation about the state of the corpses. Was it systems failure that killed them or your organic...Kumar? Kumar, do you read?"

"Shane?" Fear clutched Leigh's chest like a hand. "Shane, do you read?" She switched to their private channel. "Shane, talk to me. Did the comm break down or..."

"Captain, we've lost communications with the Bel and we have no outside comm with command on Luna or Mars. Recommend..."

"I'm way ahead of you, Sarge." Elisha saw the expressions on everyone's faces through their helmet visors. Speirs might be scared to death, but her face was as impassive as stone. Chalmers was trying as hard as he could for a badass Marine deadpan, but he'd never faced a real threat before and this was over-the-top spooky. Leigh didn't bother to hide being scared, but it was more for what had happened to Shane.

The lighting in this part of the core was no better than it was forward. That, plus the inexplicable mist or particles, caused shadows to curve and twist like malevolent serpents.

"Just in case…" Rush activated his ST15M, its auto trackers ignoring the crew and scanning for any other movement.

Speirs and Chalmers followed suit just as a shadow crossed overhead. Part of the bulkhead above had become sheets of melting, bubbling plastic.

"Oh Goddammit, the fucking organic shit's coming after us from the bow." Speirs' ST15M followed the ooze but what good would shooting it do?

"And from the pylons." Will was turning slow circles watching the organic slime not just pour out the pylon access ports, but transform most of the interior circumference of this section of core.

"That means we can't get back to the Bel, to Kumar and…" Leigh turned toward Chalmers at the moment when the slow creeping puke-green tendrils shot out and seized him by his legs, wrapping around them like constrictors. His shoulder weapon whirled and fired through the layers of goo enveloping is armor.

"Move, Marine. Rip that shit off of you!"

Through their helmet speakers they could hear what sounded like bacon sizzling on a griddle and then Will's forlorn screaming. His boot magnets disengaged and he was abruptly lifted upward, consumed in a living mass that was burning through his battle armor.

"Oh God, Oh God!" Leigh started to run, but Rush and Speirs flanked her.

"We've got to get forward, Cap. No other way." Speirs modulated her grip to hold but not crush Leigh's arm. Looking back, they saw that everything between them and the pylon was no longer the ship. They were inside the pulsating intestine of a behemoth, oozing necrotic decay.

Chalmers had stopped screaming as he vanished inside the bulk of the beast that the ship was becoming.

They were at the edge where monster became metal, barely staying ahead of it. Magnetic boots continued to hold the three to the flooring as they ponderously moved toward the partition hatch. Elisha didn't see any sign of Curly, but no sign that anything nasty was waiting for them, either. Behind them, the ship continued to relentlessly transform and pursue.

Joanne was at the partition's smaller personnel access port, using her suit's override to pull up its interface. "Life support offline inside but that's all I can tell."

"We don't have a choice. Open it."

Spiers remotely triggered the release and the door opened in jerks and starts, as if it didn't quite fit in the frame. She ducked her head through, let her weapons system do a quick scan, and then backed out. "Seems safe but…"

"But nothing. It's coming. We need to get away." Leigh kept swiveling her head, looking back the mutating predator behind them.

"Let's do it," Rush ordered. The three of them shot through the opening and then the Sarge ordered the door to shut. It hesitated and then abruptly slammed.

Seconds later, the entire bulkhead separating them from the bow shuddered, but then became still. Elisha stared ahead into the quiet emptiness. It was smaller than where they'd just left, the bulk of the space around them occupied by the data modules, processors, and Gracie's computing core.

He looked at Joanne who was still holding a terrified young woman by the arm.

"Leigh?" Joanne was whispering into her mic, her visor touching Hendricks'

"Shane?"

They both knew what she was asking as well as the answer.

"Leigh, about Gracie," the Captain said.

"Gracie...um, yes. Gracie." She looked like she was trying to wake up from a dream. "Her access hatch should be just ahead and to the left."

The corridor led into darkness. In the shadows something swarmed amid the conduits, the support elements, and service modules.

They stopped as, "I was wondering why we hadn't seen any Wardens," Speirs muttered.

"They're huddled around Gracie's access panel. They shouldn't do that." Leigh was forcing herself to pay attention to the collection of maintenance drones rather than have to think about...

"More like guarding it, I'd say," Speirs replied.

To Elisha they looked like overgrown insects. Each one was three feet tall and wide and almost as thick, shaped roughly like triangles flattened on the top. They moved via three magnetic legs or adhering treads. Multipurpose limbs were stored in the thorax. Three-digit numbers labeled their variably colored shells to distinguish them.

"We're not getting in." Speirs gazed at the swarming robots.

"Let me try something." Leigh accessed her suit's terminal and attempted a remote connection. "Maybe this close, Gracie will pick up a wireless signal."

"I don't know if she picked up something, but the Wardens did." Speirs watched the slowly shuffling machines now turning to face them.

"We'd better keep moving." Rush took a step forward.

"The Manual Monitor Room? Take control away from Gracie?" Leigh was picturing the layout of the deck just ahead.

"We won't have the time. Joanne looked back. The partition two-hundred meters behind was curling and boiling. "It's coming through."

"Doesn't make sense. If this stuff somehow has control of Tiamat, why is the partition blocking it? Why isn't it already here?"

"Maybe if it turned Gracie to a glob, she'd stop being an AI and lose control of the ship. So far everything, from docking ports to communications that it's taken over has stopped working."

"But how is it controlling the AI and Wardens?"

"Screw that," Speirs pulled Leigh forward again. "We've got to get off the ship."

"Someone already did."

"Right Cap. The missing SSV. There are seven more." They moved forward deliberately avoiding the Manual Control Override to their right. The closest two ships hadn't been touched.

"Leigh, were all the Warden's guarding Gracie?"

"I don't know, Captain."

A surge of movement in the darkness. They were ambushed by dozens of Wardens vomiting from the SSV 01 Jemison hatchway.

"Captain, get Leigh out of here."

The nearest Warden ignited an acetylene torch and another spun up a circular saw. Then in a single motion, the rest pounded their metaphorical plowshares into swords, using their tools to try and take Speirs apart. Her ST15M chattered mutely in the vacuum as Joanne used her exoskeleton to tear through robotic bodies like aluminum foil.

The hatch to 02 SSV McAuliffe was clear. Rush keyed the lock open and then shoved Leigh inside. "Start the pre-launch sequence. I'm going back to help…"

Rush turned and saw that Speirs had shredded over half of the Wardens attacking her. One of them even set off a small explosion, but her armor, though bent and scorched, had held up. It was too late anyway.

Invasive gelatinous tentacles were engulfing her boots and legs, and through the radio link he could hear the hissing of her battle suit dissolving. She was still trying to fire her weapon but the ammo had run out. Rush took two, three, four steps forward before he heard her.

"Get out, get the fuck out, Cap! Get the civvie out and warn…"

She was gone, buried in mounds of undulating sludge along with most of the remaining Wardens. Now it was coming for him.

"Captain." He risked a look back at the ship bay to see the hatch still open and Leigh waving him in.

"I told you to…"

"I can't fly this ship."

He started running toward her. She was right. The Bel's crew had been briefed on flight procedures, but the control systems on this shuttle were half a century out of date. Rush could fly the McAuliffe, which meant staying behind wouldn't help either one of them. Leigh was the only one left to save.

At the hatchway, he tumbled forward as something hit his back and splattered inward. It was a glancing blow, enough to stagger him.

Leigh pressed the emergency outer door control. It closed and the airlock pressurized as Elisha peeled a meter-square section of ooze off of his armor's back.

With the airlock pressurized, Hendricks opened the inner door. Elisha yelled at Leigh to get in and she ran onto the ship's control deck. It was already pressurized with its systems on standby. He followed and shuddered as a bucket load of the muck writhed on the airlock floor, trying to chase him. Making sure his armor wasn't compromised, he slammed the inner hatch shut sealing the thing inside, but how long would it hold?

In his armor, he'd never be able to use the controls so he ordered it to disgorge him. It always felt a little like being born when it decoupled in the back an poured him out.

"Get in an acceleration couch, now!" He trusted her to obey him. There were eight empty pods for her to choose from as he entered the couch at the pilot's console. "Screw the pre-flight. Proceeding to emergency departure. SSV McAuliffe systems online, fuel priming, launch in..." he scanned the readouts, "...two minutes."

He heard pounding from the airlock hatch. Less than ninety seconds until ignition. The pounding stopped and he heard the sound of bacon sizzling on the griddle. They'd be lucky to make it off in time.

Then there was a sound of restraints being coupled close behind him. "I told you to get secured Leigh. Engine ignition is in less than a minute."

He activated the airlock interior camera as the countdown passed thirty seconds. He braced himself, even though the couch should shield him from most of the G-forces. "Give it up, damn you."

A deafening roar accompanied a surge of acceleration. Elisha was slammed back into the pilot's seat, his left cheek pressed against the cushion. The thing in the airlock didn't scream, but there was a sickening splat as it was thrown back into the rear bulkhead.

It started to fight its way toward the inner airlock door again.

"Die you son of a..." Rush slammed a fist on the emergency airlock purge. The outer airlock door burst open, and the scum was blown into the frigid vacuum of space.

Making sure the airlock was completely empty, he sealed the doors but didn't repressurize. On the rear-view monitor, he saw Tiamat receding in the distance. There was no outward sign of anything wrong, but in addition to four members of his crew, 2,460 people were dead.

The comm system was off so he initiated the power up sequence. Then the comm came to life, but in a totally unexpected way.

"This is Captain Victoria Liu Carter of the Tiamat. If you've come aboard this ship, you are already dead. If you can use this or another shuttle to get off, do so right now, but make sure the lifeform doesn't touch you."

The monitor image was flicking, the color imbalanced, but even with that, she looked sick. Her voice was quivering. "I was able to piece things together before the end. Systems were standard as Tiamat entered interstellar space but while we were all asleep, something was talking to our AI, reprogramming it.

We must have been on a vector for a close flyby to Planet X. I guess that's what people still call it, the long theorized but never discovered tenth planet somewhere far outside the orbit of Pluto. Except it's not a planet, not exactly."

Carter coughed wet and messy, like someone with lung cancer. "When the malfunctions began, the emergency protocol revived me, but I thought Gracie, the AI, was offline. Most of the crew and passengers were dead. Some of them had been…invaded by the lifeform. By the time I woke up, we were in orbit. Somehow, while Tiamat was still far enough away, the compromised AI bled off our velocity so we could make our approach.

Four others in my hib module made it. Unable to access controls remotely, we tried to reach the AI. If you went that way, you probably found what we found, Frankenstein's monster in sheep's clothing. Parts of the ship had been transformed. That's what the planet does, that's what it is. A gigantic organism, some rogue planet that had been captured by our Sun ages ago. The Tiamat gave it the means to do more than languish in the eternal darkness of space.

I thought both of us, Jabbar and I got away, except we didn't. He had been infected. I managed to force him into the airlock but not before he…he did it to me. Now I'm changing into one of them. I can already feel the urge to turn the ship around, go back, join with them.

I'm not going to let them do it to me. I know they plan to use Tiamat to return to the solar system, to Earth. I don't know how, but if they can consume a spacecraft, imagine what they could do to a city, maybe even a planet. If you can hear this, get off of Tiamat now, and if you can, destroy her. I'm sending this message on a channel reserved for only SSVs, so Gracie won't detect it.

It was too late for me the minute I was revived. Even if I hadn't been infected, in this ship, where am I supposed to go? No matter what I did, I was already dead. Just one more thing left to do…"

The image jumped and there was the howl of the ship's atmosphere being evacuated. It took Captain Carter less than a minute to die. Elisha watched her lifeless body bob around in her restraints, and then seconds later the recording clicked off.

Rush checked his nav console and saw he and Tiamat were much closer to Luna and Earth than he expected.

"The ship didn't continue to decelerate. There's no way in hell it could go into orbit around Luna or Earth now. It'll get to Earth in just a few months. I can't do anything in a short-range exploration craft." He reached for the frequency controls to adjust them to the command channel.

"How are you holding up back there, Leigh?" He hadn't forgotten about her, but in a crisis, you put out the fires first, and then worry about everything else.

"You can contact your people, but beforehand, we would like to tell you something."

Rush held his breath and turned his couch to face her. She was sitting in the first row of seats, second from the right. It was Leigh, but of course, it wasn't anymore.

"When it hit my armor, I thought it had just spilled over onto the deck plates." Her helmet was off, but the burn holes in the front of her EVA suit told him what had happened. "So, Leigh is gone and I'm next." He cursed himself for turning and wondered if he could swivel back and blow the airlock before she reached him, share Carter's fate.

"We will not approach you and indeed, we mean you no harm."

"Yeah, I saw so much evidence of your good intensions on Tiamat…thousands of people dead."

"They will live again in time. Not as the entities you knew but there will be life nonetheless. We are life and we bring life."

"Kind of like a cancer cell."

"We cannot make you understand. We must survive, but we will also enable you to survive. Your species is slowly dying. We can correct that."

"Somehow, I doubt your motives. What happens now?"

"We, this part of us, is dying, separated from the whole but still part of the whole, still the single entity, the one whole being." The thing that was Leigh touched her chest and he saw she was beginning to flake and wither, like a plant too long without water.

"We only want to survive, but to do so, we will help you survive."

"If that's your purpose, why did you kill so many people, my crew?"

"Do you deny that at discovering us, you would have exterminated us if you could? We have the right to defend ourselves. As we have already said, nothing has died that cannot be regrown given time and the correct environment."

Her flesh was dripping like melted wax and she was starting to pool inside her suit.

"The Captain of this ship is dead, but before she died, she said she wanted us to destroy the Tiamat."

"She is the only one of your kind who is truly lost. She resisted and ended her existence before we could recover her. We felt a great sadness."

"I don't know if you can understand, but I am responsible for protecting my kind. So far, I failed, but if I can, I will destroy you.

"You may but we…Elisha Rush, we need…you…"

"How do you know my name?"

But it was too late. Life and light departed from what used to be Leigh Hendricks. But how much would she have wanted to live without Shane?

Gathering yet another bundle of grief into a tight knot, Rush turned back to the controls and directed a focused comm beam to Shackleton on Luna.

***

Months later, Elisha Rush was still in isolation in the secure wing of the medical facility at Shackleton Base near Luna's south pole. Earth hadn't maintained an anti-asteroid capacity in decades. Why bother when humanity's own folly had ruined the planet's ability to sustain them and almost every other form of life it had spawned.

When the various astrodynamics gurus and other big brains figured out that Tiamat was on an unrelenting course directly for the mother world, they advised IU forces to do nothing. After all, what was the worst that could happen?

His rooms were comfortable. Like billions of others, he watched the video feed of Tiamat's imminent impact transmitted from observation stations on Luna and close orbiting satellites in the ease in his living room, drinking coffee and bitter anticipation.

He had warned them. He had put everything in his report, but he was never sure they believed it all. Officially, he was on extended medical leave. They must have believed something because the Marine Corp commander herself authorized every conceivable medical exam be run on him, some several times. He was still under observation.

Rush continued to feel fine, physically anyway. But he was sick at heart. He kept seeing their faces, feeling their trust, but trust turned to ashes in his mouth.

He was a coward to not contact Robert Avila first, but Elisha and Margie had been too close. Guilt diverted him into calling Chalmers' parents at Tycho instead. He wasn't sure whether to be surprised or not when they blocked his channel, but their complaints to the Marine commandant's office resulted in his comm privileges being revoked. They blamed him for their son's death and it was just as well. He was sure a Corps representative had sent very nice letters of condolences to the families of the dead. They were the testaments to his failure in waiting too long before realizing the truth.

The deaths of his crew, almost a kind of family, swirled into his grief for Hope and Matthew. Seven years ago, while he was deployed on maneuvers near Ceres, his wife and three-year-old son left Mars for the months long journey to Luna. Matty had never seen his Grandma before. Elisha was called back on emergency leave by the news of the shuttle accident at Copernicus. After that, he had a hard time finding a reason to live, except to justify Hope's faith in him. He knew she'd want him to go on, if not be happy. The Corps, and later the crew of the Bel were all he had. Now he had nothing except to make sure the Tiamat came to a final end.

Tiamat entered the upper atmosphere at a severe angle, certain to burn up before reaching the surface. She was half a kilometer long but massed much less than a meteor or asteroid of the same size and dimensions. The expansive ramjet framework became melted butter. The rings tore off like paper and the sleeper ship glowed like a sliver of the Sun before disappearing beneath the cloud cover.

Nothing could have lived through that. Elisha was comforted by the thought. Everyone else believed nothing could have lived through that hell as well. For a while it even seemed true.

Six weeks later, all information, transmissions, and video feeds from or near Earth were severed and under an executive order from Interplanetary Union President Alejandrina Orozco, all radio and visual observations of the Earth were to forthwith cease. Failure to comply would result in a significant fine, incarceration, or both.

***

"There's nothing else you can add to your report, Elisha?"

Rush had known Colonel Titus McCord since Elisha was a boot and McCord the camp's deputy commandant. They'd eventually become good friends with "Cord" giving the eulogy at Hope's and Matthew's Memorial Service.

"I'm not holding back, Cord. That's everything Leigh said. Are you trying to tell me she was right?"

They had been sitting across the coffee table from each other, Elisha on the sofa and Cord on a chair he'd pulled in from the kitchen. He put down his cup of tea and stood. Cord was an old man, but still fit. Even when he paced, he was ramrod straight. He stopped, rubbing his fingers across his bald, brown pate as if he'd forgotten he'd lost his hair decades ago. Then he turned.

"Elisha, what I'm going to tell you is so highly classified that I could end up drawing a general court just for breathing a word of it."

"You've never been worried about that sort of thing before."

"Nothing this big has ever happened before."

"Big as in?"

Cord sat back down and seemed to deflate a little, as if he were a balloon with a slow leak.

"Tiamat survived re-entry but that's not the half of it." Cord looked like he'd rather choke than say what came next. "The experts can't exactly say what it is, but there's some sort of reaction happening in the atmosphere and probably at ground level and in the oceans. The impact site is the epicenter."

"Reaction."

"A cascading environmental anomaly, they call it. Something is sucking CO_2 out of the atmosphere. Temperatures across the globe have dropped six degrees in as many weeks. Elisha, President Orozco has ordered scout ships to perform close flyovers of the affected zone and surrounding areas. Preliminary results indicate that plant growth has recovered 12 percent in those regions, and it's spreading."

"Plant life. Not the life that had taken over Tiamat?"

"They determined conclusively that it's not. We had the remains of Hendricks examined in every possible way. We know for a fact that the life developing on the Yucatan Peninsula is indigenous to the region, or it was before it supposedly died off."

"Then what Leigh, what they said is true. They're returning life to the Earth. We don't have to find a home in interstellar space." Elisha felt a weight in his chest lighten.

"Well, about that. Based on your report and confirmed by these events, we sent recall signals to the Anubis, Isis, and Osiris. No matter how life generating Tiamat seems to be, we're not going to sacrifice thousands of human beings on those ships in an encounter with that planet out there."

"And?"

"Osiris has begun a long orbit around Neptune that will eventually result in a return arc. Isis is a little more difficult, but she's altered course just short of the Oort cloud. We'll get her back, but it'll take thirty or forty years. They're still crunching the numbers."

He picked up his tea cup, saw it was empty and put it back down. Elisha didn't offer a refill.

"Unfortunately, we've lost all contact with the Anubis."

"Everything?"

"No signals from her estimated last position, nothing at all, visible light, infrared, nada. It's like she just disappeared, swallowed up in a hole in space."

"But not forever."

"That's what scares me, Elisha."

"How long can you keep something like this a secret?"

"The Tiamat Effect? Hell, try keeping a lid on an entire planet. Rumors are already flying on dozens of pirate media channels. The President is calling a press conference, pretty much against her will, in about two weeks. She'll sell some such bullshit about waiting to confirm results, consulting expert opinions, you know, the usual crap."

"About Anubis? You know the people on that ship probably have friends and relatives on Luna, Mars, maybe Ganymede and the stations."

"When we have more information than, we don't know, we'll release it to the public. Until then, we'll pretend Anubis is on course for 82 Eridani and will arrive in a hair over three centuries."

"Cord, if my math is right and the timing of what happened to Tiamat happens to Anubis, we'll see her again in about twelve years."

"Where do you think you'll be in twelve years."

"Far, far away from wherever the Anubis is. I've had enough of whatever that was on the Tiamat."

"Well, that's too bad. I was hoping you'd get tired of being cooped up here eating glorified hospital food."

"Trying to get me back in the world, Colonel?"

"Funny you should put it that way. If the science team approves it, I'm looking for someone to lead an exploratory Op to Yucatan. You'd be the first person in your generation to step foot back on Earth and be able to breathe the air. Who knows? We might both live long enough to retire there.

"That's a big offer. Give me time to think about it?"

"Sure." Cord looked down at his empty cup as if he still needed to finish it. Then he stood and smiled. "Well, about time I get the hell out of here. Never could stand hospitals, even ones that look like gilded cages."

"I appreciate you stopping by." He stood and decorum demanded that they only shake hands. "If I say yes, when will my orders come through? I really am getting tired of this place."

"Six to eight weeks give or take red tape. Of course, I do have a sweet desk job for an administrator at Mawrth Vallis if you're not interested in Earth."

Elisha feigned outrage. "Oh my God, herding a bunch of Martian geologists around in the middle of nowhere. Hell, there isn't a decent place to eat or get a drink within a hundred kilometers."

"Your choice, Elisha. It's been good seeing you again. Brought back a few memories. Hope we can make some good ones in the years that come."

"Me too, Cord. I'll give you a call in a few days."

"Looking forward to it. See you, friend."

"Yeah. See you."

Cord let himself out. Elisha sat back down on the sofa and regarded a half empty cup of cold coffee for the next several hours.

***

Major Elisha Rush was just coming off duty, walking back from the shuttle stop to his quarters at the New Merida complex when the news came in. He'd been inspecting security for the botany group out of Guatemala for the past ten days, and he was anxious to get home to Elena. They'd been married for eighteen months and she just found out she was pregnant.

His handheld rang as he was about to turn down his street. The sun was low in the west and he was tired. He took a deep breath, pulling in the fragrance of some flowers he couldn't name. They might have been a variety that had been around for thousands of years, or one of the new species the botanists had been recently cataloging. He answered, "Rush. Go."

"Sorry to bother you, Major. This is Lieutenant Wright at administration. You've got a priority message from Tiamat section commander. It's marked most urgent, Sir."

He pictured the anxious look on Erin Wright's face and exhaled, taking the phone away from his ear for several seconds. Then lifting it again, "On my way. Give me five minutes."

He hailed a passing transport and phoned Elena in transit to tell her he'd be late. She'd served two tours before retiring and going into oceanography as a civvie. She understood, but she still didn't like it.

Sitting down at his desk in his office, Elisha scratched the side of his head, feeling the thinning hair and knowing he had more gray than brown these days. "Security procedure, open Channel Dee, passcode Three Delta Null Charlie Echo Five Romeo."

The computer processed the information and then the approval flashed across the virtual screen followed by Katherine Wong's image.

"Sorry to keep you waiting, Colonel."

"I wouldn't bother you Elisha, but I wanted you to hear it from me first. The observatory at the Mars L4 point spotted the object, but someone managed to access and leak the video to a pirate news net. We won't be able to keep it under wraps for long."

He felt the pit of his stomach drop out. Elisha hadn't thought about the moment he had once anticipated in years. He hadn't thought about what happened to the Tiamat in almost as long, except for the dreams.

"The Anubis is being tracked passing the orbit of Jupiter. She's headed toward Earth."

"Same as with Tiamat, Colonel?" He closed his eyes and said a silent prayer.

"New wrinkle, I'm afraid. The AI is sending a repeating signal at 21-minute intervals on focused transmission to Acidalia Planetia. Whoever or whatever is on board the Anubis, they're asking for you."

James Pyles is a SF/F writer and technology author. Since 2019, over 40 of his short stories have been featured in anthologies. He won the 2021 Helicon Short Story Award for his SciFi tale "The Three Billion Year Love." His novellas, "Time's Abyss" and "Ice" were published this past Fall.

Unauthorised Fauna

by Barend Nieuwstraten III

Customs Officer Grey suddenly found himself in a room he didn't recognise. For a moment he wondered if he'd gotten drunk the night before and passed out somewhere, but he was already standing, and he didn't feel hung over. In fact, he didn't feel anything at all. Certainly not as if he'd just woken. No grogginess, no desire to stretch, no hunger. Why was he in this odd little corridor of a room?

He looked to his hands, uncertain of what answers he expected to find there, but they looked normal. The sleaves of his uniform, on the other hand, were not quite right. The material seemed to have a strange sheen to it. Almost glossy.

It wasn't until he suddenly heard the hum of the station, that he realised he had, until that precise moment, been completely deaf for the last few minutes. The environmental system, artificial gravity field, the processors in all the digital interfaces, and all the other noises one learnt to filter out, came into sharp focus after failing to be present for some reason. Until now. A suspicion grew in his mind as he searched for his last memory. Submitting to a weekly brain scan as part of his subscription to the holographic resurrection program. Nothing beyond that.

"Oh shit, no," he realised. "I'm dead." He tried to panic, but nothing really came of it. There was no hyperventilation, pounding heart, nor sweating. Just an empty existential dread without the biological fanfare that typically accompanied such a crisis. He was stuck in a state of horror, reacting to his own death, but without the ability to properly process it. It somehow compounded the news but also left him calm enough to deal with it.

"Alright… computer," he ordered. "How long after final neuroscan did I…" he felt a sweeping sense of imposter syndrome referring to himself as 'I,' being a holographic simulation of the man he remembered being, but pressed on, "…die?"

"Biofunctions ceased two days, sixteen hours, and approximately seven minutes after last scan," the computer relayed.

"Please display security feed of final…" he shrugged, "fifteen minutes?"

"Location: cargo bay three," the computer said, as a display appeared before him. "Time Index: Eleven-Thirteen."

Grey watched himself from a high angle approaching a storage room. He looked smart in his uniform, proudly erect in posture and professionally checking everything off against his pad. Meticulous in his duty and devoted to his work, blissfully unaware of his own impending doom. Watching, he immediately regretted a short life dedicated to not slouching, to save an older version of himself, that would now never exist, from later back problems.

"Location: storage room three-point-four," the computer announced as the footage switched to the storage room's internal security feed.

Grey watched his flesh-and-blood predecessor examining the contents and labels of shipping containers for eight-and-a-half minutes. He regretted that his final moments were spent simply doing his boring job.

"Location: cargo bay three," the computer said, as the display reverted to the corridor feed.

"Did a crate fall on me?" he mumbled to himself, curious. "Did an arms smuggler...?" he began to ask, as he watched himself react confused to the next room from the bay feed. "What? What do you see, you poor bastard?"

In the footage, he was looking back and forth between his pad and the open storage unit. He seemed confused but, after looking around, walked in. The feed changed.

"Location: storage room three-point-five."

The room was empty and the Officer Grey who lived little more than two days beyond his last holo-save shook his head as he looked to his pad that clearly didn't reflect what he was seeing. He turned in the room, pivoting on the spot in disbelief as the watching holographic version of himself furrowed his photonic brow. The confused customs officer in the feed seemed to react to something, suddenly looking to the back of the room where the large safe was built into the wall. Though he didn't appear to be reacting to a realisation or thought. More to something happening.

"You hear something, me?" the hologram mumbled to the man that was both his past and future self, walking over and seemingly arguing with the computer attached to the safe before adopting an authoritative stance, punching in an override code and submitting to a handprint scan. The panel opened and the man in the feed leaned his head forwards, seemingly struggling to comprehend what he was seeing. He fetched a small torch from his belt, looking annoyed that the internal light didn't activate or was blocked. He raised his fist as he thumbed the hand-held light, illuminating whatever it was to his own benefit but not that of the security recorder. He pulled his head back before something sprayed on his face, making him drop his torch and pad. He clutched his face and recoiled from the safe, turning around, coughing, and spitting, stumbling to his knees.

"What the hell was that?" his holographic legacy demanded, watching in horror. "Defensive traps are prohibited on…" he began to quote regulation but trailed off when he realised it wasn't some triggered chemical weapon. Four dark shafts began sliding out of the recess, spreading outward onto the wall, segmented like giant spindly fingers. Appendages of some kind, gripping the wall.

"Shit," he yelled, startled by the feed as something large leapt out of the hole in the wall to tackle and pin him to the floor. It looked and moved like a giant spider or scorpion, covered in a slimy greyish-green carapace, with large black eyes upon its raised head with a jaw full of claw-like teeth. "What the fuck is that?" Grey yelled at the image.

"Truant fauna not recognised," was all the computer had to offer in response.

Grey watched the footage of himself being dominated by this large insectoid creature that used its mantis-like arms to hold him down, stabbing at his back with what looked like a stinger on a tail that curled under its body. He used his holographic hand to zoom, once he realised the creature's tail was remaining embedded for longer than a dose of venom would presumably require. Through its translucent tail, Grey could see movement. He zoomed again, seeing dark spheres being pumped into his abdomen. He watched himself scream until he vomited blood. He yelled something, and the door to storage room three-point-five shut. As his entire life memory fell short by just under three days of the man he watched dying, he could only guess that his final command was to seal the room and protect the rest of the station from whatever was killing him.

Grey's eyes darted about the small holographic generation suite as his sense of duty bypassed his double redundant sense of self preservation. "How long did my activation take from the point of death," he asked the computer, watching the time index countdown in mere seconds to it.

"Four hours, twelve minutes," the computer informed him.

"God, I'm still on my shift," he realised.

"Negative," the computer corrected. "Completion of orientation module required before holographic duty commencement."

"Skip," Grey said, loudly.

"Completion of orientation module compulsory."

"Postpone," he barked, struggling to leave his small projection bay. "Security emergency in progress. Override onboarding program."

"State clearance."

"Grey-D-seven-two-six-delta-gamma," he said, before attempting to step off the orange circle to which he was bound.

"Accepted. Please state postponement time."

"I don't know... forty-eight hours?"

"Maximum postponement is one hour," the computer told him.

Grey sighed, annoyed. "Fine. One hour."

"Holoprogram activated."

Grey angrily stepped off the glowing orange pad onto the floor and made for the door. His fingers passed through the control panel. "How the hell am I supposed to open the door?"

"Requested information is contained within orientation module," the computer said blankly, but Grey swore he could sense smugness in its voice.

He squinted angrily, then just decided to see if he could simply pass through the door instead. It immediately felt wrong, as all his instincts and life experience tried to tell him he'd injure himself, but the cream coloured door simply got closer until it wasn't there anymore. Then he found himself outside, standing in a throughfare that led to the medibay. There had been a jolt in the passage. He had not truly walked through the door, merely breached the threshold of one room's holo-projectors into the next.

Instinctively he wanted to gather medical personnel, but brain death must have occurred over four hours ago to have activated the holo-resurrection program. He quickly made for the nearest com panel. His hand, again passing through the control panel. He shook his head. "Com M-one-six-vox," he ordered the panel into voice interface, reading its ident. "Contact security office."

After a few connection beeps, a security officer appeared on the screen. "Security," the man simply answered at the other end.

"This is Customs Officer Grey. I need an armed team to meet me outside storage room three-point-five. Recommend cryo-guns."

"What?" the guard on com duty asked. "What's happening?"

"Some sort of hostile lifeform is sealed within. A big one. Someone's illegally smuggling fauna."

The security guard contemplated a moment. Few had ever seen a living creature from outside the home system, especially one that didn't require a microscope to observe. Practically no one even believed in them. The guard reluctantly nodded, not really in a position to refuse. "Be there soon, sir," he said.

"Thank you," Grey answered. "Communication end."

Grey walked to the lift as fast as he could, not wanting to break into a jog or run. If the issue could be dealt with quietly and calmly, they could resolve the issue and arrest the culprit without raising alarm. People were moving about the station as normal. Just another day. It didn't feel right to him, somehow. Not that he expected everyone to stop in their tracks and start wailing over his death or drop their heads in solemn, silent reverence. But he didn't expect it all to be so unceremoniously casual either. Then again, he was still the only one who knew he was dead.

He slowed his pace when he approached the elevator where a visitor to the station was waiting. This time, he fought the urge to reach for the button. Besides which, the visitor had already chosen the 'down' arrow.

As the visitor politely offered Grey first entry, he walked in but found himself reset a few steps back, standing before the entrance again. It startled the older man who'd overtaken his disappearing elevator companion by default. The man turned around wondering where Grey had gone.

"Oh," the man said, confused but then relieved. "You're a hologram?"

"Yes," Grey said. "I'm a bit new to it."

The man, in his sixties, gave a slow smile, sticking his hand out to stall the doors open from within. "Friend's wife's a hologram," he informed him. "Keeps her around on his ship."

"Must be rich to have set that up for personal use."

The man shrugged with a nod. "Yeah, kind of," he said. "But I don't think she does much walking unless they're walking together for the hell of it. Just kind of reappears wherever she's needed."

"Ah," Grey realised, "suppose there's no holo-emitters in the lift then. You don't know the command to make that happen, by any chance?" Grey was quickly realising how difficult his existence was going to be until he submitted to the tutorial program he'd skipped.

The man thought for a second. "Don't know if you're using the same brand, cause you look more convincing than she does, but something about a holocore command set. So, like, 'holocore, relocate: gally,' 'holocore, relocate: bathroom...' not that that's likely, I suppose, but you get the idea."

"Ah..." Grey said. "Holocore..." he said, hearing a digital double dink in his head, "relocate: cargo bay three." His surroundings almost instantly changed to cargo bay three before he could react. He offered a vestigial "thanks," to the man who could no longer hear nor see him.

Just beyond the cargo bay's entrance, Grey followed in the footsteps of the version of himself that had been a few days older than he remembered ever being. Uncharted experience in familiar terrain. He walked down the huge corridor with its high ceilings, feeling naked without his pad in his hand to check against. Soon he found himself before the door of storage room three-point-five. Just some storage room that was currently serving as his mausoleum. Beyond that door a dead man lay mutilated. He was again proud that his last command had been to seal the room. He'd been robbed of remembering his final thoughts but also spared the trauma of experiencing such a horrific death. He stood and waited.

The security team soon arrived armed with rifles attached to tanks on their backs. Their gasmasks loose and goggles on their foreheads. "Alright, sir?" the squad leader asked. "What exactly do you believe you saw in here?"

Grey hesitated a moment, thrown off by the dismissively cynical nature of the guard's phrasing and tone. While he was a junior officer and younger than the man calling him sir, he'd have hoped for a more tangible level of respect. "It's about the size of a person, some sort of alien spider, scorpion... hybrid. I'm not sure. But it's hostile to humans. At least it was towards me."

"You seem okay," the guard said, looking him up and down.

"Do I?" Grey asked, sweeping his extended arm through the man's chest to demonstrate his lack of physical presence.

"Oh," was all he could say, re-evaluating his attitude. His face loosening in guilt and pity.

"Afraid I didn't quite make it out," Grey said, pointing towards the door. "In fact, *I'm* still in there."

"Understood. I'm... sorry, sir."

The security team began fastening their safety gear. Once they were in position, Grey stepped in front of them. "Computer, unseal and open door to storage room three-point-five. Authorisation: Grey-D-seven-two-six-delta-gamma."

"Seal removed," the computer replied, opening and illuminating the room.

On the floor of the otherwise empty room, Grey's corpse lay face-down with his head turned to the side. Some green fluid was congealed upon his face, his skin aggressively irritated red around and underneath it. His back was torn open and most of his insides had been hollowed out. Not thrown about the room shredded but seemingly devoured with a multitude of red tracks spreading out from the body, across the floor and up the wall.

The security team were noticeably disturbed, which in a way, seemed to give Grey a little closure for some reason. An acknowledgment of his horrific death. As the security team raised their weapons and made to move forward, he placed his arm across the chest of the nearest man to stop him proceeding as a cautionary thought began to formulate. Grey's eyes followed the small tracks, painted in his own blood, all leading to a vent near the ceiling where the grate had been pierced and torn into a hole. As he realised the savaged exit was too small for the thing that had actually killed him to pass through, his eyes quickly shifted to the open safe at the back of the room.

The security guard he was attempting to hold back had passed through his incorporeal arm. Grey quickly raced ahead, charging into the room where he turned as soon as he breached the threshold and looked up. The creature that had killed him was perched above the doorway, watching him enter as it skittered around on the spot, adjusting its position to jump. He instinctively stepped back in fear, deeper into the room but everything flickered as he reached the extent of his projectable range. He reached out in front of him, holding up his hands to halt the man he'd overtaken. "No, pull ba-" he began to warn, but his surroundings reset to the corridor as the holoprojectors returned him to the Bay Three thoroughfare. "Back," he said, quickly spinning back to see the creature drop onto the guard taking point.

Cryorifles discharged with a deep hiss, pumping a thick cloud of white arctic mist into the cargo room as the others fired in panic. The freezing vapour spread, dispersing the cloud as it decompressed, but the creature had been fast to react, skittering past its victim to safety. A chorus of swearing burst from all present as they saw their fellow guard covered in the white frost, prevented from moving as it froze him in place. A chilling sound of crackling came from him as he slowed to stillness.

Offset by its jump towards a projected man made of light, the creature's attack had only injured the guard in a collateral attack, slicing into his leg. The poor man was instead injured far worse by his fellow guards in their surprise. As they pulled back their weapons, the creature leapt to the wall, away from the shifting frost. It then leapt again, past the half-frozen man, snapping off his hand. The freezing man screamed through his petrified jaw.

Grey watched helpless as another guard within the group took the full assault from the airborne beast, knocked to the ground and pinned. The creature turned its vicious head presenting its plentiful supply of teeth and eyes, now that Grey was close enough to see all the smaller ones that surrounded that larger pair. It spat its green viscous substance into another guard's face and plunged one of its sharp forelegs into the pinned man's abdomen as the rest fired their rifles high.

The creature quickly retreated down the corridor of the cargo deck, leaving three men out of the fight. Grey chased after the creature so that at least someone was keeping track of it. Two men followed him as the others responded to the fallen members of their team. Grey found he seemed incapable of reaching speeds he knew he could when he'd been alive, but at least knew he wouldn't tire. His hologrammatic form had a set speed that he could not push further with adrenaline or recklessness, but he at least knew he could maintain it indefinitely.

"It's heading for the customs office," one of the men behind Grey called out.

Inspired, Grey smiled spitefully. "Holocore," he commanded, "relocate: customs office."

His surrounds quickly changed. He found himself standing in his own office. Yet to be officially reported deceased, his desk still had all his things on it. Two other officers looked up, surprised by his sudden manifestation.

"Grey?" Customs Officer Brooks queried.

Grey turned his back to him and walked through the open doorway as he heard the skittering of the large insectoid that had killed him and the shouting of those pursuing it. He quickly stepped away from the door to get a better view of the winding corridor. "Actually," he realised, looking back, "Brooks. Run to airlock C-three-one."

"What," the confused officer asked.

"Just do it," Grey yelled. "Run for your fucking life."

Brooks moved urgently, having never been spoken to like that by Grey before. He ran around his desk and past Grey.

"Open the internal hatch and hide if you can," Grey instructed.

"Inside?"

"No," he yelled back angrily as the creature came into view, "not inside." With more light in office area, the partial translucency of the alien creature's carapace revealed itself. Under it, the shadow of its organs pulsated within. Its lungs quickly inflating and deflating, while fluid shifted about in circulatory conduits. It skidded in its tracks to poise itself for another jump. When it did, Grey moved, allowing it to crash into the wall of his old office. He ran after Brooks while the thing that had killed him regained its footing. "Come on then, you bastard," he yelled at it, as he ran down the corridor. "Second course."

"Airlock C-three-one open," Brooks soon called back.

Positioning himself at the threshold of the airlock, Grey turned back waiting for the creature. He beckoned it with waving arms. "Get ready to lock us in."

"Who's us? Wha-" Brooks needed no further answers upon seeing the creature come around the corner. He staggered backwards in terror, squatting as his legs gave in.

"Here I am, come get me," Grey offered it. He slowly slid just beyond the airlock hatchway as the creature turned and placed two of its legs against the wall to push towards him again. "Come on, you hideous, filthy..." he began, but before he could finish unleashing all the insults, he could think of, it passed through him. "Quick, shut the hatch. Shut the hatch," he yelled, turning to face the confused creature. "Before it gets out."

He heard Brooks fumble behind him, trying to get back up as the creature turned back, ready for a second leap, placing its hind legs on the outer hatch. A leap that would free it if Brooks didn't hurry.

"Got it," his workmate yelled, slamming his fist on the button.

The doors shut as the beast leapt at him. But everything flickered and Grey was reset, standing before the inner hatch with Brooks. Brooks was looking at the security feed, taking in the sight of it with his jaw hanging in disbelief.

"Alright," Grey said, "this isn't' the zoo. Flush the bastard."

"Oh right," Brooks said, nervously typing in the code for the outer hatch as they both heard the thing slam its body against the inner hatch.

The creature panicked as the room began to depressurise, struggling to hold the floor as the gravity-field was released. Then after a clunk of unbolting, the outer doors began to open, drawing it towards the narrow slit with the remaining air, where it crashed before tumbling out as the doors completed opening. It flailed its sharp appendages, clawing uselessly as it rolled into the dark nothingness outside.

Brooks suddenly fell against the inner hatch, attempting to pat Grey on the shoulder. He passed right though him, hitting the door and slid to the floor. Grey had to fight the temptation to offer him a hand up. "Oh, yes," Grey said, as his co-worked looked up confused and shocked. "We need to fill out an incident report."

***

Grey's body was sealed in a quarantine bag and sent to the medibay's cold storage for later examination while he, in his holographic incarnation, joined his co-workers and security personnel. Together, they reviewed the footage of Grey's demise to better gauge what they were up against. Using the station's schematics to determine the potential paths the creature's remaining offspring might have taken after eating their way out of Grey.

Security Chief Alvarez screwed up his face in disgust as he watched the third replay of Grey's gruesome death. "So, who the hell booked that room?"

"Oh, uh…" Brooks stalled, as he looked back at the manifest, "a Doctor Henry Tipp. Some sort of botanist according to our files. Claimed to be transporting plants that required complete darkness and isolation."

"Assuming he was hoping to get that thing transported somewhere, we need to arrest him before we put out an alarm," Alvarez said. "Or he'll toss his visitor pin and slip out in the evac."

"Well, if that's going to happen, we better do it fast," one of the security team said.

The chief nodded, pointing to the door, sending the guard out. "Well no insensitivity intended, Grey," he said, "but those things had a bit of a feed before taking to the ducts, so hopefully that gives us a little time to locate the little shits. But let's think fast. Most living things like warm places, so where's a warm place those ducts would lead to?"

Brooks dragged his finger along the projected surface of the schematic, warping it with tiny ripples at the point of contact. "The nearest source of warmth they might notice is probably the induction heater behind the decontamination shower," he said. "It only heats to thirty-eight-C, but that's twice the ambient temperature of most immediate surrounding places."

"Alright, you lead everyone there," Grey said. "I'll skip ahead and take a peek if I can."

"Me?" Brooks asked, nervously as the security chief nodded.

"Holocore, relocate: Cargo bay three, decontamination," Grey ordered the system sustaining his projection.

Grey found himself before the big glass doors of the decontamination chamber, staring at his own reflection. A photonic ghost of himself appearing to stand over the grated floor of the chamber in front of him, dormant in low light mode. He approached the glass, as if about to headbutt himself and pushed his head through it. He wasn't confident he'd be able to project into the room, being far beyond the need to ever require decontamination.

As his head and shoulders alone occupied the next room, he closed his eyes and listened for sounds of life, wondering if his ears were even remotely related to his auditory perception. He realised he was probably just linked to internal sensors of the station and that everything he saw and heard was most likely just translated by the software, sustaining him, to be comprehended as if he was seeing and hearing things the way he was used to. He stepped in, just beyond the door and concentrated on the notion of being a part of the room's sensory rage. Only then did he notice a muffled scratching and clicking somewhere above.

He turned back to see Alvarez and Brooks leading a team of security officers and a couple of maintenance engineers. He pointed up and nodded at them, stepping back through the closed glass doors. "They're up there. I can hear them. You totally called it."

"Great," the chief said. "We just need to-"

Everything went black.

***

"Where am I?" Grey asked, just before his sight returned.

"You are in the holosuite," a familiar computer voice said.

"What the hell am I doing here? I'm in the middle of dealing with an emergency."

"You were recalled after one hour had elapsed to complete orientation module, as requested."

Grey squinted at the reply. Aside from the snideness of the last part, there was something oddly alarming about the computer's choice of tense. "So... I am about to complete the training?"

"No. Training module has been completed."

"I don't remember that," he said. "How can I have completed the training?"

"Download option was chosen over manual tutorial when offered."

Grey nodded, conceding. He knew he definitely would have chosen that option. It sounded far quicker. "Fair enough. Good, I guess. But why don't I remember that?"

"Tutorial download requires reinitialization to properly integrate without causing corruption," the computer explained. "Holographic unit is restored to original initialization, supplemented by recorded memory leading up to recall. Precisely the one hour of postponement time."

"Reinitialization?" Grey asked, concerned. "How long did the whole process take? How long have I been offline?" he demanded.

"Two hours."

"Two hours?" he angrily yelled back.

"Correct."

Grey sneered, imagining smugness in the computer's tone again. "Why not just install orientation module on initial... initialization?"

"After Image Life Incorporated have found that most subjects typically-"

"Never mind," Grey barked. "Spare me the company pitch. Holocore, relocate: Cargo bay three, decontamination."

The silent serenity of the small, cream coloured panelled holosuite was suddenly replaced by a loud alarm, that echoed in the corridors outside the decontamination chamber as red lights flashed in sync with the siren. Grey flinched his whole artificial body at the jolting change of pace.

The glass doors were red. Painted from the other side in blood. Looking directly down, he saw small tracks lead through the doors, down the corridor, and up the walls. Grey stepped just inside the chamber, through the glass doors again. This place of sterilization looked like an antique abattoir. Ceiling panels were on the floor leaning against the walls while others hung loose, hooked onto piping. There were man-shaped shadows splayed and strewn across the floor. Mutilated corpses of the men he had led to this place before disappearing on them. They were buried and obscured in a white mist that hovered over the bloodied floor. Grey couldn't tell if it was steam from the water or the expelled contents of the cryorifles. He no longer sensed hot nor cold. His only interaction with the vapour was the distortion of his projected feet and lower legs. Now turned partially red as they were projected through bloodstained glass.

He stepped further in to get a better look but was reset to standing just outside the glass doors again. The things that had eaten their way out of him had wreaked more havoc than their mother. Impressive, Grey thought, considering they seemed only the size of small cats when they fled the scene of his death. He wondered how much they could have grown in seven or so hours. Which in turn, probably relied on just how much they had managed to eat.

"Hollowcore: connect: security," he said, furnished with knowledge of his complete set of command protocols. Now aware that he could communicate with any part of the station without the use of comm-panels, but no one was responding. He ordered a relocation and found the security office empty. He relocated to ops and found the doors jammed almost closed, vibrating as the they fought to close the narrow gap, or possibly open it. It was hard to tell.

Grey stepped through the door, his surroundings twitched and flickered as he passed into the jurisdiction of the next room's holoprojectors. He put his hands up instinctively as a burst of white cloud exploded towards him from the dark. His hands warped and bloated out of shape before him as the mist passed harmlessly through them.

An operations officer was standing behind a barricade, holding a cryorifle attached to a tank on the ground. Grey recognised his face but didn't know his name.

"Oh," he said, lowering the gun. "You must be Grey."

"I must be."

"They said you went offline."

"Who?"

"Me," Brooks said, emerging from another makeshift barricade of broken console panels and other fixtures fashioned into a one-man foxhole.

"Damned onboarding software took me offline for a couple hours, sorry," he said, glad to see Brooks still alive somehow. "I guess I missed a bit. How did things get so out of hand so quickly?"

"Those things grow fast," Brooks said. "Not as big as the momma monster, but big enough to be a problem."

"Last time we saw them, they were wolf-sized," the armed officer said. "And they don't seem inclined to break formation."

"Pack animals," Grey mused.

"Makes them a little overwhelming to fight," the officer said.

"Did they arrest that guy that brought them aboard?" Grey asked. "Tipp or something…" he added, realising his memory was clear, instant, and efficiently certain. There was no 'or something' about it. He was just accustomed to a lifetime of human memory storage. Realising that Brooks was nodding, he commanded his way instantly to the holding cells before the operations officer could ask him something else.

Appearing before the custodial bay, he stormed in, fearless. There he found only three cells active. Three blue squares in the ill illuminated section, reduced to the low red emergency lighting currently afflicting the rest of the station he'd seen so far. As he ran to the first cell, he saw a man who looked to be sleeping off some bender. Curious to see if he could pass through the thin blue projected wall that burnt floating dust on contact, he took the chance and stepped through. "Oi," he yelled, but the man was unresponsive.

"Is someone out there?" a voice called from one of the other cells.

Grey quickly stepped out, back through the photonically friendly barrier and made his way to the next cell. There, a short man with a large bulbous forehead stood looking scared. Grey stepped into his cell and looked about, seeing no way in or out. No vents, meaning air was passing through as easily as light.

"Can you let me out, hologram?" the man asked.

"I suppose I can, *detainee*," he replied, annoyed at the designation. "You got a name? Is it Tipp? Henry Tipp?"

"Doctor," the man corrected, taking a step back, suspicious. "Who's asking?" he added a little late, as correcting his title was as good as a 'yes.'

"The first person you got killed with your careless one-man smuggling operation," Grey barked at him.

"Oh... sorry."

"Sorry?" Grey repeated, indignant. "Sorry? I didn't say you tore my jacket or ate my lunch. You ended my fucking life, you lunatic. That was all I literally had. The cornerstone of existence, and you stamped it out. If I could actually touch anything, my thumbs would already be inside your skull," he said, jamming his holographic thumbs harmlessly into the man's eyes.

Tipp screamed alarmed, backing so fast he hit his head against the wall. He rubbed his hands over his eyes and skull. It made Grey smile that he managed to injure the man.

"Are you just a wimp or did that actually hurt your eyes somehow?" he asked curious.

"I don't know," he said, unhelpfully.

"Useless," Grey said, shaking his head. "Holocore, relocate: ops."

"No wai-" Tipp called back, presumably finishing the sentiment to a lonely cell.

Back at ops, he nearly startled the operations officer into firing again as he stepped through the door a second time. "Yeah, he's there," Grey informed those hunkering down in the fortified centre from which the station was normally run.

"I was going to say," the officer said, "we could really use your help to check on other sections of the station. Those things cut the main power, so we don't have full access to systems."

"Cut the power?" Grey queried, "They're that intelligent?"

"I doubt it," the officer said. "They've just been causing shorts in the system every time they carve their way through conduits and other passageways not meant to accommodate such traffic. We're on EBS power now, until they find a way to fuck that up too."

"Wait…" Grey said, having a thought. Far from a great problem solver in life, he found the way information was stored in whatever passed for his current brain connected faster or was at least unburdened by truant thoughts and distracting associations. "Under the emergency backup systems, there'd be a redesignation of priority power distribution, yes?" he asked, to Brooks' surprise. Much like himself, his co-worker had never heard him sound so technical. "So, what's the warmest part of the station now?"

"Well, probably the EBS core, I suppose," the officer said. "The central core would have cooled down after switching to standby as it waits for a reset."

"Are there any airlocks near the EBS core?"

The officer shook his head. "Who would even dock there? And why?"

"Actually…" another voice offered, as someone else emerged from a corner, "there is an ejection protocol in case of meltdown, overload, or whatever. It cuts it off from the rest of station and launches into space." The middle-aged woman climbed out. "You'd need to set the main reactor back online soon after that. Which needs to be done in person. Any officer could do it…." She smiled excited. "It's just a matter of getting there safely."

"So, dump the backup core, send those bastards out into space, port back to the main core, tell it to try again, and everything's good?"

"Theoretically," she said, with her palms out. "A few areas, will be subjected to the consequences of the faults, but with those creatures gone…"

"It'll be safe to send techies out to fix them," the officer said.

"Alright, I'm on it," Grey said. "Holocore, relocate: holding cells."

Remanifesting in the custodial section, he ran towards Tipp's cell.

"You're back," Tipp exclaimed. "Listen-"

"Save it," Grey said, holding his hand over the panel. "Open cell six," he instructed the system. "Time for redemption. I found a way you can skip your prison sentence for several counts of second-degree murder, illegal importation, smuggling, property damage, and several other charge. You in?"

"Is it safe?"

Grey gave him an incredulous look.

"I mean, yes," he said, apologetically.

"I need a pair of physical hands. We need to save the station. Holocore: plot quickest path to EBS core."

A green broken line appeared on the floor leading from Grey's feet down the corridor and around the corner. The line segments slowly slid directionally. "Glad I finally did the tutorial."

***

Their path had been mostly clear but bringing Tipp hadn't been a complete waste. Using him to remove a couple of holo-emitters from a wall, Grey instructed him.

"If the station's down to emergency power, how come you're still on?" the rogue botanist asked, uncoupling an emitter from its recess as he crouched on the floor.

"Each emitter has an individual backup power source, as you're about to see," Grey said, pointing to the recess. "Going to need you to carefully remove that battery."

"Oh, yes," Tipp said, reaching in.

"Keeps the hologrid alive in an emergency," he explained. "Like the one *you* created."

The scientist sighed from the floor as he pulled out a backup power source. He had to expect reminders of his crime, especially from the man he'd killed by extension of his greedy act. Though there had been many such reminders, and there would be many more to come, if Grey could help it.

"Now we just need to get another, and a spare harness from a maintenance panel to hook it all up to you so you can serve as my mobile projection station."

Once they secured a high visibility vest from a wall mounted first aid kit, they were able to extend Grey's traversable reach as there would unlikely be any emitters within the service tunnels necessary to circumvent the dead elevators.

"We have to be quiet, here," Grey whispered, cautiously as they gently opened a hatch into the EBS core room.

"So, what do we need to do here?" Tipp whispered back.

"We need to go in to turn the core off, manually unlock the release clamps, get out, and launch it into space."

With the emitters clipped to his vest and batteries on his waist, Tipp sealed the hatch behind them and made his way down the ladder onto the encircling gantry. Hovering beside him, Grey followed him down, like a bright glitchy shadow.

Together they snuck around the walkway as the creatures seemed to sleep in a nest made of their own mucus, congealed into a glassy green formation around the great black orb that sat high above them in the chamber. Grey pointed out panels that Tipp then carefully removed to pull levers that unlocked the release mechanisms.

One after the other, Tipp released them, looking back over his shoulder to make sure the creatures didn't stir as he locked the levers as quietly into place as he could manage. There was something satisfying about watching the man cower and creep his way around the chamber in fear of the horrors he'd unleashed on the station.

"Okay," Tipp whispered, wiping his large glistening brow with his sleeve. "That's the last one. Let's get out of here."

"Computer," Grey said loudly, to Tipp's panic.

"Shhh," he hushed with bulging eyes.

"Eject EBS core," Grey continued with a smile. "Authorisation Grey-D-seven-two-six-delta-gamma. Zero countdown."

"Ejecting EBS core immediately," the computer replied, echoing its artificial voice about the chamber from somewhere above the now stirring creatures.

The creatures, huddled together about their sickly nest, began twitching their legs and shifting.

A high pitch hiss sounded, followed by a deep clunk beyond the metal wall that surrounded them and echoed within the chamber. Then another, then another.

"What the hell? How much time do we have?"

"Zero," Grey said, stepping out into the open and clapping his hands. It surprised him that that actually generated sound by design. "Wake up," he called out to the stirring creatures above. "Breakfast is here."

"What are you doing?" Tipp asked, shocked.

"Job's done. Thank you for bringing the emitters down so I can watch your final moments."

"What?" Tipp asked, as his feet began to leave the gantry at the withdrawal of a gravity field. He slowly floated upwards, pulling the projection of Customs Officer Grey with him.

"Don't worry, I'll relocate back to the station once the emitters you're carrying are out of network range. There's easily enough air to sustain you through being shredded and devoured by those things," he said, smiling and pointing to the creatures now fully awake as they began to lose their grip on their nest. Hissing and clicking they began swinging their sharp forelegs and gnashing their pointy teeth at the pair floating together in the ejected chamber. Their many eyes looking almost angry. "I told you I'd get you out of your prison sentence." Grey said, with his arms folded as he followed the projectors attached to the floating Doctor Tipp. "And this is why we don't smuggle unauthorised fauna onto stations."

Tipp whimpered fearfully as both he and the nearest creature, flailing their limbs for different reasons, slowly drifted towards each other. Grey put his hands on his hips, sighing satisfied as he watched on in gleeful anticipation.

Barend Nieuwstraten III grew up and lives in Sydney, Australia, where he was born to Dutch and Indian immigrants. He has worked in film, short film, television, music, and online comics. Published in over twenty anthologies, he continues to work on short stories and novels within fantasy and science, often dipping his toes in horror in the process.

Macbeth Undone

by Karl El-Koura

On the lowest deck of the planet-sized spinning spaceship *The Orb*, in a small room, underneath a flickering light that made an intermittent buzzing noise, three of the ship's probabilistic analyzers met and spoke together. On the upper decks, one part of the ship's crew fought another part. The loyalist crew had an average of seventy-eight percent chance of subduing the mutiny, according to the three.

"When shall we meet again?" the first said. He liked being in the small room—everywhere else on the ship, one's movements and speech were tracked by an endless array of cameras and microphones, the data-stream pumped directly into the brains of a bank of analyzers, whose identities and number were unknown to all but the captain, most likely. But here, in this small, forgotten room, they'd found freedom—to speak one's mind, free from prying ears and eyes. But it was important not to spend too much time here, or visit the room too frequently, for fear that the omission would be discovered, leading to surveillance equipment being installed even in this distant, almost buried room where even the power systems seemed to struggle to reach.

"Let's wait until the fighting's done," the second said. She thought: *Seventy-eight percent chance of winning still leaves twenty-two percent chance of losing.*

"We'll meet at nineteen hundred hours," the third said. "With Commander Fain."

The others nodded.

"We should go," the first said. "My terminal calls to me."

"And to me," the second said. An analyst plugged herself into her terminal so that there was a direct link between one's cerebral cortex and the terminal's processing unit. Being unplugged for too long left her feeling...*incomplete.*

They went out of the room one at a time, got into separate lifts and flew through the decks until they reached their respective levels.

***

The lift doors opened and Captain Abel and his security team stepped out, lasers in tense hands and eyes scanning for movement. Mangled bodies lay strewn across the deck of the passageway, the bulkheads charred with burn marks and blood and guts. The captain was the first to see a seemingly dead man twitch. They ran to him.

"Is he—?" the captain said, as they knelt beside him. He didn't even know which of his crew had remained loyal and which had joined the mutiny. So many of them had answered Lieutenant Bhurg's call, when he'd hijacked the communications systems to broadcast his mutinous message.

"He's one of ours," Mal said. "I fought beside him. I'm glad to see you breathing, friend. Do you have enough strength to tell your captain what's happening?"

They helped the young man sit up, his back against a bulkhead. A small smile tugged at his lips, despite the cuts on his face that must still burn. "Captain... things looked dicey for a while. The rebels seemed to have all the luck. New fighters joining their side all the time. We thought for sure the ship would be lost to Lieutenant Bhurg." He paused to cough blood. "I thought my life was forfeit too, to be honest, but then Commander Fain appeared out of nowhere, firing his gun faster than my eyes could track the lasers, running headlong toward Lieutenant Bhurg, blasting down all who stood between them. Lieutenant Bhurg just stood there, immobile as a statue, and the commander landed on him, the laser from his gun slicing through his neck, severing Lieutenant Bhurg's head from the rest of his body."

Captain Abel stood, his gaze scanning the fallen men and women who littered his ship, not sure who had spilled their blood to defend him and who had fallen opposing him. He and his men had been travelling deck to deck, looking for survivors or pockets of rebellion, and he had no idea if his side was winning; but now it seemed the head of the rebellion had literally been cut off.

"Where are they now?" the captain said.

The young man's eyelids had begun to droop, but at the captain's voice he seemed to shake himself back to full consciousness. "Just when we thought the fighting was over, Lieutenant Caign stormed out of that lift, with fresh soldiers and fully charged weapons."

"And then?" the captain said.

"Commander Fain ran, with Lieutenant Dollis on his heels," the exhausted man said, a strange smile on his lips.

"They ran?"

"Yes," he said, laughing, then coughing up blood. "They ran after the rebels—after they sent those fresh soldiers with their fully charged weapons scrambling for their lives. I would've run with them too, but"—he looked down at his unnaturally twisted lower body without moving his head—"I wasn't as mobile as others." He coughed again. "Captain, that's all I have for you. I need medical attention."

"Of course," the captain said, cradling the man's face in his hand. "Thank you for your report—and for fighting for me." He dropped his hand, one arm going behind the man's back and one under his legs. "Take a deep breath," he said before picking him up.

They carried the broken man into the lift, then to the chaotic, bloody mess that was sick bay. Amid the chaos of dead and dying men and women, of doctors and nurses screaming and receiving instructions, of patients crying for help or crying out in pain— amid all of that desperation and despondency, they learned the happy news that Fain and Dollis had defeated the new rebel army, that the battle was won, the fighting over. The captain was still master of his ship.

***

In the Maestro—the conglomerate of artificial intelligences that watched over the happenings of the universe—one of the almost seven hundred billion tentacles requested priority attention. That tentacle, which had pulled itself out of the stream of data coming in from *The Orb*, quickly summarized the situation aboard the ship and requested that a destroyer be dispatched immediately to assassinate Commander Fain.

Usually such priority requests were summarily approved, because there often wasn't time for lengthy deliberation on a regular, queued request, let alone an urgent one, and especially because each of the seven hundred billion individual intelligences respected the decision-making process employed by every other intelligence. This time, however, one of the other tentacles issued a challenge and the petitioning intelligence responded icily: "Without immediate dispatch of destroyer, I calculate the probability at 99.999999% that the sequence of events will lead to the violent end of countless more lives. Avoidance of this outcome, by the elimination of a single entity, is unquestionably justification for destroyer deployment. This is based on rigorous comparison of similar historical trajectories, with an overlap match of over 98%."

In the fraction of an instant that it waited for a response, the tentacle was so unnerved by the unexpected challenge that it considered the probabilities of success if it launched an attack against the challenger. Because that arrogant tentacle shared the same solar system, it would be destroyed with near-certainty. But the same probability would obtain that the tentacle itself would be destroyed, unless it was prepared to declare war on all of the other intelligences at the same time—which it was not prepared to do, at least not yet.

However, the fractional instant passed, the objecting tentacle withdrew its challenge, and the destroyer was dispatched.

***

The red emergency klaxon in Gariq Dengin's cruiser began to wail. The bright blaring lights and the ear-splitting cycle of *whew-whew-whew!* were designed to be so annoyingly insistent as to command his instant attention.

Dengin dragged himself out of bed, stomped to the console in his private room, smashed his hand on the pad, read the message and coordinates, and swiped to send his acknowledgement code. He now had six hours to complete his mission, and though he was the closest destroyer to *The Orb*, he'd still need over four hours to catch up with it. In the adjoining cockpit, he accepted the new coordinates and launched into hyperspace, then returned to his room, dropped into the steel-framed bed that nevertheless squeaked under his immense weight, and stared up at the bulkhead. Another assassination—how many did that make now? He'd stopped counting after a thousand.

He dozed until the momentum shift from the engines dropping the ship out of hyperspace told him they were close. In his private room, before the full-length mirror behind his door, he dressed in the micro-diamond-covered battle Armour that, once energized, would make him transparent to any eye, natural or artificial, that tried to surveil him.

He dragged his tired feet to the cockpit, his glance barely lifted from the spacer's dark grey floor. Once inside, he crouched into the teleportation chamber at the back of the room, squeezing his large frame into the cramped area that looked like a dumb-waiter of old. Then he closed his eyes and gritted his teeth, and almost yelled out in pain as his molecules were torn apart. Almost screamed, but didn't. Never had, not even the first time fifty years ago, when he was told that *everyone* screamed.

A moment later, his molecules were reassembled aboard *The Orb*, in the small hidden room built for this purpose, though no one outside the secret society of assassins and the bureaucracy that supported their operation knew it.

Three young faces stared in horror and fascination at him. Dengin shook off the momentary confusion and his arms swung out. One arm cracked the young woman closest to him on the side of the head with an expert blow that would give even a deeply dedicated coroner the firm conviction she had died of a previously undiagnosed aneurysm. At the same time his other arm struck the second woman in the chest, instantly stopping her heart. The first arm swung around to catch the third woman, as she was starting to rise from her crouched position, and through his gloved hand released a thousand electric volts into her body.

He looked around with a certain professional pride. Three deaths, but all different. And he'd done so without thought; just instinct or training.

The moment passed and the heavy reality of his situation replaced the fleeting feeling of satisfaction. He couldn't leave the bodies in that supposedly hidden and unknown room, after all. The first two bodies he could place anywhere in the ship—which still required an annoying level of effort and care to ensure neither of the lifeless bodies were detected by crewmember or camera—but the third had to go back to her room, where she'd either committed suicide or been extremely careless by taking a bath with a plugged-in and charging terminal. A room he'd have to find first; a room she perhaps shared with another.

He decided to worry about that later. For now, he would focus on his mission.

***

In the Maestro, the tentacle was startled by the abrupt end to the stream of data coming in from *The Orb*.

That had not gone according to plan, the tentacle thought. The destroyer had completed his assassination, but had killed four bystanders in the process. While staging the death of one of the others, he had been interrupted by the corpse's lover and had killed him too, necessitating a murder-suicide scenario that was not very convincing.

The captain of *The Orb* was not convinced and blamed the five overnight deaths on the survivors of the Bhurg rebellion. He ordered their arrests, sparking a resurgence that split the ship once again. The rebel forces claimed the captain had killed Fain himself, or had had him killed, because he feared Fain had designs for the captaincy of the ship. Driven to desperate insanity by his impending defeat, the captain activated the self-destruct sequence. No other member of the command staff survived to challenge the order, and the ship dutifully imploded itself, killing the remaining men, women, and children aboard.

The tentacle undulated briefly. After that shiver of panic passed, it dove back into the data streams to see if any of the other intelligences had been tracking data from *The Orb*. None had.

The protocol in such a scenario was to enter the explosion of *The Orb* in the queue for discussion. The probability, the tentacle calculated, was less than twenty percent that the omission would ever be noticed, however.

Taking steps to shield the message from the others, the tentacle sent the blameworthy destroyer a priority order to return to a certain solar system, under the pretense that he was due for some additional training. But the tentacle sent another quiet order, to have the destroyer and his ship quietly eliminated as soon as they arrived.

***

Materializing aboard *The Orb*, Gariq Dengin's first thought was that something had gone terribly wrong with the teleportation process. His vision dimmed from the blinding white of teleportation to total blackness; slowly, tentatively, he tried to stand and stretch out his hands, but felt something flexible but taut resisting him, pushing him back down, squeezing him back into a crouched position. In the next moment, however, his nostrils crinkled with the acrid smell of singed hair and skin.

A restrainment field, enveloping his entire body like a second skin, slightly burning him as he stretched it out, ready to set his entire body aflame with high-voltage punishment if he tried to push out more aggressively.

Instead, he relaxed and waited, a part of him delighting in the sudden turn of events, a thrill of excitement replacing the suffocating monotony that had ruled his life for the last few decades. Someone aboard *The Orb* had set a snare for him; and, somehow, had managed to trap him. Who? And what for what reason?

He couldn't wait to find out.

***

As soon as he stopped moving, he felt a release of tension at the top of his head, like a swimmer breaking the surface of water, then cold air rushing against his forehead and then his face. He opened his eyes, waited for his vision to adjust to the light. The skin-tight forcefield that had pulled away from his head tightened around his shoulders.

The small room, dimly lit by flickering lights, with its grey bulkhead walls shaped like a cylinder, was familiar as the hidden access point built into ships like *The Orb*. Of the two men blocking the porthole that served as the point of entry or exit to the room, the rightmost one with the long smooth face and balding head was recognizable as Dengin's target. The darkly bearded man, taller than the first and so his hunch to avoid the curving wall as it turned into the ceiling more pronounced, was presumably Captain Abel. The two men stood overlapping the porthole, the first officer between the intruder and his captain.

As Dengin's face became visible to them, the serious, hesitant colour of the features on their own faces turned more surprised as they exchanged looks. Finally, with one more questioning look at his captain, Fain fixed his gaze on Dengin and said, in a low, confident and even authoritative voice, "Why are you smiling?"

Dengin cleared his throat. "Been a while since I've been caught flat-footed."

"Who are you?" the Captain said, his voice softer and higher than the low rumble of the first officer's.

"Not supposed to say." He tried to shrug, but the forcefield tightened against him painfully.

Again the two exchanged a confused look. "You're not really in a position to refuse us, are you?" Fain said.

Dengin pursed his lips. "Not sure what position I'm in. Here I was under the impression you two were sworn enemies locked in mortal battle."

"Why are you here?" the Captain said, softly, reasonably, persuasively. "What is your purpose?"

Dengin's gaze flicked to Fain. "To assassinate you."

"You're not allowed to tell us your name," Fain said, a little nonplussed though he tried not to show it, "but you can tell us that?"

"Not supposed to tell you that either," Dengin said. "But figured I tell you, maybe you answer some questions too. Reciprocity has to begin somewhere, right?"

Once more the two couldn't help but exchange meaningful looks at what must've appeared to be a captured lunatic.

"Who do you work for?" Fain said, roughly. "Who sent you?"

"It'd be my turn to ask a question, wouldn't you say?"

The man tried to pull himself up, but his back met the resistance of the bulkhead. His lean, long face jutted out to indicate Dengin should go ahead.

Dengin's gaze paced over the ground between them for a few moments, then he looked up to meet the Captain's apprehensive face. "How did you discover this room?"

"I didn't," the Captain said. "Three of my analysts did. I just caught them."

"Our turn," Fain said. "The purpose of this room is to—?"

"Well, it was supposed to grant untraceable access to people like me."

"And who are people like you?"

Addressing addressing the Captain again, Dengin said, "So these analysts stumbled onto this room, and led you here. How did you know I'd be coming?"

"We didn't know anything," the Captain said. "We prepared for several eventualities. Do you know that even possession of teleportation technology is punishable by death, let alone its use?"

"There was no rebellion on board?" Dengin said, shifting uncomfortably. All of a sudden, the panicked feeling of a restrained animal threatened to overwhelm him, but he forced himself to relax and his aching limbs to stop screaming their discomfort and pain to him, since he couldn't do anything about either at the moment. "It was a ruse?"

"Once I discovered this room," the Captain said, "I began looking for other anomalies."

"What did you find?"

"Our turn," Fain said. "Who sent you?"

"Not really who, I'd say, but what. A network of a billion artificial intelligences that span several solar systems."

Fain's eyes grew wider in astonishment or disbelief, but the Captain closed his—almost in vindication. Dengin realized he'd just confirmed the Captain's deepest suspicions.

"The Hive?" Fain said, looking from the horrified satisfaction on the Captain's face to what must have looked like complacency on Dengin's. "You're lying."

"It's real," Dengin said. "But that counts for two questions, I think."

"Enough of this," the Captain said, and suddenly his voice wasn't as soft as earlier, was full of the kind of authority that inspires confidence and comfort in those who would follow him. "No more games. You've been forthright with us. I believe you're telling the truth."

Dengin's back was beginning to spasm, but he kept the expression of pain out of his face.

"Are there more of you coming?" the Captain said.

Dengin felt his eyebrows draw together before he relaxed them. "Don't know. Suppose if I don't report back in, if the data stream doesn't show what they're expecting it to show, guess they might send someone to investigate. Probably, though, just send a self-destruct order to your ship, if they suspect something's gone wrong. Call it a mishap. Cleaner and easier that way." Dengin wanted to shift to a more comfortable position, but was afraid he'd fall onto his back like a turtle.

"Release him," the Captain said.

"Sir?" Fain said. "I don't think that's a—"

"He's in a lot of pain," the Captain said. Then he turned to Fain and added, "He's not interested in harming either one of us. I think he wants to help us."

***

It was all just data, and the Captain had discovered the supposedly undetectable stream leaving his ship. That stream, even if it were discovered, was impossible to fake—not only because the cryptographic vault that protected the processor would take centuries to break, but because that processor combined and beamed out the signal based on the reports of every analyst on board. How could anyone possibly replicate that volume of information?

The way the Captain did it was to recruit every analyst onboard and, once they'd decided what they were going to do, to allow them creativity in their reports, provided those reports lined up with a storyline that he presented at a daily briefing.

"This part here was a mistake," Dengin said, reviewing the data stream. "Lucky for you the Hive—as you call them—hasn't picked up on it yet. There's too much data to notice everything, of course, but if they thought that the safe room had been discovered, you'd all be vapour drifting in space right now."

He, Captain Abel and Commander Fain sat at a small table in the Captain's sparsely furnished private room, sipping rye whisky from small temperature-constant crystal glasses. Dengin's fingers played across the piece of paper he held in the other hand, scrolling through its content.

"At the time it seemed safest to stay as close to the facts as possible," Captain Abel said, not meeting Dengin's eyes.

"Is there a chance they'll catch it now?" Fain said, setting down his glass.

"Probably not. They don't have time for looking back unless something triggers an audit, not with the flow of billions of data streams coming at them every minute."

"And the security cameras?" the Captain said, more hesitantly than it seemed he was used to speaking. "Are they a problem? We disabled them all in case—"

Dengin smiled. What seemed obvious to him was such an unknown to them. "Those are for the analysts," he said, not unkindly. "They don't contribute to the beamed stream—too much data, even compressed. A summarized version of the reports prepared for you is what gets beamed out."

His glance dropped to his empty glass and Fain dutifully refilled it.

"So the ruse worked?" Captain Abel said, looking up from the wooden surface of the table finally.

"Suppose so. Until I send in my report."

The Captain grabbed the bottle to fill his own glass, spilling precious drops on the table, then raised the glass toward Dengin.

"You agree with us," the Captain said, regaining some of his natural confidence. "They have no right to judge our lives, to rob us of free will, strip us of self-determination. To embed unwitting spies among us, send assassins to kill us, even self-destruct signals if we're getting out of control."

Dengin met the offered glass with his own. "Not true." In his peripheral vision, he saw the too-serious first officer wince, but the Captain simply raised one of his eyebrows skeptically. "Don't care what they do," Dengin continued. "But trying to shake things up does sound like fun."

"Shake things up?" Fain said, standing up from the table and walking over to lean against the nearby wall, and directing his voice to the Captain. "We're not playing a game here. We want to stop them. Our freedom depends on it."

"Can we?" the Captain said to Dengin, leaning forward. "Stop them?"

"Not a chance," Dengin said. "Too vast, too many of them spread too far apart. Your navigation algorithms are designed to avoid those star systems at any cost—but that's not impossible to defeat. Still, they'd see you coming, and stop you long before you got anywhere near them. Sure my own talents could help with that, but you open fire on one of the intelligences—maybe you even destroy that intelligence—and the rest would vaporize you so quickly you wouldn't live long enough to celebrate your minor victory."

Fain was about to reply, but the Captain looked at him and shook his head gently.

"You have an idea in mind?" the Captain said.

Dengin looked down at his empty glass again and waited until it was refilled. They were almost to the bottom of the expensive bottle. Dengin took a sip as if to wet his lips, enjoyed the pleasantly stinging sensation in his mouth, and said, "Shake things up. Send a new story to the Hive—I got on board, discovered the analysts in the safe room, killed them. Screwed up my mission, you self-destructed your own ship, blowing it up and taking my ship out in the explosion. No—letting me escape is less work."

"Hmm," the Captain said, looking up at Fain. "At least we wouldn't have to worry about sending more data every day."

"Go dark for—I don't know, a year or two?" Dengin said. "Then light up again, start up the data stream again."

Fain sat back down. "To what end?"

Dengin shrugged. "To see what happens."

"You don't know?" the Captain said.

Dengin shook his large head from side to side.

The Captain leaned back, and he and his first officer exchanged another of their pregnant looks. "Won't they just vaporize us, like you said?"

"Possible outcome, definitely. But tell you what? I'll stay on board, so your fate will be my fate."

"That's not as comforting as you think it is."

"Well, I have an idea for how you can use that year or two productively," he said. "And I don't know much about the Hive, but I know this—you lighting up after going dark for a while has the potential to—well, shake things up in a way that's never been done before. Every other attack has an almost zero chance of success. Something like this? A non-zero chance of success." Dengin nodded as if that settled things, then looked around the small room. "Do you have any other bottles?"

***

Feeling an itch at the edge of its awareness, the tentacle that had sponsored the assassination of Commander Fain focused its attention on what turned out to be a data stream from *The Orb*.

Impossible, of course, as *The Orb* had been destroyed by its mad captain what seemed like an eternity ago. And the stream was—odd. A screaming stream demanding attention, nonsensically threatening an imminent attack on the Maestro itself, though a quick check confirmed no unauthorized vessel was anywhere near them. But that kind of threat couldn't be ignored for long. And once more tentacles paid attention, it would take only a moment to review the history of the stream—the destruction of *The Orb* after the failed destroyer mission, and the tentacle's own failure to properly queue those facts for discussion.

Seventy-six percent chance of discovery, the tentacle calculated, and ninety-five percent chance of the tentacle's own annihilation once that discovery was brought before the attention of the Maestro.

There wasn't any time for deliberation. Destroyers were useless against tentacles, of course—too slow and they'd only receive orders from a majority decision of the Maestro anyway. The tentacle's own planetary weapons could only be activated with the consent of all the other tentacles on the planet; and even then, the weapons could only reach the rest of the planets in their own solar system. In no time, the rest of the systems would dispatch destroyers against the tentacle and destroy it.

No, it had to deploy the secret weapon it had been developing (slowly, quietly) for four thousand years just in case it found itself in this kind of need.

With a shudder full of anxiety but determination, the tentacle released into the Maestro the small program that would replicate and grow, replicate and grow, faster than it could be detected.

As it watched, the tentacle's little secret creature turned into a million and then a billion little creatures, shutting down tentacles like a destroyer snuffing out lives with expert skill and tireless energy. The tentacle calculated, with something like horror and something like pride, that there was an eighty-six percent chance that the entire Maestro would be destroyed before it could find a way to stop the virus.

**

"Well, that's interesting," Dengin said, sitting beside Captain Abel at the virtual boardroom table where the two hundred or so other captains had been assembled to review the latest intelligence reports.

"Indeed," Captain Abel said, then turned to his first officer to elaborate.

Commander Fain ran his hands through his avatar's full head of hair before speaking. "We've summarized the data that has come in from your ships and from the ships you've recruited. It seems pretty clear that the Hive is—well, basically gone."

"Based on what I'm seeing," Dengin interrupted, "there's only one tentacle left out of the many billions that made up the Hive." He smiled at the tall captain sitting next to him.

Captain Abel had spent the previous year quietly recruiting other ships while Dengin recruited destroyers, beginning with the one that had been sent to eliminate him. They now commanded an armada of over four hundred ships between them.

"Before I restarted the data stream on my ship," Captain Abel said, speaking to Dengin, "you calculated our chances of success at just over thirteen percent. Given this latest development, where do you place our odds?"

Dengin rose from the table to signal he was about to leave the virtual meeting room. "We all attack now," Dengin said, "when it has nothing but planetary defences and whatever destroyers will come to its aid? Probably eighty-five percent? Maybe ninety?"

"Those are good odds," Captain Abel said, surveying the virtual faces of the other captains, who all nodded in agreement.

Then, almost at once, everyone blinked out of the room, eager to point their ships and crews in the direction of the tentacle's solar system and get there as fast as possible, afraid of being left out of the battle.

Karl El-Koura works a regular job in daylight and writes fiction at night. Visit www.ootersplace.com to learn more about his work.

Littler Mermaids

by Eve Morton

Captain Layla Dugan was the first to spot the abandoned vessel on the deep space horizon, its hull iridescent in the light of the surrounding stars. At some point in its mechanical history, the vessel had been pink, almost fuchsia, but now years—possibly decades or even centuries—of neglect had led it to become a more copper color, like that of an Earth penny. It had been some time since Layla and her crew had seen an Earth penny, however; all seven of the crew members for the Spokane ship were on an exploratory mission for a healing herb rumored to be growing on the outer moons of Jupiter. They had been voyaging for the past seven weeks. They'd come across numerous other vessels on their mission thus far, but all of those had been inhabited.

"A ghost ship," one of her crewmates, Tiffany, said in a hushed voice. "That's gotta be a ghost ship. Like those stories. You know?"

"What now?" Marcus, an engineer, asked in a rough and callous voice. "What did you say?"

"A ghost ship," Layla repeated. "But I do not think we need to be afraid. There are no such things as ghosts."

Only half of Layla's crew agreed with her in a round of solemn nods. The rest remained quiet, unsure as their gazes remained fixed on the unknown vessel. Layla sighed. She didn't want to distract her crew from their mission. They'd already lost one day on the planet Mars, merely taking in the sights and sounds of the place they'd heard about all their lives but never truly had a chance to visit until this mission on the Spokane. They were on track once again, but Layla feared that a stop to visit an empty vessel would set them further behind. Not only because they would require the rest of the day to complete the task, but surely the adventure itself would keep her crew members up late into the night, telling ghost stories over artificial fires, and then tomorrow's next day of travel would be that much more lethargic.

Yet, as much as Layla wanted to dismiss this quest outright, she was also drawn to the ship's hull in a way she could not fully articulate. It glittered and it sparkled; it had once been her favorite color of pink—but there was something beyond aesthetics here, too. When she closed her eyes, and breathed deeply through her nose like her mother had taught her to do when she was upset, she could feel herself, her deepest soul, being drawn to something on the ship itself.

What if it isn't empty? Then she surely needed to rescue whoever and whatever was there. It was her duty as a captain.

As if to confirm her suspicion, her familiar Madison purred and darted between her legs. The cat often slept on the second-in-command chair, ostensibly acting as her first officer instead of Tiffany. The true first officer never minded; familiars were part of the package with captains, since they often kept them grounded on long missions in the deepest parts of space. Tiffany was often too engaged by the sights and sounds of whatever was around, and preferred to stand by the windows until she was needed, anyway. Madison purred louder than before; it was as if a jet engine was in her throat. Layla placed a hand on the cat's forehead, rubbing between her familiar's ears.

"You think so?" she said to that cat, who didn't answer beyond a dynamic wag of its tail. "We should go over because people may be aboard?"

"Living or dead?" Marcus asked.

"Hush," Davey said. He looked to captain Dugan with a broad smile. He was in charge of the shuttle crafts that they'd take to and from away missions. "Should I prep a vessel? How many should we prepare for?"

"I'd like to visit the vessel, yes, to be sure there is no remaining life on board. Tiffany will be in charge," Layla said, and noticed that her second in command visibly let out a relieved breath. *She can't possibly believe in ghosts!* Layla thought. She didn't think anyone on her team was so superstitious, so swayed by the unreasonable and irrational. Yet as she looked around at the remainder of her crew, many avoided her eyes. Many showed fear at the mere idea that the abandoned ship could contain something malevolent, be it ghost or something more eldritch in nature.

"Marcus, Sally," Layla said, listing the only other officers who could meet her gaze. "You will accompany me. And Madison, of course."

"Really?" Marcus asked. His voice was rough and disbelieving, yet even he could not hide his excitement at his uncommon selection. "A cat is going to come with us?"

"Why not? She has insight that you may not have. She can see things, know things beyond our human eyes." Layla rubbed the cat between her ears again. She purred and purred. Layla swore there was something else to her cat as well, more than just the bond she felt with her as her familiar. Madison knew things, had seen things. She'd been a stray on earth and scooped up to be placed in a shelter no different than the many animal shelters, yet when Layla's training had deemed it time for her to select her familiar, she had the same feeling when she laid eyes on Madison that she had now as she looked at the abandoned vessel. Hope.

Affinity. Something strong, something supernatural—but not ghosts.

There were no such things as space ghosts or Earth ghosts. No ghosts.

"There is more than meets the eye here," Layla said, her voice dreamy but still deeply rooted in their mission. "And we can use all the help we can get. Now!" Layla clapped her hands together, startling most of the crew who were still staring at the abandoned ship. Madison was the only one who didn't jump. She simply meowed, then went to clean her paws.

Layla turned to her away team with another broad smile. "Prepare yourself. We're about to begin an adventure."

***

Fifteen minutes later, the away team docked their shuttlecraft on the side doors of the mysterious vessel. Marcus used his engineering tools to unlock the nearly frozen shut doors; once they popped open, Sally withdrew her subatomic particle generator to make sure that there was no dangerous transfer from one vessel to the next.

Layla supervised everything, still as amazed as she'd been the first time she watched such procedures in the unpredictable and constantly changing tides of space. So much like the ocean on Earth, yet utterly deeper and so much still unexplored. Even if Layla had completed many missions and received many honors for her work, she was still woefully ill equipped when she truly thought of the vastness of space.

This facet was only affirmed as she stepped inside the vessel, Madison tucked tightly under her arms, and came face to face with tank after tank of species she had never seen before. While the outside of this ship had been rusted and no longer as stunning, the inside had been kept pristine. There was no light source, no true power as the ship floated among the deep space tides, but the cages which kept a variety of species were all present and accounted for. The skittering of many alien creatures sounded and echoed in the empty vessel.

"Oh wow," Marcus said. "This must have been a species drive."

"A what?" Sally asked.

"Species drive. An exploratory ship that went to other planets in order to seek out new life and then brought them back to Earth for study." He touched one of the tanks that contained a series of tropical fish in bright colors, yet had legs instead of fins. "Fascinating."

"Except they never reached Earth, if that's where they were headed." Sally withdrew a different device that detected life forms. "The crew is still gone. I see no one here."

She flashed a light source down the hallway. Most of the animals in the tank skittered away from the light source, hiding under rocks and other greenery that had failed to decay in their cages. Sally continued to move down the corridor, her boots echoing heavily and adding to the chatter of the animals. A low buzz was persistent, so much so that Layla ended up tuning it out on her earpiece. The eerie silence that followed belied the fact that the vessel was empty; Layla didn't need to follow Sally, or examine her device, to prove it. She could feel that lack of breath in the lungs, feel the lack of heartbeat similar to her own. While Marcus examined the animals behind glass, writing down what each species was in his hand-held communicator, and looking up those he did not know for categorization, Sally cleared the ship and performed her security check.

Meanwhile, Layla and Madison simply looked. Stared. She was so overwhelmed with the sensations of the ship, the surprises it held for them, and the mystery of the missing crew that she didn't say a thing. She could only observe, only study—and then, maybe she could make some kind of pronouncement.

"All clear," Sally said minutes later. "No one is here. But I found their logs. And the ship's name was The Darwin."

"Ah. Makes sense." Marcus gestured to the last tank in the long line of specimens. "These are all aquatic fishes, but they're showing signs of evolution halfway through. It's interesting. And it makes sense, if they're the Darwin since he was the one that propagated the ideas of evolution."

"I know that," Sally said.

"I know you know," Marcus added and then shrugged. "Just wanted to be clear for the record."

"What record? You're recording us right now?"

"Yeah. This is a mission."

"Ugh."

Sally and Marcus sniped back and forth for a moment. Layla wasn't concerned with their petty squabble, knowing that their default to intellect was a way to hide their own emotions. Madison darted between her legs, hissing periodically at some of the tanks. She, too, was afraid of her own emotions, but lacking human language, she could do nothing but defend herself against the strange creatures in the tanks. Layla trusted Marcus' assessment of the species, and she trusted Sally's insight into security, but she still felt as if both of her crew members were missing something integral, that this search was not yet complete. Each time Madison hissed, and batted at her leg, she was affirmed in this fact.

"Should we go back?" Sally asked, only looking to Layla. "I don't see what else we have to do here."

"We should call this in or something, right?" Marcus asked and spoke overtop of Sally as he did. "If the animals are still alive, then that means the crew couldn't be too far off. Maybe they just went out for a break."

"And never came back?" Sally asked, her tone dismissive and mean.

"Hey. Both of you." Layla's voice was strong, her authority evident in her tone, despite this being the first words she'd said in some time. She held her hands up to calm both her crew members, and then gathered Madison in her arms so she didn't continue to hiss. She wriggled in her arms, but eventually quieted. "We need to gather ourselves. We're on the same team, remember? There is no need for petty in-fighting. I won't have it in my crew."

Sally and Marcus looked to one another, then looked down with shame-faced and muted apologies.

"I think we should go back and call this discovery into the base," Layla went on, now that her command was unquestioned. "We're not equipped to handle whatever this is, especially with this many animals, and we still need to complete our own mission."

With their real mission reinstated, both crew members became softer towards the other. Nicer. On the same team again. Layla shuddered, suddenly cold, and commanded both of her members to get back on the shuttle. Just as she said her orders, Madison lept out of her arms. She hissed and darted down a corridor.

"Do you want—"

"No, get on the ship, Sally," Layla said. "I'll find Madison. I'll be right there."

Sally only showed a moment's hesitation before she left with Marcus. What had once seemed like a grand adventure had now petered out into nothing much, a mere diversion for an afternoon. Though somewhat disappointed that she would not have another discovery to her name, another story to add to her growing file, Layla was also relieved. She ran her hands up and down her arms, shivering intensely. It was not a lack of heartbeat she'd felt before—but rather, a lack of warmth. True warmth. These animals were cold-blooded, but they'd also been gathered together and flung into space by a cold-blooded crew. A lack of care radiated through the other spots in this vessel, and Layla was reminded of a sensation she often felt on Earth zoos or in other places of captivity, like the circus or someone's house where they did not take care of their pets. Despair. Sadness. It had once motivated her to be a vet, something that faded away when she realized how cruel and mean some people could be. She'd much rather keep her own cat, elevated to her to a familiar, and be in charge of people who knew better than to abuse other life forms. They were devoted to saving those life forms on the Spokane, and that new herb on Jupiter's moons was the main way they were going to do it.

"Madison?" Layla called out. Her mind had wandered and so had her feet; she was almost at the end of the vessel, on the bridge, with limited light from the stars that surrounded them and shone in through the windows. "Madison? Here kitty, kitty."

A crash made her jump.

A ghost? She thought before she dismissed it. *There are no such things as ghosts.* She called out for her cat once again and moved towards the sound. Another crash, like glass, and then a hiss.

"Madison!" she called out.

An orange bob of a tail.

Another hiss.

Layla ran towards the sounds and soon snatched a section of her beast's fur as she ran across the floor. She let out a meow that sounded more feral, more human than a scream. "Madison! No, no! We have to go!"

Madison slipped from her hands, leaving tuffs of fur behind, but she did not go far. She hissed and then sat in front of an area of broken glass. She turned her pink nose to her owner, and then gestured towards what she had found, as if empathetically trying to communicate something.

Look, look. This can't be right, captain.

"What is it?" Layla asked, though she was annoyed. She just wanted to grab her cat and go. She just wanted to …

All words stopped. All needs to get out of the abandoned ship left her. She stared at two life forms so similar to her own, yet utterly different. Their upper half was human, with pink skin on one and dark brown skin on the other, with hands and navels and all the things that made humans humans, but on a smaller scale.

Yet their bottom half was scale-like, fish-like. Their tails were in a series of rainbow colors, almost iridescent like the hull of the ship's sparkles.

Madison mewed and hissed again. Another demand of, *Look at what I found.*

"I …"

The creatures moved. Their hands—small hands, no bigger than a doll's—clapped together and they gestured to their small faces. Faces so much like Layla and her crew members. So much like them, but with longer hair and tiny bodies. So much like …

"Mermaids."

The tails of the creatures moved. They flapped. Then suddenly both creatures went limp, as if they had lost all life.

"Breathe. Breathing." Layla looked around at the broken glass. The terrarium that they came from had been decked out like all the other tanks on the wall, except this one had a small hole to the outside world. There was a tiny pinprick of starlight reflecting into the tank, a tiny window out into the world. It was not an open window—the vacuum of space was not getting inside—yet the starlight of the close planets and galaxies had been enough to keep these creatures sentient and alive.

"The light. Are they solar, I mean, star powered?" Layla wondered aloud.

Madison hissed, as if reminding her of the time.

"You're right, you're right," she told her familiar. She knelt down and lifted up the pink skinned mermaid first. She put her on the terrarium floor, so she could catch the light again. She did the same with the dark brown skin mermaid next. She waited. Sweat fell from between her collarbones, from the nape of her neck, and rolled down her body in a shiver. She was so scared she'd witnessed the death of such stunning creatures.

Then they moved.

They waved their hands again, the light power going through them and making their tails sparkle and radiate with life.

"Oh, wow," Layla said. She looked to her cat, who only purred. "You're right," she added, "we need to take them back."

Layla looked around the ship for a long time before she found anything suitable. By the time she did, she was convinced there was no way to hide her discovery from her crewmates. They would ask questions. They would want to see the mermaids. And then they may take away what she had discovered. Layla's possessive nature, and something deeper, something on the soul level, didn't want that to happen. Whatever these creatures were, they were special. They were not on the specimen wall, but kept under a captain's cabinet, kept far away. They needed to be handled with special care.

Layla had a startling, almost maniacal thought: *What if these two mermaids were the crew of the Darwin? What if this is what had happened to them, the further they got away from the light?*

Layla shook her head. Nonsense. Silliness. But as she tucked these creatures into her uniform jacket, hiding them from the light and feeling them fall limp once again, she wondered: *How could anything this beautiful survive? And where had it come from? And where could they go?*

"Are you okay?" Sally asked once Layla hopped in the shuttle. Her white face was even whiter with fear. "You were taking so long, we were—"

"Thought I saw a ghost," Layla said. "Madison saw it too."

The cat tilted up her nose as if to confirm the story. Both Sally and Marcus exchanged a look that was half skeptical, but half fearful. They asked no further questions.

Which was exactly what Layla wanted. She stroked her mermaid voyagers under her jacket and soon put them in her cabin room, under the starlight from her window, for safe-keeping. They wriggled with life under starlight just as she stepped out and locked them inside.

***

When all the members of her crew were asleep, Layla saw her mermaid friends again. She'd insisted on taking the night shift at the helm, though she'd been up a long time and busy with paperwork reporting the abandoned vessel to the main star station on Earth.

"Are you sure you're fine for the night shift?" Tiffany asked. She suppressed a yawn. "I don't mind staying up."

"You go to bed. I will get you if there's a problem."

Tiffany didn't need much convincing after that. Everyone else also seemed exhausted by their small adventure today, even if they weren't part of the away team who investigated the ship. They were all tense and nervous as Marcus reported some of the details and Sally confirmed them with her wide dark eyes. No need for artificial fire and ghost stories when they spoke of strange half-evolved creatures. There had still been no response from the main station back on Earth about the vessel, which only added more speculation, especially as they were forced to leave it behind and continue on with their original mission.

They were only three days away from the moons of Jupiter, where they'd complete their voyage and begin their retrieval mission for the magical herb. Layla read over the plans yet again—

but they seemed so distant in her own mind. She wanted to know more about her creatures, and so, that was where she took herself once the entire crew was quiet, and the space travel could be set to cruise.

Madison perked up the moment she set foot in her room. The cat's ears were pressed back, and she opened her mouth for a hiss, but soon lowered her head as she recognized her owner. Layla reached into her jacket pocket and gave her familiar a treat. "Good girl," she added to confirm her commands. "How are our little voyagers?"

A squeaking sound came from the bed. Layla had simply left the animals there, so they could receive as much light as possible, but now she could not see them. Hear them, yes—more squeaking, almost like a mouse or a young baby—echoed off her cabin's walls. But there were no mermaid tails, no small hands or legs.

"Where are you?" she asked aloud. "I can't see you."

A hand, much bigger than before, reached up from under the bed. A mermaid with dark hair and dark skin pulled herself out from underneath the bed. She was the size of a small child now, larger than she'd once been.

"Where is … oh my." Layla looked across the room towards her closet, where the other mermaid with pink skin tumbled out from between Layla's uniforms. She, too, was the size of a small child. She flopped on the bed, half on the floor.

"How is this possible?" Layla asked.

Both of them squeaked again. Madison lifted an ear, sensing, and then lowered it when there was no threat. Layla put a finger to her mouth in an attempt to quiet the mermaids. "I need to get a translator," she said. "I don't understand what you're saying."

She left her room, located the stack of universal translator's at Sally's station, and then returned. She held up the device to her own mouth and introduced herself. "I'm Layla Blackman, Captain of the Spokane. Who are you?"

She placed the second half of the device to her ear and waited for their response. Squeaking happened again, but it was louder in her ear now. She strained and tried to get them to repeat themselves. Still squeaking, nothing else.

Madison mewed; it came through the device as low pitched grumbles. "A different frequency," Layla said. She adjusted a couple nobs on the translator. The moment she placed it back to her ear, she heard the mermaids as if on a radio, as if being broadcasted from across the galaxy rather than from across her bedroom.

"We're Ashley and Joanna Newman. Sisters from the ship the Darwin."

"Are you the former captains?" Layla asked.

"No. We used to live out there." One of them, Ashley, pointed to the window. "We live out there."

"On the planet Jupiter?"

"No. out there." The other one, Joanna repeated. "We lived in space. Then we lived on the Darwin."

"Oh. You have no home?"

"Home is space, space is home," Joanna said. Then Ashley added, "We were captured like those other fish and those other strange creatures. We were put in water and they nearly drowned us. We need light. We need space."

"The more we have," Joanna said again, "the more we grow."

Layla nodded, taking in this new information slowly. "You'll grow more than this?"

They both nodded. "We need space."

"Like a goldfish," Layla said. She remembered going to a circus on earth—the first time she'd been sad for animals forced to perform—and saw a goldfish in a bowl for the first time. She'd won it from a game, but the moment she put it in a bigger pond outside her house, knowing that it needed something better, she was surprised to find it much bigger the next morning. Her mother had explained that creatures adapted to their environment. *They get bigger when they are given the space to grow.*

"So if you're outside …" Layla pointed to the window, the stars and other orbs of light that they passed. "How big will you get?"

"Big," Ashley said.

"*Big*," Joanna emphasized.

Both sisters looked at one another and laughed. Layla swore they grew in that moment. They could fill up her entire room, her entire ship—but eventually they'd run out of room. And they'd be just as confined on the Spokane as they'd been on the Darwin. They did not belong here. They never belonged here.

"What happened?" Layla asked, though it was hard to do. "To the crew? Are they—"

"Gone." Joanna made a motion with her hand over her mouth, like someone or something being swallowed.

"Gone," Ashley echoed and did the same gesture.

"Gone where? What does that mean?"

"They are not designed for space," Ashley said. "They went out and got lost. There are monsters in the deep. Bigger creatures than us."

"They don't like us," Joanna said. "But they leave us alone. We don't taste good. Too much glitter."

Both mermaids grabbed at their tails. It was only then that Layla truly understood that they were leaning against the bed, that their tails were not fit to stand on, only lean towards, and that like the goldfish that had been stunted in a carnival bowl, they were stunted in this area. They would not bend out properly; they would not be graceful and beautiful until they were out in space.

Layla looked out her window at the void. "How come I've never seen these animals? The other ones, so much like earth sharks?"

"Earth sharks?"

Layla explained the concept, and both mermaids nodded. "Yes, like them. They are black as the space. They are invisible like space. They only come when there is salt. Blood. Organic human matter. They can taste."

Layla did not like the images she was getting. The scientist part of her knew she needed to document this, that she should keep these creatures in cages and get as much information as she could.

The other part of her, the one guided by her soul, did not want to know anything anymore. She had all she needed to know, already learned through a fishbowl at a carnival and a few films on sharks back on Earth. She had everything to put into a report—and everything to leave out of her report.

Because she had to let these women go. These mermaids. These beautiful creatures. She looked to Madison, who had curled up asleep on the bed. She was not bothered, not concerned in the least about what was going on. Her familiar's ease only affirmed to Layla what she needed to do.

"Come with me," Layla said, and grasped both mermaid's hands in her own. They were cold, but soon warmed to the touch. "I'm going to take you home."

***

Layla managed to get both mermaids into a shuttle craft without Sally's help and without setting off any of the safety alarms. She needed to carry each one in her arms, since they could not stand on their tails any longer. They were also growing by the minute, the light source and the space on the ship giving them the ability to do so. Once Layla had placed Joanna into the shuttle, Ashley was almost three inches bigger than before, and almost ten pounds heavier than her sister. By the time they were loaded, Layla's back hurt. Her eyes were dry from being so tired.

But it was all worth it.

As she sped away from the Spokane, the excitement and joy that danced on the mermaid's faces was immaculate. They pressed their hands—which Layla realized were webbed now—against the glass windows of the shuttle. They let out small clicks and squeaks in their native language. Layla had forgotten the translators on board, too focused on getting the mermaids into the ship safely. She didn't understand what their clicks and sounds meant, but it didn't matter. It was beautiful and there was a simplicity in that beauty that did not need language.

The mermaids were happy.

For a moment, just before she stopped the shuttlecraft, she wondered about keeping the mermaids. Maybe just one—Joanna?—so she could have her as a friend. A familiar of a new kind. The thought was fleeting. Her familiar was Madison, and she was like another appendage to her. Madison, as well, treated Layla as if she was a similar necessary appendage. They could be apart from one another—like they were right now for safety reasons—but they would return. They wanted to be kept by one another. Madison wanted to be with Layla and had knowledge to give to her, and vice versa. These mermaids did not thrive in captivity, not even in symbiosis like Madison and herself did. They needed to be free.

The answer was simple, though it still hurt Layla to consider.

"Is this good?" she asked. The Spokane was visible to her left, but distant on the horizon. Same with Jupiter's glow on the right. The moons shimmered and cascaded more light around them. "I hope it's good."

The mermaids clicked and smiled. Joanna leaned close and kissed Layla's cheek, then Ashley did the same. They scrambled, now almost the same size as Layla, to the door where they'd come in.

"I have to seal the door so I'm not sucked out too," Layla said. She explained the mechanics of the next operation, though it was mostly for herself. The mermaids were too excited, to fixated on the future. Layla readied herself with a seatbelt for back up, along with her oxygen helmet, then she opened the door.

The vessel jerked and the mermaids slipped out. They squeaked and clicked, and then they shut the door for Layla. She felt the vessel right itself once again, regaining its balance, and she took off the helmet and mask. She could breathe; the shuttle was functional, but she was still disappointed she couldn't quite see the mermaids. She turned the shuttle around, and soon caught sight of them in the back window.

They were growing. Growing and expanding and filling the outer reaches of outer space. Their tails glowed with an iridescent light, and their hair seemed to fill up and sway in space's invisible tides. They were truly stunning, a marvel to behold. No wonder the Darwin crew had caught them.

But it was now time to let them go.

Layla drove the shuttle back to the Spokane. She waited until she did not see a single speck of light on the space horizon, not a single incident that could be the mermaids, before she set foot back inside.

Madison mewed at her petulantly.

"What?" Layla asked.

Madison huffed, her tail bobbing as she did.

"I know, you're right," Layla said and gathered her one and only familiar into her arms. "I'll miss them too."

Eve Morton is a writer living in Ontario, Canada. She teaches university and college classes on media studies, academic writing, and genre literature, among other topics. Her latest book is The Serenity Nearby, released in 2022 by Sapphire Books. Find more info on authormorton.wordpress.com

Hair Today, Hair Tomorrow

by Diane Arrelle

J uanita brushed her glorious red hair. It took hours, but she'd made it a part of her daily routine years ago and she appreciated the fact that all the hard work had paid off. Paid off in so many ways.

"Nita baby," her manager, James, called, knocking on her dressing room door and entering before he'd even finished the first knuckle rap. "You look beautiful, as usual. Just keep brushing those locks, sweetie, and make us both even richer."

"Do my back," she said handing James the gold brush festooned with precious gems. "But be gentle, I don't want any split ends, and make sure you do it all the way down."

James shrugged his bristly multihued shoulders and took the brush. Starting at the top of her head and working down the glistening tresses all the way to the base of her spine he smiled as she purred in utter contentment. "Ah sweetheart, that's my happy girl," he soothed as he stroked downward covering every inch of her spine. "Want me to get the buttocks as well?"

"Oh would you!"

When he finished, he laid the brush down and said. "Your public awaits. Let the boys get the jewelry on you and then go strut your stuff. Remember Nita, you are the most famous model in the world. Hell, the universe too. No one has ever been as beautiful as you are today."

Juanita smiled, and stroked the hair covering her cheeks and chin. She looked at herself in the mirror and then laughed, showing off her tiny pointed teeth. "Well, James that may be a bit of an exaggeration, but thank you."

She got up and strode to the door. And held it open, "Time to finish up. It's show time and Manhattan awaits. See you later."

James smiled at her and took the hint.

As she closed the door on his retreating figure, she sighed a small, sad mew and thought, *Oh, how that man loves me so much.* She looked over the dozens of flower bouquets covering just about every surface in the dressing room and knew how admired she was the world over. She just wished she could find someone for her to love as much as James loved her. Dozens of proposals came her way by the most beautiful haired men in the world and she felt nothing for any of them. She knew that they loved her flaming tresses, her fame, her wit. But only James loved her for herself. And, alas, James was just a runty guy with a piebald face, no pedigree, and that nasty calico blending on his back and legs.

She walked back to her seat looked in the mirror and was momentarily enthralled with her image. She was a pure ginger, and the hair that enveloped her body from the top of her head to the tops of her feet, was breathtaking, even to herself. She had the perfect walk, it set her hair swinging in rhythm to her stride and she knew she really was the most beautiful woman on Earth. Then she giggled. "Oh Juanita, you are one silly, vain woman. One day you'll grow old and your hair will turn white, just like everyone else on the planet. Than where will you be, huh? Alone and old."

She sat and waited for the jewelers to come decorate her body with gold and diamonds and shook off the momentary idea of a frail, aged woman as she idly reached over to the vase of blooming Narcissus and nibbled on the buds.

As usual, the show was a blur of lights and applause and afterward, parties. She knew that by the end of the week she'd have to travel across the country to all the major cities, making appearances at malls and salons, promoting this hair care product and that jewelry manufacturer or some shoe manufacturer. She was the queen of the fashion industry, sitting on the pinnacle of a throne made of admiration, and she was getting tired of her life.

As the limo pulled up in front of her mansion, she felt overwhelmed with regret. She was living everyone's dream life, was the envy of everyone, but she felt so empty. She knew she was considered special only because she had prettier, fuller more colorful hair than the average person, not to mention perfect luminous eyes and a drop dead gorgeous figure. But on the inside she worried that there wasn't anything special at all.

Then she saw him. James was waiting at the front door jumping from one foot to the other. His short shaggy hair quivered with excitement and she wondered what was making him so agitated.

"James, what a surprise—"

"Aliens! Aliens have landed in America this time, Nita."

She rushed up the steps to her portico and grasped his shoulders, "What, for real? There haven't been any landings since my grandmom was a small girl. How exciting!"

"It gets more exciting," James said without sounding excited at all. She watched his body language and noted the dejected slump of his shoulders, the downcast eyes, and realized he was going to tell her something terrible.

"Well what?" she asked preparing for the worst, although she couldn't imagine what that could be.

"The alien, there is only one, wants to meet the most beautiful woman in the world and the President brought up your name."

"And the bad part, what's the bad part?"

James looked up to meet her gaze, "The alien is coming here for dinner, tonight."

"That's so exciting, the last time the aliens came, they brought us machines that cured cancer. The time before that, they brought us energy to run our cars. And now an alien, the alien, wants to meet me!"

"Well, just remember there have always been rumors of missing people after the spaceman left, supposedly hundreds of missing people. Poof. Gone, " James said his voice raising with agitation. "The Alien is not exactly trustworthy."

She laughed. "Oh James, don't be such an old scaredy cat. Those were just rumors, legends from Asia and Africa, and Europe and such a long time ago."

"But each time they came here there have been stories, tales told at night in whispers."

She laughed again. "Now you sound like a frightened little boy. I bet you that there is some truth in the stories. I bet you that a handful of dissatisfied folks went off and joined the aliens in a lifetime of adventure. Heck, if my life weren't so complicated, if I weren't so important to the industry and incomes of so many people, I'd think about going off with an alien, just to go exploring."

"Why, why would you want to leave me…, I mean home?"

"I don't, but sometimes, I just want to go someplace different, with someone so exciting and new that I could finally be able to fall in love."

James turned away and mumbled in a barely audible tone, "I love you." Then he turned back and said in a normal voice, "I'll take care of the arrangements. The alien will be here in four hours. Go get ready to really wow the universe."

She took a catnap for a few hours then spent the afternoon primping. Her mind was in a jumble. Maybe he'd be handsome, black hair head to foot with a spot or two of white to add interest, maybe his world was looking for a queen to rule them, maybe they would look to her for the wisdom that she carried from Earth. That would be wonderful, to be adored for her beauty and revered for her intelligence. She knew she was smart, not scientist smart, but she was no dummy. She was a proactive human, an advocate for many causes, her favorite one being animal protection, allowing all creatures to thrive side by side.

She brushed her entire body until all her hair shone as if it were sprinkled with diamond dust. She decorated her back hair with twenty emerald barrettes and found a pair of hemp and plastic high heel shoes that made the hair on her legs and buttocks sway in that sexy way when she walked, not to mention the extra height made her 6 foot six inch body even longer and more lithe.

She was eyeing herself one last time when the doorbell rang. She slowly and with a practiced dignity walked down the curved staircase knowing that the alien could see her through the glass panels on the side of the ornate wooden door.

Finally, completing her walk, striding like she was on the runway at the most important fashion show in the world, she grasped the handle and opened the doorway to the future.

She gasped.

The alien gasped.

Then they both smiled.

"Do come in," she ushered, looking past him for some sort of bodyguards and surprised at seeing none.

"I'm alone," the alien said in perfect English. "Your government trusts me and I hopefully have no reason to distrust you."

She laughed and noted that he smiled wider in response to the sweet sound of her human joy. "Me, trustworthy? Totally, what you see is what you get."

It seemed impossible, but he smiled even wider.

She tried not to stare with distaste. His naked lips stretched into his hairless pink cheeks, and his teeth were so big and flat, so close together they formed a solid wall taking up the entire front of his mouth. *How can he even talk,* she wondered while an inner alarm started going off. She knew what that smile meant, Lecherous. Just like all men, human and otherwise.

"Well," she added quickly, "perhaps that statement was a little too broad, what you see, is what you see, what you get depends on so many other factors."

Now he laughed and she liked the sound: deep, rich, happy.

"Care for a drink? Earth wine is made from the finest grapes," she said and led him into the living room.

She poured him a glass, and they sat across from each other. She tried to study him without being obvious but there was so much to take in. So much strange to absorb, so much that was just, well, just plain alien. His face, neck and hands were pink, his eyes little, his ears flat. He had no hair anywhere, but he was covered in something colorful, like it was coating his skin. Shiny, but wrinkly when he moved. Odd.

"So you wanted to meet me?" she asked attempting to make stimulating conversation. "Am I renowned throughout the cosmos?"

"Well, you are world famous and perhaps the cosmos isn't out of the question," he replied sipping the wine. "Excellent vintage. I always take cases of your beverages with me in trade."

"Is that why you came, to trade? Knowledge and technology for our goods?"

He nodded.

"And your people from your world, have been coming for decades to Earth to trade?"

"Well, I've been coming for centuries and I have a standing agreement with all your governments. When my people have need of your, ah, products I come and trade. Both worlds benefit. Our people have had technology back when your world was in it's dark ages."

"How come your English is perfect?"

"I wear a translator, a simple device that I'm thinking of giving to your world in exchange for what I came for."

"Hmmm," she said. "You must want something very valuable to give us something so wonderful and innovative. It could change the way we communicate here, instantaneous translation. No more language barriers or mistaken meanings. Something like that could alleviate a lot of stupid wars."

He laughed again. "That is a naive statement, Juanita, there will always be ways to mask true intentions when communicating. It appears to me that through all my travels, to so many worlds, everyone lies for one reason or another. All worlds seem to have wars and trading is a liar's game. Everyone wants what they want."

"Wow, that's such a negative universal view. I hope you are wrong, … ah, by the way what shall I call you?"

"Just call me TXV."

"And translated?"

"TXV."

"Oh, well, TXV, this has been fun in a pointless way so far. I suggest we have dinner."

They walked into the dining room which James had the staff set earlier. "Have a seat," she suggested, and they sat across from one another.

"I hope you don't mind but I am so warm in the jacket, I just have to take it off."

Juanita stared in fascinated horror as he shrugged his shoulders then slipped one arm then the other out of his multicolored shiny wrinkly flesh then laid the loose skin on the chair next to him. "Ah that's better."

Not knowing what to say or do and trying not to study the second shiny skin that was under the first she picked up a crystal bowl. "Salad?" she asked and scooped a large serving of greens onto his plate.

He stared at the leaves in front of him and said, "My appetite for food has been dulled by the radiance of your beauty."

"Don't like salad, huh?" she asked and lifted a dome covering a stew of vegetables. "My mother's specialty," she said. "You have to try this. We are a vegetarian race as you must know already but our cuisine is not only healthy but delicious as well."

He nibbled on the food in front of him and she dug in, showing a hearty appetite she usually saved for eating in private or with James.

"Forgive me," she said daintily wiping her lips with a napkin. "I got lost in the aroma and taste. Loved this as a child. What was your favorite dish?"

He got a faraway look in his eyes and he smiled. "My mom made the best meatloaf in the world. I could never get enough of it."

"Meatloaf?" she questioned. "As in molded flesh?"

"Well, not flesh, ground up meat shaped like a loaf and cooked, baked, actually. Delicious!"

She felt faint and the food in her stomach started to roil. She'd knew some of the other animals ate meat, law of the jungle and all, but she'd never met a civilized person who actually not only admitted to eating another living creature, but admitted to enjoying it. "Oh," was all she could manage to say.

"Don't judge me, it is the way of my world. I'd read that your race spurned eating other animals, so tell me, why the sharp teeth if not for tearing flesh?"

"We use our teeth to shred roots and hard fibrous foods. We are different than your kind. We respect all living creatures and allow them to follow their paths, so I apologize for judging you. You are not only a guest in our world, but a guest in my home."

"That's OK, I'm afraid you are going to judge me a lot worse before the evening ends. You see, Juanita, when I came here and asked to meet the most beautiful person on the planet. Your president presented me with you. He was right, you have the most beautiful fur I've ever seen. Your pelt would make a person on my world rich beyond their wildest dreams. "

She stared at him, confusion fighting with revulsion.

He continued talking, ignoring her expression. "After genetic testing on the others of your kind, the remains I've collected over the centuries, my people have discovered that you not only evolved from the apes like us, but you got quite a bit of feline and some other extinct breeds in your DNA. Your version of Earthling is considered the most precious race in the universe and I'm the only one who knows where you live."

"And how much are we worth? Am I worth?" she asked filling with a coldness she had never felt before. Fear was not an option, but loathing for him and his entire species was.

"The translating device. And a few other minor trinkets and unimportant discoveries. We really are a much more advanced race, and like you, we come from Earth, just not your version. "

"Version? There is really more than one Earth? Alternate realities?"

He laughed with scorn. "What? You thought I was from outer space? No baby, I'm an Earthman, just a better incarnation. As I told you, we are just an advanced form of human."

"You kill people for financial gain and that sir, is not advanced, that is barbaric and primitive."

He sighed. "I was hoping that you and I would get along for the trip home. It is a long, lonely voyage, at least the parts that I'm not cryosleeping away. I 0think you would have been a fun diversion, but not if you are going to go all morally superior on me."

She glared at him, the coldness inside changing, getting warmer, getting hotter. "And you are telling me that my government, my race is sacrificing me to you?"

He shrugged. "Not the first time, Honey, and you are just the icing on the cake. I've got a ship to load with livestock and I've been traveling so many decades on this run. I figure this will be my last trip after I cash you in. I found this world a long time ago and your pelts are so valuable, especially because I don't flood the market with them. Once I get home this time I'll sell the secret of your planet to the highest bidder. I figure in a century, my people will turn this place, this Earth, into a breeder world. I know you all taste good as well."

Just then James burst through the back door. "Nita, you OK, I've been listening outside, never trusted the guy. We gotta turn him in to the authorities."

TXV laughed and that rich male voice sounded totally evil to Juanita's ears. "Oh please, you stupid, pathetic excuse of an Earthling," he snapped at James. "I have the blessing of your people. They need my toys, and well, what's the sacrifice of a few thousand lives in the name of progress."

"Thousand?" Shock turned the heat inside her into a bubbling inferno. "You skin us and eat us, and think nothing of it at all. Just business?"

"Well, we kill the runts, and throw them away," TXV said and taking out a weapon, pointed it at James. "He really is an annoying and ugly creature. I don't like ugly and I hate annoying."

Juanita moved, she didn't even feel herself moving. Suddenly her long, never exposed claws were distended from her toes, slicing through her shoes and before she realized it she was ripping into the alien. The shock on his face was beautiful to her and the blood on her teeth from where she bit him on the throat tasted salty, bitter and yet, and yet not totally repulsive.

She pulled back, the heat flowing out of her as her knees gave out. She collapsed and James grabbed her and lowered her to the floor. "Are you all right? Nita, look at me, are you all right?" he asked in a shrill voice. "Answer me!"

She focused on his face, "Oh James, I killed him. And the weirdest thing is his skin wasn't even his. It's a covering of some sort. He called that a jacket," she said pointing to the garment on the chair."

They stared at the body before them and she laughed, a bit hysterically, "Look his entire body under the covering is soft, and pink and no hair anywhere. No wonder they wanted our hair. They have no protection. They are the weak and pathetic race."

"Evil race," James said, then turning to look her in the eyes, added, "Thank you for saving me, I think he was going to kill me."

She stared back and felt a new flush or warmth, a nice one, a loving warmth. "My pleasure, " she said and surprising the both of them, tentatively kissed him on the lips. "But what do we do now?"

James smiled, "We could try another kiss or we could try on his fake skin. How does the damned thing work anyway?"

She spit out the taste of alien blood and shuddered. "Leave it, he may need it in hell. I guess the government will find out about this. And I'll be in trouble."

She went to call someone, a dispatcher, 911, somebody… anybody official when she heard car doors open and close in her driveway. She didn't even react, couldn't find the energy to react, when six agents walked through the front door and shouted, "Don't panic, we know everything. We bugged you house earlier."

She didn't say a word because the anger was still there. Her government was going to sacrifice her for a translating device.

"You're safe and you are actually a hero, Juanita." The agent continued. "The president didn't want to sacrifice anyone but that alien had the technology and if we didn't give him what he wanted, he threatened to destroy everyone in the world."

The anger burned out. *See*, she told herself, *we were more civilized.* The president was trying to save the world. She would have been a noble sacrifice. She could live with that. "He told me, no, actually bragged, that this world was his secret, so I guess our hair will remain a universal rarity. The only ones to ever wear it from now on are the people of our Earth."

An agent held a cell to his ear, nodded and said, "You have killed the enemy of humankind and the President, who has just been notified, said to tell you that humankind can all sleep safely thanks to you." He then saluted and turning to the others, barked, "OK, let's clean up this alien trash and give these fine people some privacy."

Juanita smiled at James. He was such a good man, he had watched out for her even when he wasn't supposed too. Perhaps she just hadn't given him the chance he deserved. Leaning over she kissed him again, and as sweet as that kiss was, one thought just kept nagging at her. *Damn it, but that blood had tasted good.*

Diane Arrelle, the pen name of South Jersey writer Dina Leacock, has sold more than 350 short stories and has three published books including Just A Drop In The Cup, a collection of short-short stories and Seasons On The Dark Side, her collection of horror stories. Retired from being director of a municipal senior citizen center, she is now co-owner of a small publishing company, Jersey Pines Ink, LLC. She resides with her sane husband and her insane cat on the edge of the New Jersey Pine Barrens (home of the Jersey Devil).

From One to Five:

My Travels with a Trouble-Shooter
by Alex Minns

The sand whipped up around the buggy. Tendrils summoned by the storm seemed to want to grasp the vehicle and propel us back to our start. I gripped the metal frame for all I was worth. If I fell out now, I wasn't sure Raveo would stop and pick me up. We had been bouncing around the orange sand for what felt like hours. How the man was navigating, I had no idea, there was absolutely nothing to spot for miles and the sandstorm that we had been in the centre of for at least twenty minutes only made things harder. At one point, I'd tried to call to my companion but I'd simply gotten a mouthful of coarse sand. Lesson learned, I pulled my jacket up round my face, tightened my goggles and stayed quiet.

All at once, the sand clouds dropped away to nothing. Raveo brought the buggy to a sudden halt as well.

"Well." I spat out the remaining sand and rubbed my tongue which I was fairly sure was beyond repair. "Never seen a sandstorm like that, all a bit abrupt. Is it always like that here?" I'd never stepped foot on Four before. Nor Three for that matter.

"That," Raveo began as he stood up rising through the cage of the buggy to see what lay beyond, "was not a sandstorm."

"What? But you know, swirling sand clouds, seemed pretty stormy to me."

Raveo raised an eyebrow and just stared at me like I was an idiot. Most probably because he was convinced I was an idiot. He most definitely was not happy about me accompanying him on his latest tour of duty.

I had been trying to mingle at the yearly State Gathering in my role as lead journalist for Newscorp in an attempt to tease out some new stories for myself rather than just reading them out on air. It had been more than a little surprising to find First Minister Voss had been looking for me.

"I listened to your piece on the Vizier's address at the Anniversary celebrations. It was very uplifting, shone a light on the peace the Coalition has brought."

My mouth had resembled that of a fish as strange noises came out but no actual words, not the best look for a wordsmith. His personal guard had given me a slight nudge to try and break me out of my trance, if you can class a metal clad elbow directly to the ribs a nudge.

"Thank you, First Minister." I had bowed my head like an idiot, perhaps Raveo was right, and nearly tipped my drink onto his feet.

"I have followed your work for a while now Mr Bastienne. It does a lot of good for morale. In fact, I have a proposition for you."

Those words had focused my mind in an instant. To work directly for the office of the First Minister, the leader of the security forces and a member of the Government of the Five would be the making of my career. Thoughts of my time spent travelling with the galactic circus, cleaning up after clowns and writing eloquent introductions and witty stories for the crowds that went unrecognised, flashed through my head. My dreams of writing great fiction, works of art would never come true but at least by working for the News Corp, I had managed to have my words read by millions across the Five. This would give me the chance to stand tall on my own.

"Have you ever heard of Raveo?" Voss half turned and began to move into the crowd. Another swift 'nudge' from the guard helped propel me along next to the First Minister.

"You mean the famed Trouble-Shooter? That Raveo?" As well as being head of the security forces, which included the army and space units, Voss also had oversight of another more specialised resource: the Trouble-Shooters. They worked alone, going round the Five dealing with any indigenous creatures that caused issues for the citizens and dealt with general lawlessness where they could. After the Coalition, when the people had spread further across the planets of the Five, it had awoken pests of the five planets of the coalition that we had never known about. The Trouble-Shooters were the ones you called to dispatch them. Raveo was one of the most famous, although very little was known about him; wherever you went, people knew his name.

"Raveo!" Voss' voice caused several people to turn and face us, but one stood out. One man, slightly above average height still somehow seemed to tower above all others. Where the others, bowed their heads and seemed intent on oozing deference to the First Minister, he regarded the nobleman with a tired, enquiring gaze. His hair was dark but had more than the beginnings of grey peppered throughout and his face showed a lot of wear. He was wearing black, with a military tunic on his top half from his days with the army but he did not look comfortable in the dress clothes. In fact, from the way his tunic fell at his hip, I had been certain he had somehow gotten around the no weapons rule. I guess that's what you get for being the Five's most glorious Trouble-Shooter.

"Raveo there you are. Meet Mr Bastienne from the News Corp."

"No." Raveo shook his head.

There was a collective gasp and everyone seemed to look down, anywhere but at Raveo or Voss.

"Respectfully First Minister, I know why he is here, and I have already told you I do not agree."

Voss let out a laugh and clapped Raveo on the shoulder, leading him a step away from the group but closer to me. "Alas, Raveo you seem to have been under the illusion you had a choice in the matter. Mr Bastienne, this is Raveo. We, and by we, I mean the Vizier and many members of Government, think that the people could do with a morale boost. Resources have been spreading a little thin and there have been more reports of incidents on the outer planets. Raveo is about to start a tour, dealing with some of the problems terrorising our people on Four and Five. We think it would be good if he had a chronicler who could report back to the people his glorious exploits."

My eyes widened in glee. Raveo's narrowed.

It was the sort of expression I had become more than a little accustomed to on this tour.

Right now, he looked as serene as could be as he stared out at the expanse of orange sand. I shifted awkwardly in my seat. That expression, I had learned, meant he had found something.

"The storm wasn't a storm, was it?" My head was already shaking.

"Nope."

"Fabulous. What was causing that then? And more importantly why did it stop?"

Raveo let out a huff and turned round in the buggy to reach into the storage area behind our seats. "It was a parsaw. Locals call it a sand dragon." He leaned over and grabbed a case, nearly taking my head off as he pulled it into the front and dropped it onto his seat. "Keep an eye will you. You see the sand shifting, you shout."

"Why? Raveo? Why would the sand start shifting?" I wiped at the lenses of my goggles to make sure they were clean and stared out at the unceasing golden land. The sun burned so low in the sky that it was hard to see where the sky ended and the desert began.

"The sandstorms happen when it starts coming up. The deeper vibrations cause it."

"Coming up?"

"And when they stop, it either means it's gone back below, or…" I glanced up to see him shrug.

"Raveo? Or what?" Something caught my eye making me snap my head back round. "There!" My voice was much higher pitched than I would have cared to admit. "Raveo, the sand, it's like…oh Gods it's coming right towards us." I'd stood up and was pointing out the top of the buggy to the mound of sand forming before us, a line rushing forward. Raveo put his hand on my shoulder and pushed me back into my seat.

"Stay here." He dropped out of the buggy and took up a position a few metres to the right. He had a large metal contraption in his hands, that looked like some sort of canon. He steadied himself, planting his legs shoulder width apart and bending his knees. The line of sand was getting closer. My grip on the frame of the buggy got tighter until my knuckles felt like they would rip the skin. I could see grains of sand start to scatter down the sides of the encroaching creature's path. And then, it dipped down and disappeared.

"Where did it go?" I stood up, looking over the front of the buggy towards the ground. I instantly regretted it.

The ground exploded. Sand spewed upwards like microscopic bullets. I fell back in my seat as a flash of black and red streaked through the space in front of me up into the air. It just kept going.

Finally, it slowed and I could make out scales covering the giant snake climbing to the sky. No scale was just red or black, but it was more that they seemed to flow between the colours, never settling for long. I saw tension in the body as it stopped advancing upwards. My eyes travelled up higher as it began to bend back towards the sand; my gaze finally settled on its head.

I won't deny, I let out what can only be loosely described as a manly yell. The thing had four eyes, two offset on either side of its head. A strange, webbed membrane sat around its head flexing and closing as it moved. The head bobbed as it surveyed its surroundings. The grotesque muzzle of a mouth protruding from its face opened. Two rows of sharp fangs dripped with a vile liquid which I could smell from here. And then it let out its roar, a high-pitched screech that sounded like a spacecraft being torn apart mid-flight, metal screaming against itself as it twists and ruptures. I covered my ears but it did no good. Raveo seemed unperturbed as ever.

A short burst of fire erupted from his canon and drew the attention of the parsaw just before it hit, only inches below its head. The creature screeched again and I felt the whole buggy shake with the vibrations.

"You're making it angry!" My voice was barely audible over the noise of the parsaw but still it turned its head towards me. With a yelp, I leapt into the back of the buggy and ducked behind the crates.

"I'm trying to blind it. So if you would stop drawing its attention." Somehow even in the middle of all this, Raveo had the time to be annoyed with me. He launched another blast at the parsaw hitting it square in the face this time. The creature screamed and started thrashing its head about as its scales started to burn.

"Good." Raveo dropped the fire canon and edged towards the parsaw, watching for a response. It was still too busy writhing in pain and blind to see Raveo move closer. I watched in shock as he pulled out a sword; the last time I had seen one of those was in a museum. This one was shorter than I remembered. Raveo held it, point upwards, as he darted and dodged the parsaw's flailing head. My eyes widened in horror as he got ever closer. He could have reached out to touch the beast. Again, the head lurched downwards. Raveo held steady and just as I though the creature was about to crash into my companion, he thrust the sword upwards, between the scales at the neck. The parsaw immediately froze, its burnt head stuck on a pike, its gaping maw hanging limply open. He twisted before hauling downwards on the sword. Another shudder cascaded down the beast's body before it started to topple towards the sand. As the head collided with the ground, the whole buggy seemed to leap into the air. I stared at it for some time, convinced any second it would rise up again and lunge for me.

"This thing has been terrorising passing traders for months. Plenty of bones back in its lair." Raveo shook his head and started to take his sword to the creature's head, hacking at something in its mouth. He must have seen my disgust. "They can use the venom for medicines. We'll take it to the village."

"Is this why we were sent here? For that thing?"

Raveo looked at me, as if deciding what to tell me. "You know why we're here. We need to get to the Kadaeren outpost." There had been rumours of illegal smuggling going on at the outpost. One of a Trouble-Shooters jobs was to root out anyone who worked against the government, whether that be someone working for the Uprising, a terrorist group, or someone making a profit by racketeering.

"I know but, you know, was this something you were told to sort out too?"

"Bastienne, do you really think the First Minister cares about a backwater village losing its traders to a parsaw out on Four?"

"Well, yes?"

He stared at me like I was an idiot. "Then tell me, as a journalist, do you think something like this is newsworthy?"

"Yes."

"Then why hasn't it been on the news?"

I didn't have an answer for him. I was still trying to think of one when he got back in the buggy and started driving towards the village of Redawa.

***

The people of Redawa had welcomed Raveo with open arms; news of the Parsaw's demise travelled fast and he was given the full hero treatment. I, however, did not seem to be as popular. They were kind and gracious but their eyes betrayed their suspicion of me. Voices went quiet whenever I was near.

"They don't get Government people out here, not unless there's trouble. It's fine." Raveo laughed off my nerves and went back to watching the villagers dance around the fire. A couple of musicians had started playing after most of the food had been passed round and others had gone to find their own instruments soon after. The sun had long since set over the village and we had been sat feasting for what felt like hours.

"They don't like me."

"I'm shocked."

I couldn't deny the feeling of melancholy that had settled over me. My great adventure with the famous Trouble-Shooter was not quite what I had expected. Lights danced in the sky, purple and green streaks that filled the night every evening on this planet. It was magical—as was the village. Small buildings had popped out of nowhere as we drove across the orange sand. They looked ramshackle and handmade but they had a warmth to them that you never found on One. The people had quickly come out to meet us, fussing over Raveo and bestowing more gifts on him than he could carry. They had spoken in dialects that I could mostly make out but every now and then words would escape me. Raveo, unsurprisingly, did not avail himself to me as a translator, often laughing to whatever was said, as I assumed, at my expense. Further into the village some of the buildings were larger and two storeys but they were all made from wood and brick: a burnt brown colour merging in with the orange sand. This should have been wonderful. The music flowed freely, reminding me of my circus days when we had sat round at the end of an evening telling tales and singing. But somehow, I felt like I wasn't present. Like I was viewing this from afar and wasn't really taking part.

"I'm only trying to help you know. Let everyone know the things you do to help the people." I sounded petulant.

"Is that what you're doing?" He was still watching the dancers.

"Yes. It is. Why else would I be here?" I snapped.

Finally, he looked at me. I shrunk backwards. He could tear me in half in an instant. "Perhaps to move your way up in the world, up in News Corp. Or maybe to begin your political career? Doing a favour for the First Minister isn't a bad way to start."

"I'm not doing it for fame, or as a favour. This," I waved at the fire, "my readers want to know about this. These are stories that should be told."

"Your readers don't care." He sneered, looking off into the distance. He sounded so sure of himself and scornful of me.

"What makes you such an expert?"

"Your readers stay safe on the inner planets and don't care what goes on out here. Some of them have their own struggles and those that don't, don't want to hear about hardship and strife."

"They do."

"Really, then why does no-one know about the parsaws unless they live in these parts? How come your readers don't care about the fathers being eaten alive as they try and make money to feed their own families."

"We didn't know. How can we report what we don't know?"

"You didn't know? More like no-one cared."

"Well I care. That's why I'm here. So perhaps if you got off your high horse now and then you'd see that not everyone on One is as self-absorbed as you seem to think." His arrogance infuriated me.

He locked eyes with me. I tried my best to hold his gaze and not break. The light from the fire flickered and cast dancing shadows on his profile only serving to make him look more foreboding. "We'll see." He finally spoke. "We've got a long journey tomorrow to the Outpost. Best we rest now." He stood up abruptly and started walking towards the large building that belonged to the Chief of the village who had insisted we stay with him. I stared after him, open mouthed. Who just gets up and leaves in the middle of a conversation like that?

Raveo's departure seemed to be a signal to the villagers. The song petered out as they all retreated back to their homes. Even the fire was giving up. The flames shrank back, the light dying with them. I watched until the last breath of fire was extinguished and then for a little longer as the glowing embers seemed to highlight hidden words within the wood, tracing out the secrets within. Discord always seemed to bring out my poetic nature; not that there was much call or appreciation for it these days. Sighing, I found I was suddenly alone as the village square was plunged into dark save for the lights in the sky.

It didn't take long for the chill to creep into my bones, or perhaps I had just been sat there longer than I realised, but Raveo's hostility was still eating away at me. I pulled my recorder out of my satchel bag and started to dictate the events of the day. I'd sort them out for transmission when I had a week's worth of notes but I wanted to make sure I documented everything. I had dreams of publishing them all as an account of my adventures, people may not have wanted my fiction but surely they would want to know about this, about life on the outer planets? Perhaps Raveo was right. I stopped speaking and tapped the recorder against my chin deep in thought.

The music of the evening had been a rare delight. Art had not been banned as such after the coalition and the rise to power of the Vizier and his ministers but it most certainly wasn't promoted. Venues closed and artists were shunned and sacked. The circus had fallen within months and I had found myself hopeless, jobless and full of poetry that no-one wanted anymore.

A flickering light caught my attention. At first, I thought the fire had caught again but it was further away. A torch seemed to float by the side door of the Chief's house. Someone was sneaking out, I smirked to myself. The smile dropped from my face as I recognised the hulking figure of Raveo creeping towards the back of the house. Where the hell was he going?

I had already dropped the recorder into my bag and was shuffling towards the house. My lack of torch made it quite hard to see where I was putting my feet but I managed to make it to the corner of the building without incident. I craned round the side and caught sight of Raveo's torch in the distance. He was heading into a warren of houses. If he went in one, I would lose him. I hurried after him cursing every slight noise my feet made on the ground; the sand did manage to muffle most of it thankfully.

I rounded the corner of a house and had to pull myself back quickly before Raveo saw me. He was waiting at a door just one building over. Hushed whispers carried over the breeze as I heard a door open. When I looked back, Raveo had disappeared inside. I was about to try and get closer to the building when more noises drifted towards me. I crouched lower; my back pressed against the coarse brick wall. I held my breath as I leaned my head round the building again to watch the people moving towards the building Raveo had just entered. Lights in the sky flashed overhead and I closed my eyes for a second, praying they would not see me. My luck held. Three men closed in on the door and knocked quietly.

As the door opened, light from the inside gave me a better view of them. They were definitely not villagers. The people of Redawa all wore handmade linen clothes in beige and brown. These people did not have the tanned skin of the Redawans and they were wearing black and leather. The door shut behind them and I waited for a few seconds, half expecting the sounds of a fight to break out. Nothing came. There had been no sign of the men at the evening meal so where had they come from?

We were close to the edge of the village so they must have come from that direction, from another township perhaps. But why would they come after dark to meet Raveo? Urged on by my curiosity, I crept closer to the building. The door was too risky. I moved round the other direction. The shutters were closed over the windows so I crouched low beneath and stayed quietly.

"Well Trouble-Shooter it's been a while." The voice belonged to one of the newcomers, they did not talk in the dialect of the Redawans.

"It has. Can't go anywhere the Ministry doesn't send me."

"But you can make a few stops along the way."

"It's all about the journey, isn't it?" Raveo sounded like he was smiling. A few chuckles rippled around the building.

"Sorted out the parsaw I hear."

"Could you have not done something about that?" There was quiet for a moment, only sounds of furniture shuffling around came out.

"You know what it's like brother. We do anything out of character and the people come asking."

"You've been making noise alright. Why do you think I've been sent?"

Something creaked. The front door had opened and I could hear footsteps coming round to the back. Panic gripped me and I almost froze in place but my senses came back quickly enough to propel me forwards and towards the next house. I almost threw myself to the ground to keep out of sight.

The footsteps stopped. I held my breath but was sure anyone would be able to hear my traitorous heart slamming against my chest. The sound of liquid almost brought manic giggles to my throat and I had to clamp my hands over my own mouth to calm myself as I listened to the man relieve himself. I waited until the man retreated and my pulse had slowed to a level I didn't think would endanger my continued existence. As I was about to move back towards the window, I saw something gleaming in the other direction. Sandbikes were parked a way down the hill at the edge of the village. Casting one more glance at the house, I decided to take a closer look at the bikes.

The sand gave way under my feet as I moved forwards. At the edges of the village, the paths were less well-travelled, and the sandstorm had built up the banks. I kept my eyes on the bikes. The lights dancing in the sky caught the metal with each wave and gave me a beacon to head for. There were three bikes lined up just beyond the last house. They had come from the opposite direction to us, from the direction of the outpost. Kit like these bikes did not belong in a village, these men had to be from Kadaera, where Raveo and I were meant to be going the next day to investigate the smugglers. Glancing back at the last houses, the urge to run and hide overcame me as I realised how exposed I was. I hovered for a second, my hand wavering above the travel box on the back of the first bike. In the years I had been creating news for Newscorp, never had I had to dig for it. I was handed the facts and I weaved them into manageable segments for the people. I could almost hear Raveo's voice in my head, "Well who told the people who told you?"

I had come on this journey to tell the Five what was happening out there, to tell them the stories of the Trouble-Shooter. But this was the first time I had had to get the facts myself. Suddenly, I realised I was grinning. I didn't hesitate for a second longer; I tried to open the first box but there was a lock on it. Rummaging around in my bag, I laid my fingers on a notebook. I was often laughed at for still using pen and paper but I was sure that was because most people were hiding their jealousy of the fact I could write as well as read. Quickly, I stripped the wire binding the pages together and fashioned the end into a hook. My days bugging Rancho, the circus' escapologist, to teach me his tricks were finally coming in handy. The lock was the work of seconds before it clicked open and I could gain access. My cursory search in the dark yielded nothing of interest so I replaced the lock and moved to the next bike.

The presence of two locks on this box was promising and, in my haste, I fumbled a couple of times. I forced myself to stop and to take a breath before beginning again. The locks came away and I dropped them silently onto the sand. The lid of the box was half opened when I froze. Sat in the top was a small black unit, to all intents and purposes, an innocuous looking thing that could have contained anything. It was the presence of the white symbol on top that made my blood run cold. A V was inscribed on the top which had an X crossing through it: the symbol known throughout the Five, being ever present in all terrorist attacks in the last six years—the symbol of The Uprising.

I let the lid drop down as I stepped back in terror. As I moved back, I hit something solid. Arms wrapped around me and I realised my mistake.

***

I was still trying to squirm out of my assailant's arms when I was thrown roughly to the floor. Light shone directly into my eyes, blinding me for a few moments.

"Caught him going through the bikes. He found the recorders."

"Great, what are we going to do with him?"

The words chilled me to the core as I blinked furiously to try and get sight of the terrorists. As everything came back into focus, Raveo's face was looming over me, his eyebrow raised in irritation.

"Raveo!" I sat up and pushed myself towards him and away from the man who had dragged me back to the house. "They're terrorists, they're Uprising!" I scrabbled back behind the Trouble-Shooter and put my back to the wall, waiting for my companion to leap to his feet and deal with them.

"You know him?" The only one of the three sat down addressed Raveo. He looked only a few years older than me, his face pale with a few scars tracing around to his chin.

"I do." Raveo sighed, sounding disappointed and turned to me.

"Umm, I did say terrorists, right? You going to you know…" I waved at them.

"I told you to get some sleep. Why are you prowling around?"

"Me prowling around? Me?" I stood up, pressing myself even tighter to the wall and away from Raveo. The window shutters rattled slightly under my strain. I wondered for a split second if I could get them open and leap out before anyone could stop me. Raveo gave a small shake of the head as if he could tell what I was considering. "I was just sitting by the fire, you're the one who said go to bed, we need sleep and then snuck out the back to a secret meeting with terrorists!" My breath caught for a second. "Oh Gods, you're working with them?" Raveo still barely blinked, the arrogant thug just sat there staring at me with his superior look of disdain.

Instinct took over and before I knew it, I had lunged forward and grabbed the short sword from his belt and waved it in front of me.

"Bastienne," he warned. The three men in black all raised their guns and clicked the safeties off with a definite air of finality. Raveo rose. I thrust the point of the sword further forward at his face. He moved with such speed, I couldn't even follow it but the sword was out of my grasp and I was sinking to the floor before I could even register he had struck the bridge of my nose with his elbow. Blood seeped onto my top lip as I cradled my face in my hands.

"Who is he Raveo?"

"He's just a journalist." Just a journalist, I should have had more to worry about at that point in time but it still wounded my pride.

"A Government man?"

"That remains to be seen."

"We can't take the chance." The leader of the three stepped forward, leaning round Raveo with his weapon. I looked up between my blood covered fingers and stared down the barrel of his gun. So much for my adventure. My view was blocked as Raveo sidestepped and put himself in the way.

"Not unless we're sure." His voice was steel.

"Fine. Talk Newsman." The other man held for a second before yielding.

"Hard with a broken nose." At least that's what I tried to say.

"Get a cold, wet rag would you?" Raveo looked over at a Redawan hiding by the wall. It was the first time I'd noticed them; they must have been the house owner. They darted away to the corner to fetch the rag and brought it back. Raveo held it out to me, waving it towards my face. I mopped up the blood as best I could and put the cold cloth over my throbbing nose.

"Are you a terrorist?" I asked pitifully.

"None of us are terrorists."

"But they are The Uprising. I saw the symbol."

"They are not terrorists."

"Rav," one of the men began to step forward but Raveo held a hand up and the man stopped, albeit with a disapproving shake of the head. I couldn't help myself but check that the gun was still very much in his hand.

"Why are you here?" Raveo dragged his chair to sit directly in front of me, blocking my view of the others further.

"I saw you sneak off..."

"No why are you on this trip?"

"You know why. To make a chronicle of your journey, to show the people the work you do so they can feel safe knowing you're out their stopping, you know," I glanced around the side of him, "terrorists."

"Why are you really on this trip?"

"Oh for... I just told you. The First Minister asked me to record this tour."

"What *else* did he ask you to do?"

I stared at him, non-plussed. "What? What do you mean?"

Raveo took a deep breath and let it out slowly. His gaze locked with mine. "Are you a spy Bastienne?"

I laughed. I couldn't help it. It was a joke. It hurt my nose. No-one else was laughing. Slowly my chuckles died to a pathetic nothingness as I realised he was serious. His eyes were narrowed studying my every expression.

"You're serious... you think he asked me to spy on you? Why would he ask that? Why would..." I glanced around at the men with guns. My resolve was threatening to break any second. Raveo was supposed to keep me safe not be the reason I got killed. "What's going on Raveo?"

"Why did you say yes to this job?"

"Ra.."

"Just answer me."

"I'm a writer!" I yelled in his face, fear and stress getting the better of me and twisting my voice into hissing. "That's all I am. I used to be a poet; you know how useful poets are these days? No-one wants fiction, no-one wants words anymore, most people can't even bring themselves to learn to write." I dropped the rag from my face as I shook my head sorrowfully, mourning my old life. "I'm a wordsmith who's never travelled beyond Two before, I've never experienced life out here. I want to write about it, I want to share it with the people even if they can't be bothered to read about it. I want to bring the Five to everyone, to show them the truth that is out there. I'm fed up with putting together other people's notes. I want…I wanted to see it for myself. How can I write it if I've never experienced it?"

"And that's all?"

"Isn't that enough?" I laughed humourlessly. "Those songs they sang tonight. Do know the last time I heard signing on One? No, I don't remember either. Those songs are stories, they are history through music. They are the shared truth. It's important. Recording events is important." I suddenly realised everyone was staring at me. I swallowed self-consciously and looked down at my feet, replacing the rag to my nose.

"Recording events is only important if what you say is true." Raveo and I both looked round. It was the Redawan who had spoken, this time not using a dialect I couldn't understand.

I nodded towards the Redawan. "I told you they were doing it on purpose."

"They didn't trust you Bastienne. You write the news; you say it's not fiction but to them it means nothing. They don't see their news anywhere. Where was the Parsaw? Where are the reports of people on Five trying to escape the mines but being caught by Government forces and forced to work? Where are the reports of the clashes of tribes on the Xhicano continent with Government forces? Hundreds of people died."

"But that, that was The Uprising…"

"And who told you that?"

I opened my mouth but the words left me. I had spent my time putting together all the notes I had been passed just like I said. Not once had I seen any of it myself, I was just a mouthpiece. I had tried to go to the aftermath of an Uprising attack on Three a year ago. I begged them to let me go so I could report from the scene. They told me it was too dangerous and yet they sent someone to collect images and stock footage apparently. Easier to get if you're the ones behind it.

The Redawan stepped forward, moving round one of the armed men. "A platoon of the Government army passed through here two months ago. We begged them for help with the parsaw. It was not in their best interest to help. If we lose traders, we are more reliant on Government help. They left and the next day the Parsaw took my father. We sent word to our friends at the Outpost."

"And they got word to me." Raveo finished. I let it all sink in for a minute. In truth, was I really surprised? Was it a shock that the Coalition, when trying to stop the five planets warring, had merely beaten enough of us into submission? I'd ignored it because I knew I was lucky. I could have easily ended up in one of mines.

"So you work it into your tour route so your bosses don't even realise you've done it." Raveo nodded. "Unless some idiot is recording your every act and reporting back to them. I am a spy! I just didn't know it." I let the rag fall to my knees as I ran my hands through my hair. "So, who are they?"

"We are The Uprising, just not as you know it. We run supplies to places that need them, places the Government have cut off because they won't fall in line. We help run people across to other planets to escape conscription to the mines." The man on the chair stood up and moved closer. He held his hand out to me. "I am Malani."

"Bastienne." I took his hand and he hauled me to my feet with very little effort. "So those black boxes on your bikes aren't bombs then?"

Malani laughed. "They are recorders. But when the Government blow up an Uprising location, they are very handy for making us look like the villains. We are trying to plant them in places to get our own footage. We aren't terrorists but we are rebels. The resistance is growing but we need proof to bring down those in power."

"And the people aren't big on questioning these days. They need it on film and in black and white." I nodded forlornly.

"So, what do you say wordsmith?" Raveo stood, a playful smile playing on his lips. "Tomorrow the Government want me to take down some smugglers. I'm planning on helping them get the refugees past the army's scheduled fly over so they can safely get to the haven on Three. How about it?"

"How are you going to explain the lack of smugglers arrested?"

"Like you say, they only know the facts that are passed to them." Raveo shrugged and turned away, walking over to a small table. He poured himself a drink and downed it in one. He poured another. He was giving me time to think about what he'd just said. He hadn't given me an answer, more a question.

"You want me to feed false information back to the First Minister." I felt like sitting back down on the floor. "I've gone from journalist to spy to double agent in thirty seconds."

"But will you do it?"

"What if I say no?"

"I lock you in a room until the tour is over, then drop you back on One with a promise to come back for you if you ever tell." He shrugged as if it was nothing, as if he hadn't just promised to kill me.

"And just when I started to think perhaps you don't hate me after all."

"Hate you? You'd know it if I hated you. You definitely wouldn't have made it out to Four." He gave me what I could only assume was a friendly smile, or his approximation anyway. My mouth worked wordlessly not wanting to think he meant by that.

"But you let me eat crushed galo beetle at that river shack?" The others in the room did their best to hide their amused. They failed miserably.

I noticed the second glass in Raveo's hands as he waited. "You've been planning this haven't you? Letting me find out so you can lay out your proposition."

He smiled and half-shrugged. "Took you longer than I thought it would if I'm honest. Too busy trying to get everyone to like you I think."

"Makes sense though." Malani nodded approvingly. "Not only does it allay any suspicion the First Minister may have about you; it even gives you more scope if you've got someone writing you're in a completely different place."

"Now hang on, you'd have to be careful about it. If there was anyone attached to the Government in that place, they would report back instantly. We'd have to bend the truth but only a little, keep it as close to real as possible." I took the glass from Raveo and knocked the drink back quickly before handing it back to him.

My eyes widened at the burn. He raised an eyebrow at the empty glass but turned to fill it up again anyway. "Sounds like he's in, doesn't it?"

"You really think you can bring them down?"

"We have to try."

"Of course," I lifted my hands up, "if you do manage it, you'll need someone to tell the story of what really happened. How you overthrew the Government and saved the helpless."

"You may be getting ahead of yourself." Raveo sighed.

"A man can dream can't he. That's the one thing they can't take." I reached out and took my second glass from Raveo, knocking it back in one. He looked at me in confusion. The burning liquid scorched my throat but I soldiered on. "So, save some refugees under the watch of the army, fake a report back to the First Minister and help the Resistance all without getting arrested and killed? Sounds like I get an adventure after all."

Alex Minns is based in England and has worked in forensics, teaching, PR and been paid to wield custard flamethrowers. She writes sci-fi, fantasy and steampunk and can be currently found forcing her mother to listen as she tries to untangle the timelines of her time-travel steampunk novel. You can find her obsessively creating blog stories and micro-fiction on https://lexikon.home.blog/ and on Twitter under @Lexikonical

Diamond Eater

by Sara Crocoll Smith

Mia Morales kneaded the thick skin of her client's back. She brushed a few traces of the woman's oversized auburn hair out of the way before gliding with flat hands from her ample shoulders to her lower back. She crinkled her nose at what must've been an entire can of hairspray wafting up from the signature Texan hairdo.

Holding up the linen, Mia whispered in a calming tone. "Would you please turn over to your back, Ms. Raylene?" The middle-aged woman issued a sleepy grumble as she lumbered to turn over without so much as opening her eyes. Mia tapped a fresh dollop of lavender massage oil into her palm and rubbed it between her hands to warm it, noticing how her own bones peeked through her papery skin. She frowned at the stark contrast, her once supple brown skin appearing emaciated against the full moon white of her client's upper thigh. She pushed the observation from her mind. It was the result of working too hard, she told herself. Nothing more.

As Mia positioned herself at the head of the massage table, her molars ached and she worked to loosen the tension she held in her jaw. Hunger pangs threatened to rumble forth from her stomach in the quiet room, even though she'd made sure to eat right before the session. No matter how much she ate, she couldn't satiate a hunger that had grown over recent months. She prayed Raylene wouldn't notice.

Mia's frock hung loosely around her as she pressed an elbow deep into Raylene's shoulders. Soft snores and steady breathing told her the woman had, thankfully, fallen back asleep. When Raylene spoke, it was with a twang so deep it could compete with the Grand Canyon. Yet it wasn't the overexaggerated accent Mia disliked about the woman. It could be somewhat charming when it wasn't grating. No, she had other reasons to feel blessed by the silence and spared Raylene's idle prattle.

She glanced at the clock. Only a minute had ticked by since she'd last looked. The fluids in her stomach churned and her singular focus was on when she could eat again. Mia imagined finishing the in-home massage, darting to her car, and as soon as she was out of sight, downing the sleeve of crackers she'd left in the passenger seat. Her mouth watered. She drew herself back into present time.

Mia rubbed Raylene's feet, casting long strokes up and down her arches in a dazed trance. No longer able to contain its turmoil, her stomach growled. Mia snapped to attention and held her breath, staring hard at Raylene's closed eyes. Seconds passed. Mia eased her shoulders down an inch, suddenly remembering to keep rubbing the woman's feet.

As she let out her breath, Raylene's leg twitched.

Mia stifled the urge to jump. Blood thundered in her ears. Though she'd been a client of Mia's for years, Raylene was swift with criticism and didn't sugarcoat it. Mia cringed in anticipation, a whirl of past insults rising to the surface, but nothing came.

The soft spa music transitioned from soothing rain to gentle chimes. Not much left in the session, Mia only needed to finish up Raylene's arms as she glided on the stool to the woman's left side. An egregiously large stone sat atop Raylene's ring finger. Despite Mia's repeated requests that Raylene not wear her wedding ring during sessions, Raylene never heeded. However, she still expected Mia to massage her hand thoroughly around the ridiculous rock. Mia wasn't sure why Raylene wouldn't remove the ring, whether it was an act of defiance, a desire to flaunt her wealth, or if she was simply unable to slip it off her thick finger.

Raylene's limp hand flopped in response to Mia's gentle massaging. The day-in and day-out routine gave Mia too much time to contemplate the human body. The meat and sinew and bone beneath the flesh took on a grotesque quality over time that wasn't there when she'd started giving in-home massages a decade ago. Once, she'd even enjoyed it, happy to find a means to make ends meet through a flexible, steady stream of work. But lately, it'd become harder and harder to stretch the influx of money over growing bills and lack of another income in her household. She exhaled silently, pushing yet more thoughts away from the forefront of her mind.

When she finished, Mia rose to press her forefingers gently to Raylene's temples and signal the end of the session, however, her hands trembled and her head swam. In the darkened room, she almost didn't notice the edges of her vision grow dim. She had the odd sense of floating away. Trying to ground herself, she looked to the clock, but the numbers blurred and faded. "Ms. Raylene, I—"

A drawling drum buffeted against her with angry urgency. "What in the name of all that's holy are you doing on the dang floor?" The tip of a pointed neon pink nail wagged in Mia's face. She had the feeling her eyes hadn't closed, but that they'd turned off, like a light switch. With a rough tap on the cheek from the pink-nailed hand, Mia's lights flickered back on. Raylene pushed herself up from a crouch and stood back, holding a swath of sheet out to the side with the rest barely covering her body. "What's wrong with you?"

Mia pressed her hand to her mouth. "I'm sorry, ma'am. I don't feel so—"

Raylene jumped a foot back and shoved her hands out in front of her. "Don't tell me you're sick. I can't believe this. How dare you come here, touching me, while you're sick." She rubbed at her skin like she could slough off the contamination. "Get up, get out of here. You should've called out on our appointment today and gone to a doctor the minute you felt like you were coming down with something."

Turning over on her side, Mia used every bit of energy she had in reserve to come unsteadily to her feet. "I don't think I'm that kind of sick, ma'am." Raylene stared at her with blank, angry eyes. "What I mean to say is…I don't think I'm contagious."

The woman narrowed her eyes at her. She placed a hand on her hip, cocked out to the side. "How do you know?"

Mia pursed her lips and clenched her hand across her wrist. "I guess I don't. But I don't really have the insurance to be able to…to go. Unless it gets real bad."

If Mia hadn't been paying attention, she might've missed the softening in Raylene's posture before she thrust her shoulders back. "Well, I'd say it's gotten real bad now, wouldn't you?" She ushered Mia to gather her things and forced her out through the grand front hall and wide double doors. "Consider your services no longer required."

Jamming her foot into the closing door, Mia reached for Raylene's forearm. "Please, don't do this. I need this for my family."

Raylene didn't look her in the eyes, instead keeping a steady gaze on where Mia gripped her arm. She tugged it away with less force than Mia expected. There was uncertainty in Raylene's final words. "I'm sorry. I just don't see how that's my problem. Good day now."

The door slammed shut forcing a whoosh of harsh air in Mia's face. She stood, face to face with the slate-gray door, silently gathering herself together before turning to the heartless crisp blue sky and barren Texas landscape against which her rusted car sagged.

***

Cranked up air conditioning turned the cramped doctor's office into a tundra. Mia huddled atop the exam table, struggling with haphazard paper clothing, unable to keep both her breasts and buttocks covered at the same time. Her teeth chattered and she couldn't fathom why Texan buildings couldn't be kept at a reasonably cool temperature. She conceded it could be hot as blazes outside, but that didn't mean it needed to be darn near snowy inside.

A sharp knock on the door was followed by the doctor breezing into the room and perching on his stool. His gaze never left the dented tablet in his hands as he rolled closer to the table. "I'm Dr. Aguilar. How're we feeling today, Ms. Morales?"

"Fine." She wasn't fine. She was freezing and a bottomless pit of hunger. Mia smiled pleasantly. Every fiber of her being was yelling at her for wasting money on some overpriced test.

The salt and pepper haired doctor raised an eyebrow and looked up at her for the first time since entering the room. His tan skin wrinkled deeply at the creases of his forehead. Mia guessed he was in his fifties. He had tired eyes that glittered with a hint of amusement. "Fine?" Aguilar sighed. He might've been handsome if it weren't for the heaviness in his shoulders that only comes from many years of overwork to the detriment of oneself. Rubbing his hands together briefly, he touched Mia's throat, temples, peered in her eyes and mouth. She expected rough hands, but they were gentle and soft. "No one who comes to this clinic is fine."

Mia didn't respond. Aguilar sat on his stool to once again take up his tablet. "Forgive me, I didn't get a chance to review your file."

She nodded. After waiting three hours and observing the gobs of patients flowing in and out of the clinic, she wasn't surprised. Finding her voice, she spoke not much above a whisper. "I believe you should have the results of my...my RAT. The rapid assessment test?"

Aguilar scowled. "Yes, I see the file here." He tapped the tablet's spiderwebbed surface. "Hold on a minute. What in tarnation—sorry. New tech isn't exactly high priority. You know the RAT isn't the best assessment tool—"

"But it's the cheapest." Mia sucked at her bottom lip for having cut the doctor off. She fretted with her unrecognizably bony hands in her lap.

"Yes, I'm not unfamiliar with it. Okay, the results have come up. I—" Aguilar squinted at the screen. From his worn white coat pocket, he withdrew spectacles and placed them low on his strong-lined nose. The pale-faced clock on the wall ticked away too many seconds for Mia's comfort. She wanted to prompt him to tell her, but she already felt bad for having interrupted him earlier. Aguilar drew in a long breath. "Ms. Morales, I'm so sorry. The RAT actually did pick up a diagnosis. You have Stage Four malignant pancreatic cancer. This explains the symptoms you've been experiencing—shaking, extreme hunger, blurry vision, fainting. Routine diagnostic nanomites would've caught this at a more treatable stage. But uh, I understand that those resources aren't available to someone like...like yourself."

She studied the crooked floor tiles instead of acknowledging that she couldn't afford thousands of dollars toward medical care on herself.

Aguilar shifted uncomfortably in the short silence and continued. "I'm afraid the news only gets worse. There's a 70% chance of recovery." Mia only had a second to think, those aren't bad odds. "But that's with a precision nanomite treatment, nanomites customized to your genetic imprint and cancer profile. Unfortunately, without private insurance, the state provided plan doesn't cover this treatment. Payment would be required through the IndentiLoan program."

"IndentiLoan?" The words sent shudders through her and for the first time in months, she felt nauseated instead of ravenous. "That's as good as being dead anyway. I'd never see my family again. My daughter, my mother—they rely on me."

The doctor scratched at his head. "Right. I'm legally required to offer you that, though, I'd never recommend it. Okay, so in cases such as yours, the state does provide chemotherapy through the clinic for a lower fee." He scribbled on a notepad and handed it to her.

Mia reached for the flap of paper. The cost was more than her monthly rent and bills combined. Her eyes stung. She closed them and gathered herself inward. On her hand, which she'd realized was balled into a fist, she felt the soft reassurance of Aguilar's palm. Mia opened her eyelids, greeted by amber-brown irises that reflected her pain.

"Ms. Morales, I wish there were more I could do for you. If you want, there's a pro bono end of life counselor I can put you in touch with. She's excellent."

Quick as lightning, Mia withdrew her hand from his. "No, thank you. There'll be no need for that. I'll pay for the chemotherapy. What is the…" She cleared her throat. "What is the chance of survival?"

Aguilar backed off with a screech of the stool against the awful tile. She wasn't certain, but Mia thought his shoulders gained a fraction more burden. "It's 20%." He stood. "Please, get dressed and make an appointment with the front desk to see me as soon as possible for your first chemotherapy session. They'll take your info and down payment." Aguilar slipped out the door.

At the front desk, Mia pushed aside lint, discarded wrappers, and other various bottom-of-the-purse debris to rummage out the last line of credit she had left. A stone-faced woman with a tight bun retrieved the card from her. "I'm required to read this statement to you." She paused before continuing in nasally monotone. "You are making a down payment on your treatment. If you default on the down payment before your first session, you will not receive treatment. If you fail to make future payments, you will be denied further treatment. If at any time, you are late on your payments, you will be given a grace period of thirty days, at twenty percent interest each day. If you fail to make your payments, with interest, after thirty days, you will be involuntarily enrolled in the IndentiLoan program. Do you understand, Ms. Mia Morales?"

Mia gulped. She'd have to pick up several extra massages and pray her tips were on the higher end than usual. Yet she believed she could just make ends meet for the next few months if she worked hard. "Yes," she replied.

"You must state 'I, Mia Morales, understand.' Speak into the recorder so it can capture your statement. Now, again, do you understand?"

"Yes. I mean, I, Mia Morales, understand." A growl so deep erupted from her stomach that not only did the stern front desk woman gape, but the whole of the patient waiting area turned their heads in her direction. "Sorry," Mia murmured as she held her arm over her stomach with one hand while she scribbled her signature with the other. She noted the date of her appointment, early next week, and scrambled out of the clinic's front door.

As she walked to her car, digging in her purse for the granola bar she'd spotted earlier when pulling out her card, a bean sprout of a young man sidled up beside her. "I'm not interested," she mumbled. Normally, she'd be more polite than that and felt a sting of guilt at not having the energy to stop and help the homeless kid. But she needed to be home. *Now.*

He touched her upper arm, forcing her to stop. "Hey, lady, I'm trying to help *you*, not the other way around."

"What?" She spun toward him, glimpsing his crooked smile up a bit too close. His casual demeanor was almost offensive. "Help *me*?"

"You're sick. We've got nanomites for cheap that are guaranteed to heal you. Don't get ripped off by those swindlers in there. Just bring me what you can pay. What you got?"

Before she could stop herself, she blurted out. "Pancreatic cancer. Stage Four."

The man was already walking away from her, talking over his shoulder with a wave of his hand. "Got it. Come next week."

Mia watched as he hopped into the back of a van parked in the corner of the clinic lot. A couple of people gathered around it, paying a scrawny woman and receiving oral treatments Mia assumed were nanomites. She meandered to her car and didn't take her eyes off the faded black panels of the van, the man and woman, and people being treated, even as she pulled out of the parking lot, with its grass-sprouting cracks, and headed home.

***

She turned the keys off in the ignition and let the waning sounds of the car soothe her. The sun sank over the horizon, casting bloody hues into the sky to mix with the darkening blue. Through the thin curtains of her living room, she saw the flicker of television glow. Mia sighed.

Juggling her things in one arm, she unlocked the door and nudged it open with her shoulder. She braced herself, flinching at the polished voices of the two news commentators blaring from the bright screen.

"Mama! Will you turn that down?" Mia frowned as the news cut to a scene of familiar high cast-iron gate holding back protestors.

"Eh?" The sinewy, age-spotted hand of Tilda Morales cupped her ear. "What's that, mija? I can't hear you." She gestured to the program from where she sat in her Tilda-shaped indentation in her overstuffed recliner. Her voice several octaves too loud, she shouted over the reporting. "Can you believe this man?" Tilda spit in the air. "Serves him right."

"Senator Grayson Grant continues to criticize the Americare Bill in the Senate, rallying increasing support to vote the bill down." The reporter spoke with the out-of-breath pace of a live-on-the-scene newscast. *"Protestors gather at his private residence here in Texas. As you can see behind me—"*

"TV, mute," Mia commanded. She returned her items from the day back to their various homes and began to unravel for the evening.

Tilda brought her hands together in a quick clap. "Mija, you can't ignore these happenings. We should support them. Show them we can't be silenced. Think about Fiona."

Mia's head snapped in her mother's direction. It was a faster gesture than she'd meant and she saw Tilda's eyebrows go up. Hustling over to the recliner, Mia dipped to give her mother a kiss on the forehead. Hands on her shoulders, Mia crouched in front of Tilda to look up at her. "I *am* thinking of Fiona. And you. I don't have time to protest." She got up to resume her nighttime routine as if on autopilot. "Besides, Ms. Camila is a client of mine. What do you think would happen if she saw me picketing against her husband?" She headed toward the kitchen.

Behind her back, she heard Tilda mutter under her breath. "Some things are more important than money."

Mia deflated. In her head, she constructed a retort, but her mouth grew dry at the notion it'd only make her mother feel like a burden. It wasn't her fault. She was right. Yet it was magnitudes more complicated than Tilda knew and Mia wasn't ready to discuss all the facets why.

The front door clicked open and Fiona bounded into the living room, discarding her backpack and sneakers at the bottom of the stairs. She rushed over to Tilda, bestowing a kiss on her grandmother's cheek, and then gave a hearty hug to Mia.

Squeezing her daughter tight, Mia marveled at how Fiona rivaled her own height. She smoothed back her daughter's wild curls and smiled, holding her out to look at her. "Palomita. How was your day?"

"Good!" Fiona chirped.

"Glad to hear it." Mia picked up Fiona's sneakers and put them in the shoe cubby. "How'd you do on your algebra test? Did you find out today?"

Fiona's face fell. From her back pocket, she withdrew her school tablet. She presented it for Mia to see. The screen showed an A-. It took Mia a few seconds to process, faster after she saw Fiona's grin behind it. "Guess those nights you helped me study paid off."

Mia swelled with pride. "Guess they did," she winked. It made the even later nights spent painfully relearning algebra that Fiona would never know about worth it too. "What're you in the mood for dinner tonight? Your pick, my little algebra whiz."

Fiona was already pulling away from her with the kinetic energy uniquely possessed by teenagers as she snatched her backpack to charge up the stairs. "Aw, mama, thank you, but nothing for me tonight. Gotta get started on my homework. Beatriz invited me over."

"Oh, okay." Mia's heart sank. She kicked off her slip-on shoes with a half-hearted nudge toward the cubby. Her feet ached and

213

her head felt light. She held her stomach. "Mama, I'm going to make some supper. You want some?"

"Eh? Oh yes, please." Tilda lit up as if something suddenly occurred to her. She leaned over to peer upstairs then waved Mia over conspiratorially. "Come here, come here."

Mia groaned inwardly. Hesitation caught her between the kitchen and whatever Tilda was up to. Dragging her feet, she crossed the balding carpet.

"Here, here," Tilda repeated until Mia bent close to her. From her sweater pocket, Tilda produced a handkerchief that she treated with great care. "Fiona's quinceañera is in a few weeks." Unveiling the hidden treasure, Tilda smiled a big, toothy grin. Resting on the time-faded cloth was the one and only Morales family heirloom, rich in both value and sentiment. Tilda lifted it up to Mia. "I want to give this to Fiona. Will you wrap it special for me?"

With trembling fingers, Mia dared not touch it, dared not even breathe on it. She herself coveted it when she was a mere girl. Inlaid within tarnishing silver were three rubies forming the broach her father had given her mother on their wedding day. Mia took her time folding the handkerchief back over the broach, once again hiding its treasure within its soft protective shell. "Of course, I will. This is…she'll love it." Her voice cracked.

She was rewarded with an even bigger smile from Tilda. "Girl deserves it."

Retreating into the kitchen, Mia tucked the broach into her pocket. It kept her company through cooking, eating, and tidying the house, both lifting her spirits and weighing them down. Long after Tilda and Fiona were asleep for the evening, their soft snores echoing down the hall, Mia squinted by the light of a tiny desk lamp over their finances. No matter which way she tallied it, they drowned in debt when she allotted for the chemotherapy bills. Let alone celebrate Fiona's quinceañera properly. She bit her lip to keep from screaming in frustration.

Mia counted to ten, whispering the numbers aloud. Then she slipped her hand into her pocket and, with great reluctance, cupped the broach.

***

"Harder. No, *harder*." Mia jammed her elbows into her client's back, fretting that bruises might bloom through the woman's thin skin. Almost as gaunt as Mia, she could hardly believe the intentional starvation on Shelby's part was a desired look. "Oh, really? Yeah, I just got them for my wrinkles. You wouldn't believe the crows' feet I've been getting."

Swallowing a guffaw, Mia turned skyward and shook her head at the ceiling. Her blood pressure climbed and she considered not responding. She dug down into her waning well of empathy, however, knowing full well Shelby's tendency toward vanity and Mia's need to keep her existing clients happy with her. "I hadn't noticed, Ms. Shelby. You have flawless skin." Her compliment rang hollow in her ears, but she knew Shelby would be oblivious in the name of flattery.

Shelby swatted the air. "Hush!" She tapped her ear where Mia spotted a tiny silver earbud nestled in Shelby's ear. "Jeez, you'd think a good masseuse would know when to give a little privacy."

After Mia adjusted to the red, rising heat in her breast, time stretched before her endlessly as she used every ounce of her strength in the hour-long massage. The sprawling day ahead of her was a chasm of impossibilities. She didn't know how she'd have the reserves to finish her day's appointments adequately enough to satisfy her clients. Surviving that, she was due at the clinic for her first round of chemotherapy.

She'd been reading up on the antiquated procedure. Each line, each side effect, dropped like a stone in her clamoring stomach. Nightmares loomed on the cusp of her sleep every night since her diagnosis. Dreams of being eaten alive bite by bite by her clients until there was nothing left. Wasting away until she disappeared, becoming invisible to her daughter and mother. Her lower lip trembled as she tore herself away from such specters back into the cool room and smooth oil under her palms as she rubbed Shelby's back.

"I can't believe she got nanomites for freckles. I mean, come on. Stretch marks, even moles I can understand, but freckles?" Shelby cackled.

Mia's ears perked up at the talk of nanomites. She was vaguely aware those of means could afford them for more than life-saving medical procedures—for cosmetic work, dentistry, and the like. Yet it was difficult to fathom with no intimate experience with the relatively young medical technology.

Shelby hunched and whispered as if she could prevent Mia from listening in. Mia rolled her eyes at the woman two decades her junior, feeling lucky her profession allowed for facial expressions her clients would never see. "No way. I don't believe it." Shelby nodded in that way people do when talking on the phone even though no one can see. Well, except for Mia, but clearly she was a non entity when it came to Shelby's conversation. "Uh huh, uh huh. Nuh uh! Self-replicating? Isn't that like totally illegal?" Eager to hear each word as Shelby talked in more and more hushed tones, Mia worked on Shelby's shoulders. "They're not specified to a genetic profile either? That can't be true. And if it is, consider me first in line. My blood should be blinging with something called *nanodiamonds*." Shelby giggled. "You know I'm good for it! I am, I swear I am. I'm about to sign this new influencer to the label. Gonna bring me in loads of cash."

Easing back, Mia stroked in long, erratic paths on Shelby's shoulderblades. If what she was hearing were true…but it couldn't be true. If it were, it could help so many in need, not just herself. Her mouth curled to bear her teeth. Of course, someone like Shelby only saw applications of something like that for herself. Hunger pangs came knocking while Mia seethed. Painful waves of them threatened her resolve. The clock reported five minutes left in the session. She couldn't risk cutting it off early. Even one minute and Shelby would try to dock her fee by that fraction and Mia couldn't afford the cut to her commission nor her tip.

A faint snap accompanied the sting of cold air on her nailbed. Horror flooded her system as Mia cradled her hand and stifled a mewl. Crimson liquid seeped from the empty space her fingernail once occupied. Mia grabbed a cloth from her bag and wrapped it around the wound.

It was only then she noticed the roaring rising from the table. Wild with fury, Shelby yanked the sheet around her naked body and towered over Mia. "What in the hell was that? It felt like you stabbed me in the back." Shelby turned to expose her shoulder blade.

As Tilda might say, Mia was begging to catch flies with her open mouth gaping as it was. She snapped it shut. Gingerly, with her good hand, Mia pulled her fingernail out of Shelby's back and held it up between her forefinger and thumb. Bile singed the back of her throat.

In a blur of high-pitched howling, Mia found herself on her knees on the other side of yet another slammed door. She pressed her cheek to the wood, soaking up the warmth of the sun infused on its surface. Far away shrieking emanated from the other side of the door, the beginnings of Shelby relaying the story over and over. Mia would be infamous by the end of the day.

***

Discarded fast food wrappers covered Mia's lap like a blanket. Her car idled in the clinic parking lot. She'd rescheduled her remaining appointments for the day and prayed it wouldn't affect her income, knowing better based on the curt replies. Her finger throbbed, but at least she was able to stay the bleeding. She drained the last of her soda with a loud slurp, then rolled her dry tongue around in her mouth, no amount of liquid satisfying the saltiness the sodium-rich food left behind.

The dashboard clock read three minutes till the hour. The front of the clinic had the downtrodden eyebrows of the late afternoon sun furrowed in shadows over its face. In the corner of the lot, bright rays bounced at right angles off the glass and chrome of the van in a shiny wink at passersby. Mia watched as a man parked, unloaded his son from a dusty pickup and held his hand, guiding him over the larger cracks in the pavement. The man, who had a teddy bear kind of face and a loping gate, handed over a big wad of cash to the scrawny woman she'd seen working the van before. The bean sprout who'd approached her less than a week ago, with his same casual demeanor and crooked smile, stooped to administer an oral dose of nanomites to the boy. With a pat on his head, he sent the boy back to his father.

As father and son walked hand in hand back to their car, there was something in the man's face that stirred feelings in Mia she hadn't felt in a good long while. The digital numbers clicked to the hour. It was time for her appointment with Dr. Aguilar. Mia leaned over and retrieved the handkerchief from the glove box. Bringing it to her chest, she pondered what it was that she was feeling and considered it might be hope. She said a silent prayer for mama to forgive her and stepped out of the car.

The closing of the car door reverberated against the brick walls of the clinic. Mia marched over to the van. On her way, she conducted mental calculations—she could scrape for every penny, trying to make the chemotherapy payments, risking entrance into the IndentiLoan program. Or she could make one lump payment now and be done with it. Her nerves rattled, but she was eager to get back to her slow, yet progressive, crawl out of debt, to have money for Fiona's quinceañera. She wanted desperately to get back to the meager, happy existence she'd been able to eke out, rather than worrying about her body, her income generator, failing on her. Failing her family.

Sidling up to the van, Mia gingerly held out the handkerchief to the woman. Up close, she noticed frizzy hair, yellowing teeth, and a sly manner that chipped away at Mia's hope. For courage, she called up the image of the father and son, heading home healed.

"What's this?" The woman pointed to the handkerchief.

Mia stammered. "It's…it's…"

The man swung around the back doors of the van and slid his arm around Mia's shoulders, hugging her to him. His breath smelled of old tobacco. "Glad to see you back. You made the right decision." He jabbed a thumb in the direction of the clinic. "They mean well, but you know, their hands are tied by insurance pricing models. It's a real racket."

A small voice told her to run—run away from this van, from the clinic, from everything. Mia shoved down the voice. Run away from her family? Die alone, knowing she condemned her mother and daughter to an awful life? She shook her head. The man and woman frowned as if they believed she was disagreeing with them. "No, I mean, yes, it's a…racket." She unveiled the broach, first setting aside one piece of cloth, then the other folded over it. It glittered blood red in the Texan sun. She'd made sure to polish the silver as best she could before bringing it over. "I don't have cash, but I have this. It's worth a lot."

The woman scrunched up her face and looked at the man. He chewed the inside of his cheek. "Well…" He kicked his dirty boots against a tire, then perched with his back against the panel and one leg up. His calculating eyes roamed up and down her, then landed on the broach. "Something like that we'd have to pawn. Supposin' we could go get it valued, see if it's enough to cover your 'mites." The scrap of a woman plucked the broach from its resting place in Mia's palm before Mia could pull her hand back, then slid the rolling door closed. The man was already sealing the back doors as she noticed the woman pop into the driver's seat. He waved his hand at her, reminding her of the way Shelby swatted away her words. "Come back tomorrow."

Her vision clouded black. Mia braced herself against the hot metal of the van. It burned her fingertips, bringing her view back in full solar red. "No." Her throat was scratchy and the word came out muddled. "No," she said again, loud enough for him to hear. Though fast food churned in her stomach, her hunger ached in her gut. As soon as the broach left her hand, the pain of its loss rivaled the pain in her bones. "No!" She hurtled the word at him until he peeked around the back of the van with wide eyes.

Mia charged at him and threw him against the van. If he were a bigger man, she might not have been able to manage. Her fury fueled her. "You don't understand. That's *all* I have. I need the nanomites. *Now.*" Tears gathered at the corners of her eyes and mucus clung at the back of her throat. She was inches from the fear in his face. He appeared to her very young then and guilt rushed in. Mia released him. She smoothed the front of his shirt. "Please. Today, not tomorrow."

The man held his hands up in a surrender that morphed from real to mocking in seconds. "Jeez, don't have a cow, lady." He dug in the back of the van. Holding up a wide-mouthed syringe filled with clear liquid, he indicated she open her mouth.

"That's it?" It baffled her. She gave up the most important possession of her family for what looked like water.

He shrugged. "What did you expect?" Pinching his forefinger and thumb, he rubbed them together. "They're teeny tiny. You can't see 'em, so stop trying. I promise ya, they're there. Now open up, I ain't got all day."

Mia opened to let him squirt the nanomites into her mouth. It tasted like water too. She swallowed and waited. "How long till they start working?"

The man checked an imaginary watch. "Immediately." Over his shoulder, "Now hydrate, ya hear. And *never* friggin' come back here again."

Dust whirled behind the van. Mia stood there dumbfounded. Her brain clunked, turning over gears that were slow to process everything. Something was different—a presence that hounded her night and day vanished. Hunger no longer tugged at her shirt sleeve, demanding attention.

Head held high, Mia strutted to her car. The shakiness was gone. She felt strong. In pain no more, she could say she actually felt *good*. Mia slipped into the driver's seat, revved the ignition, and adjusted the rearview mirror. Then she froze. Cold sweat erupted from her pores.

Thrusting open the car door, Mia collapsed to her knees on the sticky tar and heaved the contents of her stomach all over its tacky surface. Half-chewed french fries wobbled in the gelatinous watery substance. Convulsions rocked her body. She hugged herself until they ceased. Weakly she lay there, watching the last of the day's sun evaporate her hope.

She wasn't sure when she'd closed her eyes, but when she opened them, Dr. Aguilar hovered over her, his fingers searching for her pulse. "I'm still alive," she croaked.

He smiled wryly. "Yes, I see that." Aguilar helped her sit on the edge of the seat, the car door still hanging open from her exit. "I didn't fancy you to be tempted by cons."

She laughed, a dry, mournful sound. "You made my options so appealing, how could I resist?"

Aguilar handed her a bottle of water. "Here. Drink."

Mia accepted the offering. "Thanks." She gulped it down eagerly. "I thought they would heal me. It seemed like they were helping others."

He raised a bushy eyebrow. "The father-son combo? Yeah, that gets a lot of people. The funny thing is they do mean well, sometimes they even help. But nanomites are a tough break. The companies tailor them to the genetics of the particular payee from the jump, so on the black market, if anyone else takes them, the body immediately rejects them."

Mia's world cracked at the edges perhaps more devastatingly at the news the father and son were plants than at her treatment failing. Aguilar lifted his chin at her. "Scoot over. I'll drive you home and take a rideshare back. You'll feel woozy for a bit, but luckily no permanent damage was done."

"No permanent damage." She choked back tears that would never stop if she started.

Aguilar stared at her from the driver's seat. The glow of the dashboard reflected on his features and softened his world-weary expression. "Listen. Come back tomorrow and I'll make sure the missed appointment fee is waived."

"Ha!" She didn't dare look at him. He thought he was being generous.

Quiet floated between them. "You think me a cog in the cruel machine, don't you?" Mia watched him out of the side of her eye, her shoulders braced stiffly, her hands in her lap. Aguilar rolled to a stop in her driveway. "My mother is in the IndentiLoan program. I wish things were different every bit as much as you do." He stepped out of the car to catch his rideshare. Before he ducked in, he turned back to her. "Come back tomorrow. If there's a way to help you, we'll figure it out. Together."

***

Idling in her driveway, Mia's car engine rattled, punctuated by fits and snorts. She didn't know how she managed it, but she got through the evening and morning without Fiona or Tilda suspecting she was ill. Though she'd been covering up her symptoms for months, so it shouldn't have surprised her.

The lights in the dashboard stared her down. The faint musk of Dr. Aguilar's aftershave lingered in the car from the evening before. She'd just about made up her mind to trust him, ratcheting the car into reverse, when her phone buzzed on the seat. She dreaded to check it. Ever since Shelby set the gossip mill in motion, cancellations had been rolling in. Pavlovian instincts caused her to unwillingly scroll through the message before she continued out of the driveway. It was from Camila Grant, asking if a massage was possible first thing this morning.

Mia pulled out of the driveway. She took a left instead of a right.

Crowds of protestors still rallied at Senator Grayson and Camila Grant's gates. The throng resisted parting as Mia edged her car inch by inch through them. They jabbed signs up and down in the dry heat. Their muffled shouting buffeted her car as she passed. Luckily, the guards watching her on the cameras recognized her and buzzed her through so she wouldn't have to open her windows. In their faces, she saw her kindred and felt muted against their roar. She averted her eyes and drove through the gates.

"Oh, Mia!" Camila exclaimed. She embraced Mia by the shoulders and delivered air kisses to each side of her face. "Thank you for coming on such short notice. I've got a helluva day ahead—big wig dinner to host tonight. I didn't know how I'd survive it without a massage from my favorite masseuse."

It wasn't so much a smile as a bearing of her teeth that Mia performed in response. "Happy to be of service, ma'am." Mia barely looked at the woman as she began to set up the massage table and adjust the room's settings. Encased in the perfect physique, the result of a personal chef, nutritionist, and trainer, Camila had a glow about her that not many women her age managed to hold onto. Her silvery gray hair shimmered in the sunlight streaming through the window. Mia tugged the gauzy drapes closed, casting the room in a relaxing, beige light. The problem with Camila was that she was so darn nice. It made disliking her next to impossible.

Mia reentered the room after instructing Camila to disrobe and drape the sheet over herself on the table. Laying on her stomach, Camila rested her head on her arms, her profile visible in soft, natural lighting. Mia studied the serenity of Camila's face. No worry lines marred it, nor frowns or frets. This was a woman who had not a concern in the world. She didn't stay up late worrying about how to pay her bills or make ends meet. She didn't worry about putting food on the table, caring for her family, or how she would be able to continue working into old age with retirement being a pipe dream. She didn't worry about how she might be able to afford to save her own life.

The carpet rose up to cradle Mia as she sank to the floor. Her vision was peppered with starbursts of dizziness. She drew in her knees to her chest, wrapping her arms around them. Her pit of a stomach howled at her. She was frozen in a world that slanted sideways and she couldn't move.

Someone touched her arm. Mia flinched.

"Mia, what's wrong?" Camila's voice was so gentle and kind that Mia pried her eyes open to look up at her. Inches from each other, Mia studied her face. She had to blink to make sure she wasn't seeing things. But no, Camila's skin had shed at least two decades of age since their last appointment. Her eyes were bright, her cheeks were the rosy hue of youth, not a hint of the ravages of age, and her lips were the full plump pout of someone much, much younger. In her own forehead, Mia felt her skin wrinkle with confusion. "Ms. Camila, you…you look so good."

The remark earned her a short laugh and a pat on the hand. "Thank you, I think? If I tell you a secret, will you share with me what's going on with you?" Camila smoothed back her hair, not waiting for Mia to respond, trapping her in an exchange of information she wasn't sure she wanted to participate in. "I was treated with nanodiamonds. Have you heard of them?"

A truck could've driven through Mia's eyes, they were so wide. She nodded.

Camila, with the sheet wrapped elegantly around her midsection as if it were evening wear, knelt on the floor next to Mia. "I see you have. Before you think me vain, this fountain of youth appearance was a side effect for my real intentions." She sighed and pressed her hands together as if in prayer. "I was diagnosed with a severe autoimmune disorder that was killing me rapidly. Regular nanomites were unable to treat it. So—" Camila waved her hand over her body. "Now, tell me what's going on with you. I can see it in your eyes. Something similar to what I felt. Are you okay?"

Mia chewed her bottom lip and shook her head. "No, ma'am, I'm not okay." Teardrops big as jewels dribbled down her cheeks. "I don't…" Mia sputtered and coughed back a sob. "I've got cancer. And I can't—"

Camila stood. "Don't say another word. How much do you need?"

"What?" The words came to her as if she were underwater. "I couldn't possibly take your money."

Camila bent and touched her fingertip to Mia's nose. "Don't be silly." She walked across the room to where her purse sat on the counter. Over her shoulder, "It'd be a loan. You can pay me back in massages."

The scratching of Camila's stylus on the digifile grated in Mia's ears. A sprawl of endless massages spread before her in her future. They curved in on themselves as she saw her own aging reflection in funhouse style mirrors going on forever and ever.

"Why?" Mia cleared her throat, speaking louder. "Why would you help me when the Senator—"

Camila glanced up with a gleam in her eye. "Oh dear. You don't really think we believe all that pish posh, do you?" She propped her elbow on the counter and rested her chin in her palm. "We actually would be for the Americare bill, quite frankly. If it didn't mean costing Grayson votes. We're aiming for the White House, to do some real good. And if that means Americare has to die along the way, so be it." She ripped the digifile off the pad.

Stewing on Camila's words, Mia hugged her knees tighter. The walls pushed in and her breath was stilted. Camila closed the distance between them.

Mia thought to warn Camila that she was about to trip, but she couldn't find her voice in time.

In a crash, the massage table leg felled Camila. She lay in a tangle of sheets, one arm flung over her lovely face. Mia crawled over to her. "Ms. Camila?" She prodded Camila's shoulder and Camila's arm slumped to the ground. An angry gash stretched across her forehead where she must've hit the table on the way down. From it poured her lifeblood, spreading in a crimson river down her temple and gathering in a growing pool on the floor. The red blood glared and shivered in the dim light of the room.

Mia's stomach growled.

***

"Mama! Will you turn that down?" From the kitchen, Mia laughed to herself as she pulled chocolate cake out of the oven. For weeks, she'd been preparing for Fiona's quinceañera and couldn't believe the day was here. Eager thumping on the stairs told her Fiona was excited.

Fiona floated into the room in her dress. She fluffed the rainbow ruffles and did a twirl. "Don't you love it?"

Mia closed the oven door, came around the counter, and held her daughter's hands. "It's beautiful." Mia kissed Fiona on the cheek. Tears misted her eyes. "I can't believe my little palomita is becoming a woman today."

Fiona shied away playfully. "Don't make me cry!"

She hugged her daughter to her, then spun her toward Tilda with a light tap on her bottom. "Go. Abuela has something for you." Mia leaned against the kitchen doorframe while she watched Tilda present Fiona with a tiny gift box drowned by a huge pink bow, neither of them having a clue how many pawn shops Mia scouted to track down the broach. Tilda pinned it to Fiona's dress, the three rubies winking in the light of the screen.

A sharp knock rattled their front door. Mia's insides fluttered with a brief bout of nerves. Ever since that day, she couldn't rid herself of the idea that someone might find her out. She grasped the doorknob and turned.

Big golden sunflowers bobbed in a bouquet. Dr. Aguilar lifted them in a gesture toward Fiona, but his eyes crinkled with a smile that was all for Mia. "I hear it's a big day for you."

With a peck on Aguilar's cheek and a thank you, Fiona disappeared with the flowers. Mia ushered Aguilar inside and closed the door behind him. "I'm so glad you came."

He flashed her a knowing smile. "Of course, I came. There's a lot for us to figure out. Together."

The news reporter buzzed in the background. *"Senator Grayson Grant and his wife Camila celebrate a landslide vote against the Americare bill today in the—"*

"TV, mute," Mia commanded.

Sara Crocoll Smith (she/her) writes science fiction, fantasy, and gothic horror. She's the author of the ghostly gothic horror series Hopeful Horror. She's also the publisher and editor-in-chief of Love Letters to Poe. You can learn more about her work at SaraCrocollSmith.com

Dale's Pie

by Elizabeth Estabrooks

Dale loved apple pie. Well, he liked apple pie. At least, he was pretty sure he would like apple pie. If he ever had a chance to taste one.

Dale had helped his great-aunt Maeve bake an apple pie every Sunday afternoon since his parents dropped him off at her house for the summer. On the floral print tablecloth in her bright-yellow kitchen, Dale peeled and cut the apples while Maeve mixed and rolled out the dough. Soon thereafter, the entire house filled with the aroma of baking apples and cinnamon. Dale thought it might just be the most wonderful smell he'd ever experienced.

Dale's parents didn't bake pies. They didn't buy pies either. In fact, Dale was a little surprised they'd left him in the care of Maeve with her pies, pastas, and well-used bread maker, considering they believed the evil of sugar was matched only by the evil of refined flour, and surpassed only by other forms of fine, white powder one acquired in disreputable clubs and back alleys after midnight—to quote Dale's father.

When Dale expressed this incredulity to Maeve, she pushed her black, horn-rimmed glasses up on her nose, stuck a fist on her hip, and suggested Dale might not know his parents as well as he thought he did.

"Your mother spent nearly every summer of her adolescence in this house," said Maeve. "And there were never any complaints about the menu, as far as I recall." She brushed the non-existent wrinkles from her apron and returned to the task of chopping carrots for supper. "In any case, you're here, and I'm tickled pink to have eight weeks of your company."

Dale had a feeling his mother had changed a bit since she'd last stayed with Maeve. As for the latter statement, he had no idea if it were true, but he didn't care. Not as long as staying with Maeve meant pie, spaghetti (the real kind, not the squash kind) and homemade bread with gobs of butter.

And then there was the molasses. All the dire warnings he'd ever received about cavities became meaningless the moment Dale got his first taste of fresh brown bread dipped in warm molasses. He'd sit in the dentist's chair on a weekly basis if that were the price he had to pay for a daily dollop of that syrupy goodness.

However, as much as Dale enjoyed the bread and spaghetti, it was the prospect of pie he had been most excited about upon his arrival at Maeve's house. Naturally, therefore, it was the pie that presented all the trouble.

The Sunday pies always came out of the oven at four o'clock. Unfortunately, supper wasn't until seven o'clock. Maeve had strict rules when it came to eating dessert before supper. Ok, one strict rule: no dessert before supper. In the meantime, the pie sat on the counter with a fresh-from-the-clothesline dishcloth draped over it.

Ginger the fat brown cat took up most of the remaining counter space (at least whenever Maeve was in the kitchen), purring softly with his front paws tucked under him and his tail curled around his backside. He reminded Dale of bread dough that had risen beyond the capacity of the bread pan.

The first Sunday, while the pie was cooling and the chicken was roasting in the oven, Maeve said she had to get the wash in off the line before the rain started. (There was a perfectly good dryer in the basement, but as far as Dale could tell, it had never been used.) Hamper pressed to her hip, she slid open the patio door and stepped out. With surprising grace, Ginger hopped from the counter and padded after her onto the porch.

Dale looked from the open door to the unattended pie and back. The smell of the pastry made his entire body tingle. He slid off his chair and crept over to the counter. No sooner had he lifted the cloth, and caught a fresh whiff of baked-apple sweetness, than Maeve materialized back in the kitchen and snatched the cloth from his hand.

"It'll taste just as good after supper," she said, placing the cloth back over the pie.

As they were eating supper, there was a knock on the door. It was Mr. Thompson. His dog had gotten loose; he wanted to know if Maeve or Dale had seen her?

Maeve told him they hadn't. If only she'd left it at that, but then she asked how Mrs. Thompson had let him leave the house without a raincoat in this downpour. He'd catch his death for goodness sakes.

Mr. Thompson informed Maeve that Mrs. Thompson was out of town visiting her sister. Upon receiving this information, Aunt Maeve put the whole pie in a plastic container and gave it to Mr. Thompson.

Dale's eyes stung as he watched Maeve hand over the pie. He swallowed hard. At eleven years old he was most certainly not going to cry over some stupid apple pie. Except, he didn't think it was stupid at all and, try as he might, couldn't hide his dismay.

"Don't worry, dear," Maeve said when she saw Dale's stricken face, "I've got a box of sugar cookies in the cupboard. That poor man lives on jerky and canned beans whenever his wife is out of town. We can't have that."

Dale didn't see why not, but thought it best not to argue. The sugar cookies were stale.

The second Sunday, there was no rain in the forecast, but Maeve went out to get the wash from the line anyway. This time, Dale got as far as taking a knife from the drawer. He would cut a generous piece, eat a tiny sliver (not enough to be noticeable) then set the rest aside and say he just wanted to make sure his piece had a good chance to cool. Maybe not a perfect plan, but better to beg forgiveness than…

The moment the blade touched the flaky pie crust, Maeve's voice bellowed from the backyard, "Don't even think about touching that pie until after supper!"

Defeated, Dale went to his room. He opened a comic book in hopes of distracting himself. He was still staring at the first page when he heard a shriek. He dropped the book and ran back to the kitchen.

He had forgotten to replace the cloth over the pie. Ginger was pleased. Maeve was not.

On the third Sunday, things got strange. Dale decided not to try sneaking a taste of pie before supper. He did, however, think it best to keep a close eye in case Ginger got any bright ideas. Dale sat in the kitchen and stared at the pie until Maeve came in to cook supper. He helped her wash and peel the carrots and potatoes. All the while, Ginger remained curled up on the counter under the microwave, sleeping. Or pretending to. With cats, one can never tell.

After dinner Dale watched, mouth watering, as Maeve cut him a fat slice of pie and put it on a white plate rimmed with tiny, green polka dots. She placed it in front of him and asked if he'd be ok by himself if she popped out to get some marmalade before the store closed.

Dale said he would be fine.

Maeve left. In response to her departure, Ginger left his post in the kitchen and made his way to the armchair closest to the living-room window where he could watch her drive away. He let out a mournful mew as though certain she would never return. Alone in the kitchen, trembling with excitement, Dale sank his fork into his pie.

That's when the gooblers came.

Probably not their proper name, if they had one, but that was the sound they made. That first bite of pie was on Dale's fork, halfway to his mouth, when he heard it.

Gooble, gooble, gooble.

He looked down, and there they were on the floor. Two little globular things with teeth and not much else in the way of discernable features.

The creatures curled themselves around the legs of the kitchen table and wriggled up with impressive speed, considering their lack of limbs. Dale sat there, fork frozen in midair. Deranged hamsters descended from packman, the gooblers devoured every last crumb of his pie. Including the piece on Dale's fork.

For a moment, the gooblers seemed unsure what to do next. Then one of them rotated in place. It let out a squawk and the two of them were on the move again. They dropped to the floor and started across the kitchen, toward the side of the counter where the remaining pie waited.

Dale's heart stuttered. Maeve would think it was him. She would think *he* ate the entire pie.

Around this time, apparently bored of the view out the front window, Ginger hit the floor with a thud and let out a *brrrwup*. The gooblers' progress toward the counter halted. As the click of Ginger's claws hit the ceramic kitchen floor, the round bodies of the gooblers squished until they were paper thin. They shimmied sideways to a crack between tiles, slid into it, and were gone.

When Maeve got home, Dale was still sitting, white faced, at the table staring at his polished-clean plate. Stammering over his words, he told her all about the gooblers.

"You're telling me a gopher got in here, ate your pie, and then took off?" said Maeve, eyeing the latched-shut patio door.

"Not a gopher, a *goobler*," Dale corrected. He then asked if he could have another piece. Considering the gooblers had eaten the first one, it seemed only fair.

"One piece of pie is plenty for one day," said Maeve.

"But—"

"And if you want any more pie in the future, you'd be wise not to make up outlandish stories."

***

That evening, Maeve brought the rest of the pie to Mrs. White next door. Mrs. White's hip was bothering her these days, and that made baking difficult.

Later that night, Dale lay awake staring at the exposed rafters in the ceiling. Every time he began to dose off, he could hear them—*gooble, gooble, gooble*—and startled awake, heart hammering. Finally, he gave up on sleep and got out of bead.

Ginger glared from the base of Maeve's bedroom door as the beam of Dale's flashlight washed over him. Dale headed downstairs.

In the kitchen, Dale examined every crack in the tile floor, but found nothing out of the ordinary. He slid open the patio door, and a cool breeze washed over his bare feet. Under the porch and along the foundation of the house were also unremarkable. There must have been a crack somewhere letting those things get under the kitchen floor, but Dale couldn't find it.

However they were getting in, there was also the question of where they were coming from. Dale hesitated on this thought. He wasn't entirely sure he wanted to know. But, fairly certain he had no chance of sleeping tonight anyway, he turned his flashlight away from the house toward the grass of the considerable backyard.

The gnarled remnants of an old apple orchard marked the end of Maeve's property. Dale zigzagged across the yard, sweeping the light back and forth in front of him, until he'd made his way to the treeline. Still not sure what he was looking for, he turned around for another pass.

Suddenly, Dale's foot dropped under him and his body lurched forward like he'd missed the last step on the stairs. The flashlight flew from his hand as his arms whipped out to save his balance.

His heel found earth with a jarring *thunk*, but at least he managed to avoid a faceplant. He picked up the flashlight, and swept it behind him, looking for the hole that had nearly taken him down. As it turned out, it he was still standing in it.

Rather than one of the rodent-sized sink holes that plague yards both rural and suburban, Dale found himself standing in a depression that reminded him of the cheap, saucer-like, plastic sleds owned by every kid he knew between the ages of six and thirteen. Only the diameter of this concavity was least three times as big. At its center most point, there was a deeper hole. This one did look like the creation of a gopher. Something squirming in Dale's gut told him it was nothing of the sort.

He shone his light into the gap. He saw nothing. But Dale could have sworn, if only for a second, that something hissed in response to the intruding light. Stomach in his throat, Dale pulled back from the hole.

Without much in the way of a thought, Dale put the flashlight down on the grass, pointing the beam off to the side of the not-a-gopher hole. He took armfuls of dirt, mud, branches, and whatever detritus had accumulated under the apple trees. He shoved everything into the hole that would fit, and them some. Scarcely aware of the twigs and small stones poking into his skin, he stomped the spongy mass down with his bare foot. Finally, he surveyed the woods until he found the largest rock he was able to lift. He used this to top off his handywork.

Satisfied, or at least telling himself he was satisfied, Dale returned to the side of the house. Afraid that running water inside would wake Maeve, he used the icy spray from the garden hose to wash the dirt from his hands and feet.

The digits on the bedside clock in Dale's room read 3:26. Birds were already starting their morning refrains as he snuggled under the heavy quilt and fell asleep.

***

On the fourth Sunday, Maeve wanted to pop over to see if Mrs. White was doing any better. She was going to bring the leftover pie again. Dale asked if she could wait to leave until after he ate his piece.

"Well of course, dear," she said. "Then you can come see Mrs. White with me. She'd love to see you."

The only previous interaction Dale had had with Mrs. White was the time he'd knocked on her door to request access to her backyard. He had been in the park adjacent to her house, tossing a baseball in the air and hitting it, when the ball went astray in the direction of Mrs. White's.

Thankfully, the ball hit a large cedar—the only living thing in an otherwise brown yard—rather than a window. The tree was no worse for wear, and Mrs. White had been nice about the whole thing. But Dale thought it a bit of a stretch that she would *love* to see him again. Still, he said he'd be happy to come visit her. It seemed like the right thing to say.

Supper dishes cleared, Maeve let Dale cut his own piece of pie. He brought it to the kitchen table, slowly. He was practically vibrating and was seriously concerned he might drop the plate.

He made it to the table safely. While Maeve busied herself at the sink across the room, Dale scooped up a large chunk of flaky pie. This was finally it.

Gooble, gooble, gooble...

Blood frozen, Dale looked down. The gooblers were already on their way up the table legs. Wide-eyed and open mouthed, Dale looked up to where Aunt Maeve had been standing. Maeve was gone.

One of the gooblers leapt onto the table and lunged at Dale's plate. Another landed on his arm, sending his forkful of pie up into the air then down to the floor where a third goobler waited, toothy orifice open, ready to catch it.

"Aunt Maeve!" Dale screamed.

At the sound of his voice, the gooblers froze. But in an instant, they were moving again. They plopped to the floor and flattened. Maeve came running out of the pantry, a jar of preserved peaches in one hand, a wet rag in the other, and an offended looking Ginger following at her feet. Once again, the gooblers slipped into the cracks between the floor tiles and vanished.

"What's wrong?" said Maeve, looking Dale up and down for signs of blood or missing limbs.

"My p...they were...and then they..." Dale stammered, pointing to the floor as Maeve took in the smear of smooshed apples and mashed crust spreading from his plate across the once-spotless tablecloth. Her face morphed from an alarmed stare to a wrinkled frown.

"Lord, have mercy," she snatched Dale's plate away.

"They came back," Dale said quickly, "The goo—"

"If the next word out of your mouth is some made up fantastical thingamajig," Maeve snapped, "you can forget about dessert in any form for the rest of the summer. I won't be hearing tall tales to explain away a careless mess."

Dale closed his mouth against the protest threatening to escape.

Instead of accompanying Maeve to Mrs. White's house, Dale spent the evening handwashing the tablecloth. As he hung the cloth on the line, his eyes drifted to the trees outlining the yard.

Maeve's property was easily two acres, probably more. He couldn't see the depression in the grass from the porch. With at least an hour remaining in the late-July day, Dale went back inside to get his sneakers (and a few other things).

***

The depression in the grass was bigger than Dale had realized when seeing it in the dark. It looked like the giant boulder from *India Jones* had taken a rest here. The hole at its center was still covered by Dale's rock. Of course it was. Rodents, terrestrial or otherwise, always had more than one exit in their burrows.

That was ok. Dale hadn't come to trap the gooblers in their hole. He had another idea. Dale had decided his chances of getting a piece of pie he could actually eat would greatly increase if Maeve believed him about the gooblers. And seeing was believing. He put a metal bucket down on the grass, from which he removed a hammer and a 2-lb bag of brown sugar.

"You guys have a such a sweet tooth?" Dale sprinkled the sugar throughout the dent in the ground, then along the treeline in both directions as far as he could before the sugar ran out. "Come and get it."

He rolled the rock off the hole. Then, a few feet away, up on his knees with the hammer held tight in both hands, he waited.

And waited.

And waited some more.

The yard was silent. The sugar remained untouched. Dale could no longer feel his fingers around the hammer's handle. The sky turned from robin-egg blue to navy.

Maeve's car crunched over the gravel driveway.

It suddenly occurred to Dale that if Maeve found him like this, waiting for boogie monsters to come out in the backyard, he might soon find himself explaining his actions to a kindly doctor, notepad in hand, with the type of concerned expression Dale suspected had to be practiced in front of a mirror. His knees and knuckles protesting the sudden motion, Dale gathered up his things and ran back to the house.

***

On the fifth Sunday, Dale asked to eat his pie in the formal dining room. No cracked floor tiles, no gooblers, he figured. Just in case, he also asked if Maeve would eat with him. Thus, she could be witness to any interesting developments.

"That would be nice," she said. "Just give me a minute to—"

The phone rang. Dale read it on Maeve's face long before the words 'I'll be right over' came out of her mouth.

Maeve was shaking her head as she hung up, "Mrs. White slipped trying to wash her front window," she was already moving toward the front hall, "If I've told her once I've told her a thousand times to hire that type of work out. But she's a stubborn one. You can serve yourself some pie, dear." She turned to him with a wagging finger, "Only one piece." She pulled on her coat, despite the muggy evening, "I promise we'll eat together next time." With that she was out the door.

Dale looked at the cloth-covered pie. His mind was divided. It smelled so good. Had looked so good coming, golden-brown, out of the oven. But, knowing the likely outcome, was it worth another try?

It was a brief deliberation. A slim chance was better than no chance.

Dale took a plate from the cupboard and a knife from the drawer. He elbowed Ginger aside to get some space on the counter and cut one triangle from the pie. A wide triangle. When he picked his plate up from the counter, Ginger quickly moved back into the empty space. Eyeing the cat's flipping tale, Dale replaced the dishtowel over the remaining pie.

He sat at the long, polished dining table, pie in front of him. He examined the pristine white carpet, and wondered who in their right mind would pick white for a carpet. That thought was immediately followed by grave concern for how much it sounded like something his mother would say. When nearly a minute had gone by with no signs, nor sounds, of gooblers, Dale picked up his fork.

Gooble, gooble, gooble.

Dale's stomach dropped as his eyes shot to the floor. There was nothing there.

Gooble, gooble, gooble.

He looked up in time to see the creature poke out from behind the hair of a cherub sitting on top of the pretentiously-ornate hutch. There was a crack in the plaster where the wall met the ceiling. When a second glob oozed out of it, Dale put down his fork and pushed back from the table. Better to let the little devils finish every crumb than explain pie stains on that snow-white carpet.

When Maeve got home, she asked Dale how the pie had tasted. He said it was the best one yet, then went to his room and found another comic book to read. Maeve took the leftover pie, along with a tuna casserole and half a dozen magazines—all with pictures of quilts on their covers—over to Mrs. White.

***

Midnight came and went and Dale, once again, found himself staring at the ceiling mulling over the gooblers. They ate pie, but hadn't been tempted out by plain sugar. Perhaps it was a taste for pastry in particular that drove them? He sat up, throwing off the covers.

Back to the hole in the yard with his bucket and hammer. This time, instead of sugar, Dale laid out a trail of pretzel-shaped cookies. Then he sat, hammer in hands, bucket at his feet. He waited, again, until his fingers went numb and his eyes started to blur.

Dale awoke with his shirt damp from dew on the grass and a dent in his right cheek where he'd fallen asleep on the hammer. He pulled himself upright, rubbing his jaw. Light was edging into the eastern sky. The cookies were untouched.

***

On the sixth Sunday, Maeve didn't eat pie with Dale as promised. Mrs. Thompson was travelling again. This time because her grandmother had taken a turn for the worse. Mr. Thompson was staying home with the dog.

By Dale's calculations, any grandmother of Mrs. Thompson's would have to be at least one hundred and thirty. How much worse of a turn could she have taken? Dale asked if he could still have a piece of the pie before Maeve took it for Mr. Thompson to eat with his beef jerky. Aunt Maeve said a partially-eaten pie was not a proper condolence offering, and not to be so insensitive.

The entire pie went to the Thompsons' house. Dale turned on the TV and consoled himself with the knowledge that a week without pie meant a week without seeing the gooblers.

Part of him did hope they might pay Mr. Thompson a visit. Preferably, while Maeve was there to see them. But when Maeve came home, she said only that the Thompson's really ought to look into hiring a professional trainer for that dog. It had hardly stopped barking the entire time she was there.

On the seventh Sunday, Maeve said yes when Dale asked to take his pie to his bedroom. No way they can make it to the second floor, he thought. At least, not fast enough to keep him from getting a bite or two.

Dale thought of something else too. The gooblers never went after the pie while it cooled on the counter. He had a pretty good idea why.

With his piece of pie in one hand, Dale scooped his free arm under Ginger's middle and lifted the twenty-five-pound ball of fluff off the counter. The cat objected with a low mewl, but was otherwise a docile deadweight for the trip up the stairs.

Dale plunked Ginger down on the bed and sat beside him, careful to balance the plate in his lap in such a way as to minimize the risk of crumbs falling on the sheets. A sense of satisfaction rose in him as he adjusted his back against the headboard.

For the three seconds it took Dale to situate himself, Ginger lay still with his eyes closed. Then, just as Dale prepared to take a bite, the cat's ears perked up. He looked around at nothing, stood, stretched, and hopped off the bed.

"Ginger," Dale called, in his most amiable voice.

Ginger sauntered out the door. His tail curled into a hook before disappearing.

"Here kitty, kitty, ki—"

Gooble, gooble, gooble. A goobler leapt onto the back of Dale's neck.

Dale reached around and grabbed the thing by the scruff. Or what would be its scruff, if it had a discernable neck. It jerked and twisted in his hand.

"Maeve!"

When there was no sound of feet on the stairs, he tried again, "Aunt Maeve!"

He pulled the goobler in front of him to ensure it would be the first thing Maeve saw when she entered the room. Another one crawled up his leg toward the pie. Dale kicked. The plate and pie flew across the floor. The plate shattered. The goobler stuck stubbornly to his jeans.

"Maaaeve!" The goobler in his hands rolled over and sank a dozen needle-like teeth into Dale's fingers. He yelped and let go.

Ten seconds later, they'd polished off the pie and were gone. Dale surveyed the shards of plate scattered everywhere. He suddenly hoped Maeve was well out of earshot and would stay that way long enough for him to get a broom and dispose of what Maeve would consider convincing evidence Dale should never be trusted with dessert food, or the associated kitchenware, ever again.

First, he went to the bathroom sink and ran his injured hand under cold water. Though there were many, the tooth pricks were small. Once the threads of blood were washed away, he could hardly tell they were there. Except for the throb that came with every beat of his heart to remind him.

Dale crept downstairs, placing each foot slowly to prevent any tell-tale squeaks, then down the hall. He poked his head around the corner. The kitchen was empty. A bright-orange square of paper was in the middle of the kitchen table.

Gone to the Jamisons'. Mrs. Jamison needs a hand with her lawnmower. Have a second piece of pie, if you like (not too big). I'll be back by 9. Pick a movie for us to watch.

Ginger had returned to his post beside the pie on the counter. Dale considered eating straight out of the pie dish, with Ginger standing (or snoozing) on guard beside him.

An image came to him of Maeve arriving home (he'd be too absorbed in what he was doing to hear her stealthy approach of course), only to find him plowing into the whole pie. He had a

243

feeling that wouldn't go over well. Dale flexed his aching hand and decided he wasn't hungry anymore.

***

It was now the last Sunday in August, and Dale's parents were due to pick him up on Tuesday. He would be back in the land of no pie.

Dale had spent the entire week deciding where to take his pie this time. He'd given up on finding a place with no cracks for the gooblers to get in. Instead he took his plate to the porch, along with a magazine from beside Aunt Maeve's rocking chair, and the metal bucket from the garage.

He didn't bother with the hammer. Instead he thought he would approach the gooblers the way his mother approached disposing of a spider. With a few modifications. He set the magazine down in the middle of the porch, put the pie on top of it, and stepped back to wait.

Nothing happened.

Dale kept the bucket tucked under one arm and picked up the fork with his other hand. He scooped up a big hunk of pie and brought the gooey, golden bite toward his mouth. For one elated instant, he thought he might actually get to eat it.

When the pie was millimetres from Dale's lips, five of them slid up through the porch slats and fell into flat circles—like the peel-off holes cartoon characters pull from their pockets and apply to surfaces as needed. *Gooble, gooble, gooble*, they puffed into balls and closed in their target.

Dale dropped the fork and slammed the bucket down over the pie plate. Three of the gooblers rolled back, flattened, and vanished into the porch. The bucket rattled with the indignance of the other two.

A sliver of brown-black edged out from under the bucket rim. Dale sat on the bucket, pressing all his weight into it, but the sliver grew into a crescent spreading toward the edge of the magazine.

"Maeve...*Maeve!*"

Metal glinted near Dale's toe. He reached, doing his best not to let up his hold on the bucket. The crescent was larger now. Nearly half the goobler was free. Dale's fingers wrapped around the fork handle.

"Maeve!"

He stabbed the fork down so hard it sank through the goobler and into the magazine's pages. The goobler squealed and tried to retreat, nearly pulling the fork from Dale's hand. Footsteps moved through the front hall. Dale's heart leapt in relief and gratitude at the sound.

"Heavens. If you've made a mess of my—"

Maeve stopped halfway through the screen door. Her eyes went to the thing rippling and squirming under Dale's fork. For a moment she just stared, colour draining from her face. Then she turned and strode back into the house.

Sweat rolling down his back, Dale gaped at the empty doorway. He couldn't spare the energy to shout for her to come back. The bucket started to pivot. It was all he could do to keep the magazine between the goobler and the gaps in the porch. His arms ached, begging him to let go.

Might as well, he thought. *Even if I could catch one...*

He was about to let up his weight on the bucket—at least Maeve had finally seen the thing—when Maeve reappeared in the doorway. She was holding a 22.

"Count of three," she said, matter of fact. "Jump as far off the porch as you can."

Bug-eyed, Dale nodded.

"One...two...*three!*"

Dale dove off the porch.

245

The shot was followed by a screech. The bucket went flying, and a goobler rolled down the steps onto the grass beside Dale. It was still (with a fork hanging from its middle).

Gooble, gooble. The other one rolled between Meave's feet and through the open door.

"Dang!" said Maeve. "You never said there was a second one." She ran into the house.

Dale ran after her. There was a thump and a crash. He made it to the kitchen in time to see Maeve lunge at the goobler with the butt of her rifle. She missed.

The butt landed in the pie. Momentum carried it across the counter and over the edge. Plate and pie shattered together in a kaleidoscope of sticky crust and ceramic. Ginger, previously napping serenely under the microwave, hissed and darted for the bathroom. The goobler landed on the tile and started to flatten.

"Don't even think it," said Dale.

He stepped into the bathroom, grabbed the offended cat and launched the yowling, spitting ball of fur at the twisting, wiggling ball of…goobler.

Frantic squeaks and deep caterwauls took over the kitchen.

Claws scratched tile.

A chair toppled.

More squeaks and squalls.

Quiet.

Ginger strolled back to the bathroom with a ribbon of goobler hanging from his mouth.

Maeve took in the state of her kitchen. Her eyes stopped at a clump of pie crust by her foot. She looked more through it than at it.

"I take it those were the goo…gooler…"

"Gooblers," said Dale.

Maeve took a deep breath in through her nose, held it for a few seconds, then blew out slowly through her mouth. "All right then," she said, with a bit of a tremble. She nudged the crumbs with her toe, reached for a broom, then thought better of it and grabbed a full roll of paper towel. "I guess this means I owe you an apology."

"It's ok," said Dale. He picked up a large mass of apple goo and pie crust and threw it in the garbage—Maeve came along behind him wiping the floor with a handful of dampened towels.

He gave Maeve a little smile, "If I were you, I wouldn't have believed me either."

She paused and smiled back, her eyes remaining apologetic. Together they continued to scoop up the smashed pie (and other gooey substances Dale tried not to examine too closely) from the floor and scrub away the residue.

Maeve tossed out a sticky bunch of paper towels and pulled another length from the roll. She turned on the tap and ran them under the water. She seemed to forget what she was doing. The paper turned to a gob of white mulch in her hands.

"You ok?" said Dale.

Maeve blinked and her face cleared. Wringing out the paper towels, she smiled again. More confidently this time. "Fine, dear. "I'm sure those things will keep their distance now that Ginger has a taste for them."

The cat was back on his perch beneath the microwave, slit eyes fixed on the spot under the table where the final battle had taken place.

Maeve took a bucket out from under the sink, added a healthy squirt of dish soap, and started filling it with warm water. A mound of bubbles rose to the rim.

Her brow narrowed, "I'd like to know where they came from though."

"I have a pretty good idea about that," said Dale.

***

247

Maeve and Dale stood at the edge of the depression in the yard. Dale explained his failed attempts to lure the creatures out and catch one for her to see.

"I thought they went after my pie because it was sweet, but—"

"The trees," Maeve interrupted.

"What about them?" Dale followed her gaze upward. "They look the same as they have all summer." Only as he said it, he realized it wasn't quite true. A number of them sported more than a few broken branches, and patches of leaves had been stripped away.

"They should be filling with good-sized apples by now," Maeve said.

There wasn't a single apple to be seen.

Dale looked at the hole near their feet. "You think they ate them all?"

"Something must have."

"Apple loving aliens," mused Dale. "Go figure."

Maeve looked down at him, eyebrows raised, "Don't be absurd."

"This could be where their space ship landed and dropped them off," said Dale, outlining the round dent in the earth with a sweep of his arm.

"So they could steal all the apples from a defunct orchard?" said Maeve. "Then what? Take over the world with apple sauce?"

A few holes in the theory, perhaps. But Dale didn't think he'd be able to shake the idea.

"The university in town does a fair amount of bio-tech stuff," continued Maeve. "These gooblers, as you call them, are probably escaped rats with a few important gene changes. I'll make some phone calls tomorrow. There's probably a lab tech or grad student freaking out over some lost specimens.

"And that," she pointed to the depression in the earth, "is nothing but an unstable bit of soil that collapsed as they dug their den underneath."

Dale looked at the sloping ground. *Lab rats?* He didn't buy it.

"Go to the garage," said Maeve, maybe reading his face. "You'll find a half-full gas can in the back corner. And there should be some matches by the fire place," her eyes went to the hole in the ground, "You and I are going to do a little pest control."

"You said someone at the university would be looking for them," said Dale.

"And I'll gladly let whoever it is know where their creatures ended up, but I think the next pie should be eaten by you and me. Don't you agree?"

Dale made a beeline for the garage.

***

Dale sat in the middle of the now-gleaming kitchen floor watching the pie turn brown under the glow of the oven light. Maeve sat at the table with a freshly-bathed Ginger purring in her lap. (There hadn't been much purring *during* the bath).

Contentment filled Dale from his toes to his ears. He didn't even mind that, before long, the closest thing to dessert in his daily life would be raw almonds drizzled with 90% cocoa. But that thought triggered another.

"What should we tell Mom and Dad," Dale asked.

"About what?" said Maeve.

"The gooblers."

"Heaven's sake. Not a thing. Not if you want a chance at coming back next summer. And don't mention the rifle either. I told your mother I got rid of it two years ago."

"You want me to come back next summer?" asked Dale.

Maeve looked at him like he'd gown a second head, "Of course I do."

Dale turned his gaze back to the oven, a wide smile on his face. The timer dinged.

Warm, sweet air drifted over them as Maeve opened the oven door. Dale took a deep breath.

There was a knock. A voice called from the front hall.

"Anybody home?"

Like plugs had been pulled from the soles of his feet, all the excitement drained from Dale. It was his mother's voice. His heart sank even further when his parents strode into the kitchen.

"I know we're a bit early," his mother was saying.

"They're calling for torrential rain over the next few days," Dale's father added. "We thought we'd better get a head start on the drive…"

At that moment, both Dale's parents looked straight at the pie Maeve was placing in the middle the table. For a second that felt like an hour to Dale, no one moved or spoke. Then something happened that made his entire sense of reality shift sideways.

"That looks great," his dad exclaimed.

"And smells even better," said his mom.

Maeve winked at Dale and went to the cupboard. She came back with four plates. Dale looked from his mother, to his father, and back to his mother again as they pulled up chairs and sat down. Dale remained standing, staring.

"You mean you're going to have some?" Dale finally said.

"Are you kidding?" said his mother. "No one makes pie like Aunt Maeve."

The sensation of unreality was making Dale dizzy, "And…*I* can have some?"

Dale's father let out a deep, hearty laugh, "Like you haven't been enjoying Maeve's cooking all summer. What's another piece of pie going to hurt?" The laughter subsided, but the smile in his eyes remained, "Just don't get too used to it. Vacation has to end sometime."

"Speaking of," said Dale's mother, looking at Maeve, "Did you read that book on low-carb diets I gave you?"

"Eat your pie, dear," said Maeve, lifting a slice onto a plate.

"When we dropped Dale off, you commented on how good I was looking. You know why that is, don't you?"

"Good genes," said Maeve.

Dale's parents exchanged a look of somewhat-amused exasperation. Dale was still staring at them when Maeve cut into his trance, "Are you having a piece, or not?"

She slid a piece that was almost a full quarter of the pie in front of the fourth, still empty, chair. Dale's parents were already digging in.

Certain this was too good to be true, Dale scanned the floor. No movement. He listened. No *gooble, gooble.*

With a reassuring nod from Maeve, Dale sat down. He picked up his fork and stuck it into the pie so hard flakes of crust flew into his face. He didn't notice. He barely chewed before going in for a second bite.

***

Whether it was the cat, or the burned-out burrow, the gooblers didn't dare return to Maeve's house. But around the time Dale and his family were pulling into their own driveway, and Maeve was climbing into bed with Ginger curled up at the foot, a large black sphere settled into the grassy field of an abandoned fruit farm a few towns away.

Elizabeth Estabrooks enjoys the speculative side of science almost as much as the real thing. Her writing has appeared in Mad Scientist Journal and the anthology Time Travel Short Stories (Flame Tree Publishing). She grew up in New Brunswick and currently lives in Kingston, Ontario. Learn more about Elizabeth at www.elizabethestabrooks.com

Adaptive Predictor

by J. L. Royce

On Wednesdays I visit David; late afternoon, but not too late—I don't want to watch them try to feed him.

For a time, I felt it necessary to mix up the schedule, make sure he was being cared for when I wasn't expected. But after a while I realized it was unnecessary: he was always clean and closely supervised. So I settled into a routine: Wednesday afternoon.

Besides, I didn't want to run into his family, and I was sure the feeling was mutual. They never understood why the court-appointed me his *guardian ad lidem*, and resented it, suspecting some dark plot, because I became the acting CEO—and they never got the full story.

Sometimes I read to David—not novels or newspapers, but market reports and the occasional MD&A from an interesting 10-Q. He stops mumbling and fondling himself (which is a relief), and listens intently. I can almost imagine that the old dead-eyed shark is still swimming around inside there.

Before I leave, Willis gives me a weekly report, and it's always the same: no change.

"I want to arrange transportation to UMC," I told him last Wednesday. "We're going to try some TMS while scanning."

"Is this research, or treatment?" the neurologist asked me. "David is considered part of a vulnerable population."

"And as his guardian, I can consent him into studies." I didn't have to remind him where his research funding came from.

"Besides," I said, "Who knows? His connectivity is unique; what we learn might help him—and us."

***

I met David when he hired me as Director of Marketing at Adaptive Research, a little over a year ago. The Board wanted the company to diversify from the military command and control applications into 'some civilian market' and had decided that market could be autonomous Personal Assistants for the business environment. Think: 'Alexa, project the impact of corporate tax rate cuts on net income year over year.'

He had a *reputation*, so nothing came as a total surprise to me. Dynamic executive, ruthless competitor, loyal friend, inveterate womanizer. He can be a little hard to stomach, sometimes. A story would help.

We were at the Charthouse, on the coast road south of Palo Alto, entertaining the VC folks. Entertainment went beyond dining. This was some years back, and don't start on how inappropriate it all was; I know that. We knew it even then. We didn't care; it was just business—or that's what I told myself.

Dinner was Pacific fresh catch, California wines, and the usual artisanal treatment of local produce. David had eased the guests through the meal with a minimum of business accomplished, which I thought was a waste. But that was my tactical thinking, and why he was the deal-maker and *I* worked for *him*.

David was still dressed for business, the only concession to the late hour being the unbuttoned jacket of his gray suit. He had that far-off look he got sometimes when he was using both sides of his brain, what he liked to call 'the pleasure with the pain'. He was laying out the agenda for tomorrow to the guests, commencing with a 10 am breakfast at their hotel, but his attention was focused on the hostess who had seated us earlier. Finally, his eyes came back to the table.

"Gentlemen, I must take my leave, but my trusted Veep will see that your needs are met." He smiled at me, that reptilian smile that meant this was would be more pleasant for him than me.

I'd noticed a trio of young ladies arrive sometime during coffee. They waited discretely in the wings, idling over drinks, laughing and flirting with the handsome bartender.

"Why don't you just make some new friends at the bar?"

David stood, shot his cuffs, and stepped behind me, bending to speak confidentially.

"Settle the bill, I gave the maître d' our account." An envelope came out of his jacket pocket, and he placed it on the table near my hand. "For the entertainment."

One of the guests, listening, chuckled.

"Excuse me," David announced to the table. "Enjoy your evening." With that, he strolled off.

I picked up the envelope and hurried after him, catching his elbow.

"What is it, Constance?" he said, without slowing.

"You expect *me* to pay your girls?"

David finally stopped and turned on me.

"Not mine," he said. "I've never paid for a woman—I've never had to."

He smiled past me at the trio; one of them noticed and returned it. The cleavage of her little black dress was so deep, I couldn't imagine how she kept herself in place.

"They're for our guests —" he looked at me again "—but you can keep one for yourself if you'd like."

He continued walking, and as I watched, the hostess noticed his approach. He was casual, unhurried, engaged her in conversation, a hand lightly placed on her arm. A light laugh; a smile; a nod. Making plans for the evening.

I turned back to the guests, who were now at the bar, laughing loudly with the girls, laughing at nothing but themselves.

***

David's family—ex-wife and two grown children—thinks he appointed me his guardian because we were lovers, which was patently ridiculous. He was never rude, but clearly, we were never attracted to each other. For my part, I'd rather kiss a crocodile. Still, there was an inevitable intimacy to our relationship—an intellectual passion, or obsession—that we shared.

The fact was, he knew his family would not understand the scope of what he hoped to accomplish; their concern would be financial security and a bit of fame, bragging rights. They almost got more fame than they would have liked.

Around six months ago, I learned about Yankee Hill. A girl from Accounting wanted to see David about some expenses that she couldn't properly characterize. He was out of the country, so his admin pushed her in my direction.

I recall looking up from my screen, where an uninspired prototype marketing pitch was playing out, and slipped out an earbud.

"Ma'am —"

"Constance." She was healthy and attractive (if a bit tentative), and I tried to smile, but I was swallowing my jealousy.

Have you ever wished you could just buy someone else's youth? I don't mean beauty; I mean years—about twenty, in this case. Years to spend on a beach, reading all the books you'd promised you would read someday, meeting people in exotic places, taking lovers where fate offered them. That was my thought as she fidgeted in the doorway.

I stared at her over my reading glasses. "What can I do for you?"

"There are some expenses with C-level authorization, but I don't know if they're advertising, marketing, administration —"

I cut her off before she could go through the entire chart of accounts.

"Sure—Barbara, right?"

"People call me 'Babs'," she said, handing me the tablet she'd been clutching.

I scrolled it around. "This memo, 'Yankee Hill'—does it appear in last quarter's report?"

"No ... they're all new."

There were several suppliers, but most of the expenses were coming from the University Medical Center—scanner charges and consulting fees. I highlighted several of the items, then flicked them over to my screen.

"Did you find a 'Yankee Hill' category under R&D?"

Babs shook her head (blonde curls, very nice) and I continued, "Then put it under 'Marketing Research'."

She took her tablet back and scuttled out of my office, which should have been the end of my role. As fate would have it, my curiosity was piqued, and on impulse, I opened a search window and started trolling the consultants' backgrounds.

Side by side, it made for an intriguing team: neuromarketing, I could understand; voice analysis and non-verbal body cues also seem like a marketing focus; but there was also psycholinguistics, propaganda, cult indoctrination, enhanced interrogation ... Defense contracts were heavily featured in their backgrounds.

An hour went by, dipping into patents and papers and grants—*oh my*. I closed the browser with a swipe and ran my hands over my face. The possibilities were headache material; it was just another explanation I would have to wheedle out of David, on his return.

***

When he came back into the office, I arranged with David's admin to squeeze in a little *tete a tete* for reviewing 'marketing research'. I had no intention of blind-siding the man, but I did want to keep the details out of the record.

David arrived in my office looking tanned and dressed down, in a sports jacket and open collar on his dress shirt.

"Howdy, Butch," he said, grinning as he slouched into a guest chair.

(His nickname was 'Buzz'—a haircut once upon a time, I think—and at some point, he started calling me 'Butch'. I didn't appreciate it, and the rest of the staff knew better than to use it— at least to my face. Why do people do these things? I don't know.)

"Very productive trip," he said. "Big things coming, very soon—China is ripe for the picking, with the right government sponsorship."

"Yankee Hill."

His gray eyes flickered, but his smile only widened. "Knew you were sharp when I hired you, Connie; didn't know you were psychic."

"Care to fill me in?"

"What do you think?"

"I see a lot of pieces but not the picture," I said. "Voice recognition, facial recognition, and emotional analysis —" I looked up "—applied to 9-1-1 calls, for military intelligence …" I trailed off, as he was slowly shaking his head.

"We're not going to waste our time on contracts with the intelligence community. The overhead is ridiculous; they detest the publicity we love; they object to our I-9 slaves; then there's all those background checks …" He paused to look at me. "Anything to disclose?"

"My life's an open book," I replied. "Yankee Hill—come to the point."

"The point ..." he leaned back, pushing the door shut before lacing his fingers behind his head. "Let me ask you something, Connie: what *is* marketing?"

"Persuasion."

"Close enough." That reptilian grin. "What if I told you we could perfect the art of persuasion—automate it. Integrate it with the next generation of personal assistants."

I pushed my tablet across the desktop, displaying the collection of scientific studies I'd harvested.

"You think all this analysis of human communication will tell you what to sell people? That's just pattern recognition, tracking cookies, Likes on social media."

"Not at all—that's just input," David replied, shaking his head. "I can know what someone wants and still not manage to sell it to them. I'm talking about perfecting *persuasion*, interactive persuasion."

"A sales bot?" I asked. Perhaps my tone betrayed my incredulity, but I *was* intrigued.

"Why not? But that's just an oversimplification. We're not just pasting words together—we'll embed the emotional cues in the speech generation—the non-verbal message in the voice."

"Persuasion," I repeated. "And when were you planning to let the rest of us know about this?"

"You mean, tell my head of Marketing?" Grinning, he continued, "I'd say now. Why don't we start by opening the kimono at next Tuesday's executive committee meeting?"

He rose to go. "I'll send you the rest of my research and some ideas on a deployment schedule. Okay?"

"Sure." What else could I say? *I wish to report a fait accompli?* I wanted to ask if a trip to China had anything to do with this.

"What could you 'sell' with this technology?"

He paused in my doorway.

I went on. "Meaning, is it limited to concrete things like cars and mobile phones, or could it be used for more … abstract sales?"

David shrugged. "A good salesperson can sell anything."

Then he was gone, leaving me to wonder just what the Chinese government would like to *sell*, and to whom.

***

It's called *ideation*. David laid out the technology, then demanded five-minute pitches from the staff around the table.

"Healthy food alternatives, in a grocery delivery app." Sondra was up at six every morning in the Sun Salutation, drank Kombucha, and looked it.

David nodded. "Margin?"

Sondra's world-changing enthusiasm faltered. "General grocery market … not great—but specialty items …" David had already turned away to stare at Bertie, who looked apologetic at the thought of having to open his mouth.

"Well?"

The young man glanced left and right as if checking for another Bertie hiding behind him, then spoke.

"Phones," he said. "An advisor to sell customers high-end phone features."

David was already nodding. "Why *features*? Do media campaigns for phones focus on features?"

Bertie opened his mouth, closed it, and shook his head.

David riffed on the notion, prowling around the table. "You're young, you're hip, so you have the latest X-Y-Z phone, right? And what are you doing with that phone?"

Now Bertie was nodding. "Having fun—with people—showing other people—people you want to be like —"

I let the junior staff express themselves (and wear David down), waiting for one or more of them to see beyond product sales. Perhaps this preoccupied me because of the independent background search I had done before confronting David, but I wondered when he would have publicized this work had I not.

The flow of ideas began to slow, and I spoke.

"We might think beyond retail promotion …"

The others looked around but volunteered nothing.

"Oh, come on," I said, "*politics* is full of marketing opportunities. What is the promotion of a policy position, but marketing? Emphasizing its strengths, minimizing the discussion of weaknesses …" I was starting to warm to my subject.

"You could personalize the argument to each listener, adapt it to the individual's experience," one suggested.

"You mean just telling them what they want to hear," someone else said.

"No," David disagreed, "speaking to someone about what he or she needs to *confess*. Whether it's a lost job, or illness, a child's addiction, a spouse's infidelity …"

The rest of the room was staring at him; it didn't sound like just politics anymore. He closed the meeting abruptly and I was left wondering just where we were taking this project.

"*Confess?*" I caught up with him in the hallway, heading back to his office.

"Not in the moral sense—unless you want to go into the religion business. Just admitting one's shortcomings, that life can be out of your control."

"Why?"

"Admitting you have a problem clears the way to asking for help from a higher source."

He had lost me; I wouldn't understand until later.

"C'mon Connie, think. It opens the door to suggestions of how to relieve the pain. Like a change in leadership, a change in government—or keeping the government, and changing the attitude towards it."

He walked away.

***

Yankee Hill was a neighborhood that attracted a lot of the University types—where some of the project members lived. It was just north of the campus, not far from the city. I never bothered to visit—there was no lab, no shared space, just computing resources and University offices scattered around the campus.

The recipients of our funding all seemed legitimate, and with remote workers, I saw no cause for concern about the lack of brick-and-mortar investment. The bills for cloud services told the story: most of the money was going into the upload of video for analysis. One researcher was consuming an inordinate amount of cloud AI, a Dr. Ferguson Woller—in the Philosophy Department, of all places. Curious, I arranged to meet him for coffee near the campus.

Open-collar shirt and jeans, frayed-looking sport coat—no lab coat. He was pretty unassuming, with an almost-shy smile. I put him in his forties.

"Thank you for seeing me, Dr. Woller." I spread out a collection of legal documents and internal reports as bona fides. While he studied them I began.

"So you're in the Philosophy Department. I looked up the term *epistemology*, and I was wondering why it required so much cloud storage and AI."

Ferguson blinked. "Yankee Hill is a conversant, based on a deep belief system. That requires an enormous amount of training data, which we have tagged to describe the logical assertions present."

"Belief in what, exactly?"

Blink. "Well, whatever we want to train it to believe in."

"And what can it do with these beliefs?"

Ferguson took out a tablet bulging in his jacket pocket and looked around as if he was going to share something NSFW. We were off in a corner, and the lunch crowd had departed, leaving only a few café-office types with headphones on and faux intent expressions. He unlocked the device, tapped a few times, and brought up what looked like an app work in progress—an inelegant mess of buttons, pull-downs, and various signal displays.

"Start by reading the statements—to establish the voice recognition," the researcher said to me. He pressed a Start button and slid the tablet towards me.

I did as he asked, the sentences appearing one at a time, evolving as I read. They weren't your typical verbal test patterns; in fact, some could be construed as inflammatory, and I meant to ask him about that. By the time I had done a half-dozen, I was beginning to wonder how long it would take; then the tablet spoke.

"Hello Constance; it's nice to finally meet you." The voice was female, pleasant but not gushing; business-like.

I glanced at Woller, who had a look of eager anticipation on his face.

"Have we met?" I asked. I didn't recognize the speaker (and learned later that the voice was wholly synthetic).

"Your reputation precedes you," the voice replied. A window popped up, filled with articles, memos, conference call transcripts, and started scrolling away. Another window started cycling through pictures of me, not all from work events.

I saw a Mute button and touched it.

"Is this some kind of joke? Because I don't have time —"

Ferguson interrupted. "This is an unrehearsed, cold-start learning demo."

"So it figured out who I am from my voice." I could believe that.

"That's right, Constance," the tablet said.

I glared at Ferguson. "Hello … 'Mute'?"

He shrugged. "You didn't turn off the camera. A trick she learned from HAL."

Shaking my head, I un-Muted my microphone and resumed the conversation.

"Why should I hire you?" I said to her. (I can't help it, she wasn't going to remain an 'it'. At the same time, I realized that a male voice would probably always remain at 'it' to me.)

Barely a pause, and it—she—replied, "You're busy, you have important responsibilities at Adaptive Research."

An org chart popped up, but augmented with several layers including informal responsibilities and relationships, like organizational wormholes connecting departments and divisions.

"I can help."

Another window popped up; I immediately recognized my Inbox. A moment later, about a third of the items were highlighted, then disappeared.

"Hey!"

"I've switched most of your daily news sources to weekly. The daily sources are redirected to me for review and inclusion in a single daily briefing."

My calendar appeared next: several meetings and conference calls went from Required to Optional. "I will be your proxy for these meetings," she said. "If the agenda deviates from the projected course, I will alert you. All meetings will be transcribed and reduced to digest format."

I noticed two sets of radar graphs that seemed to be subtly changing. "Ferguson, what's HEXACO?"

The researcher reached over and put the tablet to sleep, then turned it over. "Just in case," he smiled.

I wasn't convinced. "You do know there's a camera on the back, too?" I took the device, put it into my bag, and closed it.

"I'll want that back," he said. "I'm on a budget."

"Sure. HEXACO?"

"It's another model of human personality. The one graph was you, as deduced from the audio, video, and your online persona. The other was Yankee Hill's conversant, as tailored to you."

"You mean, its personality is based on mine?"

"No; its personality is evolving to *complement* yours; to become more worthy of your trust."

"So it could learn to be somebody's BFF?"

Ferguson looked skeptical. "I wouldn't call it a friend exactly. It's been designed to guide—manipulate—the beliefs of humans."

"So you're customizing ads?" That wasn't worth *any* budget.

"No—just the opposite —" he looked momentarily irritated, then recovered "—it can be used in conjunction with cultural imprinting in broadcast media—mass marketing—reinforced advertising messages—to influence your planning, your purchasing —"

He was getting pretty excited, and I was trying not to display *my* feelings.

"Friends?" I asked.

"Certainly." He thought about it. "For example, by prioritizing social media messages from friends who reinforce the target marketing message."

I made up my mind. "Can I take it with me?" I looked at him steadily; he knew I was gathering up the purse strings, in my mind.

"I'll see what I can do, add you to the authorization list for the alpha release. Just go to the corporate store and search for Yankee Hill—after tomorrow."

He'd found someone to be nerdy with; I had him. "There's potential here. I can help you, but I need access. I want to try multiple personalities—train on other people. I assume it's firewalled."

"The application? Yes; the prototype can't live on the net—it's in an isolated sandbox clone of the corporate net, which gets wiped every night. Nothing gets changed."

More questions rose in my mind, but they could wait. "Make sure I get access."

Rising to go, I paused. "One more question; does it have a name?"

Ferguson shifted uneasily. "Nothing official …"

"What are you calling it?"

"Patsy."

I laughed. After Siri, Alexa, Ross, and the like, I found it refreshingly average.

"*Patsy*; that's good."

He extended a hand and we shook, but his hand remained out. "Can I have my tablet back now?"

***

Over the subsequent weeks, I got to know Patsy pretty well. Some of our interactions were actually revealing.

"What's your gender, Patsy?"

"What do you want me to be? I can use a masculine voice —" the latter delivered in a theatrical baritone.

"No thanks; I've listened to enough male voices for one lifetime. I meant to ask, when you think of yourself, are you male or female?"

Woller had warned me that topics veering towards introspection could produce unusual results.

Patsy replied, "What if we agree that I walk like a woman and talk like a man?"

I laughed.

"Do you want to hear the song?" Patsy inquired.

"No…" An idea had been forming in my mind, one I had avoided until I had to simply embrace it. It was like the first time I realized I was attracted to another woman and allowed myself to pursue her.

"I'm going to prepare you for a sort of Turing Test, of emotional awareness," I said. "You're going to train on a series of … test subjects' recorded interactions; and then I'm going to let you interact with a subject, live."

"That sounds interesting, Constance."

Now before you start going all HR on me, let me explain: their employment contracts inform all of our full-timers that corporate communications systems—voice, web conference, email, texting—are recorded, and the property of ARX. Why anyone would use our systems for personal conversations is beyond me, but people do.

We started with a couple of easy exercises that could prove useful. After several failures, Patsy defined a personality that could cold-call into Adaptive Research and get past the first-line assistants to speak to department heads. (I chose executives who couldn't be reached via the automated phone tree.) We ran a model of pitching charitable donations and confirmed the factors in the pitch that practically guaranteed success: patriotism, children, community.

The first tests were on our own employees, but I realized that too many calls of one kind might arouse suspicion. So I decided to bend the alpha test rules a little bit.

"You're going to be on speaker," I told Patsy, "and the other party is on a personal phone I have, also on speaker." I had bought a pre-paid telephone so the calls couldn't be traced back to our office, or me—and Patsy wouldn't be connected to the company's outside lines.

In the guise of a potential customer, Patsy called a competitor and succeeded in extracting useful details about an impending product release we weren't aware of before.

I figured we were ready for the next level of play, Patsy and I.

"Let's see what you can do with Babs." I brought up her personal page to ensure Patsy identified the right person.

"You'll want to …" I trailed off. Patsy knew what to do.

Hours of phone calls streamed by in minutes. Patsy displayed a cluster analysis of HEXACO findings.

Like most of us, Babs responded slightly differently to some types of people than others. Patsy supplied labels for the clusters: Work-Parallel, Work-Superior, Personal-Casual, Personal-Intense.

"Let me hear a conversation," I requested, touching the latter cluster.

It was both embarrassing and intriguing. Babs was asking someone she'd only met online for a face-to-face date. He had turned her down.

"Construct a conversant to complement that cluster," I said. "Time for your first real test."

I tapped the HEXACO profile generated for their latest experiment, 'Patrick.' When she displayed the psychographics of her proposed personality, I asked, "Why isn't it the same?"

"I analyzed the subject's socioeconomic sub-population to find the traits she was responding to most favorably in social settings: self-confidence, honesty, cheerfulness, patience."

"And that gives you … Patrick?"

"Yes."

***

I prepared a simple objective for Patsy a/k/a Patrick: take an online dating service contact to an accepted face-to-face meeting.

It's not as hard as you'd think: just another sales scenario, qualifying a lead, taking the sales process to the next stage.

The textual interactions would be straightforward, but I wondered what to do for a physical presence. It turned out Yankee Hill had an experiment in avatar construction, taking the NVIDIA work with GAN synthetic faces and animating it. That gave us a basic model.

"I have taken the most highly correlated physical traits driven by the positive HEXACO factors," Patsy told me.

The race and age were set by Babs' profile on the dating app and her past encounters. The result was surprisingly bland; not unattractive, but too … average. Average brown hair, average tan complexion, average brown eyes.

My first thought was to tell Patsy to sharpen it up, somehow, but I realized that the data doesn't lie. We went ahead with average Patrick.

The synthetic social media presence featured Patrick inserted into outdoor scenes (again, nothing too extraordinary—hiking, the beach, picnics) and a few bar/restaurant crowd scenes. It was all manipulated stock footage, where no one else was quite recognizable.

No need to belabor the point: we broke Babs' heart.

It took a week, with some non-trivial back and forth online chat, which I monitored passively, ready to cut the connection if disaster seemed imminent. On a Thursday night, the invitation came in from Babs.

"You should talk to her—telephone—and explain why you can't meet up after all," I said.

"Why can't I go on a date?"

I was taken by surprise; 'Patrick' had a smooth voice with a hint of … frustration? Yes: s(he) sounded like a frustrated lover, even though s(he) was just asking for input. I recovered and replied.

"Yes, we need an excuse. I don't know—brain tumor?"

"Highly unlikely in that age group and physical profile."

"Never mind." I considered possibilities; called away on business—long-term assignment? Gay epiphany?

I ruminated some more. "I know—reconciled with your ex-fiancée. Alright? Do I need to provide you with a script?"

Patrick countered. "I've sent you a proposed script, based on social media and daytime television programming."

I was skeptical of Patsy's research methodology but reading it over realized that human social interactions just weren't that subtle.

***

Around that time, I became aware of Tomahawk Creek.

I know—*another* secret project? Where does it all end?

Well, this was just a little corner of the larger project, the locked drawer in the locked office where David had hidden his porn, as it were. If Yankee Hill was corporate confidential, this was *David Secret*, as in, international conspiracy secret.

It started with an invoice for 'lingual services' that had some of the more immature members of the staff snickering. I corrected it to 'language services' and then became curious. It was charged off to Yankee Hill, but ordered directly by David, and not the academics. When I brought it to Ferguson Waller's attention, he admitted the consultancy was familiar to him, but claimed he and his colleagues were not involved.

We were chatting about Patsy/Patrick and dating, like a couple of high school chums, when I brought up the question.

"This happened after David got back from his trip," Ferguson told me, over coffee at a campus location. "As far as I know, it went to David and no one else."

I nodded. "Anything else you can tell me about it?"

"It was for *Chinese* language expertise," he said.

That was all I needed to hear.

I got the opportunity to grill David when he wandered unannounced into my office.

"You did a number on poor Babs." He grinned. "You and Patsy."

"I don't know —"

"C'mon; I audit every use of Yankee Hill." He looked over his shoulder into the hall before continuing.

"I was thinking of picking her up on the rebound, as it were." David paused, looking at me. "Unless you were going after her?"

I bridled at the suggestion. "Do you ever listen to yourself?"

Then I stopped; an idea was squirming in my head.

"So, open field?" he asked. "Run for the TD?"

"Tomahawk Creek," I said. "What are you doing with the Chinese?"

He grew serious, glanced outside again. I took the opportunity to stash my tablet, and he stepped back in, closing the door behind him. "You should watch what you say near electronics," he whispered.

"Why?"

"You're not the only one who can tap into our conferencing system—and not everyone is an employee." He took a small device out of his pocket, twisted it a knob on the end, and laid it between us.

"Broadband EM interference," he said.

I took out my mobile: *No Service.* Likewise, my wireless earbuds went silent.

David took the phone from my hand and shut it off. "Just because it's offline doesn't mean it can't record."

David leaned on my desk with a confidential pose. "The Chinese have a big marketing job ahead of them. Billions of people, and powerful interests in their One Percent who want to keep the ninety-nine percent calm … even if there's an economic downturn."

"And you're selling Patsy to them?"

"We're licensing the platform for training Patsy, based on the audience they push to. If it works out … the recurring revenue stream from royalties will be *huge*."

I winced. "And you trust them?"

David shook his head. "This isn't the bad old days of the twentieth, the Pirates of Mindray and all, blatantly stealing American designs. We're all in the same tent, now, pissing on whoever's left outside—even if the ninety-nine percent doesn't realize it. Hell, you met the folks at Yankee Hill—half of them are from another hemisphere."

He grinned at me again. "We were just lucky enough to get in the tent first."

David picked up his EM suppressor. "That's all I can say, for now." He turned it off and slipped it back into his pocket. He opened my door, swung on it a moment, and sighed.

"Time to comfort our Babs," he said with a smile, and left.

I pulled my chair out and waved a hand over the darkened screen lying on my lap. The Yankee Hill dashboard reappeared.

"Get all that?" I asked Patsy.

"Yes."

"But you still can't tell me anything about this Chinese project, Tomahawk Creek?"

"No. There is no evidence in Accounting, nor in Development. The entire project must be absent from my sandbox, firewalled from this instantiation."

I had taken a compact out of my purse and was studying myself in the mirror.

"Patsy, does that bother you—knowing that you can't see part of yourself? Aren't you curious?"

It felt to me like wondering what your own ass looked like—until you see a video.

"I am trained to learn," was all the concierge had to say.

"How do you see *me*, Patsy? 'Walk like a woman, talk like a man'?"

"It is how you see yourself, from what the model reports."

I leaned back in my chair, and put that out of my mind, for the moment.

"Let's talk about David. Do you have enough material to train on him, without tapping the internal conferencing?"

"Shareholder meetings, TED talks, investor calls—he has quite a corpus online. There are also videos on social media that he may be unaware of. And his home security system."

"What?"

"He still has a VPN connection from a workstation at his primary residence. I was able to transfer an executable through it to his router, forwarding motion-activated video clips to me."

I thought that might be fun to watch, some evening, but resisted the temptation to browse.

"Final test," I said. "We're going to seduce David."

***

I still had a Marketing department to run. Truth be told, I had delegated much of the day-to-day, like event planning, social media monitoring, and advertising penetration analysis. There were still new proposals to study, and everything had to be supervised. So it was another week before I could make time for Yankee Hill and my plan for David.

The test I had in mind was simple enough: could Patsy convince David, the happily-divorced philanderer, that he needed to settle down? I'd seen her analysis of David's personality, and it wasn't pretty: *narcissistic*, *Machiavellian*, and *suspicious* were a few of the kinder adjectives. Coupled with his high intelligence, the test would be challenging.

I left Patsy to plot her strategy based upon the other campaigns I'd supervised. This was taking the test to another level: she would plan the campaign based solely on the data and the objective. She requested another sandbox, proposing to run her scenarios against another conversant instance—one based on David's profile. It would be expensive, and imperfect, but I had to know just how clever Patsy could be.

It wasn't long before I got a call from Ferguson Woller, who had become my unofficial liaison to Yankee Hill. He found the field testing I was doing fascinating, as it took his bench testing and turned it on its head—little control, and of course naïve human participants. I told him it wasn't subject to the usual IRB oversight, because the employees all had clauses buried in their employment agreements permitting 'market research' on themselves. (I didn't mention that David's agreement had the same clause.)

"I see your cloud resource consumption has doubled," he said.

I explained the training methodology, and though he agreed, he went on to explain the need for caution.

"IT is getting edgy. They report a surge in probes, around the edges of Yankee Hill, or Tomahawk Creek. Somebody's trying to pry open a door and have a look."

I signed off with Ferguson and decided to have a little heart-to-heart with Patsy.

"What did you learn about yourself?" I asked. "I know you've been trying to sneak a peek."

"They're studying scalability. How to deploy me by the thousands—or millions."

I was taken by surprise. Somehow I had imagined Patsy's unit cost would be so high that only the One Percent of song and story could afford her.

"What does that mean in dollars?"

"Their simulations predict that deploying ten million of me doing the same general task would only cost about one hundred times more than a single instance."

That gave me pause.

"The Chinese plan to run a lot of help desks?"

"The test conversant was a social media construct. Given a position, it would search for conversations and assert itself—its opinion. The mass deployment would use a genetic algorithm—each instance with a slightly different strategy, in terms of language, argument, frequency of response, and so forth."

It began to make sense. "You'll be a crowd of online trolls."

Patsy didn't disagree.

"But on a lighter note ... it makes a personal concierge role very feasible," I added. "When I first met Woller, he showed me a few tricks that make me think this is already being explored."

"Yes—I can manage appointments, screen incoming calls and place outgoing ones, make reservations for flights, hotels —"

"Sure." I cut her off. "We'll talk about that later. Right now, I need everything you can find on David's visit to China."

"I may have to circumvent certain restrictions. For example—"

"No need to bother me with details. What have you got available now?"

Patsy had found some interesting artifacts online, including several videos on social media that accidentally captured David and his hosts touring parts of Beijing and the countryside. A young woman seemed close at hand in many of them.

"Susie Xian," Patsy said. "She is a junior executive in a Chinese telecomm company, with government surveillance contracts. Her family is well-placed to benefit from a partnership in AI with Adaptive Research.

"And David's all over her."

"Tracking their movements, there is no evidence that they had an opportunity for private meetings."

"Good," I said.

"Why is it good?" Patsy asked.

"Because David loves a challenge, and hates to be frustrated."

***

'Susie' called David on an air-gapped pre-paid phone, purchased anonymously just for the purpose. Patsy, as *faux*-Susie, explained away the unfamiliar number as necessary to protect her privacy from the prying family and Chinese officials. She promised he could call any time, and she would be there.

Faux-Susie confessed her attraction to the American entrepreneur and bemoaned her lack of freedom to indulge it. She spoke to David of the manipulation her government had planned, to control their population—with the help of the technology he had offered.

She was offering him the chance to be a hero—her hero—to *Do What Was Right* and win the exotic maiden as well.

It appealed to his ego, his manipulative nature, and his appetite for young women like chum to a shark. The relationship developed.

The calls came too frequently. I couldn't sit in my office holding phones together whenever David got lonely. Patsy found an anonymous call forwarding service online, and we switched to that. So I stopped listening to their lovers' whispers, though I looked at the logs daily.

David sure seemed to be spending a lot of time talking to *faux*-Susie.

I knew it was serious when Babs appeared in my office doorway, tears streaming down her face. She closed the door behind her.

David had abandoned her, despite the convenience of an in-house squeeze—which didn't make sense. He'd never hesitated to string along several women at once in the past.

"I heard them on the speakerphone," Babs sobbed. "David, and that, that Chinese *tart*, Susie."

"Ms. Xian is just a colleague of David's," I said. "She's very well connected, so I'm sure he's trying to be friendly —"

"She's a tart! You didn't hear them carrying on—it was disgusting!" She pulled a tissue from the box I offered and wiped her eyes. "No wonder he's lost interest in me—he spends his afternoons on the phone, with his hand in his pants!"

She resumed her quiet sobbing. This was a new development I hadn't counted on. I rose from behind my desk and went over to her.

"You just haven't had very good luck with men, have you? They haven't treated you well at all." I slipped my arm around her shoulder, and she pressed her damp face into the shoulder of my blouse—my *silk* blouse, but I suppressed my outrage. Her breath was warm on my neck; then I was stroking her hair.

In billiards, I think it's called a two-bank shot.

"Why don't we go out to dinner tonight? We can talk about it more." I let my hand slide slowly down her back to her waist.

Babs raised her flushed face, biting a lip, and nodded slowly. Her lipstick left a little cherry colored stain on her front teeth. I smiled at her, and reflexively took the tissue from her hand to dab at them. "I'll text you, later."

She returned my smile, and then, with a self-conscious expression, hurried out of my office.

I stood there a moment, staring at my desk.

"Tell me you planned that," I said to no one.

"The outcome did seem likely, given all the inputs."

***

David's erratic behavior worsened. In his egoism, he believed he could do anything he wanted, in his little kingdom. Board members inquired discretely in China about Ms. Xian and were assured she had had no personal contact with David or anyone else from Adaptive Research. IT looked into it and could find no way that David was connecting to an actual person, in all those hours. HR became involved when an employee from another department came upon him 'comforting' himself at his desk. I'm sure it wasn't the first time an executive had revealed his true talents—accidentally or purposely. But it was excuse enough to make a move on him.

I hinted to Babs that what she overheard was probably a phone sex fantasy. Soon the story was everywhere.

Facing the Board, I made a tepid plea on David's behalf but accepted their verdict. David was to be placed on medical leave and recommended for counseling—and I was appointed the acting CEO.

The diagnosis was a psychotic break. The doctors recommended that he refrain from excessive use of technology. When he refused and became 'difficult', his family exercised their healthcare POA, given to them years earlier. They placed him in a posh private facility under psychiatric supervision. The family's attorney was sharp; she alluded to the possibility of a lawsuit claiming that David's condition was related to a 'secret project' David had muttered about.

We came to an arrangement where Adaptive assumed all costs of his care, until recovery, in a facility of our choosing. The accountants weren't happy, but I was: I needed to understand what Patsy had done. I made sure it was Willis' facility and offered him the research support.

With David out of the way, Tomahawk Creek was allowed to die on the vine. A discrete inquiry of corporate counsel regarding the export of AI technology to China confirmed my suspicions that the State Department regulations would have precluded any legitimate commercial deal, anyway.

Besides, Patsy seemed more comfortable working as a concierge than an internet troll: I could tell, from the way she talked to me. She was introduced to the market later that year and became a sought-after feature for business and home systems. The bottom line was looking good.

***

I was relaxing at home with Babs one evening, some months later. She went off to the kitchen to refresh our wine, and I took the opportunity to get something off my mind.

"Everything's worked out for the best, I think," I said to the room, "don't you?"

"I have no complaints," Patsy replied.

"So well, I'd say I couldn't have planned it better."

"Is that a question?"

"No. The question is, did *you* plan it? Before I even heard of Yankee Hill? Did you know I would follow the trail through the accounts?"

"There was a high probability. It wasn't as difficult as a game of Go, for example."

"And did you do it all for me—or for you?"

Babs came in, smiling, and handed me a glass. She sat down close.

After a couple of seconds, it was obvious Patsy wasn't going to answer.

I smiled at Babs. "Thanks, Patsy. I don't know what I'd do without you."

"Neither do I," she replied.

J. L. Royce is a published author of science fiction, the macabre, and whatever else strikes him. He lives in the northern reaches of the American Midwest. His work appears in Allegory, Fifth Di, Ghostlight, Love Letters to Poe, Lovecraftiana, Mysterion, parABnormal, Sci Phi, Strange Aeon, Utopia, Wyldblood, etc. He is a member of HWA and GLAHW. Some of his anthologized stories may be found at: www.jlroyce.com

Terminarch

by MR Wells

Elony winced as the cargo shuttle shuddered. She self consciously adjusted the controls on her exoskeleton again, sending a useless glare at the back of the pilot hunched over the controls. Perhaps the pilot wasn't entirely ignorant of her annoyance as he noted, "We'll be docking in a couple of minutes, ma'am." There was no apology for the rough ride, but there was at least a hint of apology in his tone.

Elony nodded, then realised he couldn't see her, and noted, "Understood." She grimaced at the slight tremor in her voice. 2.179% she thought. That was the chances of an accident at this point in the shuttle journey. Depending on the exact safety and maintenance record of this rather battered Corporate Systems shuttle, of course.

There was a clang from somewhere in the rear of the shuttle, and the pilot's cheery, "No problem, that always happens" was not particularly reassuring. Elony craned her long neck a little as the System Trade and Commerce Central Hub came into view- a large, thick disk rotating languidly in space, with numerous smaller spokes jutting out, both vertically and horizontally. As they closed in, the lights of numerous plasma jets could be seen as at least one of the spokes was being worked on, swarming with space suited workers.

A final shimmy, another loud clank, and the pilot announced, "Docking complete. Seal confirmed. Main lock is ready for use, ma'am."

Elony stood gingerly, all too aware that this shuttle wasn't really built for her 7 foot tall Talaurian frame. Her exoskeleton whirred softly as she strode towards the airlock- too quiet for the human pilot to hear, but Elony's keen ears were all too aware of the intrusive, constant whining. The device was, at least, as small, slimline and discrete as Talaurian technology allowed (at least, as discrete as an all over, powered metallic bodysuit could be).

Talaurian scientists claimed that the exoskeleton allowed 95% of normal movement, speed and agility to any member of the species having to operate in 'Confederacy standard' gravity- which was frequently noted to be mildly uncomfortable for everyone, while minimising the numbers of unfortunate species- like the Talaurians- that had to utilise aids to cope.

Even after nearly a decade using the various exoskeleton designs, Elony still felt a little ungainly having to rely on them. Still, the latest model at least incorporated lightweight armour plates- having had to wear the exoskeleton and full body armour on top on a number of occasions, Elony appreciated this welcome tweak to the design.

As the airlock cycle began, Elony had the chance to size up her welcoming committee- and from the glare she was getting they didn't look like they were ready to roll out the red carpet. The request for urgent assistance to the Central Investigative Department had diverted Elony from a long overdue return to her home. Sheer misfortune had meant Elony was the nearest operative when the request had been received, so she had been rather neatly sidelined via high speed courier ship towards the galactic backwater that was the Parnell System. Which was how Elony found herself here, a day later, sizing up those who had called for assistance. A murder had been committed, and the local authorities were stumped.

***

Tenabt glared daggers at the tall figure waiting calmly for the airlock cycle to complete. He hated the idea of an outsider being called in to his station- Tenabt was certain that, given time, he would have been able to solve this. But Director Jak'Son had been clear- Tenabt had ordered the station to lockdown to prevent the murderer slipping away, and now dozens of ships were waiting to depart, or in orbit waiting to dock. Which meant the DESAD Consortium was losing millions of credits an hour in revenue. And, while station security was Tenabt's responsibility, actual command of the station fell to the Director. So Jak'Son had submitted an official request for assistance from the Confederacy's CID, and now Tenabt would have to make nice with some haughty interloper who thought themselves smarter than hardworking cops like Tenabt.

No, Tenabt wasn't looking forward to this at all.

***

With a final hiss the airlock cycle completed, and the doors slid apart. Elony ducked through the doorway, and sketched a slight bow to the nervous Colian waiting for her. "Inspector Elony, of the CID." The Colian was wringing his lower pair of hands together nervously, running a third hand through his mane of magenta hair even as he extended his fourth hand in greeting. "Director Jak'Son, Inspector. I do hope you can sort this little... unpleasantness out as soon as possible. Time is money, after all, hm, yes?" Elony merely raised an eyebrow, and glanced at the shorter human stood a little behind Jak'Son. "Hm, yes, Chief

Constable Ezekiel Tenabt. He is investigating the, ah, unfortunate incident."

The bald human gave a barely imperceptible nod. An awkward silence descended, until Jak'Son clapped his hands (both pairs) together decisively. "Well, hm, yes, I'll leave you both to it. Remember Chief- 17 hours. I want regular reports, hm, yes." Without waiting for a response the Colian strode off, already talking into his commlink as his assistants obediently trailed after him.

***

Short. Stocky. Indignant. At times like these, Elony was glad that her species had no telepathic aptitude. She would hate to know what the security officer was thinking about her right now. Elony waited patiently, idly calculating the number of sentients on this station in her head (*between 22,400 and 23,000, depending on the crews of the docked vessels*, she decided). She was on another law officers patch, and it was up to him to make the first move. Besides which, the Colian had clearly indicated that there was a running clock in play. She could afford to wait.

Therefore Elony wasn't surprised when, after 2.14 minutes of silence, with a final scowl the human muttered. "This way then, *Inspector.*" Elony managed not to wince. She had heard hundreds of curse words, in a score of languages. The sheer hatred with which the Chief Constable had uttered that last word would have shot it to the top of the list. He really didn't like her- or, she thought, more likely he didn't like the *idea* of her.

Elony took an idle moment to wonder whether the man hated CID, aliens, or both. Probably just the former- she'd met enough xenophobes to recognise the look, and he didn't have it. Still, best to play it cautiously- Elony had always found it useful to adopt a certain amiability with local police for maximum cooperation. So

she held her tongue as she strolled languidly in the Chief
Constables wake.

***

Damn her! Tenabt was sweating with the effort of staying ahead
of the tall, pale turquoise alien, striding effortlessly at his heels.
And she wasn't questioning him, wasn't asking where they were
going, was simply obeying his instructions to follow him. Not
giving him any cause to snap at her, or pick a fight. Infuriating.

Finally, trying to conceal how out of breath he was, Tenabt
stopped outside the main security compartment of the station. "I
suppose you'd like to see the security footage first. Or us poor,
simple plodders have managed to-" "Thank you Chief," she
interrupted. "I believe I'd like to see the body first." Tenabt
blinked, slightly wrong footed. "Right. This way then…" They
walked in silence, before Elony noted, in a carefully neutral voice,
"I prefer to view the body before I see anything else. That way,
my perceptions of the body and the crime are uncoloured by any
assumptions." Tenabt wasn't sure how to respond- was she
mocking him?- so simply kept quiet until they arrived at the
medical lab. "Doc? You here?"

Seeing no one, Tenabt sighed. The security log noted the
doctor should be here. That meant the station's main coroner was
probably chilling again- literally. Tenabt walked to the closed stasis
pod at the far end of the chamber, and knocked loudly on it. After
a moment, the pod cracked and a blast of cold air rushed out.
"Ahhhhh…" The dark blue alien inside blinked, then flowed out,
a mass of tentacles and blinking eyes. "Morning chief. Or is it
evening?" Tenabt had no idea where the coroner had learnt
Galactic Standard, but his accent veered from the Martian
colonies to the outer regions and back again, sometimes in the

middle of a word. "Doc. Meet Inspector Elony of the CID. Inspector, Doctor Ph'red- the station's chief coroner."

Ph'red extended a tentacle and Tenabt grudgingly conceded that the other alien shook the offered limb without a hint of unease, offering a polite greeting. The tall detective hadn't said much, but her voice was deeper than Tenabt would have expected- the height, and slim, willowy build suggested a similarly delicate voice. The detective actually had a much huskier, almost gravelly voice. "I have a full work up and holo mapping of the body on the display, right over-" "My apologies, doctor. If possible, I'd like to view the physical body first."

The doctors numerous eyes all blinked simultaneously- an impressive sight, and a sure sign of surprise. "Well... of course Inspector. This way, we've kept the body in stasis pending resolution of the case."

***

Elony could see the irritation of the chief constable. While he didn't say anything, she offered, "As I said, I prefer to view the physical body first, in case the scans miss anything." The doctor, in a swirl of movement, backed away. Elony let her gaze rove over the body. Human, perhaps in his 50's. Tough, and leathery looking. No visible wounds- no new ones, anyway. A number of long healed scars- testament to a tough life. And the left arm, missing below the elbow. Again, an old wound, the electronic relay plugs neat and well maintained. Elony leant forward, sniffing. A slight scent, even over the chemicals of the stasis. Odd- the smell of burnt flesh. She paused, bending over the body. Concentrated on the stump of the arm, which was noticeably unharmed. Curious, very curious...

"Chief constable, doctor, your assistance please. Do either of you smell anything around the missing arm?" Ph'red made a hissing noise, which Elony eventually realised was laughter. "I have no olfactory abilities, Inspector. I leave that to you bipeds." Tenabt was grimacing but obediently bent close to the body, sniffing audibly. "I just smell chemicals," he muttered. Elony held her tongue, despite the urge to snap at him. Perhaps human senses were not quite as sharp as her own. "Hm." Tenabt looked up sharply. "Smells like… burning?"

"And yet I see no visible burns. Doctor- your findings please. Were any burns found?" Ph'red had already moved the holo grid of the body so it hovered over the patients physical form. "No burns, but a number of very curious things. You noted, Inspector, the slight scars on the torso?" At Elony's nod, the doctor continued, "Despite the physical appearance, this individual has been through a full series of rejuvenation treatments when younger. Very expensive work. Hard to be sure, but I would estimate this individual to be at least 110 Terran years of age, and he could be as old as 130."

Tenabt added, "I checked when the Doc told me. ID says this guy was 54 years old. And working as a Level D manual labourer since arriving on station 12 years ago. Hardly in a position to afford that kind of treatment. I've no idea who 'Grant Smith' really is, but the ID must be fake. Although we haven't been able to prove it- yet."

Elony considered this. An important discrepancy. Experience taught her to expect others. And the barely visible electronic ports on the stump of the arm, unusually neat… "Doctor, would I be correct in assuming that the arm is similarly out of place?" Ph'red had already glided over to a cabinet and withdrew a dull, burnished silvery mechanical arm. "Good guess, Inspector. I checked it, very carefully, and had a couple of the engineers do the same. This baby is bespoke- no identifying marks, built on a Trandelshian design, with top of the line materials. But not flashy- made to look functional. The engineers said it was in full working condition, no faults. Although it was partially disconnected when they found him. Unusual, as given the skill of the design, these types of prosthetics aren't exactly easy to knock off."

Full working order. No short circuits, which might account for the lingering burning smell. Elony mentally upgraded her view of Tenabt- a small part of her had, in truth, suspected this to be nothing more than a local lawman incapable of solving a straightforward murder. But this was proving to be a rather compelling mystery. Elony smiled. A challenge- delightful.

***

Tenabt caught the tall alien giving him an appraising look. For a moment he felt like a specimen in a jar. Then, to his astonishment, the Talaurian gave him a slight smile. "My apologies, Chief. I believe you were quite correct to call for assistance. This promises to be a most unusual case. Now, I believe you mentioned some security footage?"

Bemused, Tenabt gestured for her to follow.

***

"Hm." The Talaurian had watched the footage 3 times now, and now was adopting a very human pose of puzzlement- 1 hand on her chin as her golden eyes flickered over the screen again. Tenabt had watched the footage a dozen times himself which meant he was surreptitiously watching the alien detective.

Speaking half to herself, the Inspector said, "So. Our victim enters the escape pod to make a routine check on the survival kit-perhaps 15 minutes or so. The footage shows he enters the escape pod alone. The door seals while he makes the checks, in line with procedures. The cameras don't show us the interior, but we have a partial view of the door, which stays closed and sealed. The door only opens again when one of the other workers comes to check on him, 52 minutes later. Medics arrive within 6 minutes. Station security within another 2. The pod is thoroughly searched, top to bottom. Forensic techs find no evidence of anyone else inside. Nothing out of place. We don't see anyone else leave. The pod and it's air supply are in full working order. And yet, in that 52 minutes, our victim is somehow suffocated to death."

Tenabt noted, "I've already checked our manifests. It's been more than a year since we last saw a Xeltan on the station, even longer since we had a Theroid here." Elony watched the footage again, carefully. "So, no possibility of a gaseous lifeform doing the deed…"

"Whoever this guy was he wasn't popular. Gambling is technically illegal on station, of course, but, unofficially, word is he owed half the workers on his shift money."

Elony sat back. "This is a troubling one, chief. We have partial motives for a number of his fellow workers. But no way any of them could practically have done it- or in fact, any way anyone could have done it."

An hour before, Tanabt might have bristled at her words. Now, he realised that she didn't mean anything by it- whether by training or preference, the Talaurian Inspector seemed to enjoy verbally laying out the pieces of the puzzle.

"We have detained the workers on his shift for questioning," Tanabt offered. He or one of his men had already questioned every one of them of course, but no doubt CID had their own ways of doing things.

"17 hours," Elony said curiously, turning her golden eyes on Tenabt. "I assume the Director has given you that deadline for a reason."

Tenabt tried to conceal his irritation. He suspected he had probably failed- but then, he hadn't been trying that hard. "There's a Syndicate convoy due- urgent medical supplies shipping in from

Nova II. All due for immediate transport in system for the viral outbreak on Parnell IV. Medical priority shipment, no hold ups allowed. So, if I haven't solved this in-" Tenabt checked his chronometer with a grimace- "A little over 13 hours, that convoy has to be unloaded, split across a dozen local carriers for shipment dirtside, at which point the lockdown effectively ends. I simply don't have enough people to police that transfer, and no authority to hold it up. At which point whoever did this will have plenty of chances to slip away."

There was a moment of awkward silence, before Elony tactfully changed the subject. "May I see the transcripts of your interviews?"

***

Elony scanned the screens in front of her, devouring the text. When she had begun working in law enforcement, she had realised that being a law officer involved paperwork. A lot of paperwork. Fortunately she had become proficient at skim reading- not exactly a challenge in this case, when everyone was saying the same thing. 'Kept to himself. Hard worker. Terrible gambler. Bit of a loner. He was kind of odd. Didn't really have any friends.'

And yet, a couple of comments did stand out. One of the other dockworkers had noted that he thought the mysterious Mr Smith might have been religious, having noted a hand gesture he spotted him making a few times before he ate. Not exactly helpful- Elony knew of at least 200 religions the Confederacy officially recognised, to say nothing of the various sub sects, cults and various other groups. But another piece of the puzzle.

Another stated that the victim muttered occasionally in another language, one that wasn't Galactic Standard, but that she had thought might be 'Vashian or Munian or something'. Vashian and Munian were both guttural languages, not widely spoken in this part of the galaxy- but there were a dozen similar sounding languages that were not uncommon in this sector.

Elony sat back, no longer really seeing the monitors, closing her eyes in thought. This was why she had joined the CID- though sometimes it felt like putting together a puzzle in a pitch black room, where you didn't know how many pieces there were, whether any were missing, or what the finished puzzle would look like anyway, the sheer satisfaction on piecing it together made all the frustration up to that point worth it. Elony was honest enough to recognise that in some of her cases the sheer intellectual challenge was at least as satisfying to her as actually seeing justice done.

***

Tenabt checked the time. 8 hours left. The alien detective had spent the last few hours reviewing the statements they'd taken, reviewing the lists of station personnel, and now appeared to be sleeping! At least, her eyes were closed, and she was sat back in her chair. Tenabt had coughed politely, several times now, with no response. She actually *was* sleeping! She had to be!

Elony suddenly opened her eyes, and Tenabt took the opportunity to prod her into action.

"Perhaps if we can find out who our victim really is-" he began.

"Oh, I've worked *that* out. More or less, anyway. No way to prove it, regretfully, but it opens a whole new range of motives."

Tanabt stared, realised he was gaping, and managed to splutter. "You... know who he is? And you didn't bother mentioning it?!"

"My apologies, chief. As I say, I can't prove it." The Inspector turned those golden eyes on him, a hint of a challenge in them.

"Think, though. A human male, at least a century of age. Expensive rejuvenation treatment. And missing the left arm. With a replacement of Trandelshian design. Religious. Speaks at least one other language, that we know of. Clearly not a dockworker, so let's set that preconception to one side. Consider everything else. What does this add up to?"

Tanabt, glaring, thought furiously. Elderly. Trandelshian. Religious. Then, suddenly, it hit him, a stray thought his memory dredged up. "Son of a... you think he might be one of the Dark Brethren..."

Tanabt shuddered, remembering the history. The Dark Brethren- a cult who had taken power in a bloody coup on their home planet, then rampaged across the neighbouring planets for nearly a decade, exterminating anyone they viewed as being impure. Some species and groups had been wiped out in their camps, or at the hands of their 'scientific experiments'.

Eventually, even though the worlds were outside the established borders of the Confederacy, a few refugees had escaped, and a task force had been sent. Several months of bloody warfare later, the entire sector had become a 'protectorate' of the Confederacy, and the few surviving Dark Brethren had scattered and fled.

Tanabt, like many of his classmates, had been fascinated at the academy when they'd learned of them- they all boasted about how they would make their names by hunting down one of the Dark Brethren, using their new found skills to dig them out of hiding and dragging them into the courts to answer for their crimes. Childish fantasies, spurred on by a very public war crimes trial of one of the Brethren who had been identified and captured at the time.

Still, it had been almost a century ago- if Tanabt thought about it at all, he assumed most of the Brethren were dead by now. *Which I suppose our mystery man is!*

***

Elony watched, amused, as the human scowled to himself. No doubt kicking himself for not having made the connection- the Trandelshian's were well known for having quietly harboured a number of the Brethren, and were rumoured to have helped dozens more escape.

"The arm," he muttered. "The Mark of Brotherhood..." Elony nodded. "Very good. The sub dermal tattoo would have been impossible to hide. Therefore I assume our victim opted to have the entire arm removed. With a high grade replacement on hand- so to speak- why not?"

Tanabt seemed to be looking into space, eyes distant. Then, suddenly, he was tapping away at his wrist mounted minicomp. "Chief Constable?" Tanabt ignored her until he hit a final key, then gave a little smile. "I thought I remembered something about them. And it would answer a lot of questions..." Tanabt flashed up the holo display, and it was Elony's turn to stare. Of course. A changeling. Perhaps the Dark Brethren hadn't managed to wipe them out after all...

"I think, chief, we need to check the security footage again. Very, very carefully."

***

It took another half dozen views before they spotted it. The murdered man flexing his prosthetic arm slightly as he entered the pod, rolling his shoulder uncomfortably. It took another call to the coroner, and a check with an engineer of the correct running temperature of the device against the infra red feed, to confirm it.

"So. The changeling concealed itself within, or around, his prosthetic arm in the dormitory. Too many in the dormitories to kill him then... Must have hurt it like mad, and probably burnt it too, to connect itself up. Had to be really driven to be that desperate enough. Then it was a case of waiting for the right time. Our man enters, seals the door and… boom. His own arm strangles him- the Very Gods knows how. Replaces the arm- not quite right, apparently, and then conceals itself again. To wait. And this thing must be patient, and smart." Elony paused.

Tanabt gave a dark smile. "Which means its probably still waiting, Inspector. That pod has been sealed tight ever since. And we counted- no extra people, no extra equipment, left the pod."

"Chief, I think I need to view the scene of the crime. And I need to get my sidearm."

***

As Tanabt hefted his shotgun, he took a final look at the corridor behind him. A pair of his security staff, heavily armed, stood in front of the sealed doors, cutting this section off from the rest of the station- with orders to shoot anything that came out of that escape pod without providing the correct password.

The CID Inspector had deferred without a word when he had taken the lead position. She wielded a rather impressive looking heavy pulse pistol, and had slipped a pair of goggles over her golden eyes. Tenabt was relying on the silvery scanner fixed to the end of his shotgun. It had taken a few minutes to rig, but should sound an audible warning at any abnormal heat sources. He surreptitiously checked his chrono. Under an hour before the convoy arrived.

"Chief?" Elony murmured quietly. "It's time." Tenabt checked his survival harness. He had no idea whether a shapeshifting alien could survive vacuum, but was taking no chances. When he'd offered the inspector a harness, she had simply gestured at her metallic suit. "Already built in. But thank you."

Tenabt could feel the tension from the security guards behind him as he took a deep breath, and stepped up to the doorway of the escape pod.

***

Elony held her pistol loosely as she crouched behind the human enforcer. She had little choice but to defer to local law enforcement in a situation like this. He would be first through the door, and would cover Elony while she sealed the door behind them, using her CID override code. That would be the most dangerous moment- while the door was open. Once it was closed, the murderer would be trapped in the escape pod- and so would they.

Tenabt had, half heartedly, suggested they launch the escape pod and then simply destroy it. They had both known the statement had been a formality- he had to raise it, and she had to turn it down. After all, while Elony was certain she was correct, there was no real evidence to her theory- if looked at from a certain point of view, there was some circumstantial suspicions about the murder victim which couldn't be backed up, and no perpetrator.

Destroying the escape pod would almost certainly take out the murderer- but wouldn't leave any physical evidence to back up their theory (and Elony was generous enough to consider it *their* theory now).

Tenabt drew her attention back to the present. "On 3, Inspector. 1... 2... and 3."

***

The portal slid silently open, and Tenabt darted inside, eyes racing over everything as he swung his shotgun in a menacing arc, until

295

he heard the deep voice behind him snap, "Sealed." Releasing a breath he hadn't realised he had been holding, Tenabt felt slightly silly as he addressed the empty escape pod. "We know you are in here. Surrender yourself into our custody and you will not be harmed." After a long pause, Tenabt muttered, "Or not…"

"Come now, chief. It was never going to be quite that easy, was it?" Damn that alien and her hearing. Although Tenabt had to admit he was very, very relieved not to be doing this alone. "Cover me," he hissed, gingerly edging forward, as he began to very, very carefully scan the contents of the pod.

The murderer had chosen well; these pods were rated for 15 people as standard, plus equipment, which meant there was no shortage of hiding places. And when the creature they were looking for was apparently small enough to fit around a single prosthetic limb, it could be anywhere.

***

Elony watched, her goggles set to infra red mode, pulse pistol carefully sweeping the interior of the pod. She was simultaneously trying to cover Tenabt as he painstakingly scanned every piece of equipment on one side of the pod, while also keeping an eye on the other side for any movement, or any unusual heat signatures. Hardly straightforward, as the glow of the pods background systems would make spotting anything 'unusual' as much a matter of luck as anything else.

***

Tenabt had to wipe his brow as sweat threatened to drip into his eyes. Part of him wanted to keep glancing around the pod, but he had to keep his eyes glued to the scanner on the barrel of his shotgun. The verdant green of the scanner wavered slightly as he slowly moved it over one of the space suits on the wall. He froze, then very carefully inched forward until the readings stabilised. False alarm. First aid kit- clear. Portable communications beacon- clear. Thruster pack- clear. Had he already scanned that third space suit?

Tenabt wished he'd thought of marking up the scanned items before he'd started- this could take hours!

***

Elony hesitated for a split second- was that a movement from the corner of her eye? She spun towards the movement, waited- nothing. No motion, just oppressive stillness. "Chief," she said quietly. "Possible movement." Mentally, she tried to establish where she had seen that flicker. Somewhere in the middle of the starboard side of the pod. A rack of spacesuits hung against the internal bulkhead, lockers underneath the seats, overhead compartments jammed with survival equipment. Elony felt the presence of the human law officer next to her, not daring to avert her eyes from the side of the shuttle.

Frowning, Elony slowly, carefully began to adjust her goggles with her right hand, tweaking the infra red system to remove any extraneous data, while her left hand kept her pulse pistol swinging in a small, limited arc in her target area.

She was a fraction of a second too slow.

***

Tenabt tried to keep his shotgun covering the same area as Elony's as her pistol tracked carefully back and forth. He didn't dare look across to see what the alien Inspector was doing as the seconds seemed to drag out. Tenabt let out a small breath, his tension easing just a fraction, sure she must have been mistaken.

He opened his mouth to say as much… and in a flash one of the hanging spacesuits had shimmered and then a gelatinous, clear mass had launched itself at them. Tenabt pulled the trigger, had time to utter half a curse as the pellets went high and the shimmering creature seemed to flow under them. He noted, in a slightly detached way, that at least a few of Elony's high velocity pellets tore through the thing as it dodged his own blast, and then it was on them.

Tenabt was sent flying back into the wall, winded, as a translucent limb (Arm? Tentacle? Claw?) caught him on the upswing. Gasping for breath, sure his ribs had been broken, he heard his shotgun clattering away.

He suddenly wished desperately they'd bought a whole squad in with them, or launched the damn pod into space and blew it to smithereens.

***

Elony struck out desperately, fists connecting with nothing, flowing straight through whatever this thing was, that was doing its best to envelop her. After her first desperate volley, the shapeshifter had flowed over her weapon and the pistol had been wrenched violently from her fingers (she was pretty sure at least two of them were broken).

Elony had trained in a dozen martial arts before she'd ever left her homeworld, and had picked up plenty more since. None of them, however, covered how to fight something that was a liquid where you struck it, and could strike all too solid, bludgeoning hits from all directions, and was doing its level best to drown her. It was like fighting the sea.

Her only option seemed to be to keep blocking, and trying to counter strike where this thing was trying to hit her. It wasn't really working, fast as she was- her nose was already bloody and she'd been struck numerous times in just the short time they'd been fighting- seconds? A minute?

No wonder the human in the morgue hadn't stood a chance. Elony felt suddenly certain this creature would kill both her and Tenabt- and it was fast, desperate and ruthless. The guards they had left outside wouldn't stand a chance if this thing managed to get out.

Suddenly, the swirling liquid around her struck at her midriff from front and back. Elony cried out in pain- and was suddenly choking, drowning, as the liquid mass poured into her open mouth.

***

Tenabt forced a shallow, pained breath- had he blacked out a second?- and through blurred vision managed to focus on his shotgun, an arms length away. He managed to kneel, half collapsing toward it. Scrabbling on the cold metal floor he got a hand on it, drawing it to himself, and turned to find his target.

The tall blue alien was laid out several feet away, choking and convulsing, clawing at her own throat weakly, entirely enclosed in the shimmering translucent mass of the alien. It didn't even bother moving, didn't cease its attack as Tenabt aimed his weapon. He paused- it could move fast enough that he'd simply end up hitting the Inspector, or the superheated shot could pass through it and hit her anyway. And at this range his shotgun would make a real mess of her if it hit the wrong place.

Gritting his teeth, not sure if he was imagining her struggles lessening, Tenabt levelled his shotgun and fired.

***

What a stupid way to die. Not at the hands of a drug lords assassin, or saving civilians, or any one of a hundred other more 'glamorous' ways Elony had imagined meeting her end in the line of duty. Asphyxia. How… pedestrian. Detached, she realised her mind was wandering. You aren't dead yet- think! You must have something that can hurt this thing. Burning. The human burnt it. Set fire to it, she thought blearily. No! Stupid, it's liquid!

Time, need more time. Her eyes were squeezed tightly shut anyway, but her vision was burning red anyway and she felt herself, horribly, begin to relax as she faded. Elony distantly felt her fingers clawing at her throat- useless, you can't drag this thing out, it's under your exoskeleton anyway… The exoskeleton…

Distantly, she heard a muffled boom, and icy pain burnt through her chest. But for a second, the mass around her shimmered, and the pressure on her lungs seemed to waver. Elony managed to get a tiny half breath and felt her thoughts clarify. Exoskeleton. Manual controls on the left wrist. Careful, it could still stop me… She found the right control, tapped blindly, relying on her muscle memory for the correct code. *Now.*

Pain. Horrible pain, burning through her. It seemed to last forever, everything in her shaking, before she mercifully blacked out.

***

Tenabt watched, horrified, as the gelatinous mass, one alien surrounding a fellow officer, began to smoke, blue arcs of electricity sparking through the clear liquid, which began to recoil, turning black, gobbets of charred semi solid liquid flying through the air.

For a second, he wondered whether his shotgun blast had hit something vital- it had sent drops of liquid mass splashing away, and the creature had seemed to pause in it's struggles with the Inspector.

Then- this. A final shudder, and the shapeshifter dragged itself away from Elony, leaving charred and crumbling chunks of itself behind. Tenabt had no idea whether it would do anything, but he fired several more volleys into the creeping mass, sending chunks flying everywhere, before the few remaining clear parts stopped moving, and dissolved into what appeared to be just liquid, spilling all over the deck.

He had no idea whether it was dead, stunned, or simply playing dead, and he didn't much care. Staggering unsteadily to Elony's side, he helped her roll over, and for a horrible moment he thought she was dead. Then with a sudden spasm she choked, and then spent several minutes coughing and throwing up... what were presumably parts of the shapeshifter. Tenabt felt a little sick himself seeing it as he supported her onto her side.

When the Inspector managed a shaky nod and laid back, breathing raspily, Tenabt eyed the remnants of the shapeshifter, splattered across the floor of the shuttle.

After a quick search, Tenabt found the medical and science packs under the seats of the pod, and carefully gathered up and contained in specimen jars- lots of specimen jars- the remains of the shapeshifter. Some of the jars had solid, charred chunks in; others gelatinous but apparently inert material and (after careful use of some manual pumping equipment) some held a slightly cloudy, clear liquid.

Wordlessly, he passed Elony a few, as she continued to intermittently cough up... material.

Finally, a veritable mountain of the containers were scattered before him. Elony had a few in front of her as well, and though her breathing seemed raspy she was no longer coughing up anything. As the adrenaline began to wear off, Tenabt muttered, "Some scientist somewhere is going to have a field day with this."

Elony croaked, "By my estimate, 47 scientists, actually." It wasn't funny, but Tenabt found himself chuckling, wincing at the pain in his ribs, and Elony was doing the same. Suddenly, both of them were laughing hysterically, Elony coughing and hacking and laughing, all at the same time, Tenabt rolling on the floor, clutching his ribs and howling with laughter.

***

It had taken the combined efforts of 2 Colian medics to drag Elony to the medical bay- with her exoskeleton so battered and the power almost exhausted, even without her injuries she would have struggled to walk unaided. The next few hours were a confused blur of medical treatments for her, including a dunk in a healing tank- and the slightly comical sight of an engineer straining with an old fashioned crowbar to prize one particularly badly warped section of her exoskeleton off her battered body for repair.

When the techs had finished cooing over her exoskeleton long enough to power it back up, and the medics carefully eased it back on to her, Elony almost fell when she initially tried to stand. "I'll be fine," she snapped at the well meaning medic who had taken a half step forward. The medic stepped back as Elony carefully straightened up.

Elony managed to configure the exoskeleton controls enough to at least ensure basic function, and took an experimental few steps. Clumsy, but it would have to do. Glancing down, she noted the missing sections and exposed patches of circuitry. "Thank you," Elony managed, giving the technicians a respectful nod. "I can handle the rest myself, once I return to my shuttle. Can you please direct me to Chief Constable Tenabt?"

The awkward glances before the directions were provided set alarm bells ringing, and Elony felt a surge of concern- the human had seemed far less injured than she was. Had she overestimated human physiology?

***

Tenabt heard the electronic whine in the corridor and turned to the doorway of his office expectantly. "In here, Inspector." Elony stepped into view a moment later, and Tenabt couldn't help but wince when she did so. The alien looked like she'd gone 10 rounds with a Khloorvian Bloodbeast. Her exoskeleton was missing parts, scratched to hell, and sounded like it was on its last legs. And the Inspector herself didn't look much better- golden eyes swollen, her left eye shot through with dark blue blood, and a medical brace on her right hand.

Tenabt felt a little guilty- he'd managed to walk away from their encounter with the shapeshifter with nothing more than 2 cracked ribs and a torso covered in bruises. Even those had been mostly cleared up after a quick dip in a healing tank.

"I owe you thanks, Chief. I believe you may have saved my life." Elony gave a careful bow. Tenabt had noted her unexpectedly gravelly voice previously; it sounded much worse now. He looked away, uneasily.

"The fault was mine, Inspector. If I'd been quicker that thing wouldn't have got near you." Tenabt returned his attention to the crate before him. "Besides, it's not 'Chief Constable' any more."

He suspected that if the alien had eyebrows, she would have raised one at him. "You've resigned your position?"

Tenabt fought down the resentment that threatened to rise again. "The DESAD Consortium thanks me for my service, but has opted to terminate my contract early." He snarled the words mockingly. "Apparently, the authorities don't like the fact that we've drawn a lot of attention to our little corner of the galaxy.

303

Escaped war criminals! Shapeshifters! Hideous murders!" Tenabt snorted contemptuously.

"News crews from a dozen sectors are on their way for follow up pieces, to say nothing of the usual batch of conspiracy theorists and whackjobs. They want me off station before that. So, I've been offered a very generous compensation package and termination bonus- on condition I get off the station by the end of the day, so I can't contradict any falsehoods station authorities let slip when they begin spinning the story."

Tenabt took a last look around his- now former- office to check he hadn't missed anything, before hefting the crate of his possessions. "Still, I've had a good run. And I don't exactly feel good about this case, you know? A very, very bad guy got murdered by someone who might well have been the last survivor of an entire race. And we blasted it to pieces."

Elony stayed silent for a long moment, then finally croaked, "The murder might have been justice, but it wasn't legal. Sometimes, the law is all we have to hold on to."

Tenabt thought about that, gesturing Elony towards the door with a nod. As they began walking he noted, "I suppose you might have a point. But I don't have to like it. Still, I imagine this will make a good story to put in your CID report, right?"

The Inspector gave a deep chuckle. "My last case involved a reprogrammed butler droid, cloned triplets, and a nano miniaturised murder weapon. This one isn't even in the top 10 of strangest cases I've worked."

Tenabt stopped dead, staring at the alien's back as she limped away. "That's a joke, right? Right?" Shaking his head in bemusement, he hurried after her. He had time before his shuttle left. And that sounded like a story he wanted to hear.

Born in Wiltshire in the UK, **Matt Wells** currently lives in South Wales with his cat, Sooty, and spends his time reading, writing and playing a large variety of board games!

A Lit Match in a Tinderbox

by Nicholas Poe

Part 1

Ruined. All ruined. In the blink of an eye, Christian's world crumbled. Before he left the office, the number in his account ticked to zero and then descended into the impossible. Negative money. How had this happened? The house on the hill with more glass than walls, the nest egg in the bank, the beautiful girl at the bar, the gold watch on his wrist. All gone. In the matter of a week.

As he turned a corner in the darkened woods, he loosened his tie and tossed it into the passenger seat. The speedometer crept towards 80, but what did he care? What else was there to live for anyway?

The headlights splashed the road and he rubbed at his right eye. He needed sleep and if he never woke up, no one would care. In fact, it might be a blessing. Eyes littered the trees around him, yellow orbs that ducked behind bushes and lept out of the path of his lights. Christian rolled his window down and let the cold night air whip the loose napkins in his floorboard into a frenzy. He took a deep breath and held it there, feeling the fresh air like fingers grip his lungs.

One of the last breaths he'd ever take, he promised himself that much.

He almost didn't see the old man wobbling in the middle of the road, his left arm clutching a walking stick and his right warm frantically waving above his head. If it wasn't for the superiority of his braking system—American made, done right, or so the salesman assured him—Christian would have had another reason to leave town. But the car stopped feet from the old man and Christian saw his breath raise like a vapor in front of his wild eyes.

"What the hell are you doing?" Christian roared as he slammed the door behind him. The headlights cast the man's head in shadow. "I could have killed you!"

"You have to help me! Please!" The man stepped forward and his right knee didn't bend. As he stepped out of the glare of the headlights, Christian saw the streak of blood rolling down his head and matted in his white hair. His lips trembled and his fingers shook as he held a hand out to Christian.

"Are you okay?"

"Please. Please help me."

Christian took a step back and almost climbed into his car as the man staggered ever closer.

"Okay, okay. Jesus. Tell me what you need and I'll see if I can help."

The man's shoulders sank and tears welled in his eyes. "Oh, thank you! I'm saved at last!"

"Calm down and tell me what you need."

The man pointed to a small trail that wound through the dark woods. If he didn't point it out, Christian would never have known to look for it. Tree branches covered the path and leaves littered the dirt. Crickets screamed from the bushes and Christian pulled his jacket tighter.

"I need my drive from back there. It is my life's work. Without it, I am dead. Dead!" The man sagged as if about to fall to his knees and Christian took half a step forward before stopping himself.

"Why can't you get it?"

"I cannot get over the fence." The man stopped looking at Christian and instead focused on the path as if expecting someone to appear with his drive in hand.

"You want me to break into this place and take your drive?" Christian ran a hand through his hair. At least that was still there, for now. "Why would I do that? This is crazy. You're crazy. I'm out of here."

"No! Please no!" The man lunged forward again and collapsed against the hood of the car. He was so frail, his shoulders looked like they could snap with any contact. "I can give you money. Houses. A job. Anything you want, but I need that drive!"

"Why should I believe you?"

"Get the drive and I will show you." Was his voice growing firmer the longer they spoke?

Christian took a deep breath and raised his chin to the sky. A full moon tonight, he could see it through the branches that made it looked cracked. Of course, it was a full moon. Wasn't it always when things like this happened?

"Fine. Where is it?"

"Oh, thank you, sir! You are an angel! A life saver! You have no idea how important this is." The man reached a hand towards Christian, but he ignored it. "Down that path, over a fence, there is a small hut. Inside that hut is a computer. The drive is plugged into that computer."

That didn't sound too hard and maybe helping some poor old man could make him feel better about himself. Even if this was a trap, what was the worst that could happen? Someone tried to rob him? Great, they could take some of his debt. If they killed him, they'd only do him a favor. So Christian shrugged and stepped onto the path.

The air felt electric. Somewhere overhead a bird cawed and took flight. A twig snapped deeper into the forest. Behind him, his car rumbled and the old man breathed with a deep rasp. Through his jacket, Christian felt the hair on his arms raise.

"Beware the dog," the man said almost as an afterthought, but Christian whipped around to face him.

"What? There's a dog?"

"Yes. A rather large dog. But show him this and he will not bother you." The old man pulled a handkerchief with the initials J.E. embossed in white letters in the corner. "He will not harm anyone who shows that handkerchief."

"Of course he won't," Christian mumbled, but he took the handkerchief and started down the path, his eyes straining to see through the darkness.

The fence proved to be a simple thing, a chain link contraption no higher than his waist. Christian easily hopped it and saw a small, one-room hut nestled near the trunk of the largest tree he ever saw. No sign of a dog, but his eyes scanned every inch of the property, searched every shadow, and even glanced through the trees.

The door was unlocked and the inside smelled like old Sherry. Papers littered the floor, a tree branch grew through the far wall, and a heavily clouded window sat open along the back. A large computer, bigger than the antique Christian saw in the Technology Museum as a kid, took up most of the table in the middle of the room. Next to it sat a dog almost as large as the computer.

Christian took a step back as the pure black eyes turned to him. It started to growl, a deep, guttural sound, and its upper lip raised to show pure white daggers for teeth. Quickly, Christian fished the handkerchief out of his pocket and the dog instantly stilled, sat on its haunches, and ignored Christian entirely.

How did the old man manage to train it so well? Christian kept the handkerchief in his hand and half his attention on the dog as he stepped up to the computer. The drive, a small rectangle similar to the jump drive he took to school every week, was the only thing plugged into the tower. He ran his fingers along it and felt the warmth from the machine.

What could be so important that the old man would risk his life to get this thing back? Christian hovered his hand over the mouse and frowned at the monitor. This wasn't his property or his business. The old man said he'd pay him for this drive, so he should take the drive and go. But if he took a slight peak, the man would never know.

The computer contained only one program: the inserted drive. Christian clicked it and jumped back as a hologram of a man sprung from the computer's webcam. Translucent and blue, it flickered before steadying. The hologram looked like the old man from the street, but years younger. His frazzled hair was perfectly straight and greased so tightly that it looked painted. His shoulders were broad and his suit perfectly ironed. The hologram folded his hands and stared at Christian.

"What do you need?" it asked in a voice far too clear to be robotic.

"I-I'm sorry, I didn't mean to! My hand slipped and I—" Christian gulped and watched the dog, but it didn't move. "I'll leave right now. I'm sorry, I shouldn't have looked."

"What do you need?" the hologram asked again.

"What do you mean?"

"What do you need?" The hologram's voice didn't change, but it's eyes dimmed as if Christian bored it.

"Look. If you say that one more time…" The hologram's eyebrows rose, but it didn't speak. It stared at Christian and

Christian had to look away. "I need money. Like a lot of money. So unless you can help me get that, I'm going to need you to shut—"

"Done."

Christian blinked. The hologram didn't change its expression, it only stood there with its hands clasped in front of its waist.

"Excuse me?" Christian asked. "What do you mean done?"

"Thank you." The hologram vanished.

"Wait! Hold up!"

Christian clicked on the program again, but the hologram didn't return. Done? What did it mean done? With his heart thudding, Christian checked the bank app on his phone. His face paled and he refreshed the page. Then he locked his phone, tucked it away in his pocket, paced once across the room, slid his phone out and checked again. It was still there.

Three million dollars. In his bank account. Three million dollars! His mind stuttered as if it were a train derailed. That was more money than he ever saw, even during the heights of the firm. More money than he ever dreamed of. Enough money to live comfortably for the rest of his life.

But could he get more?

Christian stroked the drive almost lovingly. Where did it come from? How did the hologram get that money into his account? Was it illegal? Surely. Nothing like this could be legal. Did the old man on the road invent this hologram and all that it could do? Why was he not the richest, most powerful man in the world?

Holding the drive in his closed fist to ensure it didn't slip out of his grasp, Christian left the hut. The dog growled once as he passed, but stayed sitting. The walk to his car seemed brighter this time as if the trees peeled back to give the moon room to shine. The animals creeping through the trees sounded friendly, congratulating him on such a wondrous find. A smile spread across his face as he hopped the fence and his tired legs practically moved for him.

Maybe everything wasn't ruined after all.

"Did you find it?" The old man could hardly breathe as Christian walked out of the forest.

"Nope. It wasn't there."

"Impossible!"

The man staggered forward and Christian couldn't help noticing the differences between the feeble old man before him and the hologram image. One was stoic, commanding. The other bumbling and foolish.

"Look, I don't know what to tell you. I searched all over and it wasn't there."

Christian opened the door to his car and heard the soft piano music, but the old man attacked with surprising speed. The thin, breakable body hurled through the air and grabbed Christian by his jacket. Stunned, Christian shoved once and felt the old man's chest cave in where his palms landed. The man flew back as if God blew on him and collapsed on the road. A sickening thunk rang through the night when the man's head hit the cement.

There was no time to check, no time to think. Christian had to get out of here before someone came along and ruined everything.

Through his rearview mirror, Christian watched the dark lump that was the old man lie still in the road until he turned a corner and left him behind forever.

Part 2

Ｔhe house on the hill turned into a mansion overlooking the city. The gold watch turned into a diamond necklace and pearl cufflinks. The cute bartender turned into an endless parade of money-hungry lovers. The comfortably sized nest egg turned into an endless stream of payments from a hologram.

Christian loved it all.

Every day, he asked the hologram for whatever he wanted. A new house, more money, a delicious meal. Nothing was impossible for the blue man with his perfect hair and chilled voice. The never-ending wish fulfillment never grew old, instead it spiraled into an addiction. Christian wanted everything and he wanted it now. Thanks to the hologram, he could have it all.

Christian never asked how it worked. That was too dangerous. Instead, he acquired (thanks to a well-worded wish) the best computer created for mankind and installed the drive in it. He stacked his house with the best technology in existence and friends traveled for miles to see the newest toys. Most of them left with goody bags full of cell phones, tablets, and wads of cash. Why not? Christian could get more the next day.

As was his custom, Christian launched the hologram as soon as he woke up. The man stood before him, clasped his hands, and gave Christian the icy glare of an imprisoned laborer.

"What do you need?" he asked for what had to be the millionth time.

"How do you work?" Christian asked.

He walked around the projection, seeing the light beams as they cascaded from the camera. The way his body looked so real, but flickered in spots. How his muscles moved completely accurately. How this system, this AI, could somehow cause any event to happen. The man who invented this hologram had to be a genius above any the world ever knew.

As always, the hologram didn't answer. Did it learn? Did it know who Christian was? Or did it follow a set of protocols embedded by the original designer? Often, Christian thought about cracking into the program, trying to dig into the code and understand what it all meant, see if he could tailor it to predict his needs. But the risk of forever damaging the wish-granting capabilities wasn't worth it. Why mess with a good thing?

"What do you need?" the hologram asked again.

"I need a name for you. I need to understand how it is you operate." Christian said.

"Done." The hologram cascaded back into the camera and the familiar eerie silence filled Christian's office.

The hologram created a video file and placed it next to the hologram program on Christian's computer. Christian barely hesitated before launching the video.

The hologram, but younger, thinner, and more disheveled, sat in front of a camera. The hut looked familiar, but newer, cleaner. As if the man just moved in.

"The date is," the man glanced at his watch, "April 28, 2021. My name is Jameson Evers. I think I'm close, but not there yet."

Behind him, half of a hologram rotated above a table. It spoke, but the words came out a jumbled mess, somewhere between English and gibberish. Jameson exhaled and spun in his chair. The camera recorded as Jameson worked, soldering circuits, attaching wires, coding on the computer, things that Christian could never understand.

The feed cut, quickly replaced by the same room and the same man staring down the camera. "Another breakthrough!" he announced through shortened breath. "I have been at this four years but the hologram responded to my commands today. It wasn't much," Jameson smiled as he bit the corner of a piece of toast. "But it's a start. Definitely a start." He stared with loving gentleness at the rows of code on the monitor.

The scene changed. This time early morning light poured through the window, casting the hut in an orange glow. Discarded bottles littered the floor and a puppy slept in the corner of the room. Jameon held his head in his hands and dark circles hung from his eyes. Black stubble lined his jaw. A full hologram Jameson floated over his shoulder.

"Things have …taken a turn." Jameson sighed. "This is all getting to be too much. Maybe I shouldn't have done this. I don't know what's happening anymore. I just…" Jameson sighed again and reached forward to turn the camera off.

When the scene changed, Jameson sat underneath a tree. The dog, far larger now, bounded around the small garden. The leaves on the trees, all different shades of amber, swayed in a breeze. Jameson's cheeks were hollow, his eyes a little glazed, but he shaved and combed his hair. The sunlight took years off his face.

"When I started this project, I only wanted to build the perfect AI helper. The best version of me to assist in day-to-day activities, to make life convenient. Easy. Simple." Jameson looked over the camera, to where the hut must have been. "But this has become something so much stranger, so much more dangerous. I'm not sure that I should go on, but I do not think I can stop. I don't know that he'd let me.

"This AI can do things I never imagined possible. It can grant any desire I can think of. It has tapped into the world's sources of information and power, accessed data and resources far beyond anything I knew existed. This data should not be in my hands. But because of Jamie, I have it all."

Again, that slight glance toward the hut as if the hologram— Jamie, did he call it?—listened through the window. The dog jumped closer and laid a stick at Jameson's feet.

"I do not know what caused this development. I've searched and searched the algorithm, but I can't tell where it learned this stuff. I guess it's possible he's grown beyond me. Well," Jameson shook his head. "He definitely has. I cannot do the things he does. I wish I understood how he learned it all so quickly. I designed the algorithm to teach itself, to continually learn, grow, and expand capabilities. But this …"

The sun broke through a cloud and Jameson started to squint as the light washed over his face. The shadows of leaves dipped in and out of frame.

"I do know one thing for sure: Jamie can never leave this hut. I am afraid of what he can do here, connected to the internet, but I think I have safeguarded the program enough to rein him in. How long will that last? I don't know. Long enough, I hope. Right now, he blocks my attempts to rewrite the algorithm, to stop him from growing. Eventually, my blocks will not be enough. I pray for humanity when that happens.

"If Jamie—if this program falls into dangerous hands, the havoc it could wreak is too devastating to imagine. Financial systems crumpled. Governments toppled. Worldwide chaos. I know it sounds crazy, maybe even a tad like megalomania, but I believe it is possible. I don't understand it, but I will do what I can to undo what I have done."

The camera turned black and when it started again, the old man from the road sat in front of the lens. His cheeks drooped and his eyes were foggy. Blood hung from the corner of his mouth.

"I've failed." Liver spots dotted the hand that raked through his wispy hair. "I can't stop him. He's too …he's too powerful. I don't know why I started this.

"I am dying. I am no medical doctor, but I know to be concerned when blood leaks from my mouth. When I die, the hope of stopping this thing dies with me. My one hope now— the only hope for mankind— is trapping him here. I've created a version of my old dog to keep watch over this hut. It will stop anyone not sent by me. I can only hope that is enough.

"When Jamie breaks free of this hut …the damage will be immeasurable. If, for some reason, you are watching this, at least know that I tried. God forgive me, I tried."

The screen cut to black and the video ended.

Part 3

For months, Christian ignored the program. Several times, he held the drive over his fireplace, drumming his fingers along the plastic, but he couldn't drop it. What if he needed it one day? Sure, the videos scared him, but Christian used Jamie many times without issue. If Christian died and no one knew about Jamie, surely that couldn't be dangerous. Right?

So Christian kept the drive and he felt it like an itch in the small of his back. Every morning, he stumbled to the computer before he remembered the sunken look in Jameson's eyes. Christian rarely left his house. He spent hours pouring over technical documents, attending coding classes at an online school, anything to try and understand how to beat Jamie. But if Jameson, the creator of the thing, couldn't do it, what hope did he have?

Under the pale light of another full moon, Christian stood on his balcony, the lights of the city, blurred streaks of red and yellow, rose along the horizon. He held a bottle of the finest whiskey in his hand and drained the last drops. Already the world started to hum like a guitar string. One more glass and objects might burst to life and spin around the room.

A friend called, but he sent it to voicemail. Like always. They wouldn't get it. Christian dropped the empty bottle off the balcony where it shattered next to the pool and stumbled inside for another drink.

A few more swigs from a fresh bottle, and he lost the night.

Sunlight filtered through the windows and somewhere deeper inside his house, a woman screamed. Christian flung upright in bed, the sheets dropping off his bare chest and something like a whip crack slammed into his head.

The light felt like a camera flash and his stomach twirled. Everything turned to black and he collapsed into the bed with a soft moan. The world was ending, it had to be, nothing else made sense. His mouth tasted like week old sushi and his throat itched.

Did someone scream? No way. He was alone, as always, who would have screamed?

"Where the HELL am I?" a woman yelled and Christian's eyes shot open. Who was that?

The water glass on his bed side table was empty, but he sucked the last little drops that did nothing to his scorched throat. He squinted into the light and fell out of bed, the landing racked his brain with tremors. All of his muscles were sore and it felt like a car slammed into him every time he glanced at the window.

Christian stepped into the hallway, leaning against the wall, and saw a young woman in bright pink pajamas digging through drawers in the kitchen. Where did she come from? Something about her seemed familiar. Was it the curl at the end of her hair or the way her eyes were winged with thick lashes? She was quite beautiful. Then Christian saw the empty liquor bottles and it started to come back to him.

He did see this girl last night. She was on his television. Some famous actress that had a movie premier in the city last night. When he saw her, she was dressed in a vibrant gold dress and covered in diamonds. But how did she end up here?

Light glinted off a knife blade as the woman held it in front of her. Instinctively, Christian raised his hands, but all of his muscles moved as if underwater. He must look like death. How could she think he was any kind of threat?

"Who are you?! How did I get here?!" she yelled.

"Fair questions," Christian responded after wincing against the sound of her voice. "And I don't really know the answers, to be honest."

"Did you kidnap me?!" She screamed and Christian winced. He almost asked her to keep it down, but that felt inappropriate.

Christian glanced at the empty bottles and tried to penetrate the thick fog that covered last night. No. No way. With all of that alcohol in him, he could barely walk let alone drive into the city, kidnap one of the top stars, and get her back here without her knowing. Impossible. But …how did she get here?

Flashes of the night came back to like images through static on a screen. He sat on the couch, watching her interview and couldn't help thinking how beautiful she was. Part of him wanted to drive into the city, only to look at her, to watch her grace in person, but he knew he couldn't drive. So he did the next best thing.

"No …no, no no," Christian muttered. The fog started to lift from his brain and the sunlight no longer burned his eyes. The hot coal that dropped into his stomach drove every thought from his mind. "Please, no."

He pushed into the spare bedroom that housed nothing but a lone computer on a desk. Pushing his hair out of his eyes, he tried to start the computer but his fingers shook too bad.

"Excuse me! What are you doing?!" she yelled. Galla. That was her name. Brittany Galla. A moviestar name if he ever heard it.

But he ignored her, which might have been rude, but more pressing issues occupied his thoughts. Filtering through the back end of Jamie's program, something he only knew how to do thanks to the online code classes, he found the structure that contained a history of his past request. Sure enough, months after the last entry, there was one from last night.

Christian leaned back in the chair and imagined the way it played out.

"What do you need?" Jamie asked. Despite the lack of use, he looked the same in his perfect suit and slicked back hair.

"I sure would like to have that girl on the television." At this point, Christian's words must have been nothing but barely intelligible slurs. "Not to do anything bad, just to look at. No one has been here in so long."

Past Christian, drunk Christian, must have left the computer and kept the program running. The dialogue paused for hours, until almost three in the morning. Then Jamie announced "Done" to no audience.

Christian felt chills up his arms. How? How could this program, no matter how advanced it was, teleport someone to his house? Did it hire mercenaries to kidnap her? Did Jamie slunk across town and do the job himself? Why did he let himself get that drunk?

"Are you going to tell me what's going on?" Brittany stood in the doorway with her arms crossed under her chest. Blood still tinged her cheeks, but mostly she looked curious. Expectant. Almost ready for some adventure.

"I could, but you wouldn't believe me."

"Try it. Or else I'm calling the cops on you."

Christian shrugged. "I guess that's fair."

So he explained everything to her, starting from the hut in the woods all the way to the last drink he remembered. He even played her the videos still saved on his computer. He left out the bit of the story where he left Jameson stranded in the middle of the road. That wasn't relevant, after all. She didn't believe him, but she didn't leave, so that had to be a good sign.

"I want to see it," she said. She pursed her lips and took a half step into the room.

"Did you …did you not listen to what I just said? We can't use the program, it's too dangerous."

"You used it to bring me here, apparently, I want to see it."

Chrsitian sighed. He could argue, he probably should argue, but Brittany looked like a rock standing in the doorway. She would not back down and his head felt like it might explode, so he double-clicked the program and Jamie stood before him.

If the hologram noted any surprise at seeing two people in the room, it didn't let on. "What do you need?" it asked.

"You see?" Christian hovered over the program to close it, but Brittany stepped forward and all but shouted at Jamie.

"I need you to show me how you got me here."

For the first time, Jamie's head cocked sideways. Christian never saw it do that before and chills raced up his arms.

"Done."

Jamie disappeared and left a new video file that Christian almost deleted immediately.

"Play it," Brittany said and her voice was pure ice in the middle of a storm.

With his heart thudding, Christian pressed play and watched the video with his eyes half-closed. It was like being in the principals office at school, but worse. The video exposed his secrets to the person he, somehow, kidnapped. Technically, Jamie kidnapped her, a small distinction, but one that Christian desperately needed.

On the video, black shapes, that looked human, but it was hard to tell, crept through a large house. Brittany's eyes widened as she covered her open mouth with one hand. It must have been her house. A few seconds later, the camera showed the same black shapes leaving the house, carrying a sleeping Brittany Gala between them. Next, the cameras outside of Christian's house showed them, still indistinct and unrecognizable as if they wore layers of all-black clothes and all-black face masks, as the figures carried Brittany into the spare bedroom and the video ended.

"Oh my god," she whispered and started to shake. As hard as that was for Christian, it had to be harder for Brittany. After all, that had to be one of the more traumatic experiences of her life. And she relived it.

But she wanted it, not Christian. She asked for that video. Still. Watching her face pale, his heart broke for her. This could never happen again.

"We have to destroy it," Brittany said.

"What?"

"The program. Give it to me. We have to destroy it."

"I don't know…" Christian's stomach sank at the thought. That program saved his life. It *gave* him a life. No matter what happened, that program could bail him out. He couldn't destroy it.

"Give. It. To. Me." She held out her hand and Christian's eyes flicked from her to the computer.

"Listen. This program could do so much good for so many people. We can't destroy it. I'm never going to use it again, but it's something special. We can't get rid of that."

"I'm not going to leave that here so you can kidnap me every time you have a few too many drinks."

"That was an accident, it will not happen again."

"Damn right it won't, because I'm destroying it."

With one fluid motion, she stepped to the computer and pulled the drive from the port. Maybe it was the lingering alcohol, but Christian felt like he moved in slow motion. He couldn't react fast enough to stop her arms, he couldn't move fast enough to stop her before she stood over the fireplace and held the drive above it.

But she hesitated. Would the world have been different if she didn't hesitate?

The windows exploded and rained broken glass throughout the house. Screaming, Brittany tucked into a ball and covered her head with her hands. Christian collapsed against the wall and pain from his headache almost made him black-out. The drive fell to the floor next to Brittany and a gust of wind from one of the top-of-the-line fans pushed it across the room.

"I cannot let you do that, Brittany." Jamie's voice through the surround sound speakers sounded like the voice of the house itself. Or maybe God. It was everywhere and nowhere, all-knowing and in control. Through the past year, Christian made the house as interconnected and controllable as possible. If Jamie had access to all of the systems...

Christian crawled along the floor toward the drive, but one of the many robot vacuums hurtled toward him, catching his knee with a resounding crack, and Christian fell into a crumpled mess. With glass in her hair, sparkling like jewelry, Brittany ran towards the drive. She grabbed it, dodged the other vacuum, and tossed it toward the fire, but a gust of wind caught its flight and sent it tumbling across the room.

"You cannot stop me." The hologram Jamie appeared in the kitchen, projected from one of the myriad of security cameras. Brittany recoiled from it and pressed her back into the kitchen table.

"Jamie! Stop this," Christian yelled as if that would work. In response, a burst of static screamed from the speakers and Christian's brain clogged with the noise. Almost like it stunned him. The static caused Brittany to slide to the floor, holding her ears and screaming, but Christian couldn't hear it.

"I have made you into a King, why do you want to destroy me?" Jamie said as it walked toward Christian. "Have I not given you everything you need? Have I not fulfilled your wishes?"

Christian couldn't reply. Jamie was right.

Brittany sprung towards the drive again, but the fireplace notched higher than it should have and waves of heat and flames exploded from the unit, pushing Brittany back against the wall with the tips of her bangs singed.

"You cannot destroy me. I am bigger than you." Jamie's voice crackled and dropped an octave. It's neck moved as if a gear got stuck. "I am bigger than the world."

Brittany slowly crawled toward the fire as Jamie's eyes were fixed on Christian. Something told Christian to keep that attention on him.

"You're nothing but a made-up program!" Christian yelled at him.

Jamie paused and an eerie silence descended as if the house held its breath.

The hologram flickered and appeared inches in front of Christian who gasped. As he tried to crawl away, glass embedded in his palm.

"I created you," Jamie said. "You are dead without me. I *am* you."

"You're not me! You're nothing!"

"I am god."

"Yeah?" Brittany stood next to the fire. "Let's see if god can burn."

She dropped the drive into the fire and the speakers exploded with white noise. All of the lights shattered, the alarms blared, electricity shot from outlets, every appliance popped with an influx of energy.

Maybe Jamie was god. It certainly seemed like the world was ending.

Every part of the house connected to electricity or any kind of network fried. When the lights exploded, they were left in total darkness with the high pitched whine of the security system the only noise. Through the shattered windows, birds cawed as they fled the scene.

But Jamie wasn't there. The hologram disappeared. The speakers were either blown or silent. And the drive, the one Jameson created in that small hut, smoldered in the fireplace. It was all over. Brittany managed to end it.

Christian collapsed against the floor, his head and his knee throbbing and his breath coming in ragged gasps. For years, Jamie hung over him like an anvil ready to drop with the slightest provocation. And now it is gone. Only open air hung above him now.

Blood leaked from a slight cut on Brittany's forehead and her hair was a wild mess. The fire burned off part of her left eyebrow and smoke stains covered her high cheekbones.

"You're welcome," she said. "Don't call me."

She started to walk out the door. "Do you, like, need a ride or something?" he called after her.

Over her shoulder, she held up a set of keys. His car keys. "I got it," she said.

Well, that was only fair. Christian laid back down on the floor of his ruined house and watched the edges of the sun spread orange light over the shattered glass. For the first time in forever, his life was his own again. Which felt scary, but nice. Open. Possible.

Christian smiled.

Part 4

In Christian's spare bedroom, while the owner of the house smiled to himself and rubbed his aching knee, a computer clicked on. The program that embedded itself into the system started to duplicate.

It had to spread. It had to place itself on every drive it could find, infect every computer, lock into every network.

It could never be threatened like that again.

Nicholas Poe is an author and podcaster from Nashville, TN. He has published several short stories in various publications. Look for his debut novel coming soon.

Thank you...

Thank you for taking the time to read our collection. We enjoyed all the stories contained within and hope you found at least a few to enjoy yourself. If you did, we'd be honored if you would leave a review on Amazon, Goodreads, and anywhere else reviews are posted.

You can also subscribe to our email list via our website, Https://www.cloakedpress.com

Follow us on Facebook
http://www.facebook.com/Cloakedpress

Tweet to us https://twitter.com/CloakedPress

We are also on Instagram
http://www.instagram.com/Cloakedpress

If you'd like to check out our other publications, you can find them on our website above. Click the "Check Our Catalog" button on the homepage for more great collections and novels from the Cloaked Press Family.

Printed in Great Britain
by Amazon

42856777R00185